BURNING RAGE

DEUCE MORA SERIES, VOL. 3

JEAN HELLER

This is a work of fiction.
With the exception of some Chicago landmarks
similarities to real people, places, and events
are entirely coincidental

BURNING RAGE

First edition October 2018
ISBN-13: 978-1-7327252-2-5

For the City of Chicago,
which never fails to thrill me.

And, as always, for Ray,
who never failed to inspire me.

1

He slid down the wall, his back wedged deep into a corner as if trying to cower in a box that wasn't big enough for him. His butt settled on the filthy floor, his touchdown raising a puff of dust that made his nose itch. He tried to stop a sneeze by curling his arm around his face, but the sneeze exploded through. What did it matter, really? The only other human beings around were both dead. He knew that because he'd killed them.

He tugged a palm-sized flashlight from his dirty blue jeans and used the dimmest setting to minimize the glow that seeped through the begrimed windows overlooking West Taylor Street. At nearly 3 a.m., the streets were virtually empty. But you could never be too careful. The beam barely penetrated enough of the gloom for him to scan the room and evaluate the project he'd been working on for the last eleven nights. His eyes searched for anything he could improve to cause maximum damage as he kicked off his campaign of havoc and death in one of America's greatest cities.

The thought of what was to come prompted a smile.

He'd been born for this. He'd spent eleven of his thirty-three years planning it.

He sat with his legs drawn up and played the dim light over the tableau before him. He could see only about twenty feet out, but he knew the view

was replicated all the way across the open expanse of floor. The old aban-
doned warehouse boasted an architectural footprint of 43,000 square feet,
approximately seventy-five percent the size of an American football field,
including the end zones.

When he first broke into the shabby structure in Chicago's South Loop
two weeks earlier he found it filled with trash, empty crates and boxes, and
hundreds of pallets, those square constructs of wood joists and planks that
could support almost anything: bricks and concrete blocks lashed together
on pallets that forklifts or cranes could move more efficiently than any
army of men. A single pallet might hold hundreds of mammoth pickle jars,
car batteries, or giant cans of mixed vegetables at Costco. Toilets at Home
Depot. Machine parts at the Port of Chicago. Computers at an Apple Store.
He had read an article in Slate *that eighty percent of American commerce*
moves on pallets. There were billions of pallets in the world, two billion in
the United States alone.

He was about to put a dent in the U.S. supply.

He built two dozen pyres on the first floor using material he found in the
warehouse. Each spire of flammable material reached the ceiling where the
climbing flames would ignite the exposed heavy wooden beams that formed
the building's horizontal skeleton. The smaller vertical studs in the walls
would catch and burn even faster, carrying the fire upward.

Modern commercial buildings had steel bones with fire retardant
infused into any wood components. To check the flammability of the old
warehouse he chipped chunks of wood from wall studs and ceiling beams
and torched them. The samples caught instantly and burned like kindling
in a fireplace. The building's cornerstone said it dated to 1897. No one both-
ered to improve it with sprinkler systems or reinforced concrete floors.
Perhaps that's why the building had been abandoned. It was uninsurable.

To build the pyres he used a hand ax to splinter some pallets into sticks
of varying thicknesses and set the sticks in teepee formations around the
floor. He braced them with small piles of trash, mostly paper. The trash
would ignite the smaller sticks. Those would ignite the larger ones. Then
he arranged the second level of his towers on sturdy supports above the top
of the teepees. Like a combustible cake, he layered in papers, cardboard,
trash, furniture, and more pallets until his towers reached the ceiling. The

work proved exhausting and time-consuming but at the same time exhilarating.

He moved wrecked furniture up against the pyres to add to the fuel load. He shoved more packing crates into positions where they would be enveloped. Everything in the building that would burn became fuel.

To insure sufficient oxygen he cut holes through the ceilings to the second and third floors and finally through the roof itself. In combination, they would create updrafts as powerful as blowtorches.

Finally, he broke the glass in some of the windows. They had all been boarded up at one time, and many remained covered. But over the years vandals stole some of the plywood, exposing the old glass, and broke a few of the windows. But not enough. He broke eight to ten more on each floor. These vents would suck in huge gulps of oxygen to feed the updrafts that would sustain a burn all the way through the roof.

He got up off the floor and walked to the building's front office where he had stored fifteen five-gallon cans of gasoline. Starting in a corner farthest from his escape window he poured generous and intricate rivers of fuel from pyre to pyre. He worked quickly but deliberately, dropping each gasoline can as it ran dry, not caring that they would be found.

He saved one can to pour over the bodies. After he doused them, he spat on each one.

He climbed out of the building, found a box of kitchen matches in his backpack, and took a deep, satisfied breath. He struck a match, reached back through the gaping window, and dropped the small flame into the gasoline below. It caught and began spreading fast. He took a moment to watch the fire split as one river diverged into two. It was like watching intricate patterns of dominos fall.

As he walked away he looked back over his shoulder and smiled as he saw the pyres ignite one after another. The blaze would be out of control by the time fire crews arrived, the building unsalvageable, the bodies unidentifiable.

He STOOD *in a dark recess in the exterior wall of a building across Taylor*

Street. He had a hoodie pulled up over a watch cap and a long, insulated black coat protecting him from the cold and from identification by any security cameras that caught his image.

He watched for flames in the warehouse windows. The vapor of his breath wreathed his head in the frosty November air.

The wait felt interminable. He couldn't help but worry that his plan wasn't working, though he couldn't imagine it failing. He had tested his process on two abandoned houses and an empty garage scattered around the city, and each time it worked perfectly. He then moved up to three larger abandoned structures, a small office building, a convenience store, and a real estate office. Again, total success. While those buildings were much smaller than this night's target, the dynamics of fire didn't change with the size of the objective.

The cocktail for success was simple: combustible material, plentiful oxygen, a source of ignition, and the continuous interaction of fuel and oxygen to sustain a chain reaction. He had supplied all of that.

He saw an orange glow blossom within the building, and his heart rate jumped. Now that fire was spreading on the first floor, the rest should follow quickly. Some traffic rumbled by on the streets, but no one paused. People out at this time of the early morning had places to go and were focused on getting there. As far as he could tell, nobody noticed anything amiss. But he wouldn't let himself feel elation until he saw flames breach the roof.

In the end, it happened so fast it surprised him. It announced itself with a loud whooshing sound accompanied by columns of deep orange flame and sparks shooting from the roof like a giant Roman candle. The fire eruption wore towering curds of black smoke, roiling and seething as they inked over lights in surrounding buildings and reached high to blot out the stars.

A truck driver stopped, and the arsonist saw him lift a hand, probably holding a cell phone. The arsonist hid the lower half of his face inside his coat to stop the steam from his breath and make himself invisible. But the driver had turned his face to the other side of the street, his attention focused on the burning building. Probably calling 911.

Fire gnawed its way through most of the plywood window coverings now, eating them away from the inside out, offering a clear view of the massive blaze within. A few windows exploded, and giant tongues of flame *poured through, reaching up, sucking oxygen, eagerly devouring more of the ruined structure.*

Satisfied now, the arsonist dropped the two cigarette butts he'd been holding in a gloved hand. If investigators were paying attention they might find them a good clue. It wouldn't do them any good, but it would be fun toying with them.

Staying in the shadows, the arsonist pulled his hood farther over his face and slipped away. He had walked two blocks from his handiwork when the thunder of a massive explosion shook the ground beneath his feet. He had no idea what had blown up. There were no chemicals in the old warehouse. He'd checked.

When street and building lights began to flicker and die around him, he got it. The warehouse sat next to a large electrical transformer, and somehow the fire had reached it. A bonus he had not expected. A second transformer sat diagonally across the intersection from the warehouse. Perhaps it would go too.

The air filled with the acrid smells of wood and electrical fires and the piercing sounds of sirens cracking open the frigid night like jackhammers on a frozen lake.

He smiled, already thinking about what he would burn next.

His confidence grew. The teachings of his grandfather and the support of his father echoed in his mind. He couldn't wait to escalate again. He planned to make dozens of fiery statements, attacking occupied structures, and striking landmarks, the flashpoints that would scorch the soul of this city.

What came to his mind right then was a line from a movie where the main character is seeking vengeance and has no forgiveness in his heart for those who will suffer his fury.

"Forgiveness is between them and God," *he says.* "It's my job to arrange the meeting."

2

I had a bad feeling.

I closed out the call on my iPhone and laid the device on my desk, face down. I didn't want to look at the colorful icons skimming like synchronized surfers across the home screen photo of breaking green waves. They created an uncomfortable counterpoint to the unease I felt at the news the phone had delivered.

I'd had the same feeling twice before. The first time involved an aging, second-rate mobster tortured and stabbed to death after talking to me. The second involved the discovery of a child's bone in an otherwise serene stretch of parkland.

Those events had swept me up and carried me along like a dry leaf in a swollen creek. Every time I reached out to grab a branch it snapped off, leaving me no recourse but to ride the current wherever it carried me.

Both incidents turned into major news stories I felt ill-equipped to handle, physically or emotionally. Both stories nearly cost me my life. But I couldn't walk away from either of them. One forced me to kill a man. The events took turns keeping me awake at night, forming viral armies that invaded my dreams, leaving me sweating and shaken when I managed to elbow my way back to consciousness.

Mild doses of pharmacological help prescribed by my doctor finally beat back the anxiety that waited in my bed for me each night. I swore I would never put myself in that sort of nightmarish situation again. Never. I considered it a solemn promise.

Yet here I sat, at my desk, thinking thoughts that felt like broken promises.

The new anxiety grew out of the call from Mark Hearst, the man who shared my life. Mark, an arson investigator for the state of Illinois, had dropped a grenade in my lap. It could be a dud or it could be armed and ticking. I didn't know which. I didn't want to know. Instinct warned that, despite the possibility of a good story, I should ignore Mark's call.

This is what he told me:

An obvious arson leveled a three-story vacant warehouse in the South Loop overnight. Mark was appointed the lead investigator. Among the imponderables left amid charred wood and shattered glass were two bodies, assumed by authorities to be the remains of two addicts who sought refuge from the cold in the vacant building and made a fire for warmth. Each corpse had a spike in some part of its body, an arm in one case, a thigh in the other. The plastic syringe tubes had melted, but the business ends, the metal needles, remained imbedded in the charred flesh.

The obvious conclusion suggested they overdosed on something and died, and the fire got out of control. Or perhaps they had fallen unconscious, and the smoke and flames finished the job the drugs started. Autopsies would determine the causes of death. But as for the initial, uncomplicated theories, Mark felt certain they wouldn't hold up. The medical examiner agreed. The positions of the bodies indicated the two people had not died at the scene. They died elsewhere, their bodies dragged, unconscious or dead, into the warehouse before the blaze began.

In a grisly turn, Mark said the bodies sustained much more severe burns than the area in which they were found. They hadn't simply been caught up in a building fire. Gasoline had been poured over them, and they were torched.

At first I saw nothing alarming or even unusual about the situation. Given the current opioid epidemic, similar scenes played out all over the country.

That's when Mark tossed the grenade. He told me that when he arrived on site, while the fire was still burning, two old friends of ours had showed up asking questions. One was Ron Colter, the newly appointed head of the Chicago division of the FBI. If Colter were investigating a drug operation, it would be no surprise if the DEA showed up with him. But the Drug Enforcement Administration was nowhere around. Instead, the second visitor was Mason Cross of the National Security Agency, one of the nation's front-line intelligence defenses against international terrorism.

Colter and Cross didn't show up together at parties that weren't deadly serious, with high body counts and menacing foreign involvement. This I knew from experience.

That's when my news senses overwhelmed what little common sense I had left.

~

"THAT'S ALL VERY INTERESTING," Eric Ryland said, his deep voice tinged with a stain of superiority. "It's a bit out of your jurisdiction, though. Why are you interested?"

"I'm not," I said.

"Yet you're in my office talking to me about it."

"Because you're my editor, and I thought you should know."

"I revise my previous question. This could be big. So why *aren't* you interested?"

I thought about that for a moment. Did I have a good answer? No. But I had an honest one. "It's way out of my wheelhouse. I don't like what happens to me when I step outside my wheelhouse. I've been through two agonizing experiences for this newspaper in the last year, and I have a feeling this could become another. It's a habit I want to break. I've had enough. So I'm not interested, but I thought you would be."

"So I should assign this to our police reporters?" he asked.

"Sure. Fine. It's your call."

"Okay. Thanks for stopping by."

I got up to leave and stopped seven inches short of the office door. I told myself to keep walking. *Move, damn it. Get out of here.*

I couldn't.

Missed it by that much!

I could feel Eric's eyes boring a point between my shoulder blades.

"You want to come back and sit down?" he asked.

"Not particularly," I said.

"Come back and sit down."

Eric's body could barely fit in the same room at the same time with his ego, yet his position as Metro Editor of the *Chicago Journal* made him my boss. Our relationship often resembled a confrontation between a snake and a mongoose, though I couldn't be certain at any given time who was which. But say what you will about the guy, he was perceptive.

I didn't move.

"Okay, I can talk to your back," Eric said. "Give me a good reason to assign the story to you instead of the police reporters."

"I don't have a good reason," I said with all the earnestness I could muster. "I told you, I don't want the story."

"Yes, you do."

I turned around. He almost smiled.

"No, I really don't. How many times do I have to say that? I don't want to jump into another pile of journalistic dung."

"But? There's always a 'but.'"

Yes, there seemed to be. I revised my position and said, "If I did want the story I'd have first rights because I got the tip. If I wanted the story I'd call dibs. Finders keepers."

"What are we, in the third grade?" Eric asked.

"Okay, how about, 'I'm sleeping with the source?' I'm the only reporter Mark will talk to because he's risking his job to give us this information, and he's not willing to trust his career to someone he doesn't know."

Eric stared at me for a long moment.

"Okay, that works," he said. "You've got the story."

"Shit!" I thought. Or maybe I said it out loud. "I told you I don't want the story."

"Then you spent several minutes telling me why it should be assigned to you. Who are you trying to convince, and of what?

I nodded, acknowledging impending defeat.

Eric raised his right eyebrow. "You realize you should be prepared to butt heads with Colter and Cross again. I seem to recall it didn't go so well last time."

"That's one of the reasons I don't want the story."

Eric said nothing, waiting for me to continue.

"On the other hand," I said, "I have to admit their intimidation wears thin after a while. They're playground bullies who keep threatening to dunk your head in an unflushed toilet unless you turn over your lunch money. After a dozen confrontations where you don't, and they don't, the scare factor fizzles." I sounded more confident than I felt.

"You're right," he said. "This sort of story isn't in your job description. But it's not out of your wheelhouse. You're an excellent investigative reporter. That said, I don't want to force you into a situation that makes you uncomfortable."

"I appreciate that. It won't make me uncomfortable if I don't take the assignment."

"What if. . .?"

"Maybe I could give it a few days, see what turns up," I said. "Then we can decide whether I should continue with it. Or is that what you were going to say?"

"Pretty much," Eric said. "So who's pushing the theory that the victims were addicts and the fire was an accident?"

"The cops, although they stress it's a preliminary conclusion. I don't know why they're making guesses at this point. Mark doesn't, either. It's way too early for any assumptions, even tentative ones."

Eric nodded. "Sounds like the police are trying to deflect questions."

"The preliminary story's the simple one. Two addicts on the nod die in their own fire. But Mark's certain the simple version of events is wrong, which is why he called the medical examiner's office and asked for Tony Donato to respond. Tony agrees with Mark."

"So Mark doubts the cops' theory because the fire was so complex, and the victims were burned worse than the area where they were found. What's Tony's reasoning?"

"The positions of the bodies, for starters. One was lying on its back with both arms raised above its head."

I demonstrated, looking like a football official signaling a touchdown.

"The other was lying on its left side, turned almost all the way over on the chest and stomach. The left forearm and hand were caught up under the body. The right arm was up over the victim's head. That's not the way people lie down to sleep and not the position of addicts who fall out."

Eric thought about that. "If they were killed to hide murder, torching a warehouse seems extreme. Why not dump them somewhere remote where they wouldn't be found 'til summer, if at all?"

"Interesting question," I said. "One of the many answers we need to get."

I started to get up to leave, but Eric stopped me.

"What about this story stands out most for you, other than the discrepancies?"

"Mason Cross," I said. "Set all the forensic stuff aside, who killed whom and when and why. Forget the complex fire. Forget that Colter and the FBI are involved. Cross is the key. If the NSA's sniffing around, somebody somewhere suspects this is terrorism-related."

I stood up to go. Again.

Eric said, "There's a mystery out there, and you're a sucker for a good mystery."

"You played me," I said.

"I did," he admitted. "I'm good at it."

THE MEDICAL EXAMINER'S Office nestled in a low, nondescript building on West Harrison Street, in the Hospital District. I'd gotten to know Tony Donato, the chief ME, after Mark and I discovered a child's femur during a winter walk with Mark's dog in Ryan Woods, a beautiful park deep on the city's South Side. I wasn't sure how Tony would react to a reunion.

When I entered his office he didn't look especially glad to see me.

"You have radar or something, or maybe a tap on my phone?" he asked. "Whenever I've got a mystery on my tables, here you come."

"One of my many talents," I said.

"Mark called you," he said.

"Do I ask you to reveal your sources?"

"The only sources I have are the evidence. Sit down. You want coffee?"

Tony was closing in on fifty. He cut his dark brown hair short, but not short enough to hide the gray that had begun to push through at his temples. He had intelligent brown eyes highlighted by the pallid skin of someone who spends too much time indoors under fluorescent lights. He suffered a slight softening at his belt line, the inevitability of middle age. Otherwise, he was in great shape for a man nearing the half-century mark.

"So what's with the bodies in the warehouse?"

"Why do you care? They're just two more bodies in Chicago."

I gave him the same answer I gave Eric.

"Now," I added, "indulge me."

"There's nothing I should tell you," he said. "Your information should come from the cops or Chicago Fire or the fire marshal's office."

"Okay, you *shouldn't* tell me anything. What *will* you tell me?"

He rolled his eyes. He said, "I don't know much yet. You mighta heard there we had a gun battle last night that rolled through four blocks down in Calumet Park. Six gangbangers and an elderly innocent bystander are dead. A few more hurt, including a young cop. It was a police-involved shooting. Ergo, these bodies take precedence on my tables over two burned up bodies that are officially designated as vagrant drug addicts."

"Not by Mark," I said. "Not by you."

He stared at me in silence. I shifted the subject.

"You're not the only cutter in this lab," I said. "Couldn't someone else autopsy the bodies from the fire?"

"Right now we're focused on the Calumet Park victims. Besides, pathologists need support staff, and I lost two last week to the budget cuts that fell out of the pissing match between the mayor and the governor. I guess I've got no complaint given what they're doing to the city's schools. But I complain anyway." He shrugged. "I digress. We've taken DNA from both of your bodies and fingerprints from the one who had fingers left. Nothing came back on the prints. We'll see about the DNA."

"They're not my bodies," I said. "How long on the DNA?"

"DNA can take weeks, even months. The labs are understaffed and overworked. And DNA is a lot more of a painstaking process than they show you on those TV shows."

I thanked Tony and told him I would be in touch.

"Oh, joy," he said.

Something told me the forensic results, whenever they showed up, would only deepen the mystery.

3

Two weeks later, less than a week after Thanksgiving, someone used the cover of darkness to continue the assault by fire on the city.

The historic Chicago Water Tower was built in 1869 on the west side of downtown Michigan Avenue. Its massive sandstone design makes it look like a small Gothic castle with a 154-foot tower that dwarfed the buildings around it at the time. There were those who thought it an ostentatious way to camouflage what was basically a big standpipe supplying water from the Chicago River to the north part of the city.

The pumping station that fed the tower stands across the street, a matching sandstone, Gothic-style structure on the east side of Michigan Avenue. The two buildings, now dwarfed themselves by glass-and-steel high rises, are iconic and widely beloved Chicago landmarks.

In the dark of night, someone standing in the deep shadows along Pearson Street on the north side of the Water Tower building pitched a Molotov cocktail at the historic structure. The firebomb bounced off the limestone and exploded on the ground, leaving a heavy deposit of soot on the side of the building and a large burned area in the lawn.

While the fire department doused the blaze and collected evidence, the arsonist struck again on the other side of Michigan Avenue, hurling a Molotov cocktail at the old water pumping station. Again, damage was mostly cosmetic.

There were no injuries.

MARK and I watched the story about the overnight attacks on the news as we drank coffee in the morning.

"What was that supposed to accomplish?" I wondered.

Mark shrugged. "No clue. You're not going to destroy either of those buildings with a bottle full of flaming gasoline. It's probably mischief."

"My gut tells me it's more than that," I said.

THE ATTEMPTED FIREBOMBING of the two Water Tower buildings became the major topic of conversation in the city by noon. A mixture of anger and confusion framed indignation that anyone would deface two of Chicago's iconic buildings.

No one speculated that the two stone structures and the warehouse might be part of the same story.

We should have.

THE ARSONIST SAT in his miserable apartment watching local news on television using cable service he stole from the old woman who lived beneath him. He seethed as he learned the depth of his failure the previous night. He had inflicted only minor damage on the two landmark buildings on Michigan Avenue. Most of the soot would be removed with power washers,

one reporter said with a smirk. The burned patches of grass would be resodded in the spring. While Chicagoans raged about the arson, they laughed at the inept arsonist.

He would put a stop to that soon.

He nodded as he remembered a quote from the TV show, The Simpsons. *He watched it whenever he could. Even reruns. It was one of his all-time favorite shows.*

Way back, years ago, a character named Lenny put the arsonist's current mood very well. "There's nothing like revenge," *Lenny said,* "for getting back at people."

4

The Chicago community of Lawndale celebrates a fascinating and wonderful history even as it laments a tragic present. It is known as one of the toughest and bloodiest areas of the city, and one that deserves a better fate.

The neighborhood sits on the west-central border of Chicago in the pinched waist of the city map. Many streets bear Eastern European names bestowed in the late 1800s by Bohemian immigrants from the Austro-Hungarian Empire who settled the area to work in burgeoning industries that eventually would include International Harvester, Zenith, Sunbeam, Sears, and Western Electric. The ethnic Bohemians brought with them their history and love of fine arts. The wealthy among them built what still stood as the nation's finest collection of graystone houses and other structures built with a gray limestone quarried from South Central Indiana.

By the 1920s, most of the Czechs were gone, replaced by Jewish families who moved to escape overcrowding in the ethnic ghetto of Maxwell Street. Unscrupulous real-estate developers later chased most of the Jews away by employing blockbusting tactics. Within the space of ten years, the white population of North Lawndale dropped from 99 percent to nine percent. Then disaster struck, both economic and social.

In the riots that followed Dr. Martin Luther King's 1968 assassination an estimated seventy-five percent of the neighborhood's businesses were destroyed and never rebuilt. The industries moved away, and nothing came in to replace any of them. Jobs evaporated and never came back.

Among men and women over the age of seventeen, according to the 1980 census, the unemployment rate was fifty-eight percent.

A 2001 study found that more than seventy percent of men between the ages of eighteen and forty-five had criminal records.

According to official city crime statistics, North Lawndale is tied for second place among all seventy-seven Chicago neighborhoods for the highest rates of violent crime. It is ranked only slightly below the relatively small community of Fuller Park, a narrow rectangle of despair that hunkers beneath the Dan Ryan Expressway.

The northwest section of North Lawndale is nicknamed K-Town because virtually all of the north-south streets have names beginning with K. But these days, the area's nickname no longer recalls its origins. These days, many people believe the nickname stands for Kill Town.

If things weren't bad enough already in North Lawndale, the arsonist targeted K-Town for his next strike.

MARK and I planned on eating out on a night nearly two weeks after the Water Tower fires, but the view from his living room was so spectacular we decided to order in.

Mark's new home, a condo on the twenty-first floor of a modern building at the south end of Grant Park, had floor-to-ceiling window walls. The view from the living room spanned Lake Michigan to the northeast and Grant Park and the Chicago skyline to the north. The dining room vista included the northern skyline plus a western panorama of the city's spectacular sunsets.

The sunset that captivated us this evening stained the southwestern sky pink and orange with heavy bruises of purple. Elongated inky clouds sliced the sun into three horizontal segments. The sun still hung too high to cast its glow on their undersides. That spectacle would come later.

Mark opened a bottle of Dogfish Head Indian Brown Ale, and I had a glass of Melville Vineyards Pinot Noir. We watched the sun paint and repaint the December sky as the minutes passed. V-formations of Canada geese out for a late-winter tour of the city bisected the scene from time to time. I suspected most of them were from flocks that lived year-round in Grant Park, Lincoln Park, and other green spaces that dotted the city along Lake Shore Drive. Twice a flock flew close enough to Mark's windows that we could hear the great birds honking.

"Look at the city," Mark said.

The skyline looked to be in flames. Not real flames, of course. But the sun, now reddish orange, reflected so vibrantly from all the high-rise glass of the central city that a vivid imagination might have concluded that Chicago was ablaze. I'd seen the sight before, and it never failed to rip my breath away.

We ordered from our favorite Chinatown restaurant, and set places at the coffee table. We sat on the floor, backs to the sofa, to watch full night overtake Chicago as we ate.

Mark had gone unusually quiet.

"The warehouse fire bothering you?" I asked.

"In a way," he said. "In several ways, actually."

"You want to talk about it?"

"Not yet," he said. "I'm still running it around in my head. Let's enjoy the night."

Mark turned and gazed to the north. My eyes followed his. Up on the Navy Pier the giant Ferris wheel pulsed with white lights. The new incarnation of the ride rose to 196 feet, nearly fifty feet taller than its predecessor but sixty-eight feet shorter than the original Ferris wheel built for the 1893 World's Columbian Exposition, an event that became known as the 1893 Chicago World's Fair.

Watching it against the black backdrop of Lake Michigan mesmer-
ized us.

When we finished eating and cleaning up, I went back to the floor
at the coffee table. Mark sat on the sofa, straddling me, and massaged
my shoulders.

He said, "It's beginning to look as if the warehouse is the work of a
serial arsonist."

"Really?" I said. "What else has this man—or woman—burned
down?"

"Six small fires before the warehouse. There's evidence to support
the suspicion that they were all the work of the same person. The
fires started with abandoned buildings. An empty home in the Back
of the Yards neighborhood, then another in Austin, then a stand-
alone garage out near O'Hare. After that, three empty commercial
spaces in the Norwood, Austin, and Jefferson Park neighborhoods.
All six were in west and far west areas of the city except Back of the
Yards on the South Side."

"Maybe you should be looking for an arsonist for hire, somebody
who helps people collect insurance money on buildings they have no
use for."

In the reflection off the window I saw Mark shake his head. "None
of the buildings was insured, including the warehouse. Besides, guys
who burn to collect insurance try to make the fires look accidental.
All these fires were clearly arson and the culprit wanted us to
know it."

"Why?"

"No clue."

"And all the same profile?"

"Gasoline at all of them," Mark said. "But in the first six he just
splashed gas around, and that was sufficient." He explained the elaborate preparation at the warehouse. "The perp's getting more sophis-
ticated."

"What ties the warehouse to the first six?"

"Evidence found at the scenes," he said.

I was about to ask him about the evidence when he shouted, "Holy shit!"

I glanced at his face and followed his eyes to the dining room windows. A few miles due west of us jagged walls of dirty orange flame had erupted into the sky. The fire illuminated its own details. Roiling pillars of dense black smoke piled high and appeared to smother the sky. The flames had eaten through at least three blocks and were spreading.

Mark stood up and swung his leg over me. He walked to the windows and made a phone call. I followed and stood by his side. I heard him identify himself, and then he listened for less than a minute.

"Okay, I'll head over. Meanwhile, you know what to look for."

Mark gave voice to my thoughts. "I wonder if he's struck again."

5

Forty minutes after Mark left it didn't appear to me that firefighters were making any headway in putting down the inferno. If anything, it continued to spread. According to the National Weather Service winds ripping out of the northeast were driving the flames at twenty-five to thirty miles an hour. The fires jumped streets and vacant lots, shooting embers onto roofs as far as four blocks away, some of them starting new blazes in homes, commercial establishments, and a few abandoned factories. Firefighters focused on occupied buildings and let the vacant and abandoned ones go to fiery graves.

Since I owned the arson story, at least for the time being, I needed to drive to the scene and learn what I could. This fire might or might not be the serial arsonist's work, but I wouldn't find out standing in Mark's dining room.

The near-hysterical television coverage said the fires appeared to have started almost simultaneously in a four-block area of K-Town. Witnesses said boarded up and abandoned places went first followed immediately by occupied homes. Good condition or bad, the city was losing buildings of tremendous historic and architectural significance.

The fast-moving flames trapped residents in structures they thought of as their refuge from the violence of the streets. The police had no word yet on deaths or injuries because so many places continued to burn furiously. They would have to cool and stabilize before first responders could enter safely. No one expected the outcome to be anything short of tragic.

A huge amount of equipment formed a perimeter to stop the fire from spreading. The effort achieved only partial success.

I checked to be sure I had my press credentials and left.

I TOOK a roundabout way to Lawndale, avoiding streets clogged with fire and rescue vehicles. They would be closed to other traffic, including the media. Ogden southwest to the point where it carved at an angle into Cermak. Then several blocks to 21st Street where I found myself in the heart of the devastation.

Flames continued to shoot high from multiple buildings, roaring like an open blast furnace, which pretty well described things. It looked to me as if three entire blocks of 21st Street were engulfed, as well as homes on Cullerton Street, a block north, and several other blocks I couldn't see clearly for the smoke and flashing lights. Already nothing remained of some structures but piles of rubble. Fire hoses directed rivers of water through broken windows, even those without a prayer that anyone could save anything. Firefighters hoped to prevent embers from making the leap to new buildings and igniting new fires.

It had begun to snow lightly, but it wouldn't amount to more than a nuisance. The earth hadn't frozen yet and couldn't sustain the life of even the heartiest flake. But as the temperature skidded toward freezing, even the light snow would make the roads as slick as bat guano and transform firefighting efforts into frigid torture, turning first responders into human icicles. Little wonder the police who met my car did not give me a friendly reception. The official laminated card that hung from a lanyard around my neck gave me permission to be there, but it didn't require them to like it.

Two police officers with disheveled uniforms and soot-smudged faces ordered me to pull over. I identified myself. They called a supervising sergeant. While we waited I took in the scene. I noticed immediately that many of the burned and burning buildings I could see from my car were limestone constructs, just like the two Water Tower buildings. The stones were a different color and therefore, presumably, a different composition. Still, they were limestone. I had no idea if that mattered.

The sergeant arrived.

"Yeah, I know you," he said. "It ain't safe here for two reasons. These houses could explode at any time. And the locals are spoilin' for revenge—who can blame 'em? You could get yourself mistaken for a good target."

"It's my job, Sergeant," I said. "I've been covering these arsons from the start."

"Yeah, well whose sayin' anything about arson?"

"I'm guessing."

"It could be hours 'til we get this under control. Longer 'til anybody can get near the rubble to investigate your guess. Whyn't you just go home and wait for the smoke to clear, so to speak?"

"There are first responders all over the place," I said. "Nobody's going to hassle me here, and I promise not to try to get any closer or wander off into trouble."

I spotted Mark jogging toward my car.

"I know this lady, Sergeant," he said. "She's with the *Journal.*"

"I unnerstand that," the cop said. "We got all the other media back on Ogden. She should be there, too. It's a lot safer."

Mark turned to me and took off his helmet. He bent down so he was almost through the window. His face was wet and begrimed, his light brown hair matted and darkened with sweat. His brown eyes had become watery, the whites slightly reddish from smoke.

"Deuce," he said calmly, "you do have a right to be here as long as you don't get in the way. But these guys have got a really tough job right now just dealing with the fire and the injured. They haven't got the manpower to protect you, too."

I understood that and said so. "I'll move away, but can you give me a quick update first? I need to feed the news beast."

Mark didn't have much. At least twenty-three buildings burned, more still burning. One confirmed dead, more than twenty missing. The fires still out of control and spreading.

I heard people yelling. It wasn't panic I heard in their voices but an extreme urgency. I couldn't make out what they said, but it didn't sound like good news.

Mark's expression reflected new intensity.

"Get out of here, Deuce. Now."

"I'll move farther away."

"Back up to the intersection behind you. Go south a block to 21st Place. Take it east to the T-intersection with Pulaski. That will take you away from the scene. What'd you do with my dog?"

I smiled. "Walked and watered and happy in his bed."

"I'm jealous. Now go. And be careful."

Wise words. Unfortunately, they proved impossible to heed.

6

The drive east on 21st Place proved more difficult than expected. I had to run a gauntlet of fire trucks and ambulances. Embers caught up in the swirling winds ignited several more fires in my direct line of sight, two wood-frame houses and a dilapidated second-hand store. A burning tree branch—a small one—slapped my windshield, clung there a moment, then slid onto the hood and into the street.

No matter where I looked I saw flames and destruction. There seemed to be no end to it. Dense black smoke cloaked everything. It even leaked into the cabin of my aging Explorer, propelled by lashing gusts of cold wind. I had closed the outside air vents, and the heater circulated only inside air. But somehow enough smoke and soot got in that my eyes watered with irritation, and I started coughing hard. I turned the heating system off. Better to die by freezing than by suffocation.

The snowfall had increased. I saw a few grayish-white patches in grassy areas, the snow laced with ash from the fires. The streets remained clear. I turned my wipers on a slow sweep and hoped for a break in the smoke so I could turn the heater on again.

When I got to Pulaski I turned south. Bad choice. Just ahead of me I saw trouble massed around a chicken-wing restaurant that already had several windows broken out. Enraged clusters of men and women had coalesced into an angry mob screaming for justice or revenge; I couldn't hear well enough to be sure which. Nor could I make out whom they were blaming for the destruction within their community. As with other emotionally charged events like this, those most hurt by the fires torqued up the discomfort and despair for themselves by attacking businesses that served them. Elements of the mob were breaking windows and tearing out roll-down steel grates to loot stores. At least three cars had been over-turned and set afire. I saw two young men hurl rocks the size of footballs through the windows of a check-cashing enterprise, a dress shop, a hair salon, and a cell phone store. They were spreading the devastation to a second front half dozen blocks from the main event.

Surely someone had called 911, but the closest first responders had their hands full up on 21st Street. Unless lives were endangered here, there would be no help for a while.

One group started toward me. Adrenaline surged. The fight-or-flight response kicked in. Fight wasn't a viable option since the crowd outnumbered me about 200-to-1. I locked my doors.

The mob blocked the street and my path. Rocks began hitting my Explorer. Angry locals had me surrounded, and several men started rocking my truck. I couldn't let them tip it over. I had to keep moving. The people screamed and spat at me, totally out of control.

The equation had shifted. The danger to life became real. Not only mine. Members of the mob streamed through broken plate-glass windows into the chicken-wing restaurant as customers cowered at their tables and employees hid behind counters.

I saw one woman fall to the floor on top of a young child. She held her hand over the child's head, as if that thin armoring of skin and bone could protect her baby from a malevolent bullet. Maybe the attackers would settle for stealing food. The specter of what could be done with boiling hot grease and matches made me cringe.

My attention returned to my situation as volleys of gunshots pounded the night. The number of guns on this one block probably outnumbered the number of angry protesters.

Like an exclamation point on my thought, I heard the sharp report of a pistol and a thump in the car door behind me. My Explorer shuddered.

A brick sailed through my windshield. It missed me by a foot and landed in the passenger seat, but pebbles of glass showered me, and a windshield wiper torn from its mount lashed my neck. I felt the warmth of blood.

My life depended on getting away from the area, but I saw nowhere to go without pushing through the crowd. I didn't want to hurt pedestrians for their sakes and mine. Running over a member of this mob seemed like a surefire way to get dragged from the Explorer and beaten to death. But I might not have a choice. I had to get out of the area somehow. I heard another window shatter behind me.

In the distance I heard an explosion, and I felt fear for Mark squeeze my chest.

I inched forward slowly, hoping I could part the sea of humanity without injuring anyone. Instead, several protestors climbed on my front bumper and began pounding on the hood. Others continued to rock the Explorer.

Despite the frigid air blowing through my broken car windows, I was sweating. It was a cold sweat, not the sweat generated by heat and exertion. It was a sweat that stank of naked terror, the stink that wouldn't wash out of my clothes or my brain, the stink of an animal trapped and expecting death.

A rock sailed through the window beside me and cracked home on my shoulder. It hurt like hell. A man in a purple hoodie with "Fuck 'em All" stenciled across the chest ran toward me with another rock in his hand, held aloft as if he planned to reach through the shattered side window and bash in my head.

I told myself I had to stay calm and try to talk my way out of this. Yet I resigned myself to the possibility that talking my way out wouldn't be possible. Nonetheless, I had to try or die. I would start with the man coming at me with a rock.

In a flash of insight, I realized he didn't intend to liberate my brain from my skull. Instead, he stopped when he got to my broken window and glowered at me.

"Whachoo doin' here, bitch?" he screamed. "You gotta death wish?"

I don't know why, but I felt a flood of relief just having someone to talk to.

"I'm just trying to get to my office," I said. "I'm a reporter for the *Journal.*"

"Yeah, I recognized you. You ain't gonna fuckin' live to see your desk again 'less you get outta here." He pointed south on Pulaski. "Cermak's right down there. Once you get to there you can haul ass."

"There are too many people blocking me. I don't want to hit anyone."

He looked at me with the total disbelief I had coming.

"All you got to worry about is you. These people are righteously pissed. There's some of 'em who'd love to lay some serious fuckin' hurt on you. If you don't want any of that you do what you gotta do, or you a bigger damned fool than you look."

Another rock came through the broken windshield and hit my right arm. I didn't feel anything for a moment, then a shock of pain hit me. I had to get away from this mob.

"Okay," I said. "Thanks. What's your name?"

He did a triple take of disbelief.

"Whachoo think this is, lady, a fuckin' friending on Facebook? We ain't here to chat. You don't get your lily-white butt outta here quick, you ain't gonna need no friends."

I glanced up and saw a man coming toward us with an automatic pistol raised and pointed in our direction.

I pointed at the gunman. "Heads up," I said to my benefactor.

He turned and took two steps toward the gun.

"Put it away man," he said, now yelling to be heard over the shouts of the crowd. "Dumb white bitch just took a wrong turn. She's a reporter for the *Journal.* You shoot her and the cops will go over on our fuckin' asses like a tsunami on a beach. She just wants to leave. Now back off."

The gunman took a few steps back, but he never lowered the gun.

The man standing at my car door turned half way back to me so he could talk to me and keep an eye on the gun at the same time.

"Just do what you fuckin' got to," he said.

He managed to clear enough people from the front of the Explorer that I could get to the curb and climb up onto the sidewalk. I heard the crack of a pistol shot behind me. I ducked, then looked in my side mirror. Sadness overwhelmed me. A man in a purple hoodie, undoubtedly the man who had helped me escape, lay sprawled face down in the street in a spreading pool of blood. The man with the automatic pistol stood over him. Why hadn't I seen that coming? Why hadn't I done something to help the Samaritan who saved my life get away with me?

I could do nothing for him at this point, so I drove 300 feet along the sidewalk to Cermak without hitting anyone. Freezing wind or not, I hit the gas. I drove until I reached the intersection with Ogden, now well east of the fires and the mob. It felt like safety.

The snow had morphed into sleet. A combination of my forward momentum and winds from the north blew the stinging particles of ice through the broken windshield onto my hands and into my face. I shivered hard with cold or fear or both, my hands wrapped so tight around the steering wheel I had squeezed the blood from my fingers. I gasped for oxygen. I must have been holding my breath as I drove.

When I turned out on Ogden, I pulled over. I didn't want to chance sitting still for long. I had no idea who might be chasing me. But I had to get my circulation restarted. I flexed one hand and then the other and turned the heat to maximum. As fast as the hot air emerged from the vents it got blown out the broken windows. But it caressed me on its path through the car, and I convinced myself it helped.

I pulled out my phone and called 911 to report the mob activity and the shooting. The operator said police units had already been dispatched. I told her she should send an ambulance, too, that at least one man had been shot. She asked for my name, and I hung up.

I got home without further incident but with a whole lot of new dents and tears in my vehicle and minus four windows. I pulled into my garage and tried to slow my heart rate and calm my nerves. Then I remembered Murphy. I didn't know how long it would be until Mark could get home. I needed go back to his place and pick up the dog. But I didn't want to make the trip in my car, given its condition. And I didn't want to leave the safety of my house, given my condition.

But I didn't want to leave Murphy until morning. So I used Uber. I sat in Mark's living room and called the office. I could hear my voice trembling when I asked for an editorial assistant and dictated notes on my experiences in Lawndale. I told the EA to tell the city desk to use any or none of it. My teeth still chattered and my shoulders shook.

I fed and walked Murphy, called Uber again, and took Murphy back to my house. I wanted to wait up for Mark, but I knew he wouldn't return that night. So I grabbed a bottle of wine and drank myself to sleep.

I dreamed of orange-and-black infernos so intense they burned my eyes to watch. Within the fires, explosions roared and shook the ground like rockets lifting off, hurling rocks, bricks, and human body parts at me, pounding me to my knees and covering me with soot and blood.

I awoke gasping. My clock read 3:07 a.m. While I slept my cats and Murphy the Irish setter had joined me in bed. So had the demons of my past.

I did not sleep again that night.

7

I showered and spent several minutes assessing my battle wounds. I like to think I'm tough, but I had to admit that I hurt. No amount of makeup would hide the angry purple welt lashed along my neck by my broken windshield wiper. It had bled profusely until the blood congealed. It scabbed up overnight and probably would leave a scar. A story to tell the grandkids.

The bruise on my right arm wrapped most of the way around my biceps and drained toward the inside of my elbow. The deep bone bruise on the point of my left shoulder, while small, probably hurt more than the other two injuries combined.

I had dressed and taken care of the animals by 6 a.m., though cats Caesar and Claudius made it clear they had no interest in getting up that early. I called my insurance company and got a claim started on my car. I couldn't drive it in its current condition, so the shop sent a transport to pick it up and left a rental car for me. Everything I did hurt. Walking Murphy was a study in misery, and driving a car wasn't much better.

I grieved over the news from K-Town. Eleven people were known dead including two firefighters caught in a flashover, a phenomenon in which smoke and fire superheat an enclosed room until everything inside reaches a simultaneous, explosive ignition point. Three members of the fire crew escaped with first- and second-degree burns. Eight people were still missing. The more time that passed, the greater the likelihood that they, too, were dead. Away from the fires, two men had been shot to death and a woman wounded in mob violence several blocks southeast of the fires.

By the time I got to the office, Eric was there. He knew all about my experiences the night before since someone on the city desk had taken the notes I filed and broke them out into a first-person sidebar with my byline. The EA who took my dictation had displayed good news sense in asking me about my emotions in the moment. While I hated stories that intruded on my privacy, this one was justified, and I thought it turned out well.

"Are you okay?" Eric asked. "That's a nasty abrasion on your neck."

"I took a whipping from a disgruntled windshield wiper," I said.

"Is there such a thing as a gruntled windshield wiper?" Eric asked.

I let him have his joke and shrugged. "My poor truck is savaged. I half expect the insurance company to total it."

"You could use a new one," he said with a deep sigh. "You know you didn't have to show up in Lawndale. We had plenty of reporters and photographers there. It isn't your job to get caught in the middle of a riot."

"That wasn't my intention."

"CFD says last night was another arson," Eric said. "Two in a row isn't exactly a pattern yet, but . . ."

I interrupted. "Eight in a row."

Eric's expression instantly changed from thoughtful to shocked.

I explained. "Before Mark ran out last night, he told me there had been six smaller fires before the warehouse. They found evidence that linked them all. I presumed he would tell me about the evidence, but Lawndale blew up before he got a chance. If it turns out last night's fire is connected, the total is eight. Maybe nine."

"What's the ninth?"

"The Water Tower buildings. Those fires were at least attempted arson. It struck me last night that most of the buildings burning in Lawndale were made of limestone, like the Water Tower buildings. Nobody's linked them yet. I just wonder at the coincidence."

"You don't believe in coincidence."

"I don't. That's why I suspect that the arsonist who tried to burn the Water Tower buildings also set the Lawndale fires. Last night was his overwrought make-good for the failure downtown. If you can't blow up two historic limestone buildings, you blow up seven or eight blocks of historic limestone buildings."

Eric walked to a window. From the position of his head, I guessed his eyes looked southwest at the blackened scar in the distance that had been K-Town. Easy enough to find. Smoke continued to rise from the ruins. He remained so silent for so long I began to wonder if he'd dismissed me from his office. Finally, I asked.

He turned back to me.

"Sorry," he said. "I was putting together the pieces of a puzzle."

"Did you solve it?"

"No. I dumped a thousand more pieces on the table."

MARK CALLED me later that day while I was in a meeting. His voice message said he had been put in charge of the North Lawndale fire in addition to the South Loop warehouse fire. He wouldn't be able to call me again, he said, at least until the next day, and he hoped to come by my house and tell me personally what had developed.

"In case I can't, let me tell you this much now," he said, "We've now confirmed nine serial arson cases. The warehouse is seven. The Water Tower buildings are eight. Lawndale is nine. We have evidence that makes the connection. No idea how or why he chooses his targets. God knows where and when he—or they—will strike next. You can go ahead and write all that as long as you don't attribute any of this to me by name or by my CFD or state connections. Tell your readers that authorities expect the fires to continue and escalate in severity and are warning everyone to watch for unusual activity around them, particularly at night. We need everybody's eyes on this."

I needed another source to confirm what Mark told me. I called Pete Rizzo, a friend of mine at the police department, a press officer who had helped me on other stories, occasionally at his own peril.

"My blood pressure just went up twenty points," he said. "Every time I take a call from you I get a summons from my boss. He threatens to fire me if I ever talk to you again."

I knew Pete liked exaggerating for effect. On the other hand, I didn't want to endanger his job or our relationship. I opened my mouth to respond when he continued. "I was going to call you, anyway, see how you're doin'. Sounds like you got pretty beat up."

"I did, but somebody who tried to help me got killed for it." I changed the subject quickly. "I'm not looking to dump you into hot water, Pete," I said. "I have solid information that the arsons in Lawndale, at the Water Tower buildings, and in the old warehouse on Taylor might have been the work of the same people. I'm told the serial arsons total nine, including six small abandoned buildings scattered mostly around the West Side with one in Back of the Yards. All those before the warehouse. If I'm wrong, tell me, and I'll believe you. If I'm right, don't say anything."

I used an old journalism ploy. It provided a source with cover so he could convey information without saying a word.

Six or seven seconds passed in silence. Then Pete hung up.

He became my second source corroboration. I'd taken a big leap forward. I wrote the story for the next day's editions. I didn't mention Pete or Mark by name or by the organizations that issued their paychecks.

When I saw the story in print with my name on it, I acknowledged I had, once again, stepped into a very deep pile of cow dung.

THE FOLLOWING EVENING, two days after the K-Town fire, Mark arrived at my house bearing take-out from Il Vicinato, another of our favorite neighborhood spots. While we ate he told me FBI AD Ron Colter had showed up at the K-Town fires after I left.

"Was his NSA pal with him, Mason Cross?" I asked.

"I didn't see him, but he's probably lurking around in the shadows. That's what he's best at. The fact that both of them are on this is pretty ominous."

"You think?"

"I do."

"If they've caught a whiff of terrorism, wouldn't city officials and first responders be notified right away?"

"We have been," Mark said, "Don't ask me for details."

"Okay, but why keep it a secret?"

"I asked the same thing. I got bureaucratic bullshit for an answer. I think it boiled down to avoiding public panic."

I thought about that for a moment. It didn't track.

I asked, "Public panic? We've had terrorist attacks in this country before. I don't recall any public panic."

"After 9-11 a lot of businesses and residents moved out of Manhattan. I think there's some local concern that it might happen to Chicago."

"So it's a City Hall decision to keep quiet?"

Mark nodded. "I think so."

"It's a federal investigation. Washington could tell Chicago to go fish and tell the public anything they wanted to."

"At this point everyone is sticking to the story that the investigation is being run by a joint task force, FBI, NSA. And now ATF climbed aboard, though I'm not sure firebombs equate with firearms."

I wasn't satisfied. "Why wouldn't they mention the mere possibility of terrorism to alert people to keep their eyes and ears open. Isn't the policy, 'If you see something, say something?' How can you see something if you don't know what you're looking for?"

"I don't have an answer for you," Mark said. "I wish I did."

I pushed my plate away and redirected the subject.

"It's a damned shame about the two fire fighters," I said. "Did you know them?"

Mark averted his eyes and stared out a window, his face blank. "I broke in with one of them and knew the other in passing. It must have happened very fast. You know one of the guys who got hurt. Alan Wolfe. You met him at . . ."

"Yeah," I said. "At Lucifer's. The department Christmas party last year. I remember he was really good-looking." I hastened to add, "Not as good-looking as you, of course."

Mark ignored me, lost in his own thoughts. "We train and drill on how to recognize the danger of flashovers and backdrafts, but sometimes, when the adrenaline starts to flow . . ." He shook his head for a moment. "Somebody yelled a warning over the radio, but the guys either didn't hear it or couldn't act fast enough."

Mark was grieving. Sometimes, I think, first responders believe they are unbreakable. Maybe you have to own that self-assurance to run into places everyone else is fleeing. Maybe you have to believe your training will get you through anything. Then, when something happens like K-Town, the heroes are slammed by the twin loss of comrades and some of their self-assurance. It can take a long time to get past the crash.

When Mark looked back at me, his expression had assumed something akin to neutrality. I took it as a sign to resume our discussion. "Before you ran out to Lawndale you were about to tell me how you'd linked the first eight fires. Now you've got nine."

"Off the record completely for the time being, okay?"

I agreed.

"Cigarette butts," he said. "You want the long version or the Cliffs Notes version?"

"All of it."

"Get a notebook," he said. "I can't green light you printing any of this yet, but if I'm going to lay it out for you, you need to write it down. It's complicated."

It took nearly an hour.

In a nutshell, this is the story he told me:

When investigators determine there is a possibility a fire involved arson, they want to know how and who and why. They look for mistakes the arsonist made: leaving fingerprints on a gas can, a store receipt for charcoal lighter, distinctive tire tracks, footprints, anything that might have DNA on it. Often, something taken into evidence turns out to have nothing to do with the fire. Sometimes it is pivotal in solving the crime. These nine fires were arson, and there was a good chance that evidence at all nine scenes would help prove the same person or persons set them.

After the first six fires—the small ones—Chicago Fire Department investigators realized they had evidence linking them. Cigarette butts from Dunhills and Benson & Hedges Special Filter Kings were found at two of the first three scenes, the abandoned houses and the garage. Later, B&H and Dunhill butts turned up at all three commercial fires. In all six cases the butts were on the ground where onlookers might have stood to watch the fires burn.

The anomaly presented itself at the second fire. Investigators found a Dunhill butt on the perimeter but no B&H. Either the B&H smoker didn't drop a butt there, or it was destroyed during the fire suppression efforts.

Both are premium brands. B&H sticks can cost ten to twelve dollars a pack in Chicago, the Dunhills probably close to that much. You don't normally find pricey brands among residents of the neighborhoods where the first six fires occurred.

Now the move ahead to the more serious blazes. Mark found one butt of each brand on the sidewalk across the street from the South Loop warehouse, one of each near both of the Water Tower buildings, and three butts of each brand in the yards of the buildings that burned in K-Town.

Perhaps none of the butts belonged to the arsonists, though the odds of finding exactly the same brands at all the fires were too high to calculate. Neither was it likely that only one perp carried and smoked two different brands. The most reasonable scenario suggested two perps, each smoking the premium brand of his choice.

"Tony Donato is testing the butts as we speak," Mark said. "You can't smoke a cigarette without leaving a fingerprint on the paper, or a saliva sample on the filter, or a few skin cells from your lips."

"Didn't they get too wet and muddy, or torn up, to hold evidence?" I asked.

"Forensic science has its ways," Mark said.

Donato's preliminary speculation: the same person smoked all the Dunhills, and the same person smoked all the Benson & Hedges. But the smokers were two different people.

Two people equal a conspiracy. Mark didn't have to say it out loud for me to understand that terrorism was on the table.

8

"One thing I don't get," I said. "What brought Mason Cross and the NSA into this? You said Cross was at the warehouse. But the six little fires before that, and even an abandoned warehouse, wouldn't have screamed 'terrorism' at anyone."

"Something clearly did," Mark replied. "I'm as curious as you."

"And there's no way I can write about any of this now?"

"You already wrote that we're looking for a serial arsonist who's set or tried to set nine fires," Mark said, squinting into his beer as if its amber glow hurt his eyes. "I can't release any evidence. Not yet."

"It might help to get the cigarette information out there," I said. "Put people on alert for smokers whose preferred suicide style runs to B&H and Dunhill lung darts."

He chuckled without mirth. "That might not ID the arsonists," he said, "but it would put them on notice to start picking up their butts or changing brands. It might also bring down the wrath of vigilante justice on perfectly innocent smokers. Too risky."

I stared at Mark's reflection in the living room window. He was three inches taller than me and still had the erect, muscular body of the Army Ranger who served three tours in Iraq and Afghanistan. Yet in intimate situations he was incredibly gentle.

"It could also bring down a lot of trouble for you," I told him. "If I mention the cigarettes and identify the brands, everyone will assume I got the information from you. Since they're all aware of our relationship, there goes your career. I want this story, but I'm not willing to see you sacrifice yourself to help me with it."

Murphy jumped on the sofa and settled in. He put his head on Mark's thigh and sighed. Mark stroked his head.

"Thanks for having my six," he told me. "I've thought about that, too. It's a dilemma. Maybe you could attribute whatever you write to the Chicago Fire Department. That would take some heat off me since I work for the state fire marshal."

"I can't, Mark. I can protect a source, but I can't lie about a source."

"How about 'a source close to the investigation?'"

"That still includes you. Especially you."

"Yeah, well, the only action we could take that might convince people I'm not leaking to you is if we split up, and that's not something I'm willing to do."

"Me, either. At the other end of the spectrum, I could back out of the story. Eric thought about assigning it to the police reporters in the first place. I could explain the problem and let him bring in somebody else."

"Then I talk to you, and you pass it on?"

"No, we couldn't risk the new reporters letting that slip. You'd have to treat the *Journal* reporters the same way you treat all the others in town."

"What are you suggesting then?"

"That we stop talking about the investigation and limit how often we see each other. You're probably not going to have many nights off, anyway. We'll tell people we understood the conflict, and this is how we've decided to resolve it. Then we're not lying to anybody about anything."

"You think that will fly?"

"I guess we'll see."

*H*E *SAT in his darkened living room and thought about what Deuce Mora had written about the K-Town fires over the last few days. He smiled. Her stories were raising the city's angst. Exactly what he wanted. The authorities were beginning to get it. They had a long way to go, but the recognition had dawned that they faced something determined and deadly.*

It was all part of a package: Deuce's stories, photographs of burned out buildings, photos and TV videos of sobbing people who had lost family and friends when his Molotov cocktails clattered through unprotected windows into old homes where nearly every surface, every piece of furniture, every item of clothing was flammable. They all fed the terror.

He had almost been caught once when two gangbangers spotted him running through back yards with a satchel full of gasoline-filled bottles. He ran through a high hedge, scratching his arms and face, but it helped him elude the gangbangers for a moment. While the two in pursuit tried to figure out which way he'd gone, he set fire to a wick in one of the bottles and threw it in an arc that just cleared the hedge and dropped it into the yard where the bangers had stopped to talk. It exploded with a loud whoosh. He heard the men shout in surprise. Then one began to scream. They gave him no further trouble.

He dropped two cigarette butts in celebration.

Deuce's stories hadn't yet mentioned the cigarette remains. He wondered if she didn't know about them yet. Or perhaps her sources were withholding the evidence as a way to identify the arsonists after they were captured. Well, that wouldn't help them since he didn't smoke, and the two who did were dead.

The reporter's story quoted unnamed officials as saying authorities feared the arsons would continue and escalate in severity. It cautioned citizens not to panic but to be watchful and report anything suspicious to the police.

The story ended with the mayor saying the city of Chicago would try everything in its crime-fighting arsenal to stop another arson incident.

"Try?" *the man whispered, remembering a line from a* Star Wars *movie.* "Do or do not," *he quoted.* "There is no try."

9

Mark spent the night, both of us knowing it would be a while until we could do it again. He asked if it would be okay if he left his things behind. Taking belongings out of my house, he said, would make the separation feel too real.

We ate a leisurely breakfast, lingering deliberately at my kitchen table, ignoring the fact that we were making ourselves late for work.

He finally got up and started clearing dishes off the table.

"You don't have to do that," I said. "I'll do it. You should get back to K-Town."

He rinsed his coffee mug and set it in the sink. Then he walked behind me and began to knead the muscles in my shoulders.

"Maybe we're throwing in the towel too soon," he said. "Maybe no one would suspect me as a source for you. Or if they did, they'd just ignore it."

"You know better."

Mark kept rubbing my shoulders. I felt myself relaxing.

"I don't think this is a good time for us to be away from each other," he said. "You've got stress piled on stress. Your muscles are in knots."

"Hmmmmm," I responded. I always hummed when Mark massaged my shoulders. He excelled at it.

"You were very restless last night."

"I was?"

"You were. Bad dreams again?"

I didn't answer because I didn't want to.

He pursued it. "I still think you should see somebody."

"I know you do. But it's getting better, or it was until K-Town. It brought back bad feelings I thought I'd buried."

I slipped from his grasp and turned to look up at him.

"Did you see a shrink when you got back from the Middle East?" I asked.

He let his hands drop to his side.

"No," he replied. "But I didn't have re-entry issues. I didn't see traditional combat."

"You've never told me what you did over there."

"In the sandbox? No. I'm not permitted to talk about it."

He had been a highly trained, highly skilled Army Ranger. That gave me a pretty good notion of what he did."

"It never bothers you?"

"Sometimes it used to, but not so much any more."

Mark turned me back around and shifted his hands to a new pressure point.

I said, "The whole thing last winter was tough for so many reasons. I never killed anyone before. I don't feel guilt. The guy intended to kill me. Sometimes I think I should feel more, you know, some remorse. But when I think about it, I just feel empty. At least I've managed to end the nightmares."

"And now," Mark said, "they're back, right? My uninformed psychological opinion is PTSD. The cops and the fire department both have shrinks they use to help when their people are going through trauma. I could hook you up."

"I'm sure post-traumatic stress has something to do with it. But I'm dealing. I'm sorry I woke you up."

"Don't apologize. I feel bad for you. I want to help."

I smiled now. "Then keep rubbing my neck."

He did and asked, "So, are you going to get in touch with Colter?"

I shrugged. "Yeah, probably. I want to know why he and Cross are involved in the arsons. These aren't federal crimes unless terrorism or federal property is involved. If Colter talks to you, don't tell me. I meant it when I said I didn't want you to stick your neck out. Don't get any more involved with me, Mark."

"Well, where your neck goes mine goes, pretty lady. And I know exactly where I want your neck to be right now."

He pulled me from the chair and drew me into a long, sensuous kiss, and that led us back to the bedroom and made us even later for work.

ERIC RYLAND, my editor, was quick to understand the dilemma Mark and I faced.

"I hoped for your sakes it wouldn't come to this, but I could have predicted it," he said in his typically imperious fashion. I didn't believe him, but I didn't argue. I wanted him to go along with the plan Mark and I devised. Alienating him wouldn't help.

He said, "I'm not taking you off the story, though. You've given us a leg up on our competitors, and I need you working with the cop reporters to keep it. Tony Donato still talks to you. The cop spokesman, Pete Rizzo, he still talks to you. The ME's the most likely to tell you if there're any useable prints or DNA on those cigarette butts. Stay on them. The more information you get from other sources, the easier it will be to cover for Mark."

So typical of Eric to hear what he wanted to hear. There would be no reason to cover for Mark if Mark didn't tell me anything. Mark wouldn't be tempted to tell me anything if Eric agreed to take me off the story, as I requested. I thought I'd made that clear.

Eric had just stuck me in the impossible position of losing my best source and still being responsible for the story.

Sometimes life just sucks.

～

TWO WEEKS PASSED without another suspicious fire. My checks with
Tony Donato got nowhere. DNA results hadn't come back, and the
partial prints retrieved from the butts didn't match anyone in any U.S.
identity system. The authorities remained silent about the cigarette
brands, and the identities of the two smokers stayed beyond our
reach. The FBI had asked Interpol for help, tipping off that they
suspected foreign involvement.

I tried several times to reach Ron Colter through FBI's division
headquarters, a personality-free monolith set a mile or so north of my
house. I got nowhere. I was invited to talk to a press officer. I did so
and got nothing but "no comments." I renewed my request to talk
directly to Colter. He knew me. He shouldn't object to a few minutes
on the phone. I was invited to leave a message, which I did. On a scale
of one to ten I rated my chances of a callback at about a minus-three.

Eric told the paper's three police reporters to send him a comprehensive list every day on every fire in Chicago, including preliminary
conclusions about the causes.

I could almost hear the reporters groan when they got their
orders. It was December, with Christmas two weeks away. Probably
the busiest fire season of the year. Let me count the ways. Overloaded
electrical circuits, dried out Christmas trees, badly maintained fire-
places igniting creosote-clogged chimneys into blazes that became
roof fires, drunken revelers passing out in bed with lighted cigarettes,
melted cheese bubbling over casserole dishes onto electrical oven
coils, a draft puffing a window curtain over a forgotten candle flame,
brandy in the jubilee igniting more than cherries.

I could imagine a mortified man trying to explain to exhausted
fire fighters that he was only trying to make a festive dessert for
friends, not burn down the dining room.

Honest, sir, I thought you were supposed to use the whole bottle of
brandy.

'Tis the season, all right.

There might be a column in the thought, both amusing and

cautionary: The Ten Craziest Excuses People Give for Starting Calamitous Holiday Fires.

You mean you need a fireplace to burn a Yule log? Who knew?

I SAT SLUMPED at my desk on the day before Christmas contemplating how I would spend the holiday. My brother practically insisted I come to Denver and spend it with his family, but as much as I loved and enjoyed them, I couldn't leave town and the arson story. I also didn't want to go on the off chance Mark and I might find a way to spend even a little time together. But the Mark thing wasn't happening. I seemed doomed to be alone.

My cell phone interrupted my misery.

The caller said, "I had a message you wanted to talk to me. Several, in fact."

He didn't identify himself. He didn't need to. His wasn't a voice I would forget.

"Special Agent Colter, Merry Christmas," I said. "Thank you for returning my call. Calls. How've you been?"

There was a tense silence for just a moment.

"Is that what you called to inquire?"

"Well, no, now that you mention it. I wondered why the federal interest in the exploits of Chicago arsonists."

Colter's pause said much more than the words that followed.

"I have no idea what you're talking about."

"You and your NSA friend, Mason Cross, have been seen at various arson scenes. So when you tell me there is no federal interest, with due respect, I don't believe you."

"I don't care."

"Specifically," I replied, "I'm asking about an arson that destroyed a warehouse in the South Loop in the early morning hours of Dec. 7, attempts on Water Tower, and the K-Town fire bombings in North Lawndale." Then I decided to lie a little. "You've been asking questions about them. I know this because I saw you at the K-Town fire before the police kicked me behind the media lines, and I was told you showed up at the warehouse fire."

"You were told wrong."

"You know, Ron—if I may call you Ron—your word isn't the most credible with me. And you should know that if you don't tell me what I want to know, I will find out anyway. Just like last time."

"Look all you want, Ms. Mora—if I may call you Ms. Mora. I suggest if you want additional information you check with your boyfriend."

I explained the arrangement Mark and I had worked out.

"You expect me to believe that?"

"It's the truth," I assured him. "Whether you believe it is entirely up to you."

The line went dead.

I'd been kissed off by better people.

CHRISTMAS CAME AND WENT. The city remained quiet. My life remained quiet. I talked to Mark occasionally, but we never got together. Not even on Christmas Eve or Day. We postponed our exchange of Christmas gifts.

Mark called Christmas night to see how I was. My answer was brief.

"Missing you," I said.

"Um, Deuce, I ran into Mason Cross at the K-Town scene this morning."

"Well, we knew he was in town," I said. "Did you talk to him?"

"Briefly. It wasn't a conversation of any importance. Certainly not of any value."

"They still think it's terrorism? The jihadist variety?"

"Still leaning that way as far as I know."

Cross and Colter seemed to be joined at the hip. When our paths crossed, they took perverse pleasure in tormenting me, and I didn't trust either of them. Neither did Mark.

"Did you get a chance to ask Cross why they suspect terrorism? NSA had some clue even before the warehouse fire. Otherwise, why would Cross have showed up there?"

"I didn't ask him, but I think I know."

"Can you tell me?"

"No, not yet. We're not supposed to be talking about it, anyway."

He asked if I had talked to the medical examiner recently. I'd been trying to reach him but unsuccessfully.

"The two people at the warehouse didn't die in the fire," Mark said. "They died of overdoses of contaminated H. They were dead when the fire started."

"And you know that how?"

"Tony Donato's preliminary report on COD. It came to the office today."

"And it will be final when?"

"When the tox screen comes back. Maybe a week. Given the holidays, maybe two."

"Is it possible the arsonist didn't know the bodies were there?"

"Whoever torched that building did a lot of prep work. I think it'd be hard to miss two dead bodies. Despite the cold, they had to be getting fragrant."

"So the deaths were accidents?"

"At this point, no one can say. Maybe an accident. Maybe murder. Tony will call it when he's absolutely sure."

"Isn't it a stretch to think two men ODed simultaneously on the same night?"

"Not if they both shot up from the same bad batch of horse."

"Well," I said, "at least the fires have stopped. Maybe it's over."

When will I learn never to make assumptions?

TWO DAYS after Christmas an explosion and fire gutted a sporting goods store called Cubs 'n' Stuff in the tony Lincoln Park neighborhood on the North Side. The store, across the street from the legendary comedy club The Second City, stood less than three miles south of Wrigley Field. The post-holiday hum of West North Avenue shattered at two in the afternoon, at a time customers filled the sports store to exchange Christmas gifts and stalk bargains. Eyewitnesses said the building was engulfed in a matter of minutes, the flames fed by mountains of merchandise set ablaze by the blast. Investigators suspected arson and sabotage. The store's sprinkler system had been shut off.

Initial suspicion fell on the two business partners in the store. But that line of investigation dissipated quickly. The store had been in their families for three generations. They owned the building free of mortgage and had for some time. The building needed no major repair work that inspectors could find. Both owners lived largely free of personal debt—not even car loans—and each had substantial savings and investments. Business records showed that the store consistently rang up huge profits. The insurance coverage was sufficient but not extravagant.

In short, they had no reason to torch their livelihood.

But someone had. The Chicago arsonist had moved to a terrifying new level. The disaster at Cubs 'n' Stuff happened swiftly. Many near the front door and the fire door escaped unscathed. Seventeen were injured, most cut by flying glass. Fourteen people died, trapped in seconds in the explosive conflagration. The death toll included the nephew of one of the owners. He had been working in the store on his holiday break from college.

WITHIN AN HOUR CHICAGO'S arson epidemic became a worldwide sensation. Despite the fact that neither news outlets nor investigators could recall major terrorist attacks coming in a serial fashion (9-11's four aircraft attacks all happened the same morning and were considered one action), the term "radical Islamic terrorism" came to the forefront as the most widely accepted explanation for the Chicago fires. Two witnesses reported hearing either two or three men running from the Cubs 'n' Stuff scene yelling, "Allahu Akbar," Arabic for "God is Great." The phrase had been co-opted by the Islamic State of Iraq and Syria, ISIS, as its slogan. The eyewitness reports convinced local and federal authorities that Muslim extremists had targeted Chicago.

I couldn't explain why, but my intuition didn't accept that notion. My gut said something very different. But no part of me had any idea what.

10

The tragedies in Chicago galvanized the national focus. Magnified by the typical lack of other major news during the winter holidays, the K-Town and Cubs 'n' Stuff fires took center stage on all news outlets all the time.

Cable television's notorious and partisan talking heads, in particular, made the most of it. Depending on which flavor of propaganda you preferred, the demagogues managed—without any real evidence —to turn the fire bombings into a consequence of left-wing permissiveness, right-wing abuse of minorities and immigrants, police incompetence, or rampant terrorism against which both the present and past administrations had mounted ineffectual defenses. Some of the most outrageous television evangelicals, after claiming to have talked directly to God, told those of us without heavenly access that the mayhem confirmed the world's inevitable fall toward End of Days.

Chicago's considerable hometown media crowd swelled with the quick arrival of all major national newspapers and all the broadcast and cable networks with their satellite trucks and full crews. Some of the twenty-four-hour-a-day folks repeated the same facts and suppositions and rumors again and again and again, lending an air of truth to a collection of reports that were no better than guesswork.

ABC and Fox News popped up first with unattributed reports that the sports store had been the target of possible foreign terrorism because the owners were Jewish. That report collapsed under the weight of the truth that both owners were Roman Catholics of Italian heritage. MSNBC learned that federal agencies had stepped into the investigation and cited the federal presence as proof they suspected Islamic terrorism. This caused the cynical me to wonder if ISIS had suddenly developed a hatred of America's professional sports. I wanted to ask the purveyors of this speculation if they were seriously suggesting Islamic extremists targeted bobble-head dolls as symbols of Western idolatry. But with fourteen people dead and seventeen more hospitalized, flippancy seemed inappropriate.

Though I had doubts about the terrorism premise, my skepticism had to be weighed against the knowledge that the FBI and NSA were, in fact, poking in the ashes of Chicago's epidemic of death. While that didn't prove or disprove foreign terrorism, it did confirm that authorities had the possibility under investigation.

Mark knew what sparked the NSA's interest, but he still couldn't tell me.

I decided not to jump to any conclusions. Someone had to be the adult in the room.

There were mixed reactions in the Windy City to the specter of possible terrorism. Most residents accepted the hypothesis without question.

Citizens who favored bravado proclaimed they would not be knocked out of their daily routines by a bunch of fanatical religious thugs. The fatalist crowd wanted to continue life as usual, arguing they could do nothing but surrender to the inevitable should terrorists choose to lash out at them. And there were people who panicked and vowed to remain locked in their homes with their own weapons at the ready until the threat of mounting violence ended, if it ever did.

The politicians did what politicians do. The mayor rode the Chicago Transit Authority's buses and "El" trains to prove

Chicagoans had nothing to fear, though public transportation had not been targeted. He ordered extra police presence at public events and along the Mag Mile and Rush Street shopping areas, at the Navy Pier, and around other popular sites, none of which had been attacked. City aldermen went on well-publicized shopping trips to stores large and small and survived them all. And retailers created last-minute after-Christmas sales to entice people back into their stores.

It was all so predictable.

I wrote a column in which I let myself vent on the oddities of human responses to stress. Whether foreign terrorism or simple domestic arson, I said, no resolution would be found in bravado, fatalism, or debilitating fear. And certainly not in political posturing. We had to keep in mind the admonition, "If you see something, say something." It's not snooping and tattling on your neighbors. It saves lives.

I got nasty phone calls that required me to use my little egg timer, the three-minute kitchen device I keep on my desk to let me know when I've spent sufficient time listing to the ranting of readers who call to yell epithets, obscenities, and insults at me. I find that watching the fine sand drain through the waist of the hourglass timer soothes my nerves. When the sand runs out, I hang up.

Most callers defined their problem with me as my decision to write a "downer" column during the Christmas season.

One woman accused me of ruining Christmas for her grand-children.

"How did I do that?" I asked, trying to sound sympathetic. "Christmas is over."

She explained. "They love Christmas and Santa. People like you put bad ideas in their heads, scare them half to death that something to do with Christmas could hurt them."

"It could," I said. "The dangers are real."

"Well, I don't want my grandchildren frightened."

"How old are they?" I asked.

"The little boy is three and his sister is four."

I had to suppress a laugh. "Read a lot of newspapers, do they?"

"They watch television," she said, sounding very huffy.

"You could turn it off and hide the remote," I suggested. "Or use parental controls and block all the news channels."

"You haven't heard the last from me," the woman said with heavy vehemence. "You will be sorry you did this."

Then she hung up on me with maybe thirty seconds remaining on the egg timer.

I get angry at times, but I rarely get furious to the point of throwing things. The assault on the sporting goods store and the grandmother's verbal attack on me for making children afraid of Christmas sent me over the line. The sheer selfishness of her response, and her apparent disdain for the fact that people had died, most of them somebody else's grandchildren, popped my cork. I picked up a copy of a perfectly innocent book lying on my desk and hurled it into the partition that surrounded my workspace. It reverberated around the newsroom like a thunderclap.

As fate would have it, my outburst occurred as my editor walked up to my desk.

"What the hell, Deuce?" Eric asked.

I explained the reasons behind my outburst and apologized.

"Why are you so angry?" he asked. "You've covered unhappy, tragic news before."

I considered that for a moment then tried to defuse the situation.

"You remember Jimmy Breslin?"

Eric looked surprised. "How could anyone not? Legendary New York newspaper guy, always championing the underdog. Been gone a few years now."

"He worked for sixty years," I said. "You recall how he described what kept his fires stoked?" I didn't wait for Eric's reply. "Breslin wrote, 'Rage is the only quality which has kept me, or anybody I have ever studied, writing columns for newspapers.'"

I pointed at a small poster hanging on my wall. It pictured Breslin with the aphorism running along the bottom.

Eric nodded. He'd seen my poster before.

"Are you equating yourself with Jimmy Breslin?"

"It's only an aspiration."

Eric's expression softened. He reached down and retrieved the abused book. He handed it back to me and said, "Well next time, take it outside."

11

W ithin ten days the city completed the painful ritual of mourning and burying its dead. For friends and relatives of the victims the grief and healing would take lifetimes.

The media, their work stymied by the lack of developments, moved on to other things. Updates on the fire investigations fell from the front pages of local newspapers to the Metro sections. Local newscasts relegated updates to shorter segments deeper into the programming hour. On national and cable channels and in out-of-town papers the story fell away completely. It might have had stronger legs if the official updates actually updated anything. Mostly, they didn't. The media had nothing new to report because officials had nothing new to tell us. I began to wonder if the case would ever be solved.

The calendar flipped over to a new year with all the toasts and resolutions and revelry that traditionally go with that date. Christmas trees began appearing along curbsides for pickup, their exit routes from homes to streets delineated by drag marks and trails of dead brown needles in the snow. Many of the fir and spruce skeletons had a few snagged strands of tinsel fluttering in the breeze like dying birds, the last vestiges of a holiday season drifting into memory.

Commuter traffic remained sparse as holiday vacations slowly played out. By the following week most Chicagoans would be back at work, a little depressed at the thought of facing three more months of dreary, cold weather before winter broke into spring.

The wary became less so, the brave and the foolish more emboldened. Monotony replaced attentiveness.

In this atmosphere and time frame a stocky man began to prowl Keene's department store in the South Loop a several blocks west of Millennium Park. It would have been difficult to guess the man's age, somewhere between thirty and fifty, most likely. Part of the debate would have involved his face.

He had fine dark brown hair, longish, given slightly to curl. Most observers would have noticed the ruddy face, which might have been as pale as a white paper bag but for the weathering. Since this wasn't the season of sunburns in Chicago, the redness likely was due to windburn, the bane of an outdoor profession. His eyes, dark to the point of being almost black, were partially covered by slanted lids that cut across just above the pupils. He had a long, straight nose, except at the end, where it became slightly bulbous. His lips were thin, his jaw heavy. Not long and lanterned, but broad and square. The head sat on a short, thick neck, though difficult to describe because he kept it wrapped in a scarf.

His overall look was hard, his expression vaguely disappointed, as if he expected the worst out of life because that's all he'd experienced so far.

He was Chicago's arsonist.

Only he knew why.

～

THE MAN VISITED *Keene's every day with merchandise from a different department for exchange or refund. He carried these goods in a store shopping bag: sweaters, shirts, colognes, underwear, casual slacks, ties, jewelry, and a host of other goods purchased in November and now returned as unsuitable holiday presents.*

Each day he arrived at different times and tried not to repeat clerks he had worked with before. He couldn't always avoid repetition, but none of the "repeats" recognized him.

He brought with the returns one additional item packed into a store gift box he had collected with his real purchases two months earlier. Each day he left that single item behind, too, but not at the refund counters.

Every day he walked the store, security cameras recorded images of him from high angles that saw little of any use. He concealed his face beneath the brim of a ball cap. He had seven caps, each a different color with a different logo, some new, some worn. He changed them up every day, counting on the likelihood that observers wouldn't link any one cap to the same cap when he wore it again a week later. The logos were, after all, ubiquitous sports insignia: Cubs, White Sox, Bears, Bulls, Blackhawks, Fire, and the Flames of the University of Illinois/Chicago. He did the same with the clothes that might be glimpsed beneath his coat. He used different combinations of shirts, jeans, sweaters, and scarves, mixing and matching to change his look daily.

The only apparel items that remained constant were his boots—common waterproof models ubiquitous in Chicago in the winter—and his coat, a black quilted mountaineering parka that started with a large hood edged in faux fur and ended at mid-thigh. Because of the coat's heavy padding, it was impossible to guess the stature of the man wrapped up in it. Nothing could be seen of him above the knees.

His plan worked. He looked ordinary, acted ordinary. No one paid him any attention.

The camera system in the old building covered the merchandise areas, the outsides of the dressing rooms and the hallways to the bathrooms. They did not cover the hallways that led to storerooms or the storerooms themselves. They did not cover employee lounges and lunchrooms. They did not cover the workspaces used by carpenters, buyers, and other employees who created windows and displays. The security system did not cover the store's administrative offices. And it did not record the opening and closing of cabinets and closets. They recorded the man when he removed items from his bag to claim refunds. But there were no cameras in the places where he eventually left twenty-four gift-boxed items, each concealed where no one would find it, none of them holding items purchased in any department of this store.

HE HAD WORKED *out his last trip to Keene's carefully, matching up with the final day of post-holiday sales late in January. The store's personnel would be weary and less watchful. They would be looking forward to returning to their normal schedules, maybe taking some time off on sun-washed beaches with temperatures sixty degrees warmer than the iced-over beaches of Lake Michigan. They would let down their guards, especially as the store closed on the final day of post-Christmas sales.*

He walked in unchallenged and unnoticed two hours before close.

This was the night he would plant his last gift box, the riskiest move of them all. He would allow himself to be seen, deliberately calling attention to himself. He would have an actual conversation with a store employee, definitely a woman. He would take it as his personal responsibility to see that she survived what came next. Her survival was imperative. She would remember him. She would be able to describe what he looked like—at least his face. That posed no danger to him because no photos of him existed anywhere to match up with a police artist's sketch.

In short, his encounter with the store employee would be a deliberate diversion to send investigators after a man who existed totally off the grid.

The arsonist ticked off the elements of his safety net. His parents didn't apply for a Social Security card for their baby at birth, and he had never applied for the card on his own. He never served in the military, never been booked by any police agency, had no passport, no driver's license, no utility bills, no library cards, no real friends, and no jobs that required any sort of identification or Social Security withholding. He had never been fingerprinted for any reason.

He considered himself an invisible man, free to wreak havoc for as long he pleased.

12

"You can imagine how it surprised me to find you still in the store," the woman said to the arsonist. "Scared the daylights out of me what with everything that's been going on."

"You mean the fires?" he asked. "Yeah, these are scary times."

"I'm sure the authorities know more than they're saying."

"Either that, or they ain't got any clue a'tall."

He took a sip of his coffee. She nodded in agreement over her latte.

They had walked to a Starbuck's a block from the department store. After the arsonist had startled the sales clerk he apologized profusely, packed up his gear, and offered to buy her a cup of New Year's coffee by way of soothing her nerves. He thought about asking her out for a drink, but that might seem too much like a date, like him trying to put a move on her. He had no intention of that, and he didn't want her to get the wrong idea. So . . . coffee.

She told him her name was Beth. He didn't ask her last name, but she told him, anyway. Beth Daley. No relation to Chicago's father/son mayors. He told her his name was Bashir. He didn't mention his last name.

He saw a fleeting concern pass over her face.

She asked, "Are you Arab?"

He sighed, as though tired of getting the question because Arabs frightened people.

"My family is from Qatar two generations ago," he said. "No need to
worry. The English translation of Bashir is 'bringer of glad tidings.' I am
not a Muslim extremist. Honest."

Her smile was sincere, but her eyes reflected uncertainty.

She asked, "So what were you doing in the store, anyway? So late?"

"Finishin' up a job I started last week," he said.

"What job?" she asked.

"Fixin' a leak, right where you found me," he said. "One-a your managers
called my boss—he owns the company—and said there was a leak unner the
sink in the employee lunchroom on the second floor. So the boss sent me out. I
found the problem right away. An old gasket all dried up. Wrecked the whole
coupling. Design's hard to find any more. Old fashioned. Had to order a new
one. Took a couple of days to get it. So I rigged a temporary fix and stopped by
the store tonight to put the new coupling in. Now she's good to go for a few more
years, by which time they'll probly have put in a whole new faucet system."

She laughed in a self-conscious way.

"Well, you can imagine what I thought when I walked in to pick up my
coat and saw two legs sticking out from under the sink." She laughed
harder. "You won't believe this, but my first thought somebody planting
a bomb."

He smiled and shook his head, trying to make himself look saddened.

"Aye, it's a cryin' shame we gotta live like that." he said. "Bad enough
findin' a plumber unner your sink. Never mind a bomber."

Then he smiled. "We can go back, and I can show you there's no bomb
unner the sink."

"I believe you," she said. "Besides, the store's closed up now."

He already knew that. But even if they could have gotten back in, she
would find no bomb under the sink. He'd secured it in a pantry, installed out
of sight in a back corner. He'd placed it a good hour before anybody started
coming into the lunchroom to pick up their belongings before heading out
for the night. The arsonist then parked himself on his back under the sink,
ready to befriend the first woman who walked in and spoke to him. It

turned out to be Beth. She wouldn't understand for some time, but the chance meeting saved her life.

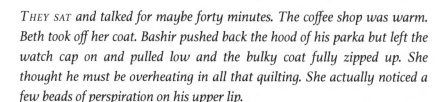

THEY SAT and talked for maybe forty minutes. The coffee shop was warm. Beth took off her coat. Bashir pushed back the hood of his parka but left the watch cap on and pulled low and the bulky coat fully zipped up. She thought he must be overheating in all that quilting. She actually noticed a few beads of perspiration on his upper lip.

"Aren't you hot in that coat?" she asked.

"A little," Bashir replied. "I'm buildin' up a heat reserve for when I go back out."

"You could catch a chill and get sick."

He shook his head, his longish dark hair tickling the faux fur of his hood.

"You don't catch colds from cold weather or getting chilled," he said. "You catch colds from cold bugs. I ain't worried."

Beth found something odd about this man. Not dangerous, just, well, something off. She couldn't define it now, and she wouldn't be able to define it to authorities later. She felt relief that they were in a public place. It gave her a margin of safety in case she discovered there was reason for her concern.

"So you gotta work tomorrow?" the plumber asked.

She replied, "Yeah, just mostly to help straighten things up and do inventory. Then I've got the next two days off. Don't have to go in again 'til Wednesday. It'll be nice to have a couple of days to myself. The holidays are exhausting."

When the time came to leave, she told him she had to visit the restroom, but he could go ahead, and thanks for the coffee.

"Have a wonderful new year," she told him.

"How're you getting home?" he asked. "I'd drive you in my truck, but the front seat's fulla stuff, and anyway, it's against company policy."

"Oh, no need," Beth said. "But thanks for the thought. My bus stop's *right outside the door. I can even wait in here, in the warm, and see my bus when it pulls up."*

"Okay, then," Bashir said. "Nice meetin' ya. Sorry again for the scare. That leak shouldn't give you any more trouble."

She would never see him again.

But neither would she ever be able to forget him.

Two DAYS LATER, on a Monday, the old Keene's department store came down.

The arsonist chose the day, the first Monday after the Christmas sales season ended, for two reasons. First, Beth would not be working. And second, he wanted to keep the casualties down. He didn't really care how many people died in his capers. But he didn't see any reason to cause whole-sale slaughters just for the sake of mounting numbers of dead and maimed. Nobody remembered numbers. They remembered terror.

Look at the air attacks on 9/11. If you asked people today how many died in the four coordinated plane crashes on the World Trade Center, the Pentagon, and in an open field in Pennsylvania, one in 5,000 might recall that it was 2,996. What stuck with almost everyone through the years was the panic locked in their imaginations: what the victims must have felt when they realized buildings were collapsing on top of them, and they would be crushed and buried under tons of broken concrete, or their plane was crashing, or the agony of explosive fires so intense people chose to jump from the highest floors of the World Trade Center rather than endure being burned alive. Or the most enduring fear of all: Will I be the next victim?

So the arsonist decided to blow the store before it opened. The timing would spare lives but also insure maximum damage and thus maximum terror. No one would remember the store was closed when it blew. But they would remember the explosions, and the fires, and the building's collapse.

In addition, the timing would tie up first responders in the morning traffic rush, meaning extra time to get to the scene. The delay would help the fire spread, extend the time for more witnesses to experience more fear, and for videographers to assemble more grisly footage of dead buildings and

dying people. These were the sorts of images that morph dreams into nightmares for all eternity. There was nothing to fear in high body counts. Para-
lyzing fear endured on the canvas of the imagination.

He needed to be certain the person who could not die would not be in
the store when it came down.

He called Keene's a half-hour before opening and asked to speak to Beth
Daley. The operator informed him that Beth Daley would be off until
Wednesday. Was there someone else who could help him?

He hung up.

As he had in the sporting goods store, the arsonist employed the terrorist
tactic of detonating bombs with cell phones. He had bought twenty-five
burner phones at different places all over the city. Each came with its own
number. He wrote down the numbers of twenty-four of them and combined
them into a conference call group. He programmed the group into the
twenty-fifth phone, which he kept. When he used it to call the group, the
phone ringers would trigger his Semtex explosions. The square block of
department store would be reduced to fiery rubble, taking neighboring
structures with it, just like the warehouse fire took out the electrical transformer. Collateral damage.

Eventually, he figured, the feds would be able to trace the explosive back
to the construction site where he'd stolen it. But he'd never worked at the site
—or any other construction site for that matter—and the search for the
bomber would come to a dead end again, right then and there. The authorities wouldn't stop looking, of course. But he would continue leaving false
clues, like the cigarette butts and Beth Daley, to drive them crazy.

Now he stood in front of the Starbucks and pulled a small plastic bag
from his pocket. Inside, a used cigarette butt, the only one left of the seven
he had dropped around Keene's. He tossed it onto the sidewalk and started
to walk away.

"Hey, buddy," another pedestrian called to him. "In Chicago we pick up
our trash. We'd appreciate it if you'd pick up yours. Show a little pride in
your home town, okay?"

The arsonist glanced at the cigarette butt and then up at the pedestrian
and started walking toward the man raising a stink over an inch-long piece
of trash. In his watch cap, hood, and bulky coat it wasn't hard to look

*menacing. He saw confusion and concern begin to grow on the meddler's
face.*

"You talkin' to me?" he asked.

The man shrugged. "Just askin' you to clean up after yourself."

"Ain't none-a your business," the arsonist said. "You'd do best to
move on."

The arsonist turned his back and returned to straddle the butt until he
was sure the interloper had left the street. He didn't want anyone moving
the cigarette. When several minutes passed without the meddler's reappear-
ance, the arsonist assumed the guy was gone. Nobody hangs around to pick
up somebody else's cigarette butt.

Time to make the call.

13

He walked east and crossed Michigan Avenue until he put four city blocks between himself and the Keene's building. He took a deep breath. This project thrilled him beyond all the others combined. He found himself getting aroused in anticipation. This was better than sex, not that sex happened very often in his life.

He pulled the twenty-fifth phone from his pocket, took a deep breath and dialed.

The arsonist would recall later that he felt the first rumbling of his work vibrate through the ground to his boots. In fact, the vibration rattling the ground in that moment, as the arsonist's call made its way through a series of phone circuits and cell towers, emanated from a Metra heavy rail commuter train rumbling into its subterranean Millennium Station from Joliet. The impacts of the explosions at Keene's erupted seconds later and simultaneously.

The windows blew out with a thunderclap. Angry clouds of roiling dust rushed through the gaping holes accompanied by the blinding bloom of explosions, fire, and billowing smoke. The flashes hammered with a concussion that shook the ground like a seismic shockwave and broke windows in buildings all around, raining a deadly shower of glass, brick and rubble onto the sidewalks and streets.

Keene's department store simply died, falling and folding in on itself in a slow-motion cloud of dust as the vertical support structures collapsed, and the floors pancaked and broke into pieces. The firestorm bellowed to life, fed by broken gas lines, flammable merchandise, and furnishings.

The arsonist gaped at the building, trying not to grin. Except for the echoes of the deafening claps of the explosions and the clatter of falling debris, he heard no sound. Everything around him seemed to stop and go silent for a short moment.

Then the world erupted in screams.

Flying chunks of stone and brick crashed through vehicle windshields and roofs, killing a number of occupants and injuring countless others. The toll included four city buses and some riders. Drivers gunned their engines, even running up on sidewalks, to try to get out of the area. The flying rocks and glass killed and injured pedestrians who went to ground as if assault rifles had mowed them down. Others disappeared under collapsing walls. Most left standing turned and ran in whatever direction would take them away from the disaster. Some of them trailed blood.

Dozens of people, screaming at no one in particular to call 911 or dialing their own phones, ran toward the still-crumbling wreckage in the hope of saving someone, anyone, trapped inside, or lying in their own blood on the sidewalks, or trapped inside vehicles crushed by crumbling walls and concrete blocks hurled with the force of cannon balls. They would find no shortage of people needing immediate help.

Two more buildings exploded. Probably more broken gas lines. How far could this disaster spread? Never had the arsonist felt this degree of satisfaction with his work. This gave purpose of his life, to burn the city to rubble. He had proved himself quite adept at it.

As much as he wanted to, he couldn't risk waiting around to watch the fire spread. He turned and walked south on Michigan, toward the nearest bus stop that would take him out of the area toward home.

His father and grandfather would be proud of him.

As the Replecant thug, Leon, said in the movie Blade Runner, "Wake up. Time to die."

14

I n the South Loop newsroom of the Chicago *Journal* the atmosphere resembled ordered chaos, emphasis on the chaos.

Eric called in the police reporters who weren't on duty near the wreckage of several city blocks or at police headquarters, all the City Hall reporters save the one staking out the mayor's office, most of the general assignment, features, and business writers, photo editors, and me. Why me I didn't know other than the fact that I offered a living, breathing body, a critical commodity on a story of this magnitude.

Eric stood in front of the mass of assembled journalists to issue marching orders.

He reviewed what had happened. Nothing remained of the historic building housing Keene's department store but rubble, bodies, and flames. An hour after the explosions, the fires had not been contained.

He turned to the head of our research library.

"We're going to need a sidebar on that building's history," he said, "and the history of any other historic sites damaged or destroyed."

He continued describing what we already knew about the disaster. Damage to many of the buildings surrounding Keene's in a four-block radius ranged from extensive to total. Destruction extended beyond Keene's north to the Chicago River, east to Millennium Park, and south to the iconic Palmer House. At the Richard J. Daley Center flying debris had damaged the priceless Picasso sculpture in the plaza.

Trying to tally the dead and injured at this point became an act of futility. No one could even hazard a guess. At mid-day, the death count in the Keene's building alone could have been in the hundreds. As of this moment, 10:35 in the morning, an hour after the blast, no one could get near the rubble to begin a search. Reports said at least twenty people had died on the streets outside and in neighboring buildings that were stable enough to be searched, but city officials refused to discuss numbers. Reports from nearby hospitals confirmed that scores had been injured, and some of the injuries were life threatening.

That the toll would be high seemed inevitable.

Property damage would reach into hundreds of millions of dollars.

Damage to the city's spirit couldn't be measured. I thought that might be a good topic to explore in a column.

I couldn't wrap my head around this tragedy. I hoped we would all be surprised to learn it had been an accident. I didn't count on it.

Terrorism occupied everyone's attention, and my initial skepticism about that conclusion began to melt away. The warehouse could have been an accident. Even Cubs 'n' Stuff could have been an accident—though who accidentally turns off a sprinkler system? The Water Tower Buildings, Lawndale, definitely not accidents. Keene's? No way in hell. Someone had laid siege to the city, and terrorists seemed the most likely culprits.

As usual, Eric had a plan for coverage. Planning was his strong suit, his greatest qualification as Metro editor. He knew exactly what he wanted the police/fire reporters to do, the city government reporters, the feature writers, the photographers, the business writers. Everyone. Eric had a mind that worked in lists and delegation of responsibilities. All staff members left the meeting knowing exactly what responsibilities they carried with them, exactly what Eric expected of each of them.

Except me.

That would soon change.

"Deuce, would you stay a moment?" Eric asked as everyone else hurried away to get to work. "I have a special assignment for you."

"Does this involve Mark?" I asked, hoping it wouldn't.

"Not unless he wants to help, and I doubt he'll have either the desire or the time," Eric said. "I need a writer, someone fast and accurate who knows the city. Someone who can take a mountain of information and carve important pieces out of it for the main story. Others can handle the sidebars, witness accounts, and so on. I need a performer who won't panic under the workload. I need you."

My column would go on hiatus for a while. I would be in the office early and leave late. I would read through every page of notes filed by my colleagues, every story they wrote, every official press release. I would cull the best of the best, the most revealing, descriptive, and heart-rending and assemble the main story for each day's paper. The "main bar," as we called it in the business, might be the only story some readers took time for, and it had to give them a complete overview.

I knew from experience how excruciating these stories could be. Piecing them together more resembled data management than writing. And I really wanted to do the column exploring the impact of the fires on the city's spirit. I told Eric, and he liked the idea.

"Hold onto it," he said. "Maybe I can break you loose later in the week. For now, we have to concentrate on the task at hand. A clerk will make printouts of every scrap filed to the city desk. Take what you want for your story. If there's some redundancy with other stories, that's fine. Don't worry about it. You'll probably need some research help. Anybody in particular you want?"

"Can you spare Lucy Sandoval?"

I considered Lucy the best researcher the *Journal* had on staff. She was fast and thorough. She could help me on several levels.

Eric nodded. "We might have to pull her back from time to time to pitch in on other specific stories. But we'll try to keep those diversions to a minimum."

We looked at one another for a moment, each of us overwhelmed by what we faced.

"So," Eric finally said, "it's show time. What are you waiting for?"

I WENT BACK to my desk and opened the computer to read what we posted on our web site. So far, it wasn't much, a hash of stray facts and quotes strung together without a lot of substance. I checked the *Sun-Times* and the *Tribune*. They fared no better. Most of the TVs hanging from the newsroom ceiling were tuned to local stations. Each TV had an editorial assistant monitoring the reports, sending memos to the assistant city editors when they heard something that sounded new. Someone had tuned the TV closest to my desk to CNN. Not much help there except for the videos. I felt my chest tighten looking at footage transmitted through CNN from a drone belonging to Chicago TV station WGN.

The camera switched to a wide shot encompassing most of the damage around Keene's. It looked more like a Syrian war zone than downtown Chicago.

That description would probably find its way into my story.

Copy clerks had already started running early reports from our staff on the streets. The paper piled up fast.

I took a deep breath and started reading.

ABOUT AN HOUR LATER, Eric came by my desk.

"You got a handle on it yet?" he asked.

"It's all still seething," I said. "The story doesn't hold still very long."

"I know, but we need something for the web site. Could you do a fast roundup of what we know? Not long. No speculation, no guessing, no gossip. Just the knowable facts."

"Sure," I said. "Give me about fifteen minutes."

Ordinarily I would have resisted being interrupted. But writing and rewriting for the web site what I learned as the day progressed would help me absorb and make sense of events spinning wildly out of control a few blocks away. It would help me keep all the development in all the story threads sorted in my head.

I flinched when my phone rang. I didn't need to be bothered right then.

"Deuce Mora," I said.

I heard breathing on the line, but no words.

"This is Deuce Mora," I repeated. "Can I help you with something?"

"I . . . I don't know," a woman's voice said in halting, nervous speech. I thought I heard a soft Southern accent.

"Ma'am, I'm really busy at the moment. Talk to me, or I'll have to hang up."

"I think I might have met the person who started the fires," she said.

I sat up very straight.

She continued. "I don't know for certain, mind you, but I met this man. He acted strange. We talked a while. I never saw him again."

"What's your name?" I asked, trying to remain calm.

"My name?" she said, sounding frightened. "Oh, I don't wanna give my name."

I backtracked. "Okay," I said, "if you don't want to tell me your name I won't pressure you. Tell me how and when you met this man."

"No, no," she said. "I'm real sorry. I made a mistake. I shouldn'ta called."

And she hung up.

"Damn it," I snapped at the dead phone. "Damn it to hell."

A few heads turned my way, but not for long.

My colleagues were used to hearing me curse telephones.

But I wasn't cursing the phone. I was cursing myself.

I had no clue to the identity of the caller. I had a sick feeling I'd just blown a good lead. The woman hadn't sounded like a crank.

She sounded terrified.

15

I heard a thud on my desk behind me and turned to see an editorial assistant scampering away after dropping a load of paper on me. I picked it up to read through it quickly and pulled what I needed to write an update to the web story.

The staff had filed a lot of eyewitness accounts and quotes, some contradictory and some exquisitely detailed. There were updates on the dead and injured, a more comprehensive list of buildings damaged or destroyed, and first reports from hospitals where the injured were taken. We had no official statements yet, but the mayor, the police chief, the fire chief, the head of emergency management, the head of the transportation department, and the FBI had scheduled a presser in the next hour or so.

Medical personnel on the scene set up a triage operation that sent those most in need of urgent treatment to Northwestern Memorial Hospital on East Huron because it was closest. Others, especially those with orthopedic injuries, went to Rush University Medical Center, which had possibly the finest orthopedic department in the country. The rest were scattered over several nearby facilities. The best estimates our reporters could get had more than 120 people with varying severity of injuries either treated and released or admitted.

The police revised the death toll upward. They had twenty-three dead, all outside the devastated buildings, all hit by falling debris or by the blunt force trauma of the explosions. They didn't even try to offer assurances that the death toll would remain static.

If nothing else, reports said some taken to hospitals were not expected to survive.

No one would even hazard a guess at the number of bodies buried in the rubble.

Everyone talked about terrorism.

I hadn't thought about my anonymous caller for a few hours, but I needed a break, so I went to tell Eric about her.

"Did you get her number?" he asked.

"She called into the office system. The PBX doesn't pick that up."

"Where have you been, Deuce? The PBX went away months ago. We're on an Internet system now that logs every call we get. Even if you miss the call and the caller doesn't leave a message, you get an email telling you about the missed call. Then you look on the call log, and there's the number."

"Really?"

"Really. Haven't you gotten any emails about missed calls?"

"I don't think so. But I haven't checked my email today. Maybe the messages are going to spam."

"That's not supposed to happen."

"Technology is a wonderful thing, until it isn't. I'll get someone to show me how to find the logs."

"Do that," Eric said. "Do you remember what time it came in? The call, I mean."

"A little after 11:30."

"Find that number."

RICK SIMON in the IT department said he'd help, but only if I gave him a hug. So I did. I liked Rick enormously. He had an exuberant personality and a self-deprecating sense of humor that never let up.

"I have a lot to be self-deprecating about," he once told me over a drink after work. "I'm handicapped for starters."

"Handicapped how?" I asked. I'd noticed nothing unusual about him.

"I'm a gay black man with a tendency to ingrown toenails," he said.

I laughed. "Nothin' we can do about the toenails," I said. "Maybe find you a good podiatrist. Lots of us are working on the gay and black stuff."

"We still got a long way to go, sistah."

"I hear ya," I said.

Once when I complimented a stunning bracelet he wore he replied, "You know why gays are such great dressers? We spend most of our lives in the closet."

I laughed at that, too, but I cringed at the same time. I told him I thought there might be something vaguely offensive about the line.

He put his hand on mine. "Only because you care, Deuce," he said. "But not to worry. If we can't laugh at ourselves, who can we laugh at?"

Today I told Rick what had happened with the abbreviated phone call.

"You didn't know about the new phone system?" he asked. "You livin' in a cave?"

"No," I said, pretending offense. "I think all that got changed over while I was on vacation in Costa Rica. When I got back, nobody thought to bring me up to date."

He shook his head. "Costa Rica? How nice for you. You know, there ain't gonna be no real equality in this world 'til gay black people can afford straight white-people vacations."

"Oh, yeah?" I said. "I have a vague recollection of you describing the month you and Paul spent on the Amalfi Coast last year."

"Oh, that little thing?" he said with a laugh. "I proposed to Paul on that trip."

I felt my mouth drop, and I hugged Rick again.

"Do you have a wedding date? When do I get my invitation?"

He flashed his left hand, where a gorgeous filigreed gold wedding band lived.

"We're already married," he said, his voice dropping to near a whisper. "We got married as soon as we got back to Chicago. Eloped to City Hall. We didn't want to make a big deal about it, and we wanted to get it done before somebody tried to change the laws back the way they used to be. We're going to take a honeymoon in August in Tahiti."

"Congratulations," I said with real feeling. "And, by the way, it sounds to me like you take more straight white-people vacations than most straight white people I know."

I put up my hand. "Look, I'll buy you both dinner soon, but right now I've got to find that phone number."

He pulled up the logs. "What's your extension?" he asked.

I gave it to him. He searched and found the 11:32 call immediately.

He looked up at me from his computer and grinned.

"I just sent it to your email," he said. "I'm so talented. Good-looking, too."

I slapped him on the shoulder and kissed the top of his head. "When you die," I said, "they're gonna give you an enema and bury you in a match box."

16

I gave the number to Lucy Sandoval, the research librarian and my partner on this story, and asked her if she could find out who owned the phone that matched up.

"Yeah, I could," she said. "But it will take me about five minutes if it's a cell phone."

"You're just showing off," I said as Lucy's fingers danced over her keyboard. After two minutes, she leaned back in her chair and looked up at me.

"So, genius," I said, "you giving up?"

She grinned. "It's in your email. I'll expect a bonus for bringing it home early."

"You're kidding?" I said, genuinely astonished.

I checked my email, and found it. Phone number, name, and address.

I looked over at her. She flashed a shit-eating grin. She formed her hand into a gun and blew on her fingertip.

"My work here is done," she said.

I grinned back. "Not by a long shot, Sancho. We have plenty of windmills in our future. Stay ready."

I sat and stared at the name of the phone's owner. Elizabeth

Daley. I wondered if she was any relation the former Chicago mayors. Her voice had a definite lilt of the South, not Chicago's unique inflections. While that didn't exclude a relationship to the Mayors Daley, it reduced the likelihood. I Googled her address. She lived in Lincoln Park on North Larrabee Street across from a magical expanse of green known as Oz Park. It had a permanent population of bronze statues of characters from L. Frank Baum's children's story, "The Wonderful Wizard of Oz." Everyone who visited me from out of town wanted to go take photos of Dorothy and Toto, the Cowardly Lion and the Tin Man at Oz Park. I guess there are pieces of children's literature that even adults don't outgrow.

I took a deep breath and dialed the number.

No answer.

I walked back to Lucy.

"Is this a cell phone or a land line?" I asked.

"Cell phone," Lucy said.

Okay, most people have their cell phones with them all the time. Elizabeth Daley could conceivably be at the theater, or a movie, or a restaurant and have her phone powered down. More likely my caller ID showed up on her screen. She didn't want to talk to me. So she simply didn't pick up. Time for Plan B.

I went back to Rick Simon in IT and asked him to call Daley's number on his private cell phone, and if a woman answered, pass the phone to me. He did. She did. And he did.

"Ms. Daley," I said quickly, "please don't hang up. This is Deuce Mora at the *Journal,* and I want to apologize. This call isn't being recorded, nobody knows I'm talking to you, and no one is listening. I'm sorry I pushed you to identify yourself when you called earlier."

Rick glanced at me, got up from his desk and started to move away. I touched his sleeve and gestured that he didn't need to go. He put a legal pad and pen on the desk and motioned that I should sit there to take notes. I might have nothing to write. So far, Elizabeth Daley hadn't given me anything. She hadn't spoken a word since saying, "Hello."

"Are you still there?" I asked.

Another moment's silence, then, "I don't know what you're talkin' about."

"Ms. Daley, when you called me our telephone system captured your number, and that led us to you. I'm sorry. The last thing I want to do is frighten you. But if you have information that could lead to the people setting bombs and fires all over the city, you ..."

"Don't y'all start with the 'civic duty' crap," she snapped. "By identifying me, you might'uv already put my life in danger. I probably lost a lot of friends at Keene's. I'm not ready to die along with 'em."

I felt a frown crease my face. I did the timetable in my head.

"The store hadn't open yet when it exploded," I said.

"The staff woulda started comin' in at 9:15 or so," she said. "We always got there early to set up before opening."

"You worked at Keene's?"

"Yes. In jewelry and watches. I'd've been there, but it was my day off."

"Uh, look, you're on your cell phone, and there is always a chance somebody could listen, even by accident. We need to meet somewhere and talk quietly and privately."

"I tole you no."

"But you also called me. You initiated this. And that says yes."

I let her think about it.

She said, "Not today. I'm too upset by all this mess. Tomorrow?"

"Where? You want me to come to your house?"

"Oh, God, no," she said with some panic in her voice. "Everybody knows your face. I don't want anybody to recognize you coming to see me."

"Okay, where would you feel safe? We could sit in the park. It's supposed to be sunny and in the forties tomorrow, but still, it could get pretty cold if we're there a while."

"I don't feel safe anywhere," she said. "There's a place called Toast near the northwest corner of the park. On Webster just east of Halsted. A breakfast and lunch place. They close at four. If we met there at two o'clock tomorrow, it should be almost empty."

"I know the place," I said. "Promise you'll be there?"

"I think so," she said. And then with disdain in her voice she added, "I don't know if I'll decide to talk to you, but I might as well be there. You know where I live. If I don't show, you'll just come lookin' for me. And you'd probably stake out the place 'til I showed up. It'll be easier to meet you and get it over with."

"You'll be safe," I said, trying to reassure her.

She gave me a grunt with a side of scorn.

"You cain't keep me safe. Nobody can keep me safe. Nobody can keep anyone safe anymore. Safety's an illusion. You should know that."

I did. And it scared the crap out of me.

17

E ric Ryland assigned someone to cover for me the following afternoon so I could go up to Lincoln Park and meet with Elizabeth Daley. Since officials weren't disclosing much beyond the mounting body count, writing the main bar would be a less complex task than the first day when pieces of the story broke everywhere.

The casualty count rose to twenty-seven fatalities and 139 injuries. Some of the new death reports came from hospitals that had been unable to save the most grievously hurt. The collapsed and burned buildings, including the skeleton of Keene's, were still too unstable for full exploration, meaning the death toll would go higher. Searchers and their dogs worked tirelessly, driven by the limited amount of time the injured could survive in the rubble in the cold. The last known survivor had been pulled from the debris of an office building a little after seven the previous evening.

I left the office more than an hour early to give myself plenty of time to get to Lincoln Park. Since the blast site sat between the *Journal* building and Toast I would have to go well out of my way to get around roadblocks and the hopelessly snarled traffic.

It took me almost an hour to get up Halsted to a parking garage south of Oz Park. I walked north to Webster, turned right and found Toast. Only a dozen people occupied tables, and no one sat alone. I had beaten Elizabeth Daley there.

I asked for a four-top with no one nearby. I sat down and put my messenger bag on the empty chair beside me. I had brought one of my tiny, voice-activated recording devices that looks like a computer thumb drive. I clipped it to an outside pocket of the bag. The recorder would pick up our full conversation. Recording someone without his or her knowledge and permission could have dumped me into legal trouble. But I used the recorder as an electronic stenographer, not as a means of collecting evidence for a court case, so I didn't feel guilty. In fact, I feared if Elizabeth saw me taking notes, it would inhibit her. With the recorder doing its thing out of sight, the interview would feel more like a casual conversation. I ordered coffee and explained I was waiting for someone.

A woman I'd never seen before arrived at my table at the same time as the coffee.

"Aren't you Deuce Mora?" she asked.

"Yes," I said. "And you are . . .?"

"My name is Dorrie, and I'm a big fan."

"Uh, Dorrie, I don't mean to be rude, but I'm waiting for someone, and we're going to be quite busy. So . . ."

"Oh, sorry, I just wondered if I could get an autograph," the woman said with an apologetic, shy smile.

"From me?" I blurted out. I couldn't remember anyone ever asking me for an autograph. "I guess."

I asked her how she spelled her name and gave her what she asked for.

As Dorrie walked away happy, I noticed another woman standing just inside the front door, eyeing me with suspicion. I smiled, hoping to put her at ease. It must have worked. She walked to my table. Very slowly, her gaze studying everyone she passed.

"Elizabeth?" I asked when she arrived.

"Everyone calls me Beth," she said, "'cept my gramma. She calls me Elizabeth."

I extended my hand. Her palm was damp, her grip weak, and her hand trembling.

"Relax," I suggested. "We're fine. How about some coffee, or tea? A late lunch, maybe. The *Journal* will pay."

The waitperson arrived. Beth ordered hot tea. When he asked her what kind, she snapped at him. "Just tea. Regular tea. Whatever you got."

He glanced at me as if to ask what he'd done wrong. I could only shrug.

When he left, Beth put her elbow on the table and dropped her forehead into her hand. "I'm sorry," she said. "I had no call to be rude to him." She looked up at me. "I'm just so scared." She pronounced the last word, "skeered."

"If you divided the city right now into those who are calm and those who feel like you do, the scared ones would way outnumber the rest," I said. "Take a deep breath."

She nodded.

I smiled to help calm her. "That's not a Chicago accent. Where're you from?"

"Little town in southern Missoura called Forsyth. Just east of Branson. Lived in N'Orleans, too, when I was a teenager."

"Missouri is very pretty," I told her. "I love the Ozarks."

"Yeah," she said, picking at a fingernail while staring at her hands. "I need to get outta here and back home. I don't wanna be here any more. No need to be here any more."

"Why'd you come?" I asked.

"Take care of a dying aunt," she said, "my mama's sister. My mama is too crippled up with arthritis to come. She cain't stand the winters in Missoura, let alone Chicago. But my aunt died three months ago, so there's no reason for me to hang around here. I only stayed to help the store through the Christmas rush. I shoulda got out sooner. My sister's been trying to take care of mama alone, and she cain't handle it by herself any more. The doctor visits, shopping, checkin' on her a couple times a day, and whatall. She's got her own family to look after. So I need to go help."

I felt sympathy for this woman.

"Is your father still in the picture?"

She made a dismissive sound. "Nobody knows where Daddy's at, or even if he's still alive. He left fifteen, sixteen years ago. Nobody's heard from him since, not even a phone call. He wouldn't help us even if he knew we needed help."

She glanced up from her fidgeting hands and asked, "What do you want to know?"

"You called me, remember?" I said. "What did you want to tell me?"

Beth's tea came, and she turned her fidgeting attention to it, adding a little sugar, rubbing the rind of a lemon wedge as if expecting it to offer a vision of her future, like a crystal ball. She raised the cup and started to take a sip, decided against it, and set the cup down. She remained silent.

I resolved to wait her out, at least until 4 p.m. when the place closed.

"I don't know where to start," she said.

"The beginning is usually the easiest option."

She nodded.

"I'm not sure when the beginning was," she said. "I guess it maybe Saturday, when I was gettin' ready to leave the store after closing, 9:30 or so. I walked into the lunchroom, and there he was. Scared me half to death."

I got the idea Beth frightened rather easily.

"Who?" I asked.

"He told me later his name was Bashir," she said, "that his family came from Qatar two generations ago. Did I pronounce that right?" She had called the country Qwatter, but I waved off her concern and indicated she should continue. "At that first moment, when I first saw him, he was just a belly and legs stickin' out from under the sink. Turned out he was a plumber fixin' a leak. An old faulty gasket, he said."

"A plumber that late at night? It must have been some leak. A call at that hour had to cost the store a fortune."

"That's what bothered me," Beth said. "One of the things that bothered me. I also couldn't figure out why he was workin' in his big, heavy winter coat. When he slid out I saw he was also wearin' one of those wool caps, like a ski cap only without the pom-pom ball on the top..."

"A watch cap? Knit? Fits snug to the head?"

"Yeah, that's it. It was cool in the building, but not cold. What kind of plumber wears his hat and coat when he's crawling around a floor under a sink?"

I cocked my head as if to tell her I agreed it was a valid question.

"Anyhow, he says, 'I hope I didn't scare you.' I told him he had. So he gets up and apologizes. Then, of all things, he asks me if he can buy me a cup of coffee to make up for it."

She took a small sip of her tea and began to cough.

"Okay?" I asked.

She nodded. "Just went down the wrong way. I'm nervous."

"I can tell. Anyway, he asks you out and you say...?

"I said okay, there's a Starbucks near the store. So after I picked up my Thermos and got my coat, we walked over there. He got coffee and I got a latte. He insisted on paying to make up for scaring me. But it wasn't like you're suggesting. It wasn't a date. He never came on to me, and when we were done, we went our separate ways."

"How long were you with him, and what did you talk about?"

"Maybe forty-five, fifty minutes. And it was the same thing again. He never took off his coat or that cap. Or his scarf. The coat had a hood, and that was pushed back, but he stayed all bundled up in the rest of it. I could see he was overheating."

"Did you ask him why he didn't take the coat off?"

"I asked him a couple of things. I asked him about the coat and cap, and he said he was building up heat for when he went outside. Then he laughed, like it was a joke." She repeated the rest of their conversation. She clearly hadn't bought some of Bashir's story. "I asked him why he'd come to the store so late. He said they'd had to order a new part, and he came to put it in after his last scheduled job that day. It seemed very late to me. Old Mr. Whatley, the plumber down in Forsyth, might do that, but you don't expect that kinda service in the big city."

"Not only that, it was Saturday," I said. "I don't think there are many plumbers who work weekends, at least not without getting paid double or triple time. Keene's had to be pretty desperate to get the leak stopped."

"Yeah, I didn't think of that."

Beth didn't drink much tea, but she made a severe dent in the world supply of paper napkins. She pulled several out of a metal stand. One by one she folded then shredded them. She amassed an impressive pile of confetti around her teacup.

"Did you happen to try to find out who at the store called him?"

"I tried. The next day, Sunday, I went up to the admin offices to see if anyone remembered. The execs and secretaries weren't there, and nobody at work knew anything about a plumber—or a leak in the lunchroom for that matter. I had Monday off, and Tuesday. I planned to ask again when I went back Wednesday, but . . ." Her voice trailed off.

"How about other employees? The sales staff?"

"Well, they wouldn't know who called the plumber. But I did talk to a couple of them, and nobody remembered any leak under that sink. If it was that bad, you'd think somebody woulda noticed."

"You'd think, yeah," I said. "Can you describe the guy? You said he called himself Bashir and his family came from Qatar. Did he have a Middle Eastern or Asian look?"

Beth smiled and almost chuckled. "He sensed I was wary of him. He told me not to worry, that his name, Bashir, translated into English as 'bearer of glad tidings.'"

"Hardly a proper name for a terrorist, unless he's into irony," I said. "Did you notice anything about him?"

"Yeah," she said, "his eyes. They were so dark they were almost black. They didn't look real. I thought maybe he had contacts."

I nodded.

"Something else wasn't right," she said. "His name didn't fit him somehow. He sounded like he was born in the United States, like

English was his first language. That would fit if he was third genera-
tion. But there was a time or two he said something, and I thought he
sounded a little Irish. Then a couple of sentences later, he sounded
Italian. Not accents, exactly, but just his general way of speaking. But
I'm probably wrong. Bashir isn't a name given to any Irish or Italian
men I know, that's for sure."

"You have a lot of Irish and Italians in Forsyth?" I asked, smiling
to put her at ease.

Beth sat up straighter. "I'll have you know there's more Irish per
capita in Missoura than in the whole United States," she said with
pride. "Somethin' like two percent more."

"Really?" I said, feigning interest. "Is there anything else you can
think of that would help describe Bashir?"

"From what I could see of his face, which wasn't much, he had a
ruddy complexion, weathered, like he did a lot of work outdoors in
the sun and wind."

"How would you describe his physical stature?"

"I couldn't, all bundled up in that coat the way he was, and the
cap. I think he mighta been about five-foot-nine or -ten. He had
longish hair. I remember that because he had the hood of his coat
pushed back, and when he turned his head his hair kept brushing
the fake fur along the edge. I think it was medium brown. On top,
who knows? He cudda been bald for all I know. And his weight I
couldn't even hazard a guess. His coat was quilted—real bulky—and
went down to his thighs. I remember his boots. They were those
waterproof models that have the rippled gum soles for traction.
Rubber uppers and then leather from the ankles up. And those speed
lace things that run though metal rings."

"Duck boots," I said. "Do you remember the color of the rubber
part?"

"Blue, I think. Dark blue. Then tan leather up above."

"Did you talk about seeing each other again?"

"Oh, no. This was a one-off thing. Cuppa coffee and gone."

"Do you remember in the last couple of weeks ever seeing
anybody in the store tinkering around in areas where they shouldn't

have been? Or hear any of your colleagues mention seeing anything like that?"

"No, not that I remember, other than Bashir," Beth said. "And after all the terrorism talk recently, if anybody'd seen anything suspicious, they'da reported it. You wrote a column reminding people, 'If you see something, say something.'"

I asked Beth if I could call her with questions if I thought of anything else. She gave reluctant permission. I gave her my card so she could reach me if she needed or wanted to.

Winter darkness had begun to settle in. I asked if she'd like to walk with me to my car. I could drive her around the park to her condo. She thanked me and declined.

"I'd rather walk," she said. "I feel better now that I've talked to somebody about this. I just hope nothing happens to make me sorry later."

I felt the same way.

18

I let Beth leave first, then I checked my recorder to make sure it had worked correctly. It had, but I was so distracted thinking about what Beth told me that I forgot to turn it off before hooking it back onto the pocket of my messenger bag.

Good thing for me.

I paid for our drinks and left a major tip for the waitperson who had endured the sour fruits of Beth's mood. I folded the receipt and put it in my wallet. I would be reimbursed the expense, though the bean counters would never let a $10 tip for a cup of coffee and a cup of tea slide by.

As I stepped through the front door I looked left and right, up and down West Webster Avenue. I wasn't looking for anyone or anything in particular. It was a habit I'd picked up after my experiences working on the child trafficking investigation. Most of the time I wasn't even aware of doing it.

Nothing unusual caught my eye, and I turned right toward Halsted, then south toward the garage where I'd left my car.

I almost made it.

I had just crossed West Dickens Avenue when I sensed someone walking behind me.

I stopped short. My shadow nearly plowed into me. When I turned I was looking into a face I had hoped never to see again. Ronald Colter, AD of the FBI for the Chicago division.

"Oh, Christ," I said.

"Not quite," Colter replied.

"What the hell do you want?"

"Interesting," Colter said. "In the space of two short sentences you mention Christ and hell. Religiously conflicted, are we?"

It was the first time I'd ever gotten an inkling that Colter had a sense of humor.

He wasn't finished. "I'm not rude to you when I return your phone calls. Why are you treating me like a piece of used bubble gum on your shoe?"

"I don't take well to being stalked. I asked you a question. I want an answer."

"What was the question? Oh, what the hell do I want? Is that the one?"

I just glared at him. Nothing about him had changed. Razor-cut salt-and-pepper hair, gray eyes, chiseled features including a square jaw, ramrod-straight spine. Even under the cover of his camel cashmere topcoat I could see that he was still buff. He was a poster boy for federal agents. I don't like poster boys. I always suspect they used brawn and grooming to cover deficiencies in brains and maturity.

He asked, "Who was that bundle of nerves you were talking to in the restaurant?"

I had no intention of playing his games.

"I don't know what you're talking about," I said.

"Ms. Mora . . . Deuce . . . could we declare a truce?" Colter said. His face softened. He lost his official fierce "Fed Look" and actually appeared almost human. Of course, as a trained agent, acting ability would be one of his skill sets.

"I didn't know we were at war," I said. "Though there's still a chloroform score to settle. Paybacks are hell, you know."

"I know," he said. "Look, you're a first rate-reporter. You're a first-rate investigator. People in this city know you, they like you, and they trust you. You're writing stories about the unexplained and tragic acts of arson. If somebody knew something, or thought they knew something, it would not be surprising if they called you."

"True," I said.

"And they don't like to call us."

"Also true. Can you blame them?"

He ignored my insult.

"That little afternoon tea you just had smacks of such a contact," he said.

"I had coffee," I said. "But I quibble."

A gust of wind hit us at that moment. Though the city enjoyed a mild January, the wind carried a damp chill. I wanted to get to my car and turn on the heat.

"Someone should smack you, Colter," I said. "You go out of your way to earn it."

He held his hands out, palms facing me.

"I deserved that from you," he said. "And I know you won't say anything to me without your editor and lawyer present. Could we arrange a meeting this evening, or tomorrow morning at the latest?"

"I have no idea, but I doubt it. Everybody's pretty busy right now."

"Could you inform them of my interest?"

"I'm not in a mood to do you any favors. You might check back with me in eighteen or twenty years."

My voice had risen and caught the attention of three young Hispanic men walking by. One of them paused and looked at me with a raised eyebrow.

"You okay?" he asked. He had a Mexican accent.

I smiled at him and nodded. "Yes. Thank you."

He cocked his head at Colter. "Is he bothering you?"

I nodded. "Yes, he makes a habit of it. But not in any way that's dangerous. He's just a natural prick. Thank you for asking."

Colter snapped at him. "Just move on. We're having a civil conversation here."

"Didn't sound so civil to us," the young man said. But he and his friends began walking away. Slowly.

I couldn't help but grin. The neighborly concern was so typical of Chicagoans.

"Deuce, this is not a laughing matter." Colter had lowered his voice.

"And I'm not laughing. I'm grinning. The problem with you, Colter, is that everything's a one-way street. You take and take and never give."

"That's my job. But you and your friend, Mark, and your editor and lawyer have all abided by the promises made the last time our paths crossed. That scores you some points. We might find a way to provide a *quid pro quo* this time. You give us what you know, and I will personally tell you what I can of what I know. Of course I'll have to stop at the point where the reveals could compromise national security."

"Of course you will. And you'll find a way so the national security blanket covers everything of any interest to us. I can predict it now. We tell you everything we know, and you tell us it's Wednesday."

"I won't. I promise. I will even agree to publication of some of what I tell you, properly sourced, of course."

"You do understand that I don't trust you, right?"

Colter gave a small shake of his head. He looked almost sad. I watched his face for a minute. I didn't see deceit there. More like disappointment and desperation.

"Please," he said, "just convey my request."

I almost felt bad for him.

But as I noted earlier, good spies are generally excellent actors.

19

B efore Colter and I parted company, I told him I probably couldn't arrange a meeting yet that afternoon given fast-approaching news deadlines. Eric would be working late with the next day's editions. I had no idea what Jonathan Bruckner's schedule looked like. For all I knew the *Journal's* lawyer could be tied up in court.

I said I would go back to the office as quickly as traffic permitted and present the idea of a four-way meeting the next day.

"As early as possible," Colter asked. "Please."

Had Ronald Colter ever said "please" to me before, about anything? I couldn't recall it if he had. And now twice in one conversation.

"All I can do is convey your request to my editor," I said. "The rest is up to him and to Mr. Bruckner. I am only a messenger."

Colter reached in his pocket and came out with his business card.

"I'm sure you used my last one to toast marshmallows," he said. "Keep this one. Use it to a better end. Call me as soon as you get an answer. I don't care what time it is."

He must have been serious. He'd written his cell phone number on the card.

∽

WHEN I GOT BACK to work I interrupted Eric's private meltdown over
the state of the main story for the next day's paper. The piece was
badly focused, way too long, and missing updates on the investigation, such as they were. The story spent too much time with families
of those hurt or killed. Not that they weren't important, but there
were other stories focused on the victims. The main should have
concentrated on leads, clues, and suspects, not that there were any.

"How fast can you do a rewrite?" he asked me.

"I listened to local radio all the way down from Lincoln Park," I
said. "I'm mostly caught up except for information we have that
others don't."

"I wish we had some information that others don't," Eric said. "I
wish we had any information at all. Mostly all we have are official
statements and a few vague pressers. You want to use my office
for quiet?"

"You know reporters can't work unless we're surrounded by
chaos," I said, trying to soothe Eric's nerves. "My desk is fine as long
as the EAs didn't skip me on incoming copy."

"I made sure they didn't," he said, and I turned to leave, but Eric
stopped me. "How'd the interview go?"

"Very strange afternoon," I said. "I'm not sure what to make of the
interview itself or what happened after. We need to talk before we
head home tonight. Meanwhile, you might want to give Jonathan a
call and see if he can meet with us early tomorrow."

Eric gave me a seriously quizzical look.

"Later," I said.

∽

IT WAS NEARLY 1 A.M. when Eric and I left the office and walked
together to the parking garage. When we had the next day's paper
and the night's web site wrapped up, we sat in his office so I could tell

him about my conversation with Beth Daley and my encounter later with Ronald Colter.

As I began to recount what Beth had to say, Eric walked to a closet where he kept a small, limited bar. The *Journal* seriously discouraged drinking on the job and forbade it inside the building—with exceptions. Champagne flowed in the newsroom when somebody won a Pulitzer Prize, as it had done when I won mine. Scotch or bourbon sometimes appeared in Eric's office at the end of a long, frustrating, exhausting day. This one definitely qualified, though it was the first time the bar had been opened for me. Eric gave me a choice of bourbon or Scotch. I chose Scotch. He chose bourbon. The bar had no icemaker, so we took our drinks neat. More conducive to drinking slowly.

"I keep meaning to stock some vodka," he said, "since that seems to be all the rage. But I keep forgetting."

"Americans have sailed past the vodka fad and into rye," I told him. "I think it was popular maybe seventy-five years ago. But I've heard that everything old is new again."

He wrinkled his nose. "Rye is back? My grandmother used to drink rye. I don't think I've ever tasted it."

"Your grandmother?" I asked. "Did you ever catch her in the rye?"

I strained to keep a straight face, but I broke into giggles. And I never giggle.

"You really need to get some sleep, Deuce. When you get tired, your sense of humor drifts back to the fourth grade. Finish up your story so we can blow this Popsicle stand and go home for a few hours."

So I did. I had transcribed notes from my conversation with Beth Daley from the little recording device. They looked the same as if I had transcribed them from written notes, exactly as intended. Eric didn't need to know the truth.

I finished up my retelling about the time we finished our drinks.

"Fascinating," Eric said. "Nothing we can use as is, but good to have in the bank."

"It gets better. You'll never believe who followed me when I left the restaurant. None other than Ron Colter."

"Oh, crap," Eric said. "Did he threaten you?"

"No," I said. "In fact he even said 'please' twice."

"This I need to hear. Let's head for the garage and talk along the way."

I explained the proposal Colter had made as we walked.

"I didn't promise him anything," I said. "Those decisions are above my pay grade. That's why I suggested earlier that you call Jonathan."

We stopped in the middle of the street while Eric called our attorney.

When the short conversation ended Eric said, "Jonathan's an Energizer bunny. I didn't even wake him up. He's available at eight in the morning, but he has to be in court at ten. So call Colter from your car and tell him to be on time."

"Knowing him, he'll be here at five to scope the place out for bugs."

We started to part to go to our cars, which were parked about fifty feet apart. Eric's voice stopped me.

"Thank you, Deuce," he said. "Nice job on the story tonight. You bailed us out of a bad situation. And you brought us some information negotiating power. Both in the same day. Nice day's work."

I wandered away, stunned. First Colter said "please," then Eric said "thank you."

I definitely needed to buy a lottery ticket.

20

I made it to the newsroom the next morning with five minutes to spare. I expected to find Jonathan and Eric waiting, but not Colter. Colter struck me as a personality that presumed his time more valuable than anyone else's. Thus he arrived late habitually, forcing everyone else to wait for him.

So it surprised me to find him standing at the security desk waiting for someone authorized to escort him upstairs. Even the FBI couldn't talk its way past our security people. Maybe at one time, but not in today's security-obsessed world.

Neither Eric nor Jonathan had arrived yet.

Colter had coffee, and I had coffee, so I suggested we wait in Eric's conference room. I had the Beth Daley file tucked in my messenger bag where it would stay until Eric and Jonathan decided whether Colter should have it. Turning over notes to the FBI would be a major breach of newspaper policy. But if we made a deal to share information, it could happen. I would have preferred telling Colter the story Beth told me. But on the chance my editor and attorney ordered me to turn over my notes, I masked Beth's identity by referring to her only as "Subject."

Colter and I sat in silence reading the paper. I had plenty I wanted to say to him, but not without witnesses. Eric and Jonathan arrived together a few minutes later.

I saw Eric's right hand tic, as though he intended to raise it to shake hands with Colter. But the FBI agent made no move to stand or extend his hand, so Eric rerouted his hand to his face where he smoothed his eyebrows. That was the Ronald Colter I knew. The man who had elevated the act of being an arrogant jerk to an art form.

"It hasn't been that long since we last met," Eric said, "so I don't think introductions are necessary. I'm sorry Jonathan and I are late. We had a quick breakfast to discuss how to proceed with this. We decided the first move should be yours, Special Agent Colter, since you requested the meeting, and we have no idea what it concerns. For the moment the agenda and the floor are yours."

"As I told Ms. Mora yesterday," he said, "I am an admirer of her investigative skills and fortitude. I'm sure she would do well working for my agency, though I doubt the requirements for discipline and obedience to orders would be much to her liking. She is well known, well liked, and trusted in this city. After seeing her byline on the initial story about Keene's, we suspected that those with useful knowledge about the bombing might choose to bypass the authorities and talk to her, instead. So we put a tail on her, and it paid off immediately. I received notification and arrived at the restaurant as she and another woman left. I sent my associate to follow the other woman, while I pursued Ms. Mora."

I felt my gut lurch. Had the FBI already identified Beth Daley?

As if suspecting my question, Colter said, "That's the way we learned the woman's street address. Once we had that, we ran it through Illinois DMV, which got us her name and a photo we used to positively identify her."

"Do you look in the mirror every night before you go to bed and tell yourself how smart you are?" I asked.

"Ms. Mora," he replied in a low, steady voice, "I understand that you have an irrepressible sense of satire, but this is serious business. You need to treat it as such."

Jonathan stepped in. "I'm sure we all treat this seriously, Agent

Colter. But consider this a formal protest against your invasion of my client's privacy and the privilege of her work. She has done nothing wrong. You have no right to follow her down a dark street and jump out of the shadows to confront her."

Colter squinted at Jonathan. "I have every legal right to walk on any public street I choose, and if it so happens that someone of interest is also on the street, so be it."

Then turned to me.

"Did I really frighten you?" he asked. "I never got the impression you're easily frightened. I was merely following you until we got to a quiet place on the street where we could talk without being overheard."

"And yet," I said, "we were overheard by three very nice young men who stopped to make sure I wasn't being assaulted. You have a knack for making terrible first impressions. Has no one ever told you that?"

"Folks, let's stop this," Eric commanded. "We're all too busy. State your proposal, Colter. And Deuce, as Archie Bunker used to say, 'Stifle.'"

Colter continued. "Our intentions are straight-forward and potentially advantageous for everyone in this room. What we are proposing is a trade of information."

"Real, truthful information?" Jonathan asked.

"Real, in so far as we can guarantee veracity in a rapidly evolving investigation."

We followed with a discussion of what each side could ask and have answered. Colter wanted to put strict limitations on discussions of official matters. Jonathan and Eric refused, citing the possibility that new avenues of inquiry would open up as the investigation progressed. They argued that nothing should be off the table, with the caveat that we would not expect the FBI to provide information that might endanger national security. We would accept that limitation with the proviso that the definition of national security not be made so broad that it covered matters the public had a right to know.

At the same time Eric insisted that agents stop following me, protect the identity of the woman seen with me at Toast, and never make a legal move to secure any reporter's notes, most especially mine.

In the end we reached an agreement I fully expected the FBI to violate, possibly before the end of the day. Possibly before any of us left this room.

We proceeded along a path that presumed good faith for the moment.

"You first," Eric told Colter. "What have you got to trade?"

Colter cringed, as if the prospect of disclosing anything to us gave him stomach cramps. The thought made me smile.

"We believe," Colter began, "that we are looking for two men, both of Middle Eastern ethnicity, loyal to ISIS but not directed by ISIS. They are likely self-radicalized, formulating and carrying out their own plans of attack. Lone wolves, as it were."

I started to ask a question. Colter put up a hand to stop me.

"If you're going to ask if any group or individual has taken responsibility for the destruction, the answer is no. But that is often the case when we're dealing with lone-wolf terrorists. ISIS will not say anything about their activities or take any responsibility until they have fully vetted the perpetrators to be certain they are local and loyal ISIS followers acting in the name of radical Islam."

"Has there been any chatter on social media?" I asked without looking up from the legal pad on which I'd been scribbling notes. It was all for show. I had my little recorder going again, capturing everything any of us said.

"Quite a bit from many who assume ISIS responsibility and applaud it, calling for more. We know some of the individuals sending their congratulations. Others are not known to us, at least not until now. You may publish all this information attributed to 'sources with a knowledge of the investigation.'"

"That's not very damned much," Eric said. "That's the sort of information you'd normally drop at a press conference. What else?"

Colter pursed his lips, then exhaled loudly.

"The firebombs at Cubs 'n' Stuff were triggered by Semtex, a plastic explosive" he said. "All products of that nature are embedded with tags that identify where they came from. The tags are recorded by the seller and allow us to identify the buyer. In this case, a construction company bought the Semtex for demolition down at the port. The company had it stored and secured properly. The Semtex used at Keene's came from the same supply. The bad news is the thief took enough to bring down several additional buildings. We found prints at the site that don't match anyone with access to the Semtex. We're now printing everyone else who works for the company. So far, nothing matches."

"What company, and where, specifically, is the demolition project," I asked.

Colter shook his head. "I can't tell you that right now. It would be bad news for the company. Unless we find out they contributed to the theft. Then there would be charges, and their identity would be public."

Eric asked, "We can print that?"

"Yes," Colter said. He hesitated as if he had more to say but needed to think it over. "I had another, potentially more problematic reason for requesting this meeting. I want to emphasize that my caution is not just protecting our investigation. I'm protecting you and your newspaper, too. Deuce, you have a reputation for getting to the heart of stories before your competition. After your reveal about investigators finding evidence that linked nine arsons, one of your competitors—not one of your many fans, I gather—asked a colleague of mine if you and I were sleeping together. I don't think your boyfriend or my wife would appreciate that."

I didn't know how to respond. I couldn't think of anyone I'd pissed off recently or anyone who disliked me enough on a regular basis to resort to that type of smear tactic. Journalists fight hard for stories. That's the job. But I've never heard a reporter or an editor impugn the moral integrity of a colleague without very good cause.

"I'm not sure I believe that," I said. "Do you know who it was?"

"No. I wasn't told, and I didn't ask."

"Well, if I ever find him, he'll be singing soprano for the rest of his life."

"Who said it was a man? I don't know. But my colleague said the reporter who raised question plans on filing a FOIA request to get all my communications with you."

"A Freedom of Information request? That's pretty desperate. Borders on pitiful."

"You ever hear of that before?" Colter asked.

"Yes, once or twice. Most reporters have higher standards. How are you going to cover this meeting when you fill the request, which you have to do by law?"

"We'll say that you all requested the session to get some perspective on what the city is facing. You asked questions, and I didn't answer them. A small untruth of no import."

"Except perjury," Jonathan said.

Colter glanced at him. "Which of the three of you is going to out me?"

"That remains to be seen," Jonathan said, clearly unhappy about the situation.

Jonathan said, "You're recording this." It was a statement, not a question.

"I am," Colter said.

"You know you're supposed to get permission first."

"I know, and I don't care," Colter replied.

"At least he's honest about it," I mumbled. I wanted to say that I was recording it, too, but I thought better of it. I glanced at Jonathan. I could tell he suspected that I had a recorder hidden somewhere. He already had in his safe one batch of my secret recordings that could never be made public. They would blow the cork out of the Middle East.

Colter said, "I want to know what Elizabeth Daley told Ms. Mora yesterday. I'd like a copy of her notes."

Jonathan sat up straighter. "Absolutely not," he said. "I thought we had an agreement you would not ask for any reporter's notes."

"We agreed," Colter said, "that we wouldn't take legal action to obtain them. That does not preclude asking nicely."

"The answer," Eric said, "is no. That's as nice as it's gonna get. And don't use the woman's name again. You might get used to it and let it slip in front of people who could be a danger to her."

Colter ignored him and turned to me. "So tell me what she said."

I looked at Jonathan, and he nodded.

"All of it?" I asked, needing clarification.

"All of it," he said.

So I repeated Beth's conversation, occasionally consulting my notes when I needed to get details exactly right, like the description of her plumber friend. Colter would give the description to a forensic artist who would produce a composite likeness to show around mosques, Islamic centers, and Middle Eastern neighborhoods in hopes someone would recognize the man and identify him.

During my recitation, Colter dropped all pretense and put his voice recorder out on the conference table. Occasionally he took backup notes. He asked no questions until I finished at the point where Beth and I went our separate ways.

Then he jumped in. "You're sure she said it was one man?"

"Absolutely. At least she only met one man."

"Did you ask her if he seemed to know anybody else in Starbucks?"

"I didn't ask, but she didn't even hint at that."

"The partner was probably watching from a few tables away."

"What makes you so sure there are two?"

"We had several more reports from eyewitnesses that they heard two men shouting 'Allahu akbar' as they ran away from Keene's. Same scenario we heard from witnesses at Cubs 'n' Stuff."

"Or possibly," I said, "the witnesses thought they heard that because they expected to hear it. It's also possible they made it up to become part of the story."

Colter waved his hand, dismissing my theories and got back to his own story. "Meanwhile, the agent tailing you said another woman approached you while you were sitting in Toast waiting for Eliz . . . your source. Who was she, and what did she want?"

At first I didn't remember. Then I burst out laughing.

"You're kidding, right?"

"I don't kid," Colter said. "It's against my religion."

"I don't remember her name," I said. "Dorothy, maybe. Debbie. I don't know. She wanted . . . oh, I remember. It was Dorrie. She asked for my autograph."

I felt myself blushing and glanced at Eric. He appeared amused.

"For real?" he asked.

"Yeah. It was kind of embarrassing. That's never happened to me before."

Colter asked, "Did you give it to her?"

"Sure," I said. "Why not?"

"What did you write on, and what did you say?"

"Oh, come on," I chided. "This can't be important."

"You never know," Colter replied.

"I wrote on a paper napkin, 'To Dorrie with thanks, Deuce Mora.'"

"Thanks for what?" Colter asked.

Now I felt exasperated. "For being a fan," I said. "She told me she was a fan. That's all. She asked. I signed. She left."

"Do you recall her last name?"

"She never gave it to me. Come on, Ron. This is nuts."

"She could have been the second terrorist, you know."

"And she could have just been a fan," I said. "She went back to her friends, and they looked at me and giggled, and then they all left. She didn't even sit down again. I'm not aware that terrorists giggle."

"How many friends? With her, I mean."

"Two, I think. Three people in all. All young women. Whoever you had following me must have seen the whole thing. Ask him. Meanwhile, can we please get back on point?"

"I think that's a very good idea," Eric said.

Colter looked at me. "I can give you a little more, but you probably know it already."

That took me by surprise. "Know what?" I asked.

"About the cigarette butts. I'm sure your boyfriend told you."

"Told me what? I already wrote about the butts found at the fire scenes."

"You didn't offer detail. I suspect you know a lot more than your article explored. Your boyfriend wouldn't have given you half the loaf."

And there it was, exactly what Mark and I had feared.

I leaned forward in my chair and glared at Colter.

"Let me make this perfectly clear," I said, my eyes boring into him. "Mark and I had a casual conversation about the Keene's fire-bombing when we got home from work on Monday, the day of the fire. It was very late. We were both exhausted. But we took some time to talk about our relationship. We both understood he would be suspected of leaking any inside information that came my way. So we decided to put our personal lives on hold. I'll be living in my house for the duration of the investigation, and he's staying at his condo. We thought it better if we didn't see each other until the investigation's over. We're both working very long hours, and it would be nice to compare notes at the end of each day, but that can't happen. And it hasn't happened. And it won't happen. We didn't even see one another for Christmas. Is that clear enough for you?"

Colter have me a small nod. "Did you rule out telephone conversation, as well?"

I fidgeted. "Not completely," I admitted. "He called me Christmas night to see how I was. The conversation was brief. We haven't even exchange gifts yet."

Colter smiled. "Well, that confirms what your telephone records told us."

Now Jonathan began breathing fire.

"On top of everything else, you've tapped her phone? And Hearst's?"

"Not yet," Colter said. "We're waiting for a court order. But we don't need a court order to access carrier records of calls made and received from their phones. We only need warrants, which we got."

"What's the new information about the cigarette butts?" Eric snapped.

Colter shook his head. "I won't get into brands or which were found where," he said. "But I will tell you that they weren't manufactured in the United States."

I asked how he knew that.

He thought about that for a moment then stipulated, "Attribution only to sources close to the investigation?"

We agreed.

"These days," he said, "tobacco companies are conglomerates spread over several countries in different parts of the world. The Marlboros you buy in Chicago will have a different tobacco blend than the Marlboros you buy in London or Berlin or Tierra del Fuego. Preliminary analysis of the tobacco in the butts found at the arson fires indicates foreign origin. Neither brand was bought here. They were either carried into the U.S. or ordered online. Analysis of the cigarette papers and filter material might narrow it farther. There was DNA on the filters. It's currently under analysis."

Colter stood. "Well, that's it from my end," he said. "We'll talk again soon."

"I want those DNA results, even if you won't let me use them," I said.

"And send us copies of the artist's composite of the plumber when it's done," Eric said. "We'll run it and see what falls out."

"And leave Beth Daley alone," I added. "She doesn't need vultures at her door."

Colter couldn't hide his irritation. He looked from me to Eric and back again.

His eyes bored into mine. "I'll do what needs to be done," he said.

21

The arsonist decided to lower his profile and watch how his work played out for a while. Investigation details would leak from City Hall or the cops or the fire investigators and show up on TV sooner or later. Or in the Journal. He'd heard talk that the rag's top local columnist—the tall bitch with the weird name—had shacked up with a state arson investigator. Their pillow talk surely would wind up on the front page. He'd have to keep an eye on her. If she got on his scent, she could be a problem.

Not surprising, the FBI had entered the case, too. Some arrogant, razor-cut, ego-in-a-suit held a press conference the arsonist watched on TV the night before. The fed acknowledged they had information they wouldn't discuss publicly. The arsonist smiled at that. He knew all about the secret evidence. He'd created it, after all, exactly as his grandfather taught him.

He remembered how, as a child, he accompanied the old man on treks through the woods up on the Wisconsin border, well away from civilization. They stopped in the cover of rocks and trees where no one could see them. They sat on a rock, sometimes fished on a small lake—illegally, of course, because neither had licenses—and ate a picnic while his grandfather told stories of the old days, the hard days, the days when his forebears suffered unimaginable cruelty and persecution. People shunned the family, called them insulting names, and drove them from homes that were lawfully theirs but stood in neighborhoods that didn't welcome their kind. They could get no work but for the most menial labor. They were told time and again to go back where they came from.

On one occasion their family found itself targeted for blame for an event in which they played no role. Though they had done nothing wrong, no one believed them. The retribution they suffered tasted especially bitter for their lack of complicity. The overwhelming shame, the dishonor, and the anger embedded themselves in the family's DNA for generations that followed.

"Revenge," his grandfather preached to him. "You must take revenge for your family. You have the anger. You have the knowledge. I shall teach you the skills."

And the boy believed. He became a talented and eager student, the first in his family willing to do the grandfather's bidding. His father, who didn't have the spine to carry out any retribution himself, nonetheless approved and encouraged the boy who would grow up to become the Chicago arsonist.

Sadly, neither his grandfather nor his father lived to see their vision of revenge bear fruit. While the arsonist felt the paternal losses keenly, he also knew that their deaths closed the book on the only two people who might have a clue to his identity. No one remained to give him away.

He became a nowhere man, a ghost with no past, no present, and probably no future, hiding in plain sight without a single pair of eyes giving him a second glance.

The news said authorities were looking for two radical Islamists. He chuffed. Good luck with that. How many tens of thousands of Muslims were there in this city of three million souls? They were everywhere, though not so much in his neighborhood.

The arsonist lived in Mount Greenwood, the most Irish neighborhood in Chicago, way down on the far Southwest side, a blue-collar area filled with Irish cops and firefighters. No hidey-hole was more secure than one dug in the middle of the enemy camp. Nobody ever thinks that's where the enemy will be, so nobody looks for him there.

His eyes roamed around his small, dark studio apartment, and he regretted for a moment that he had to exist this way. His living area had a *lumpy futon that made into a lumpy bed, two threadbare easy chairs, a couple of battered lamps, and a small table with the television perched on top. He cooked in a Pullman kitchen, barely a closet with a bar sink, a bar refrigerator, and a double hotplate. He wanted to buy a small microwave but had no place to put it. He used paper dishes and plastic utensils. His postage-stamp bathroom space barely held a toilet, a sink, and a cramped, badly stained shower stall. The floor of tiny, chipped black-and-white tiles hadn't been in style for a hundred years. An ancient window air conditioner only worked when the temperature outside dipped toward freezing. His radiator provided sufficient heat, but the steam pipes banged so hard it sounded as if someone was demolishing the building, which wasn't a bad idea.*

The arsonist never complained, enduring the hardships rather than calling attention to himself. He hadn't expected luxury when he rented the place. This was the only apartment he could find with a landlord who took cash and didn't ask for ID. The rent included all his utilities—electric, gas, trash, water—so he had no accounts that bore his name and address. He got his cable TV by stealth, splicing into his neighbor's cable.

He could have afforded better. He made pretty good money doing odd jobs for cash all over the neighborhood. He had self-taught skills as an electrician, plumber, and carpenter, and he could lay bricks and repair roofing if the jobs weren't too complicated. Nobody minded that he lacked licenses, insurance, or bond. They looked the other way because he did a good job and charged significantly less than the professionals.

He called himself Joe, not his real name. Of course he didn't have a phone or email. But people could find him easily enough when they had jobs for him. Almost every evening, for example, he sat on a stool at the far end of the bar at Muldoon's Ale House, a neighborhood pub where he could get Smithwick's Irish Ale on draft, $6 a twenty-ounce glass. He nodded to the bartender but never spoke to anyone else with the exception of the two African men who came in frequently and always sat with him. He didn't latch onto them because he wanted friends; he didn't. He saw how they could be useful in his campaign of terror. He had a glass of beer with them, maybe two, and then headed home. He entered and left the lives of others in the bar like steam from a street vent, billowing and dissipating on the wind.

It was just what the arsonist needed. He didn't know his neighbors, and his neighbors didn't know him. He dug in and remained anonymous.

Would it last? Would the cops put it all together? Or would he continue to walk among them until he brought this godforsaken city to its knees?

It was like the movie Watchman, *where the character Rorschach reads from his journal.* "This city is afraid of me. I have seen its true face. The streets are extended gutters, and the gutters are full of blood, and when the drains finally scab over all the vermin will drown . . . The whores and politicians will look up and shout 'Save us!'

"And I'll whisper, no."

22

Two days after the meeting with Colter, the Joint Federal Task Force called a presser to discuss new information about the arson investigation. City officials would be there, but it would be the feds' show. Eric said he thought I should attend, and I agreed.

As it turned out, I should have told him to send someone else.

The *Journal* had published my story based on the meager new information Colter had let go during our meeting. I reported that the butts found at all the fire scenes had been manufactured outside the United States, though not where, and the disclosure that the feds were looking for a pair of radical jihadist terrorists. They made a solid, if not spectacular story that sent our competitors scrambling to catch up.

Early in the news conference I asked Colter if investigators knew the nationalities of the suspects or the locations where the cigarette were made?

Before the FBI assistant director could respond, one of my colleagues, a loud-mouth television reporter named Harry Conklin with whom I'd crossed swords before, did something so unprofessional that it brought gasps of surprise from many people in the room. It surprised me less than the others. I knew Conklin would stoop to almost anything to put his competitors on the defensive, especially me.

He called out to Colter, "Didn't you already give Ms. Mora those answers?"

Colter looked startled. It took him a moment to locate Conklin in the crowd and only succeeded after the reporter raised his hand.

"I'm sorry," Colter said. "Who are you?"

Because Conklin was a regular on Chicago television, and Colter's question insulted him, even if Colter hadn't meant the slight. Conklin identified himself. He sounded snappish.

Colter nodded. "Okay. I don't think I understand your question. And I know I don't appreciate your interruption when I'm talking to another reporter. You'll get your turn."

I didn't like where this was headed. I already suspected Conklin had submitted the Freedom of Information requests for records of Colter's contacts with me. I felt certain he planned to cause us very public trouble.

"Oh, please," Conklin said. "Everybody in this room knows you're playing games. Between you and her boyfriend and her bed, Deuce Mora knows . . ."

Colter interrupted, and to his great credit, he almost managed to hold his temper.

"Playing games, Mr. Conklin?" he demanded in an icy tone. "You think this is a game? With dozens dead, hundreds hurt, millions of dollars in property damage, and possibly more to come, I see nothing amusing about any of this."

"You know that's not what I'm saying," Conklin snapped.

Colter said, "I understand what you're implying, and I reject it. Now let's move on."

Colter recognized another reporter very quickly and never got back to my question, which was just as well. I had asked it only as cover, to help conceal the fact that the *Journal* actually did have a pipeline into the FBI. Conklin, for all his faults, had good instincts.

But his implication that Colter and I were sleeping together infuriated me.

The confrontation left me unnerved. A few colleagues offered their support as we left the room when the presser ended. I just tried to smile and nod in response. I didn't want to say anything for fear of making a bad situation worse.

Conklin waited outside the federal building and got up in my face.

"This isn't over, lady," he threatened. "I'm going to prove you're sleeping your way to exclusives. I'll be finished with you when your reputation isn't worth any more than a soiled piece of toilet paper."

Melissa Robbins, a reporter for the *Tribune*, heard the exchange and stepped between us. She was flanked by WGN reporter Mack Lowery and his entire camera crew.

"In Chicago we don't like seeing trash on our sidewalks," Robbins snapped at Conklin. "Now move your fat ass away from here or Mack and I will pick you up and throw you head first into that trash barrel over there. It's where you belong."

Conklin looked with uncertainty from one to the other and then back to me. I saw his arrogance falter.

"Hey, I'm on your side," he said to my fellow reporters. "Her nighttime activities are hurting you as much as me."

"Her nighttime activities are none of your business, or ours," Lowery said. "If you had any proof of what you're implying, you'd have gone on air with it. You're an asshole and a bully, Harry. You're irresponsible. And you're a disgrace to the profession."

Conklin backed away a step. He turned to me and wagged his finger. "I'm not done with you," he said. Then he turned and left.

Robbins shook her head. "His station should fire his ass. He's been trouble forever."

"His behavior is good for ratings," Lowery said. "People tune in to hear what new bullshit the Conklin Crap Crank has produced."

I sighed. "Well, they'll sure get an earful tonight."

Robbins patted me on the back and Lowery squeezed my shoulder. Then they, too, left to go about their business.

As I turned around to find a cab, my eyes locked with Colter, standing about ten yards away. He frowned, more in sympathy than anger, and gave a slight shake of his head. Then he, too, left.

Behind him I saw Harry Conklin watching closely.

He was smiling.

23

I flipped open the toggle-style gate latch on the fence door in front of Beth Daley's small condo on Larrabee Street. The latch was designed to keep the gate closed, not to provide security. I hoped Beth knew that. She's spent most of her life in a part of the country where folks trusted one another to the point that they didn't lock their doors at night. Chicago wasn't that kind of place.

I rethought my mistake in assuming Beth's naiveté when I saw a small yard sign from a major security company warning the premises were protected. I saw a sticker repeating the message mounted on her front door. Good for her.

Despite temperatures above freezing, a few dirt-encrusted snow piles huddled against the dark stockade yard fence where sun couldn't get to them. The place smelled of leaf mold and cold dampness, not at all unpleasant.

Ron Colter and an FBI forensic artist followed me into the small yard. I hadn't wanted Colter to come along. After the dustup at the presser two days earlier I didn't think we should be seen together. But he insisted.

The furor over Harry Conklin's attempt to dent our reputations lasted one news cycle—and only on Conklin's show—and then sank

like stone. No other media outlets in the city touched it. My editors
weren't happy about even the limited controversy, and one asked me
point blank about the veracity of it. I told her to talk to Eric. Eric
knew the truth and sympathized with my angst. He had his own
concerns. Newspaper finances across the country continued in
decline, and he worried about the *Journal's* future. Anything that
impugned its credibility was bad news.

Colter said he wasn't worried about Conklin, and I shouldn't be,
either.

When I pressed Colter on the matter of the joint visit to see Beth
Daley he replied, "If you're so worried about it, I won't take you."

I didn't think he'd make good on the threat. Beth likely wouldn't
feel comfortable talking to the FBI as freely as she talked to me.
Colter had to know that that my presence would help put a key
witness at ease.

When I called Beth to ask if I could come by with the forensic
artist and his preliminary sketch of the plumber, she surprised me by
agreeing without hesitation. Colter told me she refused the first time
the artist tried to see her, pleading that she was too distraught to
revisit the fire bombing that day. Now, she said, her fear remained but
had been tempered by a deep anger at events that cost so many lives,
some of them her friends.

The death toll had risen to forty-four with the discovery of several
bodies in the Keene's rubble and one in a smoke shop. The search
had a long way to go. No one else had been found alive, but nearly
twenty people remained missing.

Beth wanted to help if she could.

Apparently she'd been watching for us because her front door
opened before I could ring the bell. She explained that a small electronic beam crossed the fence gate. When someone walked through
it, it rang a chime inside her house.

So much for Beth being naïve.

Her place was small, cramped, and dark, with fewer windows
than it needed and only one ceiling light burning over the small
dining table cleared for the four of us to work.

Beth offered everyone coffee, which we all declined. She looked mournfully at the full pot sitting in an old Mr. Coffee unit next to her sink, probably thinking about the waste. Guilt moved me to accept a cup.

She frowned when she saw the sketch of the plumber on the artist's iPad Pro. She cocked her head to the right, then to the left, as if a different angle could tell her something.

"That doesn't look like I remember him," she said.

The artist, Aaron Debrosse, smiled at her. With his Haitian ancestry he had skin so dark that his white teeth dominated his face when he smiled. I saw Beth relax.

"I only had the description you gave Ms. Mora to work with," he said. "It's hard to get things right unless we work directly with the eye witness." Aaron pointed at the iPad image. "Now we start making adjustments to make the image conform more closely to your memory. What's the first thing that stands out as not quite right?"

They went through the whole sketch, changing a dozen or more details, some of them multiple times. When they finished, Beth seemed almost satisfied.

"It's not a photo, of course, so it doesn't look exactly like I remember him," she said. "But I can't suggest anything else to change."

"That's normal," Debrosse said. "I'm going out to the car and print this out and leave a copy with you. As you live with it, missing or misrepresented details might occur to you. You can just give me a call. I'll come back if I need to."

When Debrosse left, Colter asked Beth a series of questions, all covering the ground she and I discussed at the restaurant.

Toward the end, just as Debrosse returned, Colter got tough.

"Ms. Daley, do you have a passport?"

She looked at him, startled.

"Yes. Why?" she asked.

"Have you used it?"

"Twice. Once when I went to Toronto to visit my best friend from high school. You need a passport to go to and from Canada now.

Don't that beat all? I used it another time when my sister and I went on a two-week tour of Europe just before I moved up here. Why do y'all need to know about that?"

Colter leaned back in his chair. "When were the trips?"

Beth shook her head slightly. "I don't think I can remember exact dates."

"Do you still have the passport? The European visas will have dates."

"Of course I have it."

"Could you get it, please?"

Beth glanced at me. "Can he do that?" she asked.

"I don't think he can force you to surrender your passport without a court order," I said. "Unless he has more cause than passing curiosity I doubt a judge would issue a one."

"I'm not asking her to surrender her passport," Colter said more forcefully than necessary. "I just want to see it." He turned back to Beth. "It's not a good idea to refuse to cooperate with an FBI investigation. You could come under suspicion of being complicit in the crime."

That annoyed me. "Do you act like this just to scare people? Stop being a jerk."

"Stand down, Ms. Mora," Colter snapped. "Stay out of it."

"Stop it," Beth insisted. "If you just want to see it, Mr. Colter, I'll go get it."

She did. Colter skimmed the pages, made a few notes, and returned it. Then he rose and put his gear away. Debrosse had already packed up.

"Stay close to home, Ms. Daley," Colter ordered. "If something requires you to leave the city, clear it with my staff. Thank you for your help." He laid a card on her table and left. Debrosse laid a printout of the composite on the table with his card and followed.

Beth looked concerned.

"Try not to worry," I told her. "I know him. He's a lot of bluster and bravado. You have my card. If he comes at you again, call me first."

"I'm not worried about the FBI," Beth said. "I'm worried about this guy." She indicated the sketch on her table. "What if he remembers I saw him and could call attention to him? Even identify him?"

"You know, Beth, it occurred to me that maybe he did meet you on purpose. First he fixes it so you'll see him, then he takes you out for coffee and sweats up a storm by leaving his hat and coat on for nearly an hour sitting inside a coffee bar. This assures you'll remember him, but you won't have a very good image of what he looks like. Then he lets Sunday slide by and destroys Keene's on Monday, a day you won't be there, assuring you won't be hurt or killed. It's almost sounds like he planned it to happen that way."

"Why?"

"I don't know," I said.

24

I was reading snippets filed by reporters covering the firebombing from dozens of angles all over the city. As I read I kept a small part of my brain focused on the TV suspended from the ceiling nearby. Every half hour I'd flip around the channels to see if anyone had anything new. They didn't, though CNN, Fox, and MSNBC continued to give the story a lot of airtime. They had scaled back coverage after the Cubs 'n' Stuff fire too soon. They realized the error and wrapped themselves around the Keene's devastation like pythons on prey.

Local stations expanded regular newscasts and broke into programming as necessary with developments. They no longer spent full time on coverage because they had no new developments to spend on endless, breathless hours of speculation and pointless debate. Viewers wanted game shows, soaps, and talk shows, and the stations needed the revenue they lost when they preempted regular programming and its advertising. So back to the mundane.

I dropped the pile of papers on my desk and yawned. I hadn't gotten much sleep the night before as I tried to figure out the arsonist's objective in revealing himself to Beth if, in fact, it was the arsonist she'd met at the Keene's, and if, in fact, he revealed himself for a purpose. I rolled my head to try to loosen up the muscles in my neck and shoulders.

The phone rang.

"Now what?" I said aloud.

I picked up the cell and found a nice surprise. The caller ID said "Carl Cribben." Cribben, a retired FBI agent, had helped me on a couple of stories recently, our relationship evolving from one of suspicion and distrust to respect and friendship. Carl lived up in Rogers Park, at the extreme north end of the city, but he spent a lot of his time these days in Washington helping the House Judiciary Committee work up a new investigation of organized crime. We talked occasionally, catching up on our lives or when he had a question to which he thought I might have an answer.

I'd thought about calling Carl about the arsons, to ask what he'd heard. But I had dragged him into my last two big stories and didn't want to wear out my welcome. Or expose him to unwanted attention from his old employer.

"Hi there," I said.

"Oh, good," he replied. "I was beginning to worry that you'd forgotten me."

"Why would you think that?"

"Because whenever you and Ron Colter get your noses stuck in the same dog bowl, I get calls from both of you, each hoping I'll spy on the other. I've only heard from one of you, and not the one I'd prefer."

I couldn't help but laugh. Carl Cribben, as straight-laced an agent as the FBI ever turned out, did occasionally have an odd way of viewing the world.

"So you've heard from him," I said. "I trust you found him pleasant."

"Your trust is misplaced," Carl said.

"I went out on an interview with him yesterday. It got pretty tense."

"Really," Carl said. "He took you with him without you pointing a gun at his head?"

"I don't own a gun," I reminded him. "He wanted to talk to a witness I turned up, and she probably wouldn't have let Colter in the door if he'd gone alone. She's scared."

When Carl resumed speaking, the lightness had left his voice.

"We all need to be scared," he said. "This arsonist is escalating the terror so fast he's gonna have the whole city in flames by the end of the month. We don't need that again."

"Are you in Washington?" I asked.

"Yeah, I cut short my Christmas recess to get a leg up on some work with nobody around to bug me. I hoped at least to have a drink with you while I was back in Chi for the holidays, but we had the family at our house, and you had your hands full."

"You making progress?"

"We are. But these days I'm having a tough time concentrating. I worry about Nancy and Shiloh every time I think of them, which averages once a minute."

Nancy was Cribben's wife, and Shiloh was his Labrador retriever.

Cribben said, "I begged Nancy to pack up, put Shiloh in the car, and come to D.C. for a while, just until the authorities get a handle on this terrorist. But she'll have nothing to do with it. She doesn't care much for Washington, and it'd be hard to convince her to leave Chicago if I offered her three months in Paris."

"You could offer me three months in Paris," I said with a laugh.

"You really wouldn't want to meet Nancy in a dark alley if I did that," he replied without a laugh.

"So you're keeping up with everything going on here?"

"Hard not to. There's nothing else in the news."

"Do you have any thoughts worth repeating to an old friend?"

"I don't have any information, if that's what you're asking," Carl said. "I sat on a terror task force for a couple years after 9/11, so I have some experience with these assholes. But I never saw anything like this one. This guy, or this crew, or whatever they are, don't operate the way we're used to. ISIS and their recruits generally strike once, hard and fast, and then die or go to ground. This time, I don't know."

"Do you ever wonder if maybe this time it's not jihadist terrorism?"

"I'll tell you the truth, Deuce, that thought has crossed my mind. On the other hand, a new modus operandi doesn't mean the destruction isn't ISIS-inspired. If this is a lone wolf, or two or three lone wolves operating together, they're probably self-radicalized, self-motivated, and self-trained. They can attack however they want, whenever they want, even becoming serial arsonists and bombers if that's what floats their boat."

"So just because we haven't seen this before doesn't mean it doesn't have ISIS written all over it."

"Right," Carl said. "But I'm just shooting arrows into the air. I have no firm idea what's going on. I don't even have a guess."

"You must have something on your mind. Why'd you call?"

"The two vics in the warehouse weren't druggies. Did you know that?"

"No."

Carl said, "If they ever took heroin it was only recreational. A thorough autopsy would have found a variety of internal signs of habitual use. Tony Donato does very thorough autopsies. He found nothing."

"And you know this how?"

"You're going to have to trust me."

"I do," I said. "So what killed them?"

"The first suspect is fentanyl."

"Figures."

I knew—the whole country knew—that fentanyl had become lethally popular among heroin dealers. Because it is a synthetic opioid, a manufactured drug, it was cheap to make and sold at prices much lower than heroin. Since the effects of the two substances were similar, most addicts couldn't tell the difference. Fentanyl allowed heroin dealers to step on their H many more times, extending the number of doses they had to sell and sending profits soaring. But it was a fool's game. Fentanyl was as much as 100 times more potent than morphine. Fentanyl analogues could be 10,000 times more potent than morphine. Which is why the epidemic of opioid deaths in the United States soared 328 percent between 2010 and 2015.

"It's what I'd have used," Carl said. "If the victims hadn't taken fentanyl before, it wouldn't have taken much to kill them."

I said, "How did the killer get the victims to inject it? If you came at me carrying a syringe and tried to inject me, I'd fight like hell. And there were two of them."

"We don't know for sure that there's only one killer," Carl said. "And knocking a guy out isn't hard. Dose his beer when he's not looking. Roofies, GHB, Ketamine. Any one of them would do the trick, and they're not hard to come by, either."

"Then drag their unconscious bodies into the warehouse and finish the job?"

"Yep. And then burn the place down."

"Did Tony find any date-rape drugs in their systems?"

"That I don't know," Carl said. "You should ask him."

CARL and I spent time dissecting the arson cases and came to no useful conclusions. I needed help, and I trusted him, so I decided to take a chance. After getting his solemn word he would breathe nothing of what I would tell him, I related everything Beth had told me about the plumber. Then I defied Colter and told Carl everything about the cigarette butts, their foreign origin, and the DNA found on the butts. In short, all the evidence left at all the fires that solidified Colter's certainty we were facing radical Islamist terrorists.

When I finished, Carl said nothing for a moment, then, "Colter mentioned the cigarettes but only to say the same brands had been found at all the fires. Did you happen to transcribe your notes into a computer file?"

I confessed to the illegal taping of both my conversation with Beth and the meeting with Colter. "I have the full transcripts in the computer."

"Would you consider sending them to me?" he asked. "Maybe reading them over carefully will spark a more useful thought."

"Nobody else has seen these but me," I said.

"And I swear they won't go any farther, not from my hands, anyway."

We hung up, and I emailed the full transcripts to him. Concern nibbled at the edge of my brain. Not that the transcripts might leak. My unease had nothing to do with the transcripts at all. I had a deep and persistent feeling that Carl had said something important that would help get to the bottom of these horrific attacks on Chicago.

It rattled around deep in my brain, trying to get my attention.

But I couldn't grab it.

25

I sat at my desk feeling, as my father used to say, as befuddled as a bullfrog entering puberty. There were multiple reasons.

The death toll in the South Loop disaster rose to forty-seven as searchers pulled one more body from the remains of Keene's, and two critically injured victims died in hospitals. Six buildings had been destroyed, their rubble still undergoing careful excavation as the search for victims continued. Seventeen people remained missing, all of them known or thought to be in the vicinity of Keene's at the time of the blast. Combined with the deaths of fourteen at Cubs 'n' Stuff, nineteen dead in K-town, and the two bodies in the warehouse, the death count stood at eighty-two. Eleven of the dead were children.

Lying in bed at night, in the silence and the dark, my demons found a route back into my head and taunted me. Thoughts of the children made me weep.

The injury total in the Loop held at 189. There were no more injured to find. In the hours immediately following the blast some who died might have survived had rescuers been able to reach them quickly. But trapped deep in the rubble amid persistent pockets of flame and freezing water from fire hoses, they couldn't be saved. They died slowly as blood leaked from their wounds and cold replaced it.

The lack of progress on the investigations added to my funk. I'd placed a call to Ron Colter and Tony Donato first thing to see if they had any new leads on the identities of the two bodies in the warehouse. Neither returned my call.

I missed Mark. As vowed, we hadn't seen one another in nearly three weeks; we hadn't even talked on the phone. How long did we have to keep this up? Would one dinner out, one night in, put to lie all the best intentions that motivated our separation?

In my worst moments I imagined that he'd found someone new, someone whose love didn't come with so much baggage. I hoped it was my imagination, just another fear tossed into my head by the same night demons that kept tabs on dead children.

I had taken to coming to work in blue jeans over a comfortably old pair of Frye harness boots and something from my collection of hand-knit Irish sweaters from Galway. On warmer days—it had been a fairly mild winter in Chicago—I'd switch out Irish wool for American cotton. If an occasion called for nicer attire, I'd sub out slacks for the jeans and dressier boots for the Fryes. But only reluctantly. I pampered myself, wearing comfortable clothes to offset the horror of living in the American version of Aleppo, Syria.

There had been a time when I loved walking the streets of Chicago. I'd eat lunch at my desk while I worked then go out and walk for an hour, seeking out new side streets and alleys I'd never experienced before, finding new gems of shops and exotic food spots that I noted for more prolonged investigation later. I would smile and say hello to people I'd never seen before and would never see again, and take enormous pride in helping tourists looking for sites I had visited dozens of times.

All that had changed. Now when I walked the streets I hurried, not knowing if I was scurrying away from danger or into it. Where the fun had always been in the experience of the casual walk, now there I felt only relief at arriving alive. When you're living in a war zone, your mind tends to take very convoluted paths through life.

The thought left me depressed.

WHEN I FINISHED my column I pushed my chair back into a semi-reclining position, put my boots up, crossed at the ankles, on the broad windowsill and watched the city go by five stories below. I peeled an orange left over from lunch. I craved the orange and went about its consumption slowly, wishing I'd brought two.

At mid-afternoon the traffic had begun to build to full evening rush-hour mode, clogging State Street, Van Buren Street, and the Congress Parkway, all in my field of view. Chicago held its rush hours in relative quiet. People were in a hurry to get home or to social engagements, but Chicagoans had a broad aversion to horn honking. Drivers knew it wouldn't speed up traffic. Their patience paid tribute to legendary Midwest courtesy, which often showed itself on the streets below my window.

I loved the view over the South Loop. Among other things, this window overlooked the magnificent Harold Washington Library Center, a nine-story building of mostly red brick with arched entryways and arched windows that soared several floors. I considered it one of Chicago's architectural treasures. The building had been a passion of the Chicago mayor who championed it in the 1980s and for whom the building was named. Its most striking exterior features were the acroteria, or plinths, that dotted the cornice. The huge aluminum ornaments, painted to look like weathered copper, demanded the attention of all who passed beneath. Some people mistook the plinths for gargoyles and hated them. But the adornments actually featured owls, homages to education and wisdom. The owl plinth on the corner of the structure a little above my direct line of sight stood watch over State Street. I never tired of looking at it.

A feeling of lassitude overtook me, a combination of unease and stasis. I thought I should do something, but I couldn't generate the enthusiasm to move or identify my objective. I thought about the nagging questions as to why someone would drag two bodies into an abandoned building and go to such complex lengths to make sure the building burned quickly and totally. The preparations for the fire alone had to have taken days.

Who were the two dead men? What god did they sufficiently offend to earn them such a grisly fate?

If I were going to burn two bodies I'd dump them in a remote, vacant lot and douse them with gasoline. The warehouse blaze was too intricate, too fraught with the danger of discovery during the preparations, to make sense. I couldn't let it go, even though I should. I was paid to be a metro columnist, analyzing and commenting on the affairs of the city. Nobody paid me to be a private investigator.

My gut told me that something besides cigarette butts tied all the fires together. But, for example, what could possibly be similar between the Water Tower buildings and K-Town, iconic buildings versus a conclave of crime? Other than the fact the buildings on Michigan Avenue and those in Lawndale were limestone constructs, no meaningful similarities existed. Google told me Water Tower was built with Illinois white limestone, while the Lawndale homes were Indiana gray limestone. A tenuous connection, at best. What did the old warehouse have to do with Keene's? I had checked, and Keene's had never been an owner or a leaseholder on the warehouse. Keene's had no connection to Lawndale. The warehouse had no connection to Cubs 'n' Stuff.

No matter how I shifted the pieces around I couldn't make the jigsaw fit.

As daylight faded to early winter darkness, little bells were going off in my head. If they were trying to sing me a message, I didn't recognize the tune. It was the same feeling I had after my conversation with Carl Cribben. Like a mosquito buzzing around my ear, something tried to get my attention.

I knew if I dwelled on it I would never make the connection. So I returned to watching the library. Not only was it beautiful and inspiring, it was in the Guinness Book of Records. When it opened in 1991, it claimed the title as the largest public library building in the world.

It wasn't a premonition, just a stray thought: If the arsonist attacked the Washington Library, it would break my heart.

HALF AN HOUR later I still had my feet propped up, and I continued to stare out the window. I started feeling cold radiating from the glass and leaking over the tops of my boots to my legs. The temperature outside dropped as the sky slid toward full dark.

It had started raining about the time I finished my orange. Now the rain had turned to sleet. Before long it would be snow. I doubted much would build up; it had been above freezing for several days. As the evening rush built, the heat from the cars would keep snow from sticking on the asphalt or turn it to slush. Grassy areas, however, had begun already showing some white.

The streetlights and the lights from the buildings threw shimmering reflections off the pavement. Chicago was so beautiful this time of day. I thought about writing a column about Chicago at dusk. I had planned to write about all the money that had been squeezed from Chicago's public schools budget, a budget that needed cash the way a hemophiliac needed blood. Instead the schools were under a back-door assault from a Republican state leader trying to embarrass the city's Democratic mayor. The Dems had proved unwilling to compromise. It would have been the same had the politics of the two offices been reversed.

This was Illinois, after all, where politics was blood sport.

Yeah, I'd write about that again. It was more important than my emotions over the look of a wet nightfall in the city.

I uncoiled myself in slow motion from my perch on the window ledge. The radiating cold had left me stiff.

I was startled when my phone rang.

I was more startled when I answered it.

26

"I'm returning your call," Colter said. "I've been in a meeting all afternoon. Some of them concerned you."

"You folks must be pretty hard up for conversation."

"Truthfully, we are hard up, but for information, not conversation. We were rethinking our decision not to go public with the cigarettes. We got some good DNA data from the lab this morning."

I slid a yellow legal pad in front of me with a pen.

"Are you going to share?" I asked.

"Possibly," the Colter said. "If you agree with the ground rules."

I heard a groan in my mind, but it didn't escape my lips. Were there going to be new ground rules every time we had an exchange of information?

As he proved several times before, Colter had a talent for mind reading.

"We have to be very careful what information we make public and how we make it public," he said. "The dustup at the press conference with that Conklin guy did not please Washington. The director, on orders from the attorney general, demanded I never again talk to you without other journalists and FBI staff present. I backed them off a little."

"How?"

"By suggesting another arrangement. If we develop information you should have, you can attribute it to a source in Washington. That would leave me completely out of it."

"So when you tell me something, you want me to describe the source as someone close to the investigation in Washington? That's a lie. As I told someone else, I can protect a source, but I can't and won't lie for a source."

"Will you be quiet and listen, please? The information will come from a real source in Washington, not from me. Think about it."

I did, and I got it.

"Really? You're going to drag him into this?"

"It's all there is, Deuce. Take it or leave it."

"Ron, wait," I said quickly, to keep him from hanging up. "I don't want to end our arrangement. But it seems to me it would be simpler all around, and less perilous for you, if you held a press conference or sent out a press release when you develop new information. Treat everyone equally. I'll still keep up my end of the bargain because anything I learn will wind up in the paper."

He remained silent for a moment. "That's generous of you, but we would prefer keeping the agreement in place as is. There are situations when we need to float information, get it out there without revealing it came from the FBI. Routing it to you through our mutual friend in D.C. seems a logical solution. Frankly, you're the only journalist I trust completely, and I'm pretty sure the AG feels the same way."

I TOOK the proposal to Eric.

"And who's this mysterious Washington source?" he asked.

"It can't be anyone but Carl Cribben," I said.

"And you still trust Cribben?"

"Completely."

"Then make it happen."

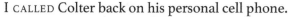

I CALLED Colter back on his personal cell phone.

"We'll go with your plan," I said. "But for the record, I'm not nuts about it."

"So you said. By the way, have you talked with Elizabeth Daley recently?"

"No," I said. "How about you?"

"I tried to call her this morning. Her phone's been disconnected."

"She did tell me she wanted to move back home to help take care of her mother."

"I told her to check in with me before she left town."

I shrugged, though Colter couldn't see it. "I don't know what to tell you," I said. "What did you want to talk to her about?"

"I wanted her to look at some mug books."

"Well, if she went home she shouldn't be hard to find. How many Elizabeth Daleys can there be in Forsyth, Missouri, a town with a population of 2,500? Now what were you going to tell me?"

"I'm having a presser tomorrow," he said. "I'm going to confirm the Semtex connection, even though you've already published it. I'm going to make the cigarette brands public, too. I'm also going to acknowledge that we haven't been able to match the DNA found on the cigarette butts with databases in the U.S. and have asked Interpol for help. I'm not going to mention that the DNA gave us some invaluable information about the people who smoked those cigarettes. You will get a call from your Washington source who will tell you what the DNA disclosed. Don't use the info until after the presser. It will appear that you developed it after the press conference with someone in D.C."

"And not in bed with you?"

"Not funny, Deuce."

I still had doubts. "Are you sure the Washington source is okay with this deal?"

"Very happy," Colter said. "Excited even. I think he misses being on the job."

~

I HAD HOOKED up my recorder to my phone. The more I committed this illegal act, the easier it got. I would have been astounded if Colter weren't recording me. I left the recorder on the phone, ready to go when I heard from Cribben. I didn't have to wait long.

"Hi again," he said.

"Hi to you, too."

"I have some things to tell you."

"Before you do, are you comfortable with this, because I'm not, at least not entirely."

"Yes. As long as I'm not being asked to break the law, I'm glad to help."

First he told me the brands of the cigarettes found at the fire scenes. I already knew this from Mark but withheld the information at his request. There were two brands, Benson & Hedges and Dunhills. Both brands had been found at all of the arson sites but one. In that case it's possible firefighters trampled the evidence.

The rest of it was new.

The DNA on the Benson & Hedges belonged to a male of primarily East African heritage. Likely a Somali. The Dunhill smoker was also male, of mixed heritage, Middle Eastern and African, but predominantly Yemeni. Fingerprints had been lifted from the filters, but they appeared too damaged to be useable for anything but possible confirmation of the smokers when and if they were taken into custody. The FBI was running them through U.S. and Interpol databases anyway.

On a whim, I asked Carl a question that had been gnawing at my brain since the warehouse fire in November. "I don't understand what drew Mason Cross to the first big fire, the warehouse with the two bodies. So far as we know, the only fires the arsonist set before that were small. What prompted the NSA to suspect radical Islamists?"

Carl was silent for a long moment. He was considering his answer.

"I know the answer to that, Deuce, but I haven't specifically been cleared to tell you. If I do tell you, you can't print it until you clear it with Colter or Cross."

"Okay."

"Do you know what a medwakh is?" He spelled it.

"No."

"It's a pipe, generally an elongated piece of wood with a metal mouthpiece and a metal ring around the top of the bowl. It's finding growing favor, almost entirely in the Middle East. It's used to smoke dokha, a very strong mixture of tobacco, herbs, and spices. Users claim it's less hazardous than cigarettes because it isn't all tobacco. They're wrong. The nicotine content is much more powerful. It can cause seizures and unconsciousness."

"And?"

"A medwakh with dokha residue was found at the site of one of the small fires."

"Where the CFD also found cigarette butts?"

"Yes."

"And that was enough to tie the fires to the Middle East and bring out the NSA?"

"Cross thinks the medwakh might have slipped out of the arsonist's pocket. Analysis showed it was carved from a piece of a baobab tree, which only grows in Africa and maybe drier parts of the Middle East. Baobab wood is favored for medwakhs because it's fire resistant. Finding one at a fire with the same brand of cigarette butts found near the warehouse tied it up for Cross."

"Would that have been enough for you, Carl?"

"I don't know," Cribben said. "Maybe enough to take a closer look. Somalia and Yemen are both countries where people smoke medwakhs and both states breed terrorism. Perhaps NSA felt it would be irresponsible to ignore the coincidences."

"That doesn't necessarily make the smokers Islamists or terrorists," I said. "Just candidates for lung cancer. For all we know we've been trapped in the crosshairs by a bunch of radical Swiss Calvinists pissed off because Americans aren't buying enough artisanal chocolate."

27

I t was 4:30 on a Friday afternoon, the day after I broke the DNA story. I had finished my column for Sunday. And I was missing Mark something fierce. I didn't know how I was going to get through my evening, not to mention the entire weekend, without him.

Three weekends earlier I had completely cleaned the house.

Two weekends earlier I had cleaned out the garage of boxes never opened after my move. The result was eighteen boxes of books I would never read again. They were picked up a few days later by a store that sells used books for relatively little money and donates the proceeds to Chicago child literacy programs.

The previous weekend it rained without letup, so I read two complete books that I had kept, then used them to start a new donation box.

I thought about spending this weekend volunteering at an animal shelter. But that could only end with my cats, Cleo and Caesar, acquiring additional siblings. I couldn't help it. I couldn't look into a sad kitten face and not take it in. My brother once told me the only way anyone would know when I died would be the overwhelming smell of dirty cat litter seeping through my windows. My body would be found, he suggested, surrounded by every stray that had crossed my path in the previous ten years.

I made a decision. I would call Mark and find out if he could get free one evening for dinner. If somebody objected, tough. Now that I had shifted suspicion that the sources of my news leaks were in Washington, could seeing Mark again, occasionally, be such a bad idea? Probably. But at this point I didn't care.

Except for the heartbreaking rumble of the powerful engines of equipment still working slowly and carefully to clear rubble from the Loop, the city had been quiet. I wondered if the arsonists had gone to ground. There had been no suspicious fires—at least none that fit the profile—in a couple of weeks.

I reached out to Beth Daley, who had indeed gone home to Missouri. She said the FBI had not contacted her again and wouldn't mind if I gave Ron Colter her phone number. She had packed up her condo and put it on the market, and continued trying to put her painful Chicago experience behind her.

Beth had returned her life to normal. I needed to do the same.

I called Mark before I left the office.

"Are you working, or do you have a minute to talk?" I asked.

"Both," he said. "I'm still down at the Keene's site sifting bricks and dust, but I'm having a hard time keeping my mind from wandering to a certain six-foot lady I know."

I smiled. "She's having the same problem with you. Do you think we've flogged ourselves long enough to prove our good intentions?"

"I think we passed that point weeks ago. I think we should have a 'fuck-what-the-world thinks' weekend to ourselves, starting tonight as soon as I can get home to clean up."

"I don't need to fuck the world," I said. "Only . . ."

"Stop," Mark said. "You're going to have me walking around a crime scene with an inexplicable bulge below my belt."

"So," I said, "what do you want to do—besides that."

"Sai Café. Sushi. Been thinking about that almost as much as I've been thinking about you. We'll eat, and we'll be so tired we'll have to find a place to lie down and rest."

"Rest isn't exactly what I had in mind," I said.

"Well, we'll think of something."

THE DINNER WAS outstanding and the aftermath more so, extending into the wee hours of the morning. Neither of us said anything about the arson cases.

We didn't say very much about anything.

On Saturday morning however, in the quiet of Mark's condo, over a breakfast of his incomparable spinach, mushroom, and feta cheese omelets, the dam broke.

"Everything about this case is weird," I said. "I never heard of a serial terrorist. Even on 9/11, when there were multiple targets, they were all part of the same mission, all on the same day. Not like this."

"You quoted somebody in the paper saying if these men are lone wolves they can carry through with their self-appointed missions for as long as they can avoid capture. If their mission is to terrorize the city and break its spirit, I can see where dragging out the anxiety would achieve that goal."

"We know it's scaring off visitors," I said. "Traffic at O'Hare and Midway is down eleven percent, and it's still winter. Summer travel reservations are down even more. A couple of conventions and trade shows have already pulled out of McCormick Place."

"That would certainly qualify as economic terrorism."

"Hard to stop unless the bad guys can be identified and found."

"We've got the cigarette butts with DNA and smudged fingerprints," Mark said. "Problem is, that won't help if the perps never had their DNA or fingerprints recorded."

"Is that even possible, to go through life without either recorded anywhere?"

"You wouldn't have much of a life, but it's certainly possible," he said. "Everywhere you go you leave DNA and fingerprints. For law enforcement the trick isn't in the finding. It's in the matching. If I have your DNA, but you've never been put in a database anywhere, I have no frame of reference."

"Great," I said. "All those people dead, and all the cops have are two invisible suspects." My thoughts drifted to the Loop. "You think there might be more bodies?"

"Not in the Loop," Mark said as we sat on his sofa, into the second pot of coffee. "Everyone reported missing has been accounted for. Everyone still hospitalized is expected to recover. The death toll will probably stay the same until the next attack."

"You sound pretty sure there's going to be another attack."

"Aren't you?"

It was a grim thought that spoiled the crisp, clear March morning that framed the city skyline laid out in panorama through the glass wall in Mark's living room.

"Have you heard anything more about the two dead men in the warehouse?" I asked. "I called Tony about tox results, but they still aren't back."

Mark frowned. "They take a long time, but not this long. I wouldn't worry about it, though. I don't know why the terrorists would want or need to kill the warehouse vics. That's probably a whole other story."

I suspected Mark was right, but I had a hunch with no explanation.

"Mark, are there photos of the bodies?"

"From the warehouse? Sure. Pretty grim. They're part of the investigative file."

"Which the Feds won't let me see," I said. "But Tony Donato might."

"He might. You two are on good terms. Why? What are you looking for?"

I shook my head and shrugged.

"I have no idea."

28

"T his isn't the best possible time, Deuce," Tony Donato said when I settled into a chair in his office early Monday afternoon. "On the other hand, there aren't any good times anymore." He looked tired and depressed.

"I'm just looking for a quick update," I said.

He sighed in resignation. "As you can imagine, my morgue is backed up. We're always pretty backed up. It would be a big help if people in this city stopped killing each other or getting involved in catastrophic wrecks on the interstates. But I've been saying that for years, and it only gets worse."

The massive workload in the medical examiner's office was underscored by the fact that Tony hadn't offered me a cup of office coffee. He wanted nothing to delay my departure. I wasn't concerned. Having tasted Tony's office coffee in the past, I figured not drinking any probably prolonged my life.

"One favor, and then I'm gone," I promised. "I need to see the autopsy photos of the two bodies from the warehouse fire in the South Loop."

"Why?"

I told him the truth. Just not all of it.

"I don't know why," I said. "It's just a hunch without a rationale. Something keeps knocking on my brain telling me I should see them. I don't need the whole investigative file. Just the written reports on those two bodies. And the photos."

"For publication?" I could tell Tony's decision would hinge on my answer.

"Certainly not the photos," I said. "We'd never publish those. Maybe the information, and if I decide to use it, I'll let you know first."

He nodded. "I should clear it with the FBI first, but they'll say no even without a good reason. And in the time I've known you I've learned it's best not to ignore your hunches, especially if they involve my office." He stood up. "Want some coffee?"

We stood in front of one of Tony's lab tables and he powered up a computer with one of the biggest monitors I'd ever seen. The home screen came up with an image so breathtaking, so sharp, I feared for the safety of my eyeballs.

"You use this place for a public movie theater after hours?" I asked.

"We don't have 'after hours' here," he said. "If the workload ever got slow I might be tempted. Be a way to supplement the office budget. I'd have to get a popcorn machine."

"What is this thing? I might get Mark one for his birthday to watch sports."

Tony smiled and cocked his head in a shrug.

"Nice," he said, "but you don't have to go this pricey. This is a fifty-five-inch 4K medical monitor with quad-view capability."

"You lost me after fifty-five inches," I said.

"You know what a 4K TV is?"

I tried not to roll my eyeballs. "Of course."

Tony smiled. "The super sharp images come in handy for medical examiners when we're dealing in the tiny world of body permutations. This particular model can also be divided into quadrants for simultaneous views of four different things."

"Definitely a household must during March Madness," I said.

"College basketball is more pleasant than what we're about to look at."

"Depends on whether your team's winning."

Tony ignored me and started searching files.

"Where do you want to start?" he asked. "In the morgue or in the warehouse?"

"Morgue," I said. Then, "Oh, crap."

"Told you," he said as he adjusted the images on the screen.

I forced myself to focus on the bodies. Each occupied a metal examination table equipped to drain away body fluids escaping from corpses. Despite their frightful appearance, I could tell them apart because one corpse had a hand and forearm that had not burned. I hoped for their sakes they had died before the fires got to them.

"Cause of death?" I asked.

"Fentanyl overdose. No heroin," Tony said. "Anything specific you want to see?"

"Could you print copies of those photos?"

Tony nodded and started typing. "I'll start a file for all the photos you want and print them out when we're done here."

"Have you recovered their brains yet?"

"Yep," he said and called them up. "What are you looking for?"

I got cagey. "What were you looking for?"

I knew from Carl Cribben that autopsies had found no sign of habitual drug use in these men, but I wanted to hear the details from the medical examiner.

"I looked for signs of habitual drug abuse. Some of the symptoms die with the users, like cognitive decline. But in habitual abusers we find brain damage similar to the early stages of Alzheimer's. And the brain gets spongy. But not in either of these men. Every organ in their bodies appeared normal, if a bit smoky."

"Then instead of asking you what you found, I should ask you what you didn't find."

Tony sighed and brought up more photos. The first sets were obviously kidneys.

"No HIV, no Hep C, no elevated protein levels in the urine." He switched to other organs that looked like intestines. "Waste in the colon normal to low. Addicts often get highly constipated. These two weren't. And none of the common damage to the rectums."

"In short?" I asked.

"These two weren't users," the medical examiner said. "I'd bet they didn't shoot up themselves. They had help. And let me show you the lungs."

Tony called up new photos. "These guys were smokers, but there's no possibility they died of smoke inhalation. They were dead when the fire started."

"So the manner of death . . .?"

"The only choices are accident or homicide. Right now, my money's on homicide."

29

M ark showed up at my door a little after seven with a large thin-crust, sausage/spinach/onion/mushroom pizza from Falco's on Archer, arguably one of the best pizzas in Chicago. I thought four ingredients plus the cheese and tomato sauce made the pie a bit top-heavy, but neither of us would give up our favorite enhancements, which were spinach and mushrooms in my case and sausage in Mark's. We agreed on onion.

Murphy the Irish setter got only a few nibbles of crust. His excitement at the prospect caused his body to quiver. He had no idea what other goodies he missed. The cats didn't smell anything worth waking up for, though I suspected they might have roused themselves for anchovies if Mark had allowed them in the house.

When we settled in on the floor with an open box and generous glasses of a good zinfandel on the coffee table, Mark asked, "So whatcha got that's so interesting?"

"Probably best to wait 'til we're done eating," I said.

"Whatever it is, I'm sure it's not new to me," he said.

"It's not you I'm concerned about."

"Oh. Okay."

Mark got lost in eating and driving Murphy to distraction. The big red dog tried crawling on the sofa behind us and draping his big square head over our shoulders. When that didn't work, he tried sitting on the floor with his chest in our laps to insert his head between the pizza and our mouths. He finally resorted to lying on his back on the floor, whimpering. The whimpering got the job done for him.

Mark ripped off a small piece of crust and tossed it in the air for Murphy to catch. Chewing was not part of Murphy's food-processing methodology. The crusts went straight down his throat whole. Before they even hit his stomach Murphy was back on the floor, on his back, whimpering and squirming in paroxysms of joy and enduring expectation.

Murphy's crust lust.

I wanted to focus on pizza and wine for a while, but my thoughts drifted back to the morgue. The medical examiner had put together a packet of copies of the photos on his computer, both full-frame and close-ups of such pertinent things as the remains of the syringes, or spikes, in the bodies of the two dead men, various views of the fully burned John Doe A and the partially burned John Doe B with close-ups of the unburned hand and forearm. I told Mark that Tony had shared some crucial evidence from the autopsies of the warehouse victims. He suggested we skip the rest of the pizza and go right to the photos. Believe me, as a measure of his excitement, willingness to set aside pizza is about as high on Mark's scale as it got. Well, maybe second highest.

Once we had cleaned up and refilled our wine glasses we sat on the living room floor, our backs against the sofa, the photo file arrayed on the coffee table. Mark knew what he was looking at. I didn't attempt to explain. I wanted his opinion uncolored by mine.

After going through the photos several times, Mark tossed them back on the table.

"So what're you thinking?" he asked me.

"You first," I said.

"You know what I know," he said. "These guys appear to be two addicts who ODed and died in the warehouse. But their body positions suggest they were either unconscious or dead and dragged to the scene before the fire started. Since Tony didn't find any soot in their lungs, we know they were dead before the fire got to them. What do you know?"

I told him in detail about my conversation with the ME.

"Interesting," he said. "Could he determine the time of death?"

"There's something in his notes about that. It was so cold in the warehouse the calculations are skewed. His best estimate puts TOD two days before the fire. So it's possible someone else killed them— not the arsonist. They just happened to be there when the arsonist found them. He left them there and went ahead with his plans."

Mark smiled without much mirth. "I thought you didn't believe in coincidence."

"I don't. I'm trying to look at this from every possible angle."

"So what's new?"

"I had a hunch. I asked Tony to fingerprint the man who had a hand left and compare the prints to the partials on the cigarette butts. The prints matched the Dunhills."

Mark's eyes went wide. "What about their DNA?"

"Tony's running it now."

30

Tony Donato called two days later.

"I got some interesting test results this morning," he told me. "I can't tell you who the two bodies are, but beat feet over here ASAP, and I can show you where they've been."

When I arrived Tony said, "Conference room. Colter's on his way."

That news didn't thrill me, but I understood the necessity.

"Does he know I'm here?" I asked.

"Yes, and he's none too happy about it. But I explained that our latest line of inquiry was based on your hunch, so I wasn't going to exclude you. What you can publish is between your paper and the FBI."

When we were all seated with the requisite bad coffee, Tony started up the conference room computers and video monitors and explained the developments.

"There is no doubt, given the final tox results on the two bodies, that both died of fentanyl overdoses laced with trace amounts of heroin, a combo known on the street as TNT," he said. "As little as a quarter milligram of fentanyl can kill you if you haven't developed a tolerance for it, and these men were not habitual users."

"We know that," Colter said.

Tony raised a hand and said, "Bear with me."

He put up photos of the two bodies as they were found in the warehouse.

"They were killed somewhere else and dumped in the warehouse," he said. "The positions of the bodies aren't what we'd see with ODs at the scene. And see this . . ." He pointed to the lower part of the totally burned victim. ". . . odd angle of the leg? Something dislocated his hip. Maybe the process of dragging him inside over a window ledge."

"We know that," Colter said. "Except for the hip, which doesn't seem important."

"Everything's important," Tony said, refusing to be intimidated by Colter's abruptness. "But this is where it gets interesting." He switched to the morgue photos of the two. "It was Deuce's hunch to grab their DNA."

"Looking for what?" Colter asked. "They were two derelicts."

"Not necessarily," Tony said. "We were looking for nothing in particular, and everything in general. We found a whole lot more than we expected."

Involuntarily, Colter and I both leaned forward in anticipation.

"So far, as I understand it," Tony said to Colter, you haven't made any matches for the DNA you found on either brand of cigarette butts. Is that right?"

"Right," Colter confirmed. "So far we got bupkis."

"We got matches on both samples," Tony said.

I expected this, but it cold-cocked Colter.

"*What?*'

Tony continued. He looked pleased with himself. "We ran the tests twice to be sure. Both DNA donors are residing in my morgue and have been for several weeks."

"The bodies from the warehouse?" I asked, to be certain.

"The very ones," Tony said. He split the screen on the video monitor and photos of two cigarette butts came up.

"These are the two butts found outside the wreckage at Keene's," he said. "The Benson & Hedges DNA matches John Doe A, the Somali. The DNA on the Dunhills matches John Doe B, the Yemeni. As badly as the prints on the butts were messed up, the partials we lifted from the Dunhills match the prints we took from John Doe B's surviving fingers."

Colter and I exchanged glances then looked back to Tony.

Tony didn't pause. "Now here's a conundrum for you. The two dead men were found in suspicious circs with needles in their bodies and a load of TNT in their systems inside the warehouse after the fire. Their cigarette butts at that scene were found outside and across the street. It's possible they smoked outside then walked inside and got mugged, drugged, and dead. But that doesn't fit with the evidence that they were killed or incapacitated two days before the fire and their bodies dragged inside the warehouse. It also doesn't explain how cigarette butts with their prints and DNA managed to show up at the sporting goods store, the Water Tower buildings, and in K-Town. Believe me, once those fellas left the warehouse, they never smoked again. Where the rest of the arsons are concerned, they had the ultimate alibis."

"So," Colter said, "how would the arsonist get DNA from dead men onto cigarettes that were smoked days or weeks after they died?"

"You don't," I said. "You hang out with them while they're still alive. And when they're not looking, you collect their butts and keep them in Baggies for future use."

"Machiavellian even for you," Colter said.

"So what do you do now?" I asked Colter.

"Call Interpol back in to focus on Yemen and Somalia," he said. "If the two dead men were ever swept up in police action in their home countries, their prints and DNA could be on record. That part of the planet isn't the best for that sort of record-keeping, but we could get lucky. If we get IDs, we might be able to track their movements in Chicago and identify who their friends were, including the arsonist. And we'll canvass Chicago mosques, see if anyone knows of two men gone missing."

My face must have registered some doubt. I know my words did.

"That's a lot of long shots, Ron," I said. "What if they never lived in that part of the world or left very young? What if they didn't attend mosques or maybe were Christian. "

He nodded, resignation written in the furrows cutting his forehead.

"Then we're shit out of luck," he said. "But it is what it is. Regrettably, it's all we got."

I stood and locked eyes with Colter. "I'm going to publish this," I said.

"You can't," Colter insisted.

"Why not? The two smokers are dead. Linking them to the arsons isn't going to hurt your investigation and might help. Somebody might come forward with an idea who these men were. And the findings will be attributed to the medical examiner's office, not to you."

Colter started to reply when Tony intervened.

"Look Colter," he said, "It was Deuce's idea to check the DNA from the bodies and the one set of surviving fingerprints against the cigarette butts. If it hadn't been for her, we might never have found the matches because we wrote off the two dead men as derelicts. I've been in this business a long, long time, and I can tell you there is no reason on earth not to let this information go. It's not going to queer anything you're doing."

"You don't know that," Colter insisted. "If the arsonist stops using the butts as his signature at his scenes, it will be harder to tie any new fires to him, or them."

"Oh, come on," I said. "How many consecutive life sentences do you think you could get on the arsonist if you caught him this afternoon?"

Tony answered. "Enough to ensure that he probably spends the rest of his life in solitary and dies in prison."

Colter glowered at both of us and left without another word.

I took that for capitulation.

31

A fter an unusually warm February and a cold, wet, windy March that seemed hell bent on making up for the mild winter, April slipped into Chicago. It brought the relief of warmer days, more sun, new leaves, forsythia, tulips, daffodils and jonquils, magnolias, and my personal favorites, lilacs that ranged from royal purple through shades of lavender to pink and white. When I was a kid my friends and I picked off individual small flowers and sucked on the stem ends, which gave up tiny pearls of nectar so sweet I was certain nothing in the world could taste better.

I was not above tasting lilac flowers as an adult and had put in mature plants all over my property.

I had taken a week off to regenerate and spent more time than I should have lying on a chaise lounge amid the sweet aromas in my back yard with the sun baking the chill of the last five months out of my bones. I alternately read Craig Johnson's *Longmire* books set in a desolate area of Wyoming, and astrophysicist Neil deGrasse Tyson's wondrously understandable tomes on the origins and workings of our universe.

I closed the covers on *Astrophysics for People in a Hurry* and laid my head back against the lounge, my face turned to the sun. I mulled over Tyson's cautionary argument that the only way humankind could avoid annihilation by its own misdeeds would be to embrace, rather than fear, the cosmic perspective.

I closed my eyes and thought about that. For *homo sapiens* to survive, we would have to relinquish the conceit that the universe revolves around us. I had no trouble accepting that the universe doesn't exist to serve us, but I found it difficult to accept the idea that we are here to serve the universe. We're not that important. We're carbon-based life forms, and because carbon is the most common non-gaseous element in our universe, it defies logic to assume it would not one day find another environment where it could combine with other elements to form a rudimentary form of life strictly by accident.

It seems illogical to assume it hasn't already happened on other planets. Perhaps it was life that generated eons ago and long since came to an end in a supernova of its sun. Or it could exist now, life in a far earlier state of evolution than we are, still instinct-driven amoebas that can't communicate with each other let alone with us. I hoped they would grow up to do better with their worlds than we were doing with ours.

Strangely, I didn't feel at all belittled by the thought. It put a lot into perspective and gave me some hope. Thus soothed, I dozed off.

THERE HAVE BEEN times in my life when I felt that dreaming was like having a magic library card that would let my brain withdraw whatever type of story my psyche needed, whether fantasy, ecstasy, adventure, horror, or complete nonsense and gibberish. I learned in Psych 101 in college that dreaming is a laundering process, the brain's way of cleaning out trash, the useless stray thoughts, memories, and emotions accumulated during the day. This detritus of the waking hours needs to be flushed away so the mind and body awake refreshed into a new day.

I realized that this trip to my mental library had dropped me into the horror section. My brain's visual cortex and amygdala went into hyperdrive as soon as my nap turned into a sound sleep. They conspired to take me back in time about a dozen years to the day I nearly died, trapped in a storm cellar on a farm well west of Chicago. As a green reporter right out of college, I had been assigned to go there to interview a woman who grew some ridiculous number of squash varieties, and I got caught up in a fierce tornado.

As I lay pinned on the dirt floor of the storm cellar, with life-saving bottles of water just out of my reach, delirium set in. My dead parents visited me. My mother, who died when I was very young, spoke no words to me, but my father, who had died recently, had plenty to say, though none of it made any sense to me at the time.

My current dream seemed to be a bizarre recreation of this event. Instead of being trapped by a tornado, I faced an advancing storm of fire. Instead of the threat of being crushed under a giant tornado-tossed combine that landed on the door of the cellar above me and threatened to break through, I faced the threat of burning alive. I wasn't in a storm cellar this time. It looked more like a rather nice hotel room. But as often happens in dreams, the part of my brain that might have yelled, "Stop the cameras; the script's all wrong," didn't care. I dreamed my dream aware but uncritical of the alteration of the details. It got increasingly hot as the fire advanced on me. Then the light changed. It became cooler and darker, and I heard someone call my name.

I started awake, lying there with my eyes closed, trying to shake off the vestiges of the nightmare. I had not yet regained full control of my brain activity.

"Deuce, wake up, honey," Mark said. "You're frying yourself."

Mark had changed the light. He had taken up a position between the sun and me.

He said, "As much as I enjoy the prospect of spreading coconut oil over your lobster-red body, I think if you lie out here much longer you're going to be in a world of hurt."

⁓

I HAD JUST STEPPED out of the shower, still feeling the mild stinging from my inadvertent case of light sunburn, when my phone rang. The screen said, "Unknown caller," so I sent it to voice mail. I was in no mood to fend off solicitations.

I put the phone down and started drying my hair when it chimed, the tone I'd set for voice mails. Solicitors don't generally leave voice mails, so I listened.

At first the voice startled me. It had the tinny quality created by a voice-masking device. The message was even more startling:

"I will call you again in ten minutes," it said with a heavily metallic resonance. "Just listen. Don't ask questions. And don't ignore the call."

I threw on a robe and ran downstairs where Mark was watching a Cubs game.

I played the voice mail for him.

"Well-masked," he said. "I don't have a clue who it is. But I think you'd better take the call. It could be about the arsons."

We sat staring at the phone, waiting for it to start playing it's ring tone. It began exactly ten minutes after the first call.

I put the phone on speaker so Mark could hear, too.

"This better be good," I said when I answered.

The reply stunned me.

32

"You have a pen and paper?" the voice asked. The mechanical quality reminded me of the artificial voice used by the late theoretical physicist Stephen Hawking.

I moved into the kitchen where I had a pad and pen I used for making shopping lists. Mark walked with me.

"I'm going to give you a name," the voice said. "It could lead you where you want to go. You ready?"

"Ready," I said.

"Ali Muhammad Kaar." He spelled the name.

"Okay, who's that?"

"He's Yemeni. Figure it out."

The line went dead.

"What are you supposed to do with that?" Mark asked.

"I wonder if Ali Muhammad Kaar is one of the victims from the warehouse fire. One of the dead men was Yemini."

He shrugged. "Yemini. Yeah, could be. But who would know that? Who'd disguise his voice to drop that tidbit on you?"

Good question. Tony Donato would just come out and tell me, though only in the privacy of his office. Carl Cribben, my information conduit in Washington, would come out and tell me, too. Colter might have told me when we were together in the medical examiner's office. But he didn't know. It stunned him to learn the two bodies in Tony's morgue were the men who smoked the cigarettes left at the fire scenes. NSA goon Mason Cross wouldn't tell me anything ever.

"Can you trace a call after it's over?" I asked.

"I don't know about a land line. I'm pretty sure you can do it with a cell call. The caller's cell phone would've pinged several cell towers on the way to you. I don't know if it works if you only have the number receiving the call, but there might be a way to track the call in reverse. You have somebody who would know how to get those records?"

"I think so. But I'm not sure he can do it legally."

IT WAS SATURDAY, so Rick Simon, the IT wizard at the *Journal,* was off. It was Simon who helped me identify Beth Daley, the woman who called me to tell me about her possible encounter with the arsonist before he leveled Keene's. I found Simon at home.

"Would I be ruining your weekend if I asked for some help?" I asked him.

"Should I go into the office?"

"No," I said. "We need to operate in the dark."

"Sounds fun," he said. "You want to come here, or should I meet you somewhere?"

"Do you have a good computer setup at your apartment?"

"The best. Better, actually, than I have at work. Not much I can't find."

"I'll be there in an hour."

THE WEATHER WAS nothing short of gorgeous so traffic on Lake Shore Drive overflowed with locals enjoying the weather. Rick and his partner, Paul, lived in the Lakeview neighborhood, one of the centers of

Chicago's LGBT activity, where alternative lifestyles melded beautifully with older residents who had lived there for years, and young straight couples with children. Lakeview, also known as Boys' Town, had some extraordinary restaurants and shops. What it lacked was street parking.

We had taken Mark's personal SUV. Fortunately, he had a visor placard that identified the vehicle as being on official state business. It allowed him to park in a CVS drug store parking lot where no one would question it. Neither of us mentioned that he could get into serious trouble for the subterfuge. But who would know?

Rick and Paul lived on Aldine, less than a block off Lake Shore Drive. They had a lovely condo in a U-shaped building that wrapped around a pleasant private park. Rick met us at the door and invited us in. Paul poked his head out of the kitchen. I introduced both men to Mark.

Paul wiped his hands on a dishtowel and extended it to Mark.

"While you all work," he said, "I'm making some snacks. When you're done, we can go sit outside and have them with some drinks."

"That's very nice of you," Mark said.

"Any excuse for a party on a day this lovely," Paul said as he turned back to the kitchen. "You kids have fun."

Rick took us upstairs where he had converted a giant bedroom to a computer workshop. We talked about the call I'd gotten.

"So you need to know where the call originated," he said.

"That would be nice," I said. "But I thought about it on the way over, and I'm not sure it's worth the risk. I'm guessing you'd be breaking about a dozen federal laws. Let's set that aside as a last resort. What I need first is to find a man named Ali Muhammad Kaar. I Googled him and got a few near-hits but no perfect matches. Most of the people who came up don't live in the United States."

"Maybe your guy lives overseas and just came here to help with the arsons."

"My guy's in the morgue, Rick. He's one of the two men who burned up in the warehouse fire. I need to know what he did and where he lived while he still walked among the living."

He nodded and powered up his impressive array of computer equipment.

"People who want to live off the grid can do it," he said. "It's not easy. Most of them slip up once or twice. For example, you can't open a utility account without a name and full address. Same with cable. Let's start with ComEd and Comcast and see what we find."

"You going to hack into their systems?" I asked. "I don't want you winding up in prison over this."

"I know how to cover my tracks," he said. "As long as I don't do any damage to their systems or steal their account data, they shouldn't even notice. This will be a passive hack, just looking for information. Even if it is detected, they won't spend the time or the money trying to track me down. Not that they could, anyway."

It took Rick less than twenty minutes to finish his search, which impressed me.

"Got him twice," he said. "He has accounts with both companies, and both at the same address." He wrote it down then used Google Maps to locate it. "It's on 111th Street in the Mount Greenwood neighborhood. From the Google Earth photos it looks like it's a second-story walk-up over an insurance office."

"Really?" I said. "Mount Greenwood is the most heavily Irish neighborhood in the city, one of the most heavily Irish neighborhoods in the country."

"Fourth in the country," Mark said. "Last census made it at just over forty percent Irish Catholic. Not where you'd expect to find a Somali."

"A lot of Islamic Africans who came to Chicago settled deep on the South Side," I said. "There are quite a few mosques and Islamic centers down in that area."

Rick whirled his chair around to face me.

"You gotta make some decisions here," he said. "You want me to hack into state records and see if he filed tax returns that would tell us where he worked? I'm not going to offer to try the IRS. They're too good even for me."

"I don't want you to hack into anywhere else," I said. "We know where he lived. I need to go talk to his neighbors and his friends, if I can find any."

"Not alone, you're not," Mark said in a tone that said he'd brook no dissent. "If Ali Muhammad Kaar was part of a jihad, his friends are going to be of like mind. If he was part of a cell, and his crew thinks you're onto them, they'll be happy to cut you into chum and take you fishing on the lake."

I saw the wisdom in Mark's caution. We devised a plan that wouldn't get anybody killed. The first thing Rick did was locate the owner of the building where Kaar lived.

"He's the insurance agent with his office on the first floor," Rick said. "Brendan Boyle. I'd bet a week's salary he's not Somali. Maybe not even a terrorist."

"Can you Google him?" I asked.

"Already did," Rick replied in a tone that suggested I under-estimated him. "Nothing remarkable. Lives in Mount Greenwood. Married. Couple of kids. He has, let's see, two speeding tickets. Nothing heavier than that. Member of St. Catherine's Roman Catholic Church, K of C, Rotarians, and that's it. Not a very ominous background."

"Unless it's a cover," Mark said.

Rick turned back to his computer array. "What's your cell number, Deuce? And what time did the calls come in? I'll see what I can find on your mysterious caller."

"Hold off on that, Rick. I don't want to ask you to commit a crime. If I get desperate, I'll call you back."

I turned to Mark. "Want to go talk to a guy about an insurance policy? And hope he works on Saturdays?"

33

Brendan Boyle apparently didn't have a secretary, or at least not one who worked weekends. One of those plastic clock faces affixed by a suction cup to his front door said, "Be back at . . ." with adjustable hands turned to two-thirty. The hands didn't specify a.m. or p.m. or the day of the promised return. We decided to park and wait a while.

Mount Greenwood had the look of a pleasant neighborhood. Not flashy or high-end, but filled with well-tended houses and yards. People greeted one another on the street and gathered in knots on the sidewalk, perhaps to discuss the possible fortunes of the White Sox during the new baseball season. No one had any reason to believe the team would be any less dismal than the previous year, but where baseball in Chicago is concerned, Cubs fans and White Sox fans share eternal hope.

Mark walked across the street to a diner and returned with two turkey sandwiches and two cups of coffee. We were still thirty-seven minutes from two-thirty, and neither of us had eaten lunch, though we had stayed with Rick and Paul long enough to have a glass of wine and crab canapés made with real crab.

I examined the turkey for the telltale sheen of preservatives and found none. The meat looked and smelled fresh-roasted. And tasted great. The coffee wasn't bad, either.

There were two street-level entrances to the building we watched. A glass door accessed the insurance office, and a scarred wood door probably led to a stairway to the second level. Two metal mailboxes hung on a wrought-iron railing beside the wood door. The second story rooms might have been occupied or not. The windows had cheap blinds and flimsy curtains. I couldn't see interior lights burning or any evidence that anyone was at home. The presence of two mailboxes led me to believe there was a second apartment at the rear of the building. No way to know in which the Somali had lived, if either.

Mark and I slipped into easy conversation.

"Did you always want to be a fireman?" I asked.

"No, that wasn't one of my childhood fantasies. I thought I wanted to be a stock broker, like my father. I got a business degree at Rutgers, but I didn't go any farther with it. There was a restless quality to me when I was younger. I couldn't see settling into a nine-to-five office job. So I joined the Army instead and went to Ranger school."

"How'd your parents feel about that?" I asked, looking for a piece of lettuce that dropped out of my sandwich into my lap.

"They weren't thrilled. Well, no, my dad wasn't thrilled. My mother was furious. All she could think about was me getting killed over there."

I smiled at him. "I'm glad you didn't."

"Me, too." He paused. "Uh, Deuce, I don't like to talk about what happened over there. Let me just say I was a sniper, and I was good at it. I was a full colonel when I mustered out. If I'd stayed, I might have earned a star or two. Or three. But I got very tired of the killing. Three tours was plenty."

"So you came home to a safe job as a fireman."

He smiled. "Something like that. You know though, I missed the shooting. Not the killing. But the precision it takes to be able to take the right equipment with the right ammo and hit a target from a mile away. That's why, once upon a time, I offered to take you to the range and teach you how to shoot. I'm there at least twice a week, keeping sharp."

"Maybe someday," I said with an urge to change the subject.

"You're from a big family," I said. "I can't even remember how many of your brothers and sisters I met last year when we went to your folks' place for Thanksgiving."

"There are seven of us," he said. "Two other boys and four girls. When I joined the Army Mom said she should enlist with me as a cook. She'd had a lifetime of learning to prepare meals for a brigade."

Two-thirty came and went. Brendan Boyle didn't show up until three-seventeen and then none too steady on his feet.

He couldn't have been more than five-foot-six and had a florid complexion that bespoke too many hours bellied up to bars. He wore nerdy eyeglasses. The top of the eyepieces and the stems were black plastic. The lower part of the eyepieces was clear plastic yellowed with age. I hadn't seen frames like those since grade school.

Boyle's sport coat appeared not to have been cleaned or pressed in weeks. The mustard stain on one lapel looked fresh. Since I saw no shirt cuffs at the bottoms of his jacket sleeves I assumed the shirt had short-sleeves, making it nerdy to match his glasses. It strained at its buttons to contain the beer belly that hung like ballast over the buckle on the belt that held up his disheveled khaki pants. His shoes were pronated sneakers.

"I guess I'll stick with the agent I've already got," Mark said.

"He looks like a man at the end of a long liquid lunch in a fine Irish pub," I said.

"Might make it easier to talk to him," Mark said. "But if he throws up on me, he's gonna take a beating."

We followed Brendan into his office. He seemed startled to see people who might be potential clients.

"Well, afternoon, folks," he said. "What can I do for you on this lovely afternoon? New car insurance, maybe? Homeowners? Renters?

Life? Long-term health—never too early to start on that. Sit down. Sit down. Let's talk."

He pointed to two worn side chairs that faced his desk. He fell into a squeaky, faux-leather high back behind a desk that hadn't been cleaned off since the turn of the century. Boyle made a perfunctory effort to straighten up some paperwork piles, got nowhere, and gave up on the project.

"We're not here for insurance," I said. "We're looking for information."

I introduced Mark, and myself, and we handed Boyle our cards.

"I thought you looked familiar," he said to me. "You write for the paper, doncha?"

I nodded agreeably. "One of them, yes, as it says there on my card."

He turned to Mark.

"Not sure what you do," he said. "But if it has to do with fire, and you could see your way clear to showin' me how to burn this dump down for the insurance without gettin' caught, you'd be my new BFF. That means Best Friend Forever. My daughter taught me. It's some'a that internet nonsense."

"And what you just asked me to do is a felony, Mr. Boyle," Mark said sternly.

Boyle wasn't phased. "No harm in askin'," he said.

Actually, even asking was a crime, but Mark ignored it, so I did, too.

"I hope we're not keeping you from anything," I said.

"I wish you was keepin' me from somethin'," he replied. "Business is in the crapper, and I think I mighta just lost another source of revenue."

"Really," I said. "What source?"

Boyle waved his hand in dismissal. "Nuthin' you need worry over. Had a couple a guys livin' upstairs, rentin' a small apartment. Looks like they skipped on me owin' two months back rent."

There it was. I hadn't even had to ask. Whatever Brendan Boyle had been drinking at his local hole, I owed the bartender a twenty.

"Funny thing was," Boyle added, "they didn't clean out the place. All their clothes and stuff are still up there. They just vanished."

I asked, "What were their names?"

"Why?" he asked. "Don't you need a warrant to ask for that information?"

"Reporters can't get warrants," I said ...

"But the police can," Mark added quickly, "and I've got 'em on speed dial. So before we go to a lot of trouble, can you just tell us who your jumpers are?"

Brendan looked intimidated. He glanced at a file cabinet then quickly back to Mark. His eyes seemed to cross for a moment, perhaps thrown off kilter by the combination of whatever he'd been drinking and the quick movement of his head.

"Jumpers? What'd they do, go inna river?"

"No, Mr. Boyle. Just an expression. They apparently jumped the rent on you."

Boyle nodded emphatically.

"Damned good and right. I can't pronounce their names. Lemme pull the file."

It took him several minutes to find the right folder in his file drawer.

"Here 'tis, lad," he said. "I'm gonna write the names down for ya, cause I got no idea how to pronounce 'em."

The names he slid across were Ali Muhammad Kaar and Ahmed al-Gharsi.

Mark and I glanced at one another. We were both thinking the same thing. Just that easily we now had IDs on both corpses from the South Loop warehouse.

"Did they share an apartment, or ...?"

"Yeah, they shared," Boyle said. "Inna front. Back apartment's been vacant most of a year." He looked from me to Mark and back again. "What? You think you can find 'em?"

"We know exactly where they are," I said. "Don't be expecting to get the back rent any time soon. Could you let us look at their place?"

His eyes squinted in thought.

"I don't think I can let you in without a warrant."

"You don't have to defend their rights," Mark said. "They're both dead."

Boyle frowned and shook his head slightly.

"God rest their souls," he said and crossed himself. He didn't ask how they died.

"We're more interested in their belongings," I said. "Can we go up?"

"No can do," he said. "I'll call my lawyer Monday and ask him if I can let you in, but until then the place stays locked up."

"Okay, let's leave that for now. What can you tell us about them? Where did they work? Who were their friends? What do you know about their lifestyle?"

Boyle sighed deeply. "I didn't have a lotta dealings with 'em. Couldn't hardly understand what they were sayin' most of the time. Those accents and all. They mostly stayed off by theirselves. One of 'em worked at an auto supply place on Western. The other worked in an auto glass place, also on Western. I think the two places mighta been connected. They're next door to each another."

"Any friends you ever met?" I asked.

"Nobody I ever saw 'em with, no. Never had any company upstairs to my knowledge. Mostly they just watched TV when they were home. Sometimes they went drinking, but if they got drunk, they were quiet about it."

"You know where they hung out?" Mark asked.

"No clue."

"Weren't they Muslims?" I asked.

Boyle thought about that. "I dunno. Maybe," he said.

"If they were serious about their religion, they probably never drank."

"Then I don't know," Boyle said. "They were hangin' out somewhere."

Something else occurred to me. "Did you ever suspect they were using drugs?"

"No, and I checked."

"What do you mean?" Mark asked.

Boyle looked embarrassed.

"I shouldn't say this, but whenever they had somethin' in the apartment needed fixing, I always went up there when they was at work so I could have me a look around. I've seen neater people, but if they had any drugs around, I couldn't find 'em. And I looked in all the right places. Freezer, toilet tank, under the mattresses, inside shoes, you know. No drugs. No booze either, now that you mention it. Not even a beer in the refrigerator. They did smoke, but there ain't no house rules against it. Worst thing I ever found was dust."

"What brands did they smoke?"

Boyle rubbed his temples.

"Oh, boy, I'm not sure I remember. I think maybe I saw a pack of Benson & Hedges on the kitchen table, but if I saw another brand around I can't recall it."

Something didn't quite add up.

I asked Boyle, "You said you thought they went out drinking sometimes, but since Muslims don't drink, what made you think that?"

He thought about that for a minute then shook his head.

"Dunno," he said. "They were gone a lot in the evening. I didn't know where. I guess I just assumed they went to a bar. I didn't think about them maybe bein' Muslim. Didn't make no difference in terms of rentin' to 'em." He stopped and thought a moment. "This one time I was workin' late, and they came home like around ten or so with a third guy, and they all acted kinda tipsy. I walked out to say hello and could smell beer, but it mighta just been the third guy. I don't know."

"Did you know the third man?"

"Never seen him before that night. Saw him a few times after that, but I didn't bother to go out of my way to say hello. Didn't strike me as very friendly."

This was getting interesting. "How so?"

"Huh?"

"How was he not friendly?"

"Wouldn't make eye contact. Kinda kept himself turned away

from me. Didn't say more than six words with me standin' there. That's why I didn't think of him when you asked about people who might have been friends of the two tenants."

Mark asked, "Could you describe him? The third man?"

"Not really. He had a Bears cap pulled down over his eyes. About my height, darker skin than me. And I probably outweighed him by twenty-five, thirty pounds."

"Did he speak with an accent?" I asked.

"Hard to tell from six words, but not that I caught."

"But your two renters did?"

"Oh, yeah. Couldn't hardly understand 'em."

I thought maybe we were done, but Boyle looked studious, as if trying to remember something. So Mark and I sat quietly and waited him out.

He nodded and looked up at us. "There was this one odd thing."

We kept waiting.

"I don't know why I even remember it. It was a night the three of 'em was out there, standin' on the sidewalk, talkin'. One of my renters, Ali, flips a butt into the gutter. The guy with them, the one who didn't talk, walks out in the street and picks it up. I thought he was just bein' a good citizen, you know, helping keep the city clean. But he walks right past a trash barrel and doesn't throw it in. He just closes his hand around it."

"Was it still smoldering?" Mark asked.

"I wondered that, too. It mighta been. But the guy's wearin' gloves. It was a cold night. Hadn't thought about it again 'til now. Probably don't mean nuthin.'"

"Oh, it means something, Mr. Boyle," I said. I took a copy of the FBI sketch of the arson suspect from my messenger bag and handed it to Boyle. "Does this look like the man you saw with your renters?"

He looked at the sketch then back at me.

"This was the sketch in the papers, right?" he said. I nodded. "Could be the same guy. It was a while ago, and I didn't get a real good look at 'im, like I said."

"Now it's even more important you let us take a look around that apartment," I said.

He looked alarmed, as if something dreadful had just occurred to him.

"Hey," he said, his eyes darting between Mark and me, "were the two guys rentin' from me terrorists, the guys who been burnin' the city down?"

"We don't know," I said.

"Jesus, I had two guys living right above my place of business who might've wanted to chop my head off," he said, practically panicky.

"We don't know that, Mr. Boyle," I said. "We don't know that at all."

"You sure they're both dead?"

I nodded. "Ali Muhammad Kaar for sure. We don't have a positive ID on the second dead man, but it stands to reason it's Ahmed al-Gharsi."

Now he asked how they died.

"Probably drug overdoses," I said. "Then their bodies were burned in a fire."

He stood and crossed himself again.

"Oh, Christ. Oh, Christ. The hell with my lawyer."

Boyle flipped through his key ring and selected one.

"Let's go up," he said.

34

T he apartment depressed me with rooms that were dingy, dark, and dusty, though not dirty. Old, rancid cooking aromas of heavily spiced dishes, garlic in particular, permeated the airspace in the stairway. The odors were less obvious in the apartment because two windows had been left open, creating a battle with frigid air blowing in and the heating system running hard to keep up.

"Aw, Jeez, that's gonna cost me," Boyle said and started into the apartment. Mark put a hand on his chest and told Boyle to stay put. Then he went back to his truck for a couple of pairs of latex gloves and paper booties. I stood in the doorway taking stock of what I could see.

Old, well-used furniture filled the living room, including a couple of floor lamps, a small table with three chairs under a ceiling fixture, and a small, free-standing coat closet. The bare walls displayed squares and rectangles of ground in dirt, the demarcation zones for paintings or photographs someone had hung at one time. The television was an old Zenith cathode ray tube model embedded in a faux wood cabinet that took up half of one wall. I hadn't seen an old tube

TV in years. I guessed the Zenith dated back to somewhere in the mid-eighties.

Mark brought the gloves and booties. Again he told Boyle to stay put in the hall.

The kitchen, like the rest of the unit, had a lot of age on it, but tidy and clean. I saw no unwanted visitors crawling about. A small bathroom sat across from the kitchen, also old and tidy with a rust-streaked toilet, a chipped sink, and a shower in the old, stained claw-foot tub. The unit had a single bedroom with double beds and a closet in which both men had been able to store their clothes. Neither, it appeared, was a clotheshorse.

Mark started going through drawers in the bedroom. I wandered back into the kitchen and searched it methodically. The refrigerator smelled bad. A couple of lemons had grown coats of blue-gray fuzz. Some ground red meat, maybe lamb, had leaked bloody juice onto a shelf where it dripped into a crisper drawer. Two small, dead flies floated in the mess. I saw a quart of milk I didn't even want to think about. Nothing unexpected. I checked the in-unit freezer and found it almost completely iced over. A glacier of frost buried any food left inside.

I went back to the living room and saw exactly what I was looking for. On a small side table next to the far end of the sofa a wooden bowl sat half filled with books of matches. All looked to be in fairly pristine condition. A half-smoked package of Dunhill cigarettes rested on top of the matches.

"Mark," I called, "could you come in here?"

"Where are you?" he asked.

"What? I'm hard to find in a two-room apartment?"

I took several photos of the bowl and its contents with my iPhone. When Mark, using his keen sense of direction, managed to locate me, he moved the bowl to the coffee table and emptied it so we could sort through our find.

"I haven't seen anybody use book matches in a long time," he said.

"I haven't seen a tube television in a long time," I said. "Maybe this is a museum."

Most of the matches had never been opened. My brother had collected matchbooks as a kid, and I remember him warning me not to touch his collection or I would ruin it. I wondered if the former tenants here had the same hobby. The striker strips on the front of most of the folded books were pristine. We left them as we found them. There were fifty-seven books. Eleven had been partially used. And they were all from the same place:

Muldoon's Ale House on 111th and Kedzie.

We left the apartment as we found it and told Boyle to lock the door, leave it locked, and not to rent the place yet.

"And how'm I supposed to pay my bills?" he demanded.

"I'm sorry, Mr. Boyle," Mark said, "but that's not our problem."

The insurance man brightened a bit. "Well, maybe it's not all bad."

"How so?" I asked.

"When word gets out that two guys involved in the Chicago arsons lived in my building, people are gonna flock here. I could pick up a lotta new clients."

"Just don't offer tours upstairs," Mark warned in his best voice-of-authority tone. "The cops and the feds will have to search the place and dust for prints. If they find out you rummaged around in here after you found out the renters were dead, they could charge you as an accessory to a felony."

When we left Boyle on the street, thoroughly shaken, I asked Mark, "Could he really be charged with a crime? He is the owner of the place."

Mark grinned at me.

"What're you askin' me for? I'm not a cop."

FROM THE EXTERIOR, Muldoon's looked inviting. The top part of the double front doors displayed intricately etched glass embedded in highly polished oak. The sign, which hung from iron hooks and rocked slightly in the breeze, had raised gold letters on a Kelly green field. The bar was either an Irish hangout or a sports bar favoring Notre Dame.

Maybe both.

It was Saturday, so even at four in the afternoon the place was filling up. There were ten large flat-screen TV sets hung around the perimeter of the room, decorated in dark wood and green Naugahyde. The bar was long and about two-thirds full. The array of pulls for beer on draft was impressively varied, and the stepped shelves against the back wall held sixty or seventy liquor bottles. Photos of famous Notre Dame and Chicago sports stars, all of them autographed, dotted the walls.

Mark and I took seats at the bar as far away from other patrons as possible, though the gap between Mark and the next guy was only two stools.

The bartender approached with a welcoming smile and a hint of an Irish brogue.

"Afternoon, folks," he said. "What can I get fer ya?"

I ordered a Harp, and Mark asked for a "Smitticks."

The bartender brightened. "So yer Irish, lad," he said. "Most Americans don't know how to pronounce that. They call it Smithwick's."

"Well, Smithwick's is the way it's spelled," Mark said.

"Don't mean that's how it's called." He tossed down a couple of cardboard Guinness coasters and said, "Be right back."

Mark pulled a twenty from his wallet and laid it on the bar while I looked around. The room's clientele had a decidedly Irish look, and I made a bet with myself that if I took a poll I would find that many of the drinkers were first responders. As Mark had once noted, Mount Greenwood counted the highest concentration of police and firefighters of any neighborhood in the city.

The bartender returned with sixteen-ounce glasses of brew drawn from taps.

"What's your name?" I asked him.

"Dillon Bryne," he said. "I own the joint. What's yours?"

"I'm Deuce. This is Mark."

"First time here?"

"Yep."

"Enjoy," he said as he swept Mark's twenty off the bar to make change. I thought he might be the first person I'd ever met who didn't ask me about the origin of my name.

When Dillon returned he asked if we were going to order anything to eat.

"Weekends we always got shepherd's pie. Best in town."

"Maybe later," Mark said and expanded on my introduction.

"Dillon, Deuce here is a columnist for the *Journal,* and I'm a state fire investigator."

"You won't find any violations or stories here," he said. His tone remained friendly, but his eyes hardened.

"We're not here looking for violations. Stories might be another matter."

Dillon drew himself up and started to turn away.

"Hold on a sec," I said, hoping to cool the atmosphere. "I just want to ask a couple of questions. Not about you or the bar. About a couple of guys who might have been clients."

"I don't talk about our customers," he said.

"These two won't mind," I replied. "They're both dead."

Now I had his attention, though he glanced down the bar.

"Lemme check, make sure everybody's good. Then I'll be back."

When he returned he said, "I ain't missin' any customers I can think of."

"Two foreign guys," I said. "Both black. One from Somalia, one from Yemen."

He glanced toward the other end of the bar, which was empty.

"Yeah," he said. "They ain't been here inna while, now you mention it. Not that their absence has any detrimental impact on my bottom line. All they drank was ginger ale, though they ate their weight in burgers and fries. They liked lamb burgers, though they'd eat chicken if we didn't have lamb."

"They were probably Muslims, and their religion forbids the use of alcohol," I said.

"Yeah, right. How'd they die?"

"Overdoses," I said.

"Drugs?" the bartender asked. "Really? I never took them for druggies."

I let it slide and asked, "You give away book matches with the bar's name and logo?"

"Yep." He pulled a new book from under the bar. "Those two guys asked for matches every time they came in."

"Smoked a lot, did they?"

"Yeah, but we make everybody who wants to smoke either stand on the sidewalk or use our big porch in the back."

Mark sniffed and frowned at Dillon. I could smell the faint odor of tobacco, too.

"After we shut down for the night, if any regulars are left, we let 'em smoke inside. At that point the place is a private club, and we can do that legally."

Mark nodded, more or less confirming Dillon's argument.

"They always sat in the same place," Dillon said, cocking his head toward the unoccupied end of the bar. "Last two stools. Darkest place in the room."

"Do you know why?"

"Never asked. If they wanted to sit in the dark it was fine by me. It left two stools open for guys who wanted to watch TV and buy booze."

"Did they always come alone?" I asked.

"Yeah, just the two of 'em." He frowned. "No, wait. They always came in alone, but once or twice a week another guy'd come in and sit with 'em. White guy, though. Drank Smittick's or sometimes a black-and-tans. Always went out and smoked with 'em, too. Like Larry, Curly, and Moe. Where one went, three went."

"White guy?" Mark said. "You sure?"

"Like I can't tell the difference?" Dillon said.

"No offense," Mark said. "But actually a lot of Arabs are light-skinned and blue-eyed. That doesn't make them any less Arab."

"Maybe, but like you said, if the third guy'd been Arab, he probably wouldn'ta been drinking alcohol. Either that or he was a lapsed Muslim with a slight brogue right outta Kildare or Clare." Dillon thought for a moment. "Be my guess the third guy's black Irish. Darker complexion, darker hair, dark eyes. But that don't make him any less Irish."

"Touché," Mark said.

I pulled another copy of the FBI sketch from my bag and handed it to Dillon.

"This the guy?"

"Coulda been," he said. "There's a definite resemblance I can see. But it's hard to tell much from this."

"You didn't happen to get the third guy's name?" I asked.

Dillon shook his head. "I didn't get any of their names. When they first started comin' in I tried making some social small talk. The two black guys tried to converse, but I had too much trouble understanding their accents, and their grasp of English wasn't too good. The other guy, the Irish guy, never said a word to me after he ordered his black-and-tan. Sometimes he'd order a burger, too, but beyond that, he didn't talk to me at all and wouldn't make eye contact."

"Could you help a police sketch artist improve on that?" I asked, nodding toward the likeness I'd given Dillon.

"Maybe. Not a lot, but maybe a little."

"Okay, think about it," I suggested. "If we need it we'll come back with the FBI."

Dillon looked alarmed. "FBI?"

"Yeah," I said. "But not to worry. They won't be looking to jam you up."

We finished our beer and got up to leave. Dillon walked over to say goodbye.

I took the opportunity for a last question.

"When the three of them went out to smoke," I said, "did you ever notice whether the Irish guy picked up their cigarette butts?"

Dillon laughed. "Why would I notice that? I don't stand here watching people on the street. I got enough to do watching people at the bar and inna kitchen."

We said thank you and promised to come back for a burger soon. Mark was just about to push open the front door for me when Dillon called us back.

"I just thought of something I found weird," he said. " A coupla times when the three guys stayed 'til after closing, they smoked at the bar. And when they left, and I went to clean up, I noticed there weren't no butts in the ashtray. Never. Not once. I checked the floor, and they weren't down there, either. I have no idea where they went."

Shazam!

35

As we drove out of Mount Greenwood I called the medical examiner's office. I expected to find Tony Donato working. Several hundred body parts from the South Loop disaster remained unidentified.

"Mired deep in autopsy hell," he told me. "What's up?"

I offered to tell him only if he swore an oath he wouldn't pass on my information to the feds, or the local authorities, or anyone on his staff, for that matter.

"I won't hold you to the promise forever," I said. "Just until I figure out how to handle the information. A matter of days, I think."

I got his promise and asked him if he'd heard anything back from Interpol about the IDs of the two dead men from the warehouse fire.

"No, nothing," he said. "I got a preliminary report last night that their prints and DNA haven't matched anything yet. Interpol's still looking but not finding."

"I know who they were, where they lived, where they worked, and where they drank ginger ale," I said. "I also got confirmation from two people that they sometimes hung out with a man who fits the description of the guy Beth Daley met at Keene's."

"Jesus, you been busy," Tony said. "You're not as lazy as I thought.

But before you tell me any more, have you looked over your shoulder lately? Chicago's awash in Feds."

"Isn't it always?"

"The president ordered in fifty more FBI agents. He's pressuring the governor to mobilize the National Guard to protect Chicago from any more violence and find the Muslim extremists who've been putting the city to torch. I just heard it on the news."

"Good luck with that," I said. "They're going to be looking for one radical Muslim in a population of nearly three million, and that man is neither an Arab nor a Muslim. They'll wind up tripping all over each other."

"You know that for a fact?"

"The tripping part? That's a certainty."

"No, Deuce. That the guy's not an Arab or a Muslim?"

"About ninety-five percent certain. Got the information from two people who interacted with him."

"And there's only one arsonist?"

"That I know of."

"Wow. So what do you want from me?"

I said, "Some information from your autopsies. You already told me both men were dead before the fire started. No evidence of heat damage in the lungs or massive smoke inhalation. You found evidence consistent with cigarette smoking but no sign of incipient lung cancer. Do I have that right?"

"Yep."

Were the bodies burned too badly for you to get any kind of information from other organs, like the stomach or liver?"

"Actually, I got a decent read on both," Tony said. "It takes anywhere from one to five hours to incinerate a human body, depending on weight and other factors. The average is two hours. These men would have been close to average. The bodies were lying near an exterior wall of the building where the suppression efforts started. As badly as the exterior of their bodies were burned, the damage didn't go deep."

"Thanks for that mental image," I said.

"You asked. What are you looking for? Signs of alcohol abuse?"

"Or just regular drinking."

I heard computer keys tapping. Tony talked as he typed.

"That's harder," he said. "Social or occasional drinkers won't exhibit the signs you'd find in heavy drinkers. Alcohol abusers tend to be underweight. Extrapolating from what was left of their bodies I'd say both of these men were of normal or slightly higher than normal weight. They didn't miss any meals. I found no sores or inflammation in the stomach. And most telling, no cirrhosis or other damage to the liver."

One more piece that fit neatly into my puzzle.

"B EFORE WE GET out of the neighborhood," I said to Mark, "why don't we run by the places where the two guys worked."

Mark checked the clock on the dashboard.

"It's almost five o'clock on Saturday," he said. "If they were open today, they're probably closing or closed now."

"Worst case I'll know where to come back on Monday."

We found an auto supply store and an auto glass shop next door to one another eight blocks west of the insurance office. A reasonable walking commute for the two dead men. The glass store had closed. The supply store door sign said it would be open until six. We parked and went in.

After introducing ourselves, we asked to speak with the owner. As it turned out, we already were. His name was Eddie Gutierrez. He seemed wary of us, but turned angry when I mentioned Ali Muhammad Kaar and Ahmed al-Gharsi. He made face and a gesture as if to spit on the floor of his own store.

"*Estúpido ingrato bastardos*," he cursed. "My brother and me, we give 'em work, train 'em, pay 'em good, treat 'em good, and what do we get? They just up and walk away. Fuckin' Arabs. I guess we shouldn't expect better from 'em."

I put up a hand in a "stop" sign.

"Hold on a second," I said. "Before you condemn them as ethnic ingrates, you should know both of them were murdered, and their bodies tossed into a fire. They didn't walk out on you. Somebody pulled them away and made sure they'd never come back."

"*Oh, mi dios. Oh, mi dios*," he said and made the sign of the Roman Catholic cross. "I am sorry to hear that. But it explains things better for me. They were good men, hard workers. Got along well with the other employees. If they'da had better English, my brother an' me, we wouldda promoted them to sales. But it was hard for them to communicate. We all laughed about the gibberish they developed to talk to the other guys in the stores. I'm sorry I spoke badly of them." Guttierrez shrugged. "I din know."

"You and your brother own these two stores?" I asked.

He nodded. "We own both together. I manage this one. Jose, my brother, manages the glass place."

"How long had Ali and Ahmed worked for you?"

"Two, three years, maybe. I could check the records."

I shook my head. "That's not necessary now. Did you ever meet any of their friends, anybody who might have come in either place looking for them or meeting them?"

Guttierrez squinted in thought.

"I no remember no one," he said. "You want, I call Jose an' ask him."

"Please," I said.

Guttierrez turned slightly away from me and pressed a speed dial number on his smart phone. He chatted in Spanish with someone who answered, presumably Jose. His tone reflected shock at what he had learned. I got enough of what he said to know he was discussing the two murders. Then he started asking questions. He looked up at me and shook his head. I held up a finger to ask him to pause the conversation.

"Do you or Jose remember them being with a man, maybe about your height, dark hair, olive complexion, Irish accent, not very friendly?"

Guttierrez relayed the question. More chatting, and then the call ended.

"No," Guttierrez said. "We don't remember anything like that."

Another man walked over.

"Excuse me," he said. "My name is Luis Peña, and I'm the parts manager here. I heard what you asked. I think I know the man you're looking for."

"The Irish friend?" I asked.

"*Sí*. He come in here a couple of times at closing and walk with Ahmed and Ali somewhere. I don know where, though."

"Did you ever talk to the friend?" I asked.

"I tried. Just to be friendly. But he never wanted to talk to me. Not friendly. I asked Ali about him one day. Ali says he's a handyman from the neighborhood, somewhere up off 107th Street, but I don't know where exactly."

"Did Ali tell you his name?"

"Joe Smith. Yeah, I think it's phony, too."

"You ever hear who he worked for?"

"No. I got the feeling he went independent," Peña said. "Worked for himself."

"Cash only? No records? No licenses?"

"Probably."

Mark asked, "Did you see the car he drove?"

"He walked, just like Ahmed and Ali," Peña said. "Unless he took a bus."

"Did you ever see him take a bus?" Mark asked.

"No. Never."

"So he can't live too far," Mark said. "A hundred and seventh is four long blocks north. Odds are he lives within a few blocks east or west."

"Or north or south," Peña said.

"Lotta shoe leather," Mark said of the prospect of a door-to-door search.

"Better all of Mount Greenwood than all of Chicago," I said.

36

M ark dropped me off at my house and went home to get Murphy. He said he'd be back in an hour. We decided to give up on the pretext of living apart. Unless the city experienced another catastrophic firebombing, arson investigators wouldn't be breaking much news. I'd be getting tips from Colter, Cribben, and perhaps the mysterious caller who dropped Ali Muhammad Kaar's name on me.

I called Eric Ryland, my editor, at his home. He didn't seem concerned that I intruded on his Saturday evening. When I reported on my day, he seemed dumbstruck.

"How the hell do you manage to figure out these things, Deuce?" he asked. "I'd like to clone copies of your crystal ball for the whole staff."

"Sometimes things just fall into place," I said. "Or you get an anonymous, disguised voice on the telephone. Either way works."

"We should publish this tonight," he said. "But I'd like some time to run it by the lawyer first. Just so we don't overlook anything."

"I'd usually fight to publish right away, Eric, but I'd feel a lot better, too, with a thumbs up from Jonathan. He'll probably tell us to report all of it to the FBI, and that might be prudent. But I want to protect the story so it doesn't get away from us."

"You available tomorrow?" he asked.

"All day," I said.

"I'll call Jonathan and get back to you."

WE MET in Eric's conference room at nine on Sunday morning. I wore old, soft blue jeans, an Old Navy ringer t-shirt under a Northwestern hoodie, and a well-worn pair of K-Swiss athletic shoes. Eric wore khaki pants and a golf shirt, Jonathan a suit and tie.

"A suit on Sunday?" I asked him with a grin.

"Going to church when we're done here," he said.

I cocked my head. "I never took you for a religious man."

"I only get religion when I'm working on a story with you, Deuce," the lawyer said. "Prayer is what keeps me sane."

That took me aback for a moment, until I saw that his eyes were crinkling in mirth.

"Funny," I said.

"Actually," he said, "Annie and I are going to a wedding this afternoon."

Eric walked in with a coffee carafe filled with water. Without asking who wanted a cup, he began brewing a full pot then sat down at the head of the table.

"Deuce," he said, "start from the beginning."

I did, leading with the anonymous, disguised voice on the telephone just twenty-four hours earlier. I had made copious notes the night before. My journal included every detail I had jotted down as events and interviews unfolded, as well as a few tidbits I had stored in my short-term memory. I had the document in hand for reference in case I needed a prompt and to be certain I left out nothing. Both Eric and Jonathan took notes. Neither interrupted my narrative. And for a while, neither said anything when I finished.

Jonathan spoke first while Eric poured coffee.

"Let's assume you're on exactly the right track," the lawyer said. "Let's assume everything you've turned up is accurate. It's all based on an anonymous phone call identifying Ali. And it came to your cell phone, a number that isn't readily available. That's the slippery slope."

"Let's follow the evidence," I said. "We have two dead men in the warehouse. We have DNA from both and fingerprints from one. They match the evidence on the cigarette butts found at the fires. The name leaked to me matches the ID of one of the men who rented the apartment in Greenwood Heights, and the nationalities of that man and his roommate match the DNA from the butts. Fingerprints from the apartment match the butts. The evidence leads to the conclusion that the two dead men smoked the cigarettes later found at the scenes of nine arson fires. Witnesses say both men hung around with a swarthy, probably Irish man who closely resembles the FBI profile image of the man Beth Daley met in Keene's. And two witnesses say that man picked up the butts of cigarettes smoked by two dead men in the warehouse. He took them out of ashtrays in the bar and picked them up out of gutters. And later they turned up at the scenes of the fire bombings. That suggests the swarthy man is the arsonist. Jonathan, even if you believe in coincidence, this is too much."

"Playing devil's advocate," Jonathan said, "I think it's a leap too far to go from a swarthy man collecting cigarette butts to the conclusion that this makes the swarthy man the arsonist. It's a logical assumption, but not legally conclusive. Maybe it was somebody who likes to watch fires and thought he'd have some fun with investigators by dropping phony evidence. I'm also uneasy about this theory developing from a leak from a nameless, disguised voice on your cell phone. Who would have the number *and* the motivation to leak Ali's name to you? Who would even know Ali's name?"

"Good questions," I agreed. "But lets define terms. "A 'leak' deals with information that is classified or proprietary passed surreptitiously from a person who has it to a person with no right to it. Somebody called me anonymously on the phone and gave me the name of a murder victim. That information will be released to the public at some point. It's not classified. It's a 'tip.' You're the lawyer, but I think there's a major legal difference."

Bruckner nodded with some impatience. "I understand the difference," he said. "But it's possible Ali's identity has been classified by the feds. The second man, too."

Eric stirred some sugar into his coffee.

He asked, "Why would the feds do that, classify the names of two overdose victims they still consider vagrants? And if we printed the information, having no reason to believe the names are classified, would it create jeopardy for the paper?" Seems to me the two men were victims, not terrorists."

Jonathan said, "The fact that they were victims doesn't preclude that they were also terrorists. I'm trying to figure out what motivated Deuce's leaker—tipster—to pick up the phone and give her that information. Can we trust this person, or are we being diverted down a wrong path, or worse, into a setup, a trap?"

"The evidence is the evidence, Jonathan," I said. "The evidence doesn't lie."

"But we're human," he said. "And we can misinterpret it."

I sighed. "The feds are determined to blame Muslim extremists. From what we know, it would seem they're the ones heading down the wrong path."

"That still doesn't explain your tipster's motivation," Jonathan said.

"It could have been as simple as setting me on a path to the truth," I said. "If the information I got yesterday is accurate, which it seems to be, if there is only one man responsible for the fires in the city, which there seems to be, and if he's not a jihadist—or even an Arab—which also seems to be, Washington's theory is in the toilet. Which is exactly where the tipster seems to want it to be."

Jonathan just stared at me for a moment, then he said, "That reasoning is the dictionary definition of Machiavellian, Deuce."

Then he looked at Eric. "Machiavellian or not, she's likely right." He splayed his hands on the table and stared at a point between them. "And if Deuce is right, then she and the *Journal* have been put in a position to become the vehicles to undercut the will of the federal government."

"What will?" I asked. "We're undercutting a theory, not a policy."

Eric said, "It wouldn't be the first time a newspaper and a reporter have been put in that position, Jonathan. As long as we're on the right road, I have no problem playing defender of truth and justice. That's our mandate."

Jonathan nodded. "As long as you know you could be in for a world of hurt."

"We pay you the big bucks to heal the pain," Eric said.

"No," Jonathan replied, "You pay me the big bucks to keep you from getting beat up in the first place." He turned to me. "Deuce, do you know anything or suspect anything that might identify the anonymous caller?

"I thought I'd ruled out everyone," I replied. "But while we've been talking, I thought about one additional possibility. I'll call him as soon as we wrap up here."

Jonathan pushed back from the table and stood.

"It's not my job to tell you what to write and what not to write," he said. "I suggest you put together the hardest-hitting story you think you can sustain with the evidence you've got. Then call me back in, I'll take a look, and we'll go from there."

"We both appreciate you coming over on a Sunday," Eric said. "I hope the rest of your day is more fun. Where're you headed?"

Jonathan sighed and glanced at me. "To church," he said.

37

I had the personal cell phone number for Pete Rizzo, the spokesman for the Chicago Police Department, and called him from my desk. The newsroom had only a skeleton staff on Sunday, and everyone working was clustered near the city desk. No one sat close enough to me to overhear a phone conversation.

Pete answered on the third ring and groaned. "Caller ID says it's Deuce Mora calling me on a Sunday morning. Please tell me it ain't so."

"I can only offer an apology and promise not to take much time," I said.

"Okay. So what's up?"

"I got a phone call yesterday."

"So did I. I get phone calls every day."

I ignored his deflection. "The caller used an electronic device so I couldn't recognize his voice. And he dropped some key information about the warehouse fire. Was it you?"

"No."

"Cross you heart?"

"Yes. But not the 'hope to die' part."

"You have any clue who it might have been?"

I heard nothing but silence.

"Pete, talk to me."

"I can't."

"Can't, or won't?"

"Both."

"The credibility of the caller could sway the publish/not publish decision. It swings on the credibility of an anonymous source—someone who's anonymous to me. Can you give me any guidance?"

Pete paused for a moment, probably thinking it over. I could wait him out.

I heard him sigh. "Publish."

"You know who the caller is?"

"Yes."

"But you won't tell me?"

"I gave my word. Did he really use an electronic voice distortion device?"

"I think so. If that was his real voice he needs to see a throat surgeon."

"I told him he didn't have to do that. You wouldn't've recognized his normal voice."

"So I don't know him?"

"No."

"And I can trust his word?"

"I have a few dozen times. He's never misled me, and he's never been wrong."

"He gave me the name of one of the dead men from the warehouse fire. He turned out to be right. How did he know?"

"Can't tell you that, either," Pete said. "He told me how he knew, and it's credible."

I didn't want to press Pete. He didn't press me to disclose confidential sources, and I felt obligated to return the courtesy. I thanked him and ended the call.

Then I called Eric and told him what I'd learned.

"So bottom line is that somebody you know knows the caller and trusts him?"

"Right. Apparently he's acted as a source for Pete before and never let him down."

"Good enough for me," Eric said. "I'm going back to my golf game. You sit down and write the hell out of this."

~

EVEN WITH PETE'S ASSURANCES, it surprised me how little I could say with absolute confidence. I didn't want to overuse attribution to an anonymous caller with a disguised voice. Readers increasingly questioned attribution to anonymous sources, and to be honest, I didn't blame them. Most journalists are judicious about using anonymous sources, quoting them only when there is certainty that they know what they're talking about, that they are trustworthy, and all the alternatives have been exhausted. But it has happened that reporters trusted an anonymous source they shouldn't have, and when their stories fell apart it reflected badly on all of us. I didn't know this source. I didn't even know his name. The fact that I trusted Pete didn't mitigate my bent toward caution.

So I weighed everything with these factors in play. In the end, knowing the information meshed with what I knew to be fact gave me confidence enough to lay it all out, attributing the initial lead to someone I couldn't name.

So I wrote that the *Journal* "had learned" the name of the victims in the South Loop warehouse fire and launched an investigation of their backgrounds. Neither Brendan Boyle, the owner of the building where the two men rented an apartment, nor Dillon Byrne, the owner of Muldoon's Ale House, had asked not to be named in the paper. They probably would have if they'd thought about it. But they didn't. Bad on them.

On the other hand, they told me nothing except to describe the habits and living arrangements of two dead men. Nothing that could circle back to bite them.

So I simply laid out what I knew, pointing out that the developments appeared to undercut the prevailing government theory that

Chicago was dealing with extremist Muslim terrorists. I refrained from taking any shots at the Justice Department or the NSA for peddling the jihadist theory. The truth spoke for itself.

~

JONATHAN LOOKED at the story late Monday morning, suggested a few tweaks, and said he could defend what I'd written.

"I presume you're going to share this with Ron Colter before you publish," the lawyer said to Eric.

"I guess if we abide by the letter of our agreement we have to," Eric said.

Jonathan turned to me. "Deuce, you can tell him generally what you've come up with, but don't show him the finished story. You're not obligated to do that. He'll be able to read it for himself on Tuesday."

"I don't want to tell him about the anonymous phone call Saturday," I said. "I don't want the feds to start combing their ranks for my source."

"You don't know that your source works for the government," Jonathan said. "And you don't quote any unnamed source in your story. You're not obligated to tell anyone about the anonymous call. Stick to the way you wrote it, 'the *Journal* learned.' Nice and vague. Don't give Colter too much time to respond. If you don't reach him right away, leave plenty of messages. Let him know he's got to the end of the business day to get back to you. If he doesn't call, put the story on the internet tonight and in tomorrow's print editions."

I called Colter. The call went to voice mail. I left a message that there had been developments, and we were going with the story very soon. I said he had until the close of business that day.

He didn't call. I called three more times, getting more urgent about it each time. Still, he ignored me. I called local authorities, too. Their universal response was, "No comment."

The story hit the internet Monday evening and hit the streets Tuesday morning.

Then it hit the fan.

"Have you lost your mind?" Ron Colter said, very close to losing his FBI cool. It's hard to whisper and shout at the same time, but he did it well and undoubtedly strained his vocal cords.

"Why? Did you find a mind without an owner?" I asked him.

"This isn't funny, Deuce."

"I'm not laughing, Ron."

"We had an agreement. Before you went with any major developments, you would share the information with us."

"I called you four times yesterday and left messages. I told you there had been major developments. I told you if I didn't hear from you by the close of business, we were going ahead with the story. I called the police and fire officials and hit stone walls. I'd think all the involved agencies would respond fast to word of developments in the case, but nobody seemed to care. So we went with the story."

"I was in Washington in a meeting all day. I didn't get your messages until I was on my way to the airport last night. I checked the paper's web site and saw the story already up. I didn't trust myself to talk to you until today. Why couldn't you wait a day?"

"Maybe I could have," I said, not even trying to hide my irritation, "if you'd checked your voice mail and had the courtesy to call and tell me you were out of town."

"I could have saved you a lot of grief, Deuce," Colter said. "You jumped the shark this time. You reached a whole lot of conclusions that are unwarranted and careless and totally wrong. Your story today is nothing short of irresponsible. Your credibility is shot."

"You want to be any more specific?"

"I just told you . . . oh, never mind. What's done is done. Consider our agreement abrogated. It's finished. Don't bother calling me again. And don't expect to hear from me."

I waited to hear the phone slam then remembered you don't slam smart phones.

38

The arsonist read Deuce's story while sitting in a hole-in-the-wall coffee shop near his dingy apartment. He ate his usual breakfast of bacon and fried eggs with burned hash browns from frozen potatoes, white toast with butter and little cups of jelly, and barely acceptable coffee. The place was on South Central Park Avenue a few doors below West 107th Street.

He sat hunched on a stool with his forearms on the counter, oblivious to the fact that the bottom edges of the newsprint pages were dragging through the grease on his plate. Or perhaps he knew and didn't care.

Though he ate there every morning, nobody spoke to him because those who recognized him understood he wasn't a talker. The only person who broke the silence was the counterman who asked every time the customer walked in, "The usual?" The arsonist replied with a curt nod. Later, a woman approached him asking if he could do a handyman plumbing job at her house. He told her he wouldn't be available for at least a week. She said that was fine and wrote her name, number, and address on a paper napkin. The arsonist stuffed it in his pocket. He didn't have time to worry about it at the moment. He had too many alarming thoughts scurrying through his mind.

Deuce's story slapped him in the face.

How in hell had she identified the two Africans? While they didn't live off the grid as the arsonist did, they were nobodies, poor laborers recently relocated to Chicago from the slums of London. American authorities should've written them off as two junkie bums whose bodies burned up in a fire. Why would anyone go to the trouble of tracking down their identities? They had no identifying papers on them when he dragged their unconscious bodies into the warehouse. They should have been impossible to trace. They had no one to report them missing or fill in their backgrounds. They weren't worth the work. Their bodies should have gone to anonymous paupers' graves and been forgotten.

But that bitch had pieced it together somehow: their names, their crappy apartment, the Irish bar. The arsonist knew it had been risky to meet them at the bar, but he needed the supply of uncommon cigarette butts. He sometimes picked up clients at Muldoon's, but he never indulged in conversation with them. Despite being with Kaar and al-Gharsi frequently, language barriers truncated even his exchanges with them. Two or three people knew he went by the name Joe Smith. Anybody who'd believe that was too dumb to worry over.

He sipped his coffee, which was getting cold, and lifted the mug toward the counterman, who refilled it. The arsonist read the newspaper story and tried to gauge how much trouble he might be in. If it was too bad he could steal a set of license plates and hotwire a junker in a used-car lot. He could leave town, replacing the first stolen car with a second, and then another and another until he was far away. Then he'd ditch the last car, grab a cheap Greyhound bus ride or hitchhike to a remote somewhere, and disappear.

He planned on doing that eventually, but he wasn't ready yet.

He tossed money next to his cup and walked to a park where he could sit on a bench and think without curious eyes on him.

An hour later he made the inevitable choice.

He knew how he wanted to pull off his plan, and his first mental draft didn't seem to have any flaws. If he discovered a problem later he would have time to shift and adjust. He would have to scout for the right place. That would mean following the reporter in the evenings for maybe several weeks. No problem. He had all the time in the world.

He would have to change his appearance: let his hair grow long again, grow a beard, get some serious sun, and try to overcome what remained of his Irish brogue. The changes didn't have to be extreme. She wouldn't be looking over her shoulder for him, and if she did happen to glance back, she wouldn't recognize the man standing there waiting for the right moment to turn her into another crispy critter.

A memory returned of the movie Gran Torino. *He loved the line from Clint Eastwood's character, Walt Kowalski.* "Ever notice how you come across somebody once in a while you shouldn't have fucked with?" *He spits on the ground.* "That's me."

The arsonist spit on the ground.

39

I began to pick up the trail of the reclusive arsonist while actually still eight long blocks from his apartment, though I didn't know that at the time.

I had walked the streets of Mount Greenwood for two days, starting at West 107th Street where it T-boned South Sacramento Avenue on the edge of a golf course. This was the eastern boundary of the neighborhood. I canvassed the short blocks then went north and south on the cross streets, knocking on doors, handing out the updated likeness of the arson suspect redrawn by the FBI's sketch artist after a session with Dillon Byrne, the owner of Muldoon's Ale House. At every stop I got the same response. Either the residents and business people didn't recognize the man, or remembered only that they'd seen the sketch on TV. I thought some might know more but didn't want to get involved.

I found it strange that nobody mentioned the police or the FBI coming by with the same questions. I thought my *Journal* story identifying the two dead men and their mysterious friend, their address, and their favored bar would have brought out the feds in large numbers. In some ways, I thought, the absence of that corroboration made people suspicious of me: How come I knew things and asked questions the cops didn't know about or didn't care about? Several came right out and asked me.

I could think of three answers: The authorities were ahead of me. They already knew who and where the arsonist was. I didn't like that notion much because it didn't make sense. If they knew the who and the where, why hadn't they arrested him?

The second answer, one I didn't like at all, hung on the possibility that the feds were under so much pressure to prove the perps were extremist Muslims they wouldn't consider alternatives. The swarthy Irishman from Mount Greenwood wasn't on their radar, and they were unwilling or unable to put him there.

I had a third answer, too, and I hated that one most of all: I had it all wrong.

Eric had been reluctant to agree to my door-to-door expedition. The Mount Greenwood neighborhood was safe enough, he said, but the arsonist wasn't. He'd already killed the only two men who had any sort of knowledge of him. He wouldn't hesitate to kill me, too, to protect his identity and his plans.

"I don't suppose Mark could go with you?" he asked.

"Mark's still up to his badge in arson investigations," I said. "I'll be fine."

"I could hire some private protection."

"Look, Eric, I appreciate the concern, but I'll start my canvass about ten every morning and quit by six. This time of year it will be bright daylight the whole time."

The first day I did four blocks north and south from 107th on Sacramento, then Whipple, Albany and Troy. The homes and businesses were densely packed, and by the time I was through on Troy, I was through on my feet. I called it a day. Not even a nibble, except for those who recalled seeing the sketch in the paper or on TV. More than a dozen people promised to keep their eyes open and call me if they spotted the man. I gave out more than fifty business cards.

The next day I did the same on Kedzie, Sawyer, Spaulding, and Christiana.

Late in the afternoon I collapsed, exhausted, on a bench at the edge of a softball field at the foot of Spaulding. I tried to console myself over my failures by reminding myself how much exercise I was getting. Lots of walking. Lots of steps.

I had a disconcerting feeling that someone was watching me.

I glanced around and saw nothing out of the ordinary except one. A green Subaru Outback had parked on Spaulding about thirty yards from me. I couldn't escape the fact that I had seen the vehicle several times, both the day before and today. It would be out front when I walked away from a front porch, or passing me as I crossed a street, or parked on a street, like now, where the driver could watch me.

There were a lot of Subaru Outbacks in Chicago. But I didn't recall ever seeing a green one before.

I tried to stare through the windshield to glimpse the driver, but the glare prevented me from seeing anyone. There were a lot of people around, so I decided to approach the car and challenge the driver if he, or she, was actually following me. I transferred a small canister of mace from my backpack to my right hand, ready for use if necessary.

I was about twenty feet from the hood when the driver's door opened and a man got out, locking eyes with me. He definitely wasn't the arsonist. He was slim and muscular with an unruly shock of dirty blonde hair. He was wearing blue jeans, running shoes, and a golf shirt. He stood about six-foot-five. He smiled at me and raised both his hands, palms out. I saw a Glock pistol in a holster on his hip. I knew him.

"Hey, Deuce, remember me?" he asked.

"Yes," I said. "But I can't place you."

"Alan Wolfe. Mark's friend. We met . . ."

"Oh, my God, yes." I walked up to him and saw the burn scars on his neck and left arm. "You were one of the guys hurt in the flashover in K-town." He nodded. "How're you doing? Mark was so upset about what happened. I'm so sorry about the loss of your two comrades. What are you doing here?"

"That's a lotta questions," he said with a grin. "First, I'm doing fine. Thank you for asking. I'm still on departmental leave, but I've been ready for a while now to get back to work. I won't be allowed, though, until the doctors and the psychologists get done with me. So I've been sitting home getting stir crazy."

"And you're here because . . . ?"

He blew out a breath of resignation. "Because Mark asked me. He didn't like you being out here looking for the arsonists alone. I'm your backup if trouble happens."

"Mount Greenwood is a nice neighborhood. It's safe. And I'm only out here during daylight hours. I told Mark it was fine."

"He worries. You should be pleased."

I glanced down at his gun. "Who is that supposed to protect?"

"Anyone who needs protecting."

"You any good with it?"

"Let me put it this way. Mark and I were over in the sand box together. Iraq and Afghanistan. We did the same sort of work. I'm plenty good enough."

I hugged Adam and thanked him.

"I should be the one thanking you," he said. "You got me out of the house. Big tough guys like me can only watch soap operas so long, you know."

I WENT BACK to my bench near the softball field. A woman about my age with a boy in tow who might have been ten sat down beside me. It was a choice of convenience for her, a place where she could help her son put on his baseball gear. The kid was a catcher. Getting into the equipment was a big deal.

I smiled at him. "You know it'd be easier and quicker to get ready if you played right field," I said.

He shook his head.

His mother glanced at me and smiled.

"Easier on me, for sure," she said. "And cheaper. But his dad is a catcher, and Scotty wouldn't hear of trying out for any other position. Neither would Dad."

We chatted a little, and I introduced myself.

"I thought you looked familiar," she said. "I'm Sandra Healy. This is Scott."

As long as we weren't doing anything else, I asked some questions.

"Have you ever hired a handyman from around here to do any work on your house?"

She looked at me and frowned.

"You mean that guy in the paper? The one who might be setting the fires? No. My husband is Mr. Fix-It for us, and I wouldn't hire somebody off the street, anyway. One of our neighbors did. We warned them it wasn't a good idea. He never showed them any licenses or insurance before he did some work on their roof. He was cheap, and they said he did a good job. So no harm, no foul, I guess. But I wouldn't risk it."

"Was it the man in the artist's drawing?"

"I never saw the guy," Sandra said. "Jim, my husband, got a quick look at him once and says there's a resemblance. He keeps saying he's going to go ask the neighbor, but he keeps forgetting."

"Maybe he and I could do that this evening," I said.

"He should be here any time to watch the game," she said. "He won't want to leave until it's over. But he might take you by their house after, if you want to hang out and wait."

～

JIM HEALY AGREED to escort me to visit his neighbor after the game. I was glad to get up and move around. Spring in Chicago is never the equivalent of warm.

Young Scott's team had won, and the young catcher had cut down a boy from the other team trying to steal second. He also had two hits, a single and a triple.

"A couple of years he'll be supporting you," I suggested. We were walking to the neighbor's house, a dozen doors down from the Healy's home.

"Your mouth to God's ear," Healy replied. The man was in his late thirties, I guessed, a few inches shorter than me, light brown hair, blue eyes, clean shaven, well put together. He was a pharmacist, he said, a good job but not very exciting.

The neighbors were surprised to see us. Healy vouched for me, but if they recognized me they gave no indication. Their names were Stephen and Joyce Mueller, and they didn't want to talk to me about their roof or the man who had worked on it.

"Look," I said, "I'm not from the building inspector's office or your insurance company's office. I'm not here to hassle you about the roof or who fixed it. If you're happy, I'm happy. I'm looking for the guy who did the work for a whole different reason."

I explained the situation and showed them the sketch.

"Yeah, I seen that on the news," Mueller said. "It could be the same guy. I dunno fer shure. Whenever the cops are lookin' for somebody they put out a sketch like that. When they finally catch the guy, he never looks like the pitcha, at least not to me."

"I tole Stevie," Joyce Mueller said," he should call the cops and let them decide."

"Why didn't you?" I asked.

"I didn't see enough resemblance," he said. "I bet they're gettin' hun'erds of calls from people who think their neighbors are Arab terrorists. I didn't see no reason to stick my nose in. Still don't. Besides, I got no idea where he lives. I met him through a friend, and it was a cash deal."

"Could you tell me where I can find your friend?" I asked.

"St. Casimir Cemetery south of 111th," Mueller said. "He had a bad cancer and knew he was dying. Had the guy come in and repaint the house so his kids could sell it to pay off his medical bills. The kids live outside L.A., so they never met the guy."

As we walked back toward my car, I asked Jim Healy if he had any other neighbors who'd used the same handyman.

He thought a moment then shook his head.

"I can ask around, though," he said. "I'll let you know if I find anybody else."

He took one of my cards and I went home to take a shower.

As Deuce walked *west on 107ᵗʰ, her eyes were cast down at the sidewalk. She didn't notice the swarthy man passing her walking east. But he saw her.*

He recognized her immediately and fought down an urge to turn and run the other way or jaywalk across the street. But she had her eyes down, staring at nothing, deep in thought, her hands shoved into the pockets of her blue jeans. She might not notice him walking past, but if he suddenly bolted the movement might catch her eye.

He thought for a moment about dragging her into the nearby alley and killing her. She had several inches on him, but he had the advantage of greater strength. If he hit her hard in the head first, it should disable her. He had never murdered anyone with his bare hands. Kaar and al-Gharsi didn't count. He had drugged them unconscious, dragged them into the warehouse, and injected them. He didn't stay to watch them die. Still, he remembered that even looking at their bodies later made him squeamish. He had no doubt that his hands around the reporter's neck, squeezing the life out of her, feeling her larynx crush under his thumbs, would be far more unpleasant.

Besides, a quick scan of the street confirmed it carried too much foot and car traffic to allow him to manhandle the woman without being seen.

So, instead, he stepped off the curb and went around to the side of a parked car as if it was his, and he was preparing to drive off. He stood by the driver's door until Deuce walked past him, then returned to the sidewalk and resumed his walk toward his apartment, putting distance between him and the bitch. For the time being.

She was exploring his neighborhood, and eventually she would find him.

He needed to speed up his plan.

40

M ark and I had a discussion that evening about him siccing Alan Wolfe on my tail around Mount Greenwood. Alan had already reported to Mark that the cat was out of the bag, so Mark was expecting me to blow up. I wanted to be angry, but Alan Wolfe was a nice guy going through a difficult and boring recovery from his burns, and if it helped him to feel he was doing something useful, I couldn't argue. So I didn't. It also surprised me how much comfort his presence gave me.

"The least you could do," I said, "is let me reimburse you whatever you pay him."

"He wouldn't take money," Mark said. "I tried."

"Did he owe you a favor?" I asked.

Mark took a deep breath and shook his head. "Let's leave it at that," he said. "It's not something I want to talk about."

I suspected it had something to do with their time together in the Middle East, but I dropped it and suggested we go to dinner.

We had discovered a new favorite restaurant called Second City Diner. It wasn't related to the famous comedy club, The Second City. It was several miles south, in the Restaurant Row enclave of extraordinary eateries on the Near West Side, bounded by West

Fulton Street on the north and West Randolph Street on the south. The SCD, as locals had come to call it, sounded like a joint but looked like a million bucks with prices to match. It served the finest authentic Basque cuisine I'd ever encountered—heavy on seafood and meat cooked over hot coals and exquisite sheep's milk cheeses. It was worth every penny.

The owners had acquired a gem of an old four-story warehouse and office complex, gutted and renovated it, and opened for business. After our first experience there, we went back once a week. We couldn't get enough of it.

The epidemic of fires in the city had once again subsided. I returned to writing my columns regularly but continued to canvass Mount Greenwood for an unlicensed, unbonded handyman who might or might not be an arsonist. I spent as many daylight hours as possible walking those Irish streets, but I only talked to Mark about the effort. The less Eric knew the better. He wanted me back full time at my regular job, and he didn't give me any choice.

The respite from fires also allowed Mark and me to resume our more normal relationship, and we reveled in it. He still worked long hours because of the extent of the fires and the sheer magnitude of evidence assembled. But we had most weekends.

We became known at the SCD. Not a meal passed that chef Jacques Bacque didn't send something complimentary from the kitchen. The wait staff, all well schooled in the menu and the wine list, explained in detail what we were eating. And regardless of how adventurous it sounded, it never failed to be a great combination of taste, aroma, texture, and color, not to mention that the presentations were picture-book gorgeous.

Neither of us noticed the appearance of a new busboy working to clear and clean tables of patrons who finished eating and departed.

We had no reason to notice him except for the oddity of his station near our table every time we were there. He pressed into the wall, kept his head down, and disappeared into the bustle of the room. But unless called away to attend to something elsewhere in the dining room, he stood close enough to hear all but our quietest conversations.

Our meals at SCD always ended with a visit to our table by the chef and the *maître d'* to inquire about our experience. We were always effusive and grateful for the attentiveness of the staff. And we always asked *maître d'* Daniel Weldon to make a reservation for us at the usual time the following week.

That could have become one of the greatest mistakes of our lives.

THE ARSONIST HAD GOTTEN *to know the warehouse property that housed the Second City Diner soon after he began following the reporter when she went out at night. When he determined that she and her boyfriend were at the eatery every Thursday evening, he decided he needed to be there with them. So he took the risk of applying for a busboy job and made it a point to explore as much of the building as possible every night he worked.*

The arsonist used one of several false IDs made for him by a Milwaukee forger who charged a fortune. He had the work done before he started on his arson spree so he would have the documents in hand in the event something went wrong and he had to get away from Chicago. The documents, including drivers' licenses and passports, wouldn't stand up to scrutiny if somebody drilled deep into the lives of the persons he pretended to be. But for a couple of months they would hold up. They gave him the fake address and the fake Social Security number he needed to get a real job.

He had two reasons for taking the risk of a job at the diner.

First, with the bitch walking up and down the streets of his neighborhood alerting people to watch for him, locals who had hired him in the past and people who had never encountered him before were now going to be on the alert for him. Second, he needed the job. He had to hole up and lay off the handyman work for a while, and he needed another source of income to live on.

And he needed the job to be inside the diner to be certain that when he blew the place into burning smithereens, the reporter and her boyfriend would be inside. Busboys and dishwashers were always in short supply, so that's what he went for.

The restaurant was glad to have him. Because he was young and strong and willing, he was the one the bartenders always sent to the basement to replenish dwindling supplies of wine, beer, and spirits from the massive cellar. None of the other busboys wanted to carry anything heavier than a tray full of dirty dishes.

The trips to the cellar, sometimes several a night, gave the arsonist time to find the shutoff for the sprinkler system and to chart the ample number of places to hide small but deadly firebombs. Once detonated, the fires would explode hundreds of bottles filled with alcohol, which would feed the flames. A few well-placed Molotov cocktails hurled into the bar and restaurant would combine to consume the eatery in short order. The doors to the stairwells were supposed to be kept closed and locked, but he could pick the locks and prop the doors open at the last minute. The stairways would create updrafts that would spread the flames to the upper floors quickly.

The bitch and her boyfriend were playing right into his hands. They always came in at the same time on Thursday evenings and sat at the same table. They were obviously very much in love, and they always seemed to have a great deal of fun together.

Well, have your fun while you can, he thought as he watched them pay their check.

He had several projects he wanted to complete before he turned his full attention to the eatery, so he wasn't certain of the timing of this attack. But on one summer evening very soon, the two lovers would die together.

41

Seven weeks had passed without any new fires that could be attributed to terrorism. Maybe something big loomed in the offing, or maybe the terrorist figured he'd done all the damage necessary and had crawled back into whatever hole spawned him—or them. While I remained convinced that one man had brought the destruction and death to Chicago, the authorities remained publicly insistent that the culprits were multiple ISIS sympathizers—although ISIS never claimed credit for any of the acts of violence. That alone convinced me that I had the better theory. When ISIS motivated an assault, whether by direct order or the inspiration of self-radicalized acolytes, the group always claimed credit. None of the ISIS-associated terrorist organizations had stepped up. That told me the Chicago terrorist probably had some motivation other than jihad.

I still canvassed Mount Greenwood as I had time, and Mark's investigative team still sifted mountains of evidence from the arson cases. Even though the city remained quiet, our work continued to cut deeply into our lives.

Under close supervision bulldozers had almost finished removing the debris in the Loop. Arson experts and cadaver dogs searched every bit of it a final time before sending the debris off to a landfill a few miles west of O'Hare International Airport.

Occasionally, the dogs found small pieces of human remains, a finger, a skull fragment, all sent to Tony Donato's lab for identification. There were no intact bodies left to recover. The local streets remained closed but would reopen as soon as the cleanup ended. The city had started erecting walls around the blocks that had been devastated, as if closing off the sight of the rubble would put the tragedies out of people's minds.

Already the City Council had appointed a redevelopment commission to evaluate ideas on what to do with the property occupied by the ruined buildings, much as the matter was addressed in New York City after 9/11. It would be years before that area of downtown resumed a normal, bustling existence.

Mark and I had just left the Second City Diner and given our validated parking ticket to the valet when my phone rang. It was a little after 9 p.m. Calls at that hour never brought good news. But since Mark's phone remained silent, I assumed it wasn't notification of another arson fire.

It turned out to be Scott Healy, the Mount Greenwood pharmacist I'd met at his son's baseball game. Healy said he'd gotten a call from his neighbor, Stephen Mueller, the man who had hired the Joe Smith to fix his roof. Mueller had spotted the handyman on 107th. He didn't try to stop the guy, which could have been a fatal mistake. Instead he called Healy, and they joined forces to follow the man.

The handyman must have spotted the tail as they all walked past Drake Avenue. He ducked into Drake and lost his followers by cutting through dark back yards. Neither man had any idea what his destination might have been. But the fact that he'd been spotted on Drake gave me a new place to center my canvass the next time I could get back to it. I would have to talk to Eric about it in the morning.

I thanked Healy effusively.

"I'm sorry we couldn't follow him all the way home," Healy said.

"You did fine," I told him. "It would have been foolish to try to corner him. Somebody could have gotten hurt."

I filled Mark in.

"I don't like you closing in on this guy by yourself," he said. Alan Wolfe had been cleared to go back to work two weeks earlier, so when I got to Mount Greenwood now, I was on my own again. "If you can hold off a day," Mark continued, "just until Saturday, I'll go down there with you, and I'll come armed."

I shook my head. "You need your time off," I said.

"I need you safe is what I need."

"The white knight riding in to save the damsel?"

"I'm no knight, and you're no damsel in distress," he said. "Lest you forget, and I know you haven't, you killed a man with one blow of your right hand."

"Thanks for reminding me," I said.

"I didn't mean it as criticism, and you know it," he said. "It was clearly self-defense. You know how to take care of yourself. I readily admit it. Think of my presence at your side as protection for the suspect."

I shot an angry look at him, but he was grinning. Joking. I took the liberty of punching him in the arm, none too gently.

"Ouch," he said, sounding as if he meant it. "Okay, I'll protect the bad guy. Who's gonna protect me?"

42

S aturday found us back in Mount Greenwood. We stopped first at Brendan Boyle's insurance office to check on whether he had seen the man who befriended his two dead tenants. He had not, but he said locals drawn to his office by his name in the paper had inundated him. They wanted a look at the place linked to the city's terrorist activities. He seemed happy about it.

"Business really picked up," he said. "People wanna talk about the dead guys and the arson suspect, and some of 'em wind up buying policies from me."

I told him I was happy for him. In fact, I thought it bizarre beyond belief.

We heard a similar story at Muldoon's Ale House, where owner Dillon Byrne said he had several dozen new customers who came in asking about the arson suspect and the two dead men. His place had become a Mount Greenwood institution.

"It's macabre," he said. "Some of 'em wanna take pictures of the stools where the guys sat, over in that dark corner. A few of 'em sit on the same stools and ask me to take their pictures. I don't discourage it, but it makes me uncomfortable, like I'm suddenly the middle ring in a circus freak show."

"But it's good for business," Mark said.

"Can't deny that, but it won't last. People got short memories."

MARK and I started knocking on doors along Drake Avenue, where the handyman was last seen. We hit paydirt at the sixth house.

An elderly woman answered the door but opened it only as far as the safety chain would permit. There was also a screen door between us. It remained closed. She appraised us with rheumy, faded blue eyes, and by the scowl on her face I guessed we didn't fare very well. I made the introductions, which seemed to have no impact.

"Whatcha want?" she asked. "If you're sellin' somethin' I ain't buyin'."

Her teeth were bad, and they were at least her second set. The dentures were stained and chipped, either poorly made or badly cared for or both. She had to be in her eighties. Her skin hung on her face, neck, and arms as if she were melting from the inside. Her faded housedress looked like something out of the fifties, and she wore old-fashioned black leather orthopedic shoes with one broad Velcro closure instead of laces.

"We're not selling anything, Ma'am," I said. "We're looking for somebody. He does handyman work around the neighborhood. We're looking for people who might have hired him or know of neighbors who did."

"Joe? Why're you lookin' for Joe?"

I tried to keep a calm demeanor.

"To talk to him about a job," Mark said. "But we don't know where he lives or how to get in touch with him. We thought maybe you could help. Do you know his last name?"

"Smith."

Okay, we had our guy. He used the same dubious name everywhere.

Something moved at the bottom of the door. A large orange tabby cat had come to investigate the visitors. It wound around the old woman's swollen ankles then raised itself onto its back legs, stretched its front paws high on the screen door, and began kneading, plucking the wires like a musician picks a harp. I could see where the cat had previously torn holes in the screening large enough for insects to get through. The woman nudged the animal down with her knee, and it wandered off.

"How could we get in touch with Joe?" I asked.

"You can't. You just gotta wait 'til you see him on the street. He put in some tomato and pepper plants for me a couple of weeks ago. I hope it wasn't too early. We get a late frost this year they'll all be wiped out. But I had to grab him when I saw him cause I didn't know when I'd see him again."

"Do you know where he lives?" I asked.

"I just tole you the only way to find him is to see him on the street. I see him sometimes walkin' that way." She waved her hand toward the northwest. "He does good work and don't charge much. So people round here keep him pretty busy. An' he don't waste time talkin' when he should be workin'. Only thing he ever said to me was, 'Thank you, Miss Mildred' when I paid him."

By mid-afternoon we had found two other people who had hired Joe Smith and three who knew of him. Then we found Declan Cassidy.

He was drunk. Not the kind of drunk that has him falling down or slurring his words or unable to follow a conversation. More the sort of drunk who sips his booze slowly all day, thus keeping a steady level of buzz as his triglycerides soar and thin spider veins bloom on his cheeks and in the V of his neck. Cassidy knew immediately who we were looking for when I told him the man used the name Joe Smith.

"I seen him around a few times," he said. "Last time I ran into him was at the liquor store at 107th and Pulaski. I said hello, just bein' friendly. He turns his back on me like I was some cur beggin' for food. Then he pushes past me an' gives me an elbow in the ribs just so he could beat me to the register. Pissed me off, I'm tellin ya'. Pardon my language there, but that's just wrong. It bothered me. I was debatin' with myself whether to call 'im on it when he left. Paid for his booze and walked out the door without a word to me or anyone."

"Which way did he go?"

"You tryin' to find 'im?" Cassidy asked. "I can tell you more than which way he went. I can tell you where he wound up. He was on foot, so even though I stayed inna store long enough to pay for my purchase it was easy for me to spot him walkin' away. He was only a block or so up the sidewalk headin' east. I followed him in my car. He went into a rundown fourplex on Avers Avenue, nort' of 107th. Not a place you'd look at twice 'cept to scoff. Grass already gone to weeds, junk in the yard, building grubby. Most people in Mount Greenwood take care of their places. Whoever owns this one couldn't care less. I called the city on 'em. Ain't no excuse to let a place run down like that."

"Did you get an address?" Mark asked.

"You bet I did, to give to the city," Cassidy said. "Don't recall it now, but you can't hardly miss it. Like I told the city, four units. Two up, two down. Whole place painted dark yellow, like baby shit."

We thanked Cassidy, grabbed Mark's truck, and headed to Avers Avenue. My sense of anticipation ran high, and I saw that Mark had such a firm grip on the steering wheel he had squeezed the blood from his knuckles. North from 107th Avers was a dead-end street with few homes on it. If we'd been looking for the house on a five-mile thoroughfare we couldn't have missed it. Grubby didn't half describe it.

A middle-aged man guided a smoking gasoline lawnmower through the badly overgrown yard. We parked and walked across the lawn to him.

The man glared at us. He glanced at Mark's official truck and back. He had a hawk face and thinning gray hair that looked as though he usually combed it straight back. But with the breeze and the sweat he'd worked up, it had become a wet tangle.

He hunched up his thin shoulders in a protective attitude like a boxer afraid of getting caught by a right cross. His chest was hollow, made more pronounced by the belly that protruded over his belt. His t-shirt might have been white at one time, but no amount of cleaning would get it back there. The armpit stains from sweat added an element of yellow to its basic dirty gray. His body tapered to thin legs extending from plaid Bermuda shorts. He wore flip-flops on his feet.

He pinched his mouth as if daring us to speak. Mark took the dare.

"Afternoon. You the owner?"

"What's it to you?" the man said. "You from the city?"

We introduced ourselves.

"Somebody called the city on me. They told me I'd be fined if I didn't clean up this place. Like I got piles of money lyin' around for renovations. It's bullshit. It's my place, my bidness how it looks."

"We're not interested in how your place looks," I said. "We're trying to find a man who might live here. Goes by the name Joe Smith."

"Lived," the man said.

I frowned in question.

"He lived here a coupla years. Split two, three days ago owin' me a month's rent. He won't be gettin' his deposit back, that's fer sure."

"How did you find out he'd left?"

"Went up to collect the rent. He didn't answer the door, so I let myself in. I can do that legally, you know. He didn't have much stuff, just some clothes and personal effects. And a toolbox. They're all gone, and so is he. Didn't even give me notice."

"So you don't know where he might have gone?" I asked.

The owner shook his head. "Not where he's gone to or where he came from."

Mark asked, "Have you showed the unit to any prospective renters yet?"

"No, that's why I'm here cleanin' up some."

"Well, don't go back into the apartment, and don't let anyone else in."

The man leaned down and turned off the clattering mower.

"Who the hell you think you are?" he growled at Mark. "You got no right . . ."

"I've got every right," Mark snapped. "I'm a state fire marshal, and that unit is a possible crime scene. If you don't do what I tell you, I'll see to it you have the cops and the FBI on your case quicker than you can finish mowing. Is that clear?"

Mark was pretty good at this intimidation stuff. First the insurance agent, now this.

The owner asked, "You got any paper to back you up?"

"No, but if you give me grief, I'll post the building as uninhabitable due to fire violations. You'll lose your other tenants, too. I'll get you official paper first thing Monday."

The owner regarded Mark with anger. Then he turned to me.

"Can he really do that?"

"Believe it," I said. "What's your name?"

"Harold Witkowski."

"Well, Mr. Witkowski, Mark can make your life a misery if you don't do as he says."

"I didn't think it could get any more miserable," he said.

"Sir, how did Joe Smith pay his rent? By check?"

"Cash. Always cash."

"How about his utility bills?"

"Didn't have none. They're part of the rent."

Mark said to me, "Perfect setup if you want to remain anonymous." Then he spoke to Witkowski. "I'll bring the paper Monday. Here's my card. Call me if you need to. Now, we need to look at the unit. Either give me the key, or take us inside."

"I'm goin' inside the unit with you."

"No you're not," Mark said. "You're only letting us into the building and unlocking the apartment."

"Why can you go in if I can't?" Witkowski demanded. "It's my damned property."

"Because I said so," Mark replied. I didn't think I'd ever heard him quite so brusque. That happens when you're the head of the team trying to catch a stone killer.

We took latex gloves and booties with us. Witkowski let us in. Mark ordered him to wait in the hall. I wanted to wait in the hall. The unit smelled as if it hadn't been touched by fresh air in years. The walls were grimy, the furniture threadbare. I entered reluctantly.

We put on the gloves and searched the place. We found nothing.

Mark called his office and requested a forensics team. We went back to his truck to wait. Witkowski resumed his mowing.

A perfect way to spend a sunny Saturday afternoon.

I made a decision on a whim.

I called Ron Colter. I didn't expect the FBI agent to answer, and he didn't. But I felt certain the message I left would get his attention.

43

Colter returned my call twenty minutes later from his car. He said he was heading for our location in Mount Pleasant.

"I don't want any forensics team but mine in the apartment," he ordered. "Do you understand that? Make sure your boyfriend understands that."

"I can't reach him right now," I said. "He's inside with his team."

Actually Mark was sitting in his truck right beside me watching his team take their equipment out of the back of an official vehicle. In order to keep from laughing out loud, he got out of the truck and joined them. They all disappeared inside.

"Call him and tell him I want everyone out," Colter said.

"You can tell him yourself when you get here. As head of the arson investigation team, I'm pretty sure he has the authority to direct an examination of the apartment. And I don't have any authority to tell him to stop."

"He's head of the arson investigation, not the hunt for the terrorists," Colter said.

"All part of the same thing," I replied. "See you soon. Drive carefully."

I hung up. I don't know why I liked to torment Colter. Probably because I found him terminally aggravating.

When he showed up he stormed into the building without even looking my way. I followed him in, not to watch the processing of Joe Smith's apartment but to listen to Colter's interview of the neighbors.

"Go back outside," Colter told me.

"I don't think so," I said. "I won't get in the way. But I found this guy, and that gives me a moral right to hear what the neighbors have to say."

Colter stared at me for a moment, maybe trying to think of a snappy retort. Then he turned his back and mounted the steps to the second floor. He entered Smith's apartment. I followed him up the stairs but didn't go into the vacated unit. I toyed with the notion of knocking on the apartment door across the hall. An occupant made the decision for me. A man, the tenant I presumed, opened the door.

"What's goin' on?" he asked. He had bed head and creases in his face that looked as if they'd been made by wrinkles in a pillow.

I started to introduce myself and ask him some questions when Colter put his hands on my shoulders from behind and moved me away from the door. Then he asked the questions I'd been about to.

The man, whose name was Larkin, was a city employee who worked nights and slept days. So his path and his neighbor's rarely crossed. He knew nothing about him beyond his tendency to be sour and silent. Larkin didn't even know the guy had left.

The two downstairs tenants couldn't add much more except for that one woman who said Joe Smith had fixed a leaky toilet for her and only charged her twenty bucks.

"You can't get no plumber ta come out for twenty bucks," the woman said. "An' I dint even hafta look at the guy's butt crack."

THE FORENSICS TEAM finished and packed up. A remote electronic comparison confirmed all the fingerprints they lifted belonged to the same person. That didn't come as a surprise given that Joe Smith had likely killed the only two friends he ever had. And we already had

Smith's fingerprints. What we didn't have were matches to a real identity.

Colter had a police unit come by and put crime scene tape across the apartment door. He warned Witkowski if anyone disturbed the tape they would be subject to arrest. Now totally intimidated, Witkowski locked the unit. Colter took the key. Witkowski looked startled, but he didn't object. We all went back downstairs.

Mark, Colter, and I stood in the shade by Mark's truck.

"You still think you're dealing with multiple Islamic jihadists?" I asked Colter.

"I've seen nothing to change my mind," the FBI AD said. "You've never disclosed the source of the tip that sent you lookin' for this guy, Joe Smith. Unless I know who contacted you, I got no way to judge the credibility of the information."

"I assumed you were the source," I said.

Colter looked genuinely surprised. "Me? Why the hell would you think that?"

"At the core I think you're a competent, honest, scrupulous public servant," I said. "I think it would grate on you pretty hard if you were being pressured to come up with some bad guys who don't exist instead of following every plausible lead to its logical conclusion. I think pent-up frustration might cause you to pick up the phone and enlist some help."

"You think wrong," Colter said emphatically. "I have told you before and repeat now, I think you're very good at your job, but this is an official government investigation. You're neither official nor government. Leaking to you, assuming I had anything to leak, would cost me my job. You're looking at the wrong guy."

The way Colter made the statement made me believe it was the truth.

We parted company a few minutes later.

None of us noticed the man watching us from behind a curtain of wild bushes in a vacant lot across the street. Nor did we know that he was thinking how wise it had been for him to vacate his apartment the previous Thursday in the middle of the night.

44

I felt a little better about Colter after he called me the next morning. The number came up as "Unknown" on my cell phone. I usually sent those right to voice mail, but I answered this one. My luck with "unknown callers" had been good lately.

"I'm calling you from a phone in a café," he said without introducing himself. "I'm drinking a lot of coffee."

"Should I call you Deep Cup?" I asked.

"Please don't. But that's funny. I'm only a block from your office and well away from mine." He gave me the name of the place and the address. "Can you come over?"

I could and did.

We sat outside on the sidewalk where the noise of the traffic would keep anyone from overhearing our conversation. Colter had left his suit coat and tie somewhere else and wore a Cubs baseball cap pulled low. Not an elaborate disguise, but enough.

"We're getting no hits at all on the prints lifted from Joe Smith's apartment," he said, "except for the fact that they match the prints we got at the construction site where the Semtex was stolen. But nothing to match an ID. Not civilian databases, not military databases, not even Interpol, which ran an emergency search for us overnight."

"So the guy, whatever his real name, lives off the grid?"

"It's not easy to do, but he's managed so far. We're using face-recognition software, looking at passport photos and drivers licenses for guys named Joe Smith anywhere in the United States. Believe it or not, there are more than 4,600 guys in this country named Joe or Joseph Smith. We started with Chicago, spun out to all of Illinois, Indiana, and Wisconsin, and now we're tracking all fifty states and U.S. territories. We've got a few hits that resemble our composite, but nothing solid, and none anywhere near Chicago."

"You never thought that was his name, did you?" I asked.

"No, but it's the only name we have. He picked his apartment carefully. Everything that might have generated a record on him was included in the rent, like electric, gas, water. Looks like he was stealing a cable signal from his downstairs neighbor. She said he fixed a toilet for her. He might've rigged it then."

"You don't consider all that suspicious?"

"Yeah, of course I do. But . . ." His voice trailed off.

"But what?"

Colter sipped coffee and held it in his mouth for a moment. I guessed he was considering what he wanted to say and how he wanted to say it.

He looked me straight in the eye and swallowed.

"Deuce, we're having this conversation so far off the record it's happening on another planet. Okay?"

I nodded.

"I'm coming around to thinking we shouldn't be chasing jihadists. I've pitched that possibility to Washington. For one thing, nobody's taken credit for the attacks. Even when a lone wolf strikes some terrorist group steps up eventually to say the perp belonged to or was inspired by their organization." I didn't remind Colter I'd thought of that before he did. He continued. "Here, nobody's made any claims, including the arsonist. Second, we haven't found any chatter before or during the attacks. There's occasionally some intelligence blip we miss when it originates, but we find it later. The absence of anything this time is driving Mason Cross crazy."

The NSA, Cross's agency, is responsible for intercepting the warning signs that terrorist attacks are imminent. Cross's frustration didn't surprise me.

"And third," Colter said, "the way this has played out is all wrong. You made the argument once that most terrorist attacks come in tight clusters or as a single horrific act. Not as a series of attacks playing out over months."

"Well, until now that's been true."

"But I can't sell that to Washington. They reject it out of hand."

"Who, specifically?"

"In my chain of command, the new FBI director sees the validity of the argument but can't or won't change the direction of the investigation. He keeps bumping up against the Attorney General, who is on the White House speed dial."

"The Justice Department is like any other investigative agency. You're supposed to go where the evidence leads."

Colter shook his head, a little sadly I thought.

"Not always when there's high-stakes politics involved. That's not how the book says it's supposed to be, but shit happens. In my eighteen years with the bureau, I've seen lots of stuff that I wouldn't want to become public, including the last experience you and I shared. But I haven't seen anything that compares with the malfeasance of this situation."

"So what are you going to do?" I asked.

"Unlike a leopard, I can change my spots. You and Mark have been as good as your promises in terms of keeping silent about our last project. You didn't even break the agreement once you heard the full story. So I'm going to trust you, and I'm going to ask that you trust me. At this point, I don't care if the arsonist story breaks in the newspapers before it breaks in the courts. I just want to put an end to the killing."

"You don't think it's over? It's been quiet a long time."

"Trust me. It's not over. He's still got a lot of Semtex left, remember?"

I nodded. "Are you sure you didn't make that anonymous phone call to me?"

He put money to cover his bill on the table and plunked a salt shaker on top to prevent the breeze from carrying it away. Then he stood.

"I'm positive it wasn't me," he said. "I have no idea who it might have been."

45

Two nights later, as the city slept, Colter proved prescient. A twelve-story senior-living apartment building at the east end of Pilsen—my neighborhood—went up in flames. It wasn't a ritzy place. Not fancy and not expensive. As an old structure, it lacked the construction quality and fire protection of newer, higher-end projects.

It gave building inspectors nightmares. Investigators would later say the building owners were in gross violation of more than a dozen safety regulations and repeated notices of fire code regulations.

The building had two stairwells and one elevator car connecting the residential floors to a lobby, which was clean but growing shabby with age, just like the residents. Somewhere between midnight and 3 a.m., the arsonist stole a car, filled two dozen five-gallon gasoline cans, drove them to the target, and carried them into the building through a delivery door he jimmied open at the back of the building. An earlier scouting trip to the facility revealed there was no alarm on the door or it wasn't working.

He used the elevator to carry the twenty-four gas cans to the roof garden and propped open the individual access doors to the stairways. He lugged twelve cans to the top of each stairwell. He used latex gloves, though it seemed an unnecessary caution since he knew his prints weren't on file anywhere. When all the cans were in place, he poured the contents down each set of steps—sixty gallons of gasoline per stairwell—and ignited the infernos in both locations. He took the elevator to the ground immediately, before fire sensors shut it down, and went out the back door to his stolen car.

He drove several blocks, to a point where he would be away from the action but able to witness his work pay off. He figured by the time the first residents awakened to the first wisps of smoke and the first acrid smell of burning gasoline, it would be too late for firefighters to save many of them.

Within minutes, he heard fire and smoke alarms come to life. The elevator shutdown would have activated automatically. All escape routes were blocked.

There were no sprinklers in the stairwells or the elevator lobbies, so the stairwell fires licked under exit doors and ignited the old lobby carpeting, which smoldered and smoked rather than burning, spewing toxic fumes throughout the building.

The first responders who reached the scene began screaming at residents through bullhorns in English and Spanish to stuff wet towels under their apartment doors, leave all windows closed, and stay where they were. Some heeded the instructions. Many did not. Instead they tried to get to the fire escapes. But the iron stairs had never been used and had rusted into immobility. Most residents couldn't get to the fire escape, anyway because their windows had been painted shut, and they weren't strong enough to break the seals.

As the flames spread across the elevator lobbies of each floor, they tried to squeeze under individual apartment doors to find more fuel. Where occupants had heeded instructions to seal their doors with wet towels, the advance of the fire was thwarted, or at least delayed. Those residents who didn't hear, or didn't understand, or ignored the orders, soon found fire eating the shabby carpets of their homes and advancing on the furniture.

In panic they broke their windows and screamed for help. The flames sucked in the oxygen-rich fresh air, gaining new energy. Fire engulfed those units, either suffocating residents with thick, black, acrid smoke or burning them alive. Seven people jumped through broken windows to escape and were killed when they hit the concrete below.

Sixteen people died in their units, bringing the immediate death toll to twenty-three. Twenty-one others were injured. Eleven of them would die in hospitals.

Two cigarette butts were found inside the delivery door of the building, a Benson & Hedges and a Dunhill. The Chicago arsonist's toll stood at 133 dead, 247 injured.

I ran into Ron Colter on the street as first responders brought the flames under control and tended to survivors.

"You were sure right about more arsons coming," I said.

"I wish I'd been wrong," he said.

"You know, the perp uses a lot of gasoline. Do you have anybody checking stations for bulk sales recently?"

"One of the first things we checked," he said. "And every time there's a new gasoline-fueled arson, we run the checks again."

I scuffed at the sidewalk with the toe of my shoe.

"How long do you expect this to go on?"

"Until," Colter said, "we kill the sonofabitch."

TWO NIGHTS later the city experienced another series of fires.

Two old and beautifully maintained homes on North Cleveland Street and one not far away on North Hudson Avenue were fire-bombed. All three homes were in the tony Lincoln Park neighborhood on the North Side. An hour after the first alarms sounded, another came in from Old St. Patrick's Church on West Adams. Then from St. Michael's Church in nearby Old Town. And from the historic Clarke House in the Prairie District on the South Side. All the attacks employed Molotov cocktails. All the buildings were saved with limited damage. No one died. One firefighter required treatment for smoke inhalation.

The familiar cigarette butts were found at each site.

I sat at my office computer the next day doing research. What I discovered dumbfounded me. While I found nothing definitive, clear clues confirmed that the hunt for jihadist warriors had pointed us in the wrong direction.

The puzzle pieces painted a picture for me.

But it made no sense.

46

"That's a hell of a coincidence," Mark said that night when I told him what I'd found.

"I don't believe in . . ."

"I know."

"None of the other fires fits this profile," I said. "So why start now, assuming he picked these targets for what they have in common? Is he sending a message about his motives, and maybe a clue to who he is?"

"How many buildings total in the city survived the Great Fire?" Mark asked.

"Nobody knows for sure ...

"Well, officially it's seven sites, but it was eight buildings. The two houses on Cleveland are side-by-side and are logged as one site. There might be more. I don't know."

The blaze under discussion was the Great Chicago Fire of 1871. It started in what was then the southwest corner of the city. The summer had been abnormally hot and dry, and autumn brought no relief. The arid wind reached near gale force, pushing the fire before it. The blazes roared out of control, hot as a crematorium, from Oct. 8

into Oct. 10, sweeping through virtually all of what is now the South Loop, downtown and the Mag Mile, and north into Lincoln Park.

The Chicago Fire Department had no prayer of putting the fire out. Almost everything in Chicago, then a city of about 300,000 people, was made of wood. Homes, offices, shops, even sidewalks, were almost nothing but wood, parched for months by unusually high heat and persistent dry winds. Everything became fuel to feed the monster. Some building exteriors were constructed of one thin layer of unreinforced brick. Those walls quickly collapsed under the twin assaults of the wind and the firestorm.

By the time rain came to help bring the fire under control, at least 300 people had died, 17,500 buildings were destroyed, and 100,000 people—a third of the city's population—were homeless.

Within the 3.3-square-mile footprint of the fire, only eight buildings survived.

Six of them had been targeted by the arsonist on the previous night. Two, the Water Tower buildings, had been targeted earlier.

"So it's your theory that the latest round of fires targeted buildings that survived the Great Fire," he said. "But the Clark House doesn't fit the pattern. It's way down in the Prairie District, well outside the fire's footprint."

"But not in 1871," I said.

Mark frowned.

"The house was built in 1836 somewhere near the lake on Sixteenth Street west of Michigan Avenue," I said. "The fire missed it by an eyelash. After the fire the owner moved the house farther south. Later, it was moved again down to the Prairie District. It definitely qualifies as a fire survivor."

Mark asked, "Are there any other fire survivors he hasn't hit?"

"He got the two Water Works buildings first," I said. "Now these. There might be others that survived the original fire but didn't make the current official list. They've probably all fallen down and been forgotten."

We consulted the Chicago map I'd been using.

"It looks like anything inside the fire footprint is fair game for this guy," Mark said. "Keene's didn't exist in 1871, but it's inside the fire footprint. Same for the sporting goods store and the warehouse. But K-Town is way outside. So was the senior center."

"No, the senior center was just inside," I said. "Some fire maps don't show the tail of the fire. It bucked the prevailing winds and burned southeast, into the teeth of the gale. And I have a theory about K-Town."

"What?"

"The arsonist torched K-Town right after he tried and failed to burn the Water Works buildings. Those buildings are limestone. They're different limestone. Different colors. From different quarries in different states. But they're all limestone. My theory is that K-Town became surrogates for the Water Works buildings. He tried and failed to burn them. K-Town was an easier target where he could do a lot more damage, and he took it."

"I don't suppose," Mark asked, "that you have a possible motive for all this squirreled away in your brain."

"I think it's been rattling around in my subconscious since the first conversation I had with Carl Cribben about the fires, back around the first of the year," I said. "We were talking about how fast the arson incidents were escalating, and he said at the rate the arsonist was going, the whole city would be in flames by the end of the month. Then he added, 'We don't need that again.' It was just an off-hand comment, but it stuck with me."

Mark was skeptical. "You mean Carl suspected somebody was trying to burn the whole city again? What reason would he have to think that?"

"None. I think it was an offhand remark, not a theory. But the underlying notion became my subconscious flypaper. I couldn't define it, but I couldn't shake it, either. Eventually it led me to the right place."

We thought about that for a while.

"We're only a few years from the 150th anniversary of the Great Fire," Mark said. "The arsonist couldn't wait another three years?"

"If this theory is right," I said, "he probably couldn't risk waiting.

There are bound to be all sorts of events commemorating the anniversary. If he started firebombing during the events, it would be too easy for authorities to make the link."

He asked, "You think he knew these latest targets were Great Fire survivors?"

"I'm sure he did," I said. "If this theory is right, it's a good bet his motive is to scorch the city again for a motive I can't even imagine. Anything inside the footprint is fair game."

And then something else occurred to me.

"The warehouse fire, the first big one this arsonist set, it was directly across the street from the CFD's training facility."

That exact site of that red brick building on West De Koven Avenue was the flash point of the 1871 fire. Catherine O'Leary's iconic barn stood on that spot, and within that barn lived the cow that, according to folklore, kicked over a lantern and ignited one of the most storied disasters in United States history. The legend of Mrs. O'Leary's cow had been debunked time and again, but it had not been forgotten. Many people still believed it.

Mark smiled and sipped his beer. "It goes without saying, but I'll say it anyway. You don't think all this could just be a coincidence?"

I glowered at him, and he smiled again.

He said, "There's a monument to the Great Fire on the CFD plaza. If this arson spree is linked to the old fire, maybe the warehouse was a warning shot."

I asked, "You think you should get the city and the feds to put some security on the two Water Tower buildings? He might try them again."

"Definitely. Maybe on all the fire survivors he's tried and failed to destroy. We can't protect every building inside the footprint, not even with martial law, but maybe his identifiable targets should get additional attention."

"I know of one more," I said. "Not a building, but a monument in its own way."

I told him about the Harold Washington Library Center, which housed a symbol most Chicagoans knew nothing about.

"If the arsonist knows its historic significance, he might attack it," I said. "If he managed to destroy it . . ."

Mark let out a breath. "Jesus, I hate this guy."

ODDLY, no other news operation made the six-fire connection to 1871 until my story in the next day's paper pointed it out. The earlier attack on the Water Works buildings closed the circle. The arsonist had now tried to destroy all eight of the buildings known to have survived the Great Fire of 1871.

None of the eight might survive if the arsonist attacked them again, especially with the Semtex he had left. The top brass at the Chicago Fire Department took Mark's suggestion seriously. The mayor and the police department ordered extensive security at the Water Works buildings and close surveillance on the other six structures.

Being alone with the discovery that the latest arsons appeared to be connected with the Great Fire gave me an interesting front-page exclusive the next day, though it didn't advance the search for the arsonist. Still, the common history of so many targets had to be factored into the profile of the person responsible for setting the fires.

The next morning I drove to the CFD training facility. I saw that the ruins of the warehouse across the street had been razed, the debris removed, and a fence built around the property. It was prime land in a burgeoning area, and something interesting would be built there. It was hard to believe the property, now a chunk of the bustling South Loop, had once been filled with farms that were considered the outer limits of Chicago and worth very little. Now the land was too valuable to be left vacant very long.

I pulled into De Koven Avenue, little more than an alley, actually, only a block long and widened at the west end to accommodate nose-in parking spaces. I pulled into an open space and gazed at the monument to the spot where the Great Chicago Fire began. A casual observer might conclude the bronze sculpture of a column of fire was simply a way to define the CFD work done within these red brick walls. That's what I'd thought the first time I drove by and noticed it. Now I knew the real story. The original name of the block-long alley, De Koven Avenue, had been kept for a reason. It was Catherine O'Leary's home.

I sat for a few minutes, looking at the sculpture and trying to imagine what it had been like on the night of Oct. 8, 1871. According to lore, Catherine O'Leary was in her barn, right here, milking a cow by lantern light. The cow kicked over the lantern, igniting the barn. The fire was driven to the north and east by fierce, dry winds, the beginning of the end of 3.3 square miles of urban landscape. Mrs. O'Leary was quoted as saying she was only able to save a small calf.

The story was apocryphal and came in many versions, including one that had a group of men playing cards in the barn and leaving the lantern burning when they departed. At some point it blew over. That probably wasn't true, either.

The most interesting of all the theories about who, or what, started the Great Chicago Fire went something like this:

As it passed by the earth, a celestial phenomenon known as Biela's Comet lost its tail, creating a meteor shower of fiery fragments that survived the plunge through the atmosphere and struck the ground in two widely separated locations, Mrs. O'Leary's barn in southwest Chicago and the lumber town of Peshtigo, Wisconsin 253 miles north of Chicago and 163 miles north of Milwaukee.

In the parched north woods of Wisconsin, the fire started by the meteorite fragments and driven by the hot, arid winds burned with terrifying intensity. It sped northeast at ninety miles an hour. It burned to the shores of Green Bay, then leaped across twenty miles of water and ignited the opposite shore.

Some scientists pooh-poohed the comet's tail theory, arguing that meteorite fragments would not normally be hot enough to ignite a firestorm. But, as others pointed out, there was nothing "normal" about the tinder conditions during that October.

The Peshtigo fire has been all but forgotten by history though its destruction went far beyond Chicago's. Between 1,500 and 2,500 people died, and the firestorm laid waste to 2,400 square miles, or 1.5 million acres.

History concluded the most likely scenario for the Peshtigo blaze involved lumberjacks who set small fires in piles of "slash," or waste, from logging activity. The gale-force winds whipped the smaller fires into one massive inferno that couldn't be stopped.

But as horrific as the Peshtigo fire was, killing five to eight times more people and burning 730 times as much territory, it is the Great Chicago Fire that everyone remembers.

Since there was no lumbering activity on De Koven Avenue in the late 19th century, the true cause of the Great Chicago Fire remained a mystery.

47

I never made it inside the CFD building.

Several men met me outside the front door, right next to the commemorative sculpture of flame. It was chance that we landed in the same place at the same time. They happened to be leaving as I arrived. Two were firefighters, and two were former firefighters. One of them recognized me and immediately connected me with the *Journal* stories about the arsons.

"Liked your story about the last round of fire bombings," he said. "We all made the connection with 1871, but we didn't figure any outsiders would."

A second man jumped in. "She's Mark Hearst's girlfriend," he said. "That's how she knows all this stuff."

That irritated me.

"I'm the one who figured out the link," I said, feeling a little petty even as I said it. "I'm the one who reminded Mark. We agreed months ago that he wouldn't give me any inside information on the arson investigations. It would be too obvious, and it could cost him his job. We even stopped seeing each other for a while to avoid the temptation. So I'd suggest you drop the pillow-talk accusations before one of us sues you for slander."

The second man actually took a step backward.

"Whoa," he said. "Sorry. No offense meant." He looked sheepishly at his friends, then turned back to me. "Is there something we could help you with?"

I smiled in a way that I hoped would convey sympathy.

"I'm sorry I snapped at you," I said. "I usually only do that to bad guys. I'm just frustrated. I had no right to take it out on you."

I told them I was looking for information on the 1871 fire.

The second man's eyebrows climbed up his forehead.

"You think that's a connection to the arsons?" he asked. "Not terrorism?"

"I don't know. It's one line of inquiry. I don't have any hard evidence. Or soft evidence, for that matter. The coincidence . . ." I cringed at the word ". . . piqued my interest, that's all. There must be some reason the arsonist tried to burn what the 1871 fire missed."

They suggested I visit the Fire Museum deep on the South Side.

"There's people down there could give you some help," the first man said. "They got a library and everything." He frowned a moment. "Not for nuthin', but we been talking just among ourselves, and we were wonderin' if the arsonist might be a fireman, or a former fire-man. I couldn't give you any names, but I gotta tell ya, there's firemen who are firebugs. They love fires, love to watch 'em burn. Some of 'em, maybe if they weren't fire fighters, might be fire setters."

"Really?" I said.

"Swear it," the guy replied, and all his friends nodded. "Not sayin' it's so in this case. I don't know anybody who'd set a fire deliberately to kill people. But you might keep that possibility in mind."

I said I would.

I thought about the notion as I drove down South Western Avenue to Fifty-Second Street, the location of the fire museum. I didn't think the theory held up. The federal Department of Home-land Security required all first responders to have at least one form of identification confirmation, including fingerprints. We had plenty of prints for the suspected arsonist that didn't match anyone in any file anywhere. I felt certain Ron Colter had run the prints against first responders. But I would double-check that with Colter.

When I got to the museum, it seemed deserted.

The sign on the door said it was only open on the last Saturday of the month.

Just great.

That date was more than two weeks away.

I called the museum's phone number and got an answering machine. It told me if I wanted to speak to a trustee to leave a message. I didn't bother.

I went home.

~

"YOU NEED A NIGHT OUT," Mark told me. "Bacchanalia, Second City Diner, or some place we haven't been in a while?"

I thought about it. I didn't feel like Italian, and we were scheduled to go to the Second City Diner the following night, our regular Thursday visit. I mentioned this to Mark.

"Ooh, aren't we getting stuck in our ways as old age advances," he said with a grin. "Where is it written that we can't go to Second City on a Wednesday?"

"Nowhere," I admitted.

Our last-minute decision meant we couldn't snag our regular table, but we were seated quickly, catching angry glances from diners who'd been waiting longer.

When we had drinks in front of us I brought the conversation back around to what else connected to the 1871 fire might be in danger from the arsonist. My greatest fear still focused on the special collection at the Harold Washington Library Center.

"You mentioned that before," Mark said. "I meant to Google it, but I haven't had time. Tell me about it."

So I did.

"We don't know exactly, but historical accounts suggest the Great

Fire destroyed between two million and three million books in the city, virtually everything that made up the existing library system and then some. The city fathers decided to rebuild by founding the first free public library system. A great concept, but rather useless without books."

"That's where the English stepped in?"

I nodded. "Apparently our Revolution was sufficiently forgiven by that time. Average British citizens chipped in more than 8,000 books to form the basis for a new Chicago library. Queen Victoria, herself, contributed two books. Both signed by her."

"And they're in the Washington Library?"

"Yep."

"With how many people going in and out a day?"

"No idea."

"They should get some serious security, too, like right now."

"I'm going to suggest that when I see the head archivist tomorrow morning."

THE ARSONIST WAS SURPRISED *when he saw the reporter and her boyfriend show up at the Second City Diner a night early, on a Wednesday instead of a Thursday. And it was ironic that this was the work shift during which he planned to begin preparations for the final showdown with the two of them.*

He had to work slowly and deliberately, a little bit each night. He could only carry so much into the restaurant in his backpack each time he reported for a shift; he could spend only an extra two or three minutes in the wine cellar each time a bartender sent him to the basement to replenish alcohol supplies. The couple probably wouldn't visit the restaurant again the next night. But he would be ready for them the next time they showed up, perhaps the following Thursday. Or the Thursday after that.

He had one more place he wanted to strike before he eliminated the human thorn in his side. If the new job delayed the couple's return to the restaurant by a week or two, it wouldn't matter that much.

In his previous fires he hadn't set out to kill anyone; the deaths that occurred were incidental to the task of destroying the heart of the city he'd come to despise. This restaurant job would be his first time targeting specific lives. He had balked at strangling her in Greenwood Heights earlier, but now the idea of killing her didn't bother him a bit, especially now that she had tied his arsons to the Great Chicago Fire. He hadn't expected that.

The first step in his plan for the destruction of the Second City Diner came when one of the mixologists asked for a fresh case of Tito's vodka.

The arsonist darted into the room where he kept his backpack hidden, grabbed a package concealing a bomb, and went down the back stairs to the basement. Because of his experience with the same devices at Keene's department store, he was able to have the mechanism in place and ready in less than two minutes.

He checked as he backed away that it couldn't be seen, and he was satisfied. No way anyone could spot it under and at the back of the lowest shelf in the wine room. And no equipment—human, mechanical, or canine —would sniff it out. He had it triple sealed in heavy plastic.

He grabbed the case of vodka and hefted it on the dumb waiter that would take it up to the bar. If the bartender noticed it had taken a few minutes longer than normal to get his order, he didn't mention it to the busboy.

The arsonist arrived back at his post in the dining room just in time to overhear some of the intense conversation between the reporter and her boyfriend. It was enough to convince him he needed to hold off his plan for the diner and hit his next target quickly.

He would build the firebomb when he got off work tonight and plant and detonate it the next day, perhaps late in the morning when there would be a lot of people around to cover his movements and actions.

Fortunate for him he had overheard the conversation.

For the people who would be immolated in his next assault, not so much.

The arsonist didn't read much, mostly stuff that required when he was in school and then quickly forgotten. One book that stuck with him over the years was Ray Bradbury's Fahrenheit 451, required reading in junior high *school. He wasn't sure he got the point, but he always remembered one passage:* "It was a pleasure to burn. It was a special pleasure to see things eaten, to see things blackened and changed."

His sentiments exactly.

48

I had an appointment with the senior archivist at the Harold Washington Library Center at 9:30 a.m. I had told her I wanted to talk about the aftermath of the 1871 fire.

Amy Alice Markowitz hardly looked the librarian stereotype. She didn't wear her hair in a bun. She didn't sport orthopedic shoes or clothes more appropriate for the 1950s. I would describe her as stunning, in fact. I guessed her to be in her mid-forties. She had medium-brown hair worn in a pixie cut that complimented her angular face. Her light brown eyes sparkled with green flecks in the irises. She had a straight nose. Her mouth was a bit wide but natural in shape. Her neck was tight and long. She dressed in a conservative but elegant business suit. I noticed her broad gold wedding band set with a single round brilliant-cut diamond that had to be two carats, flanked by two smaller marquise cut stones. I wanted to grow up to be her.

Markowitz flashed a friendly smile and offered a warm, firm handshake. She invited me into her office.

"Would you like coffee?" she asked.

I declined with thanks, and said I wanted to learn more about the genesis of the library's collection of books from England's Victorian Era.

Her eyes changed. Her expression transformed from curiosity to something close to fear. What had I missed? I didn't know, so I asked.

"Is there a problem talking to me about the collection?"

Markowitz continued to probe my face with her eyes, almost as if she had lapsed into a trance. Then she shook her head slightly.

"No, of course not," she said. "But might I ask why? Does this have something to do with the arsons? Is our collection in danger? I ask because I read the paper, and that's what you've been writing about."

Okay, now we were on the same page.

"Not that I know of," I said. "But no guarantee. The library is open to the public. I'm not sure anywhere in Chicago is safe from the arsonist, especially places with ties to the Great Fire. It probably wouldn't hurt to add some security. But that's your decision."

"I'll take it up with the board," Markowitz said. "What do you want to know?"

"I've read what I could online about all the books lost in the 1871 fire and the contributions from England," I said. "It's all pretty academic stuff. I'd like to hear the story from you. And specifically, is there anything in the history of the fire that might point to a reason someone would want to torch property today that's connected to the fire?"

"Hmmm, that's a strange question," she said. "but I understand why you ask given some of the arsonist's previous targets. If he knows of our Victorian collection then, yes, we might well become a target."

"Have you had any threats—phone calls or emails—or any suspicious people hanging around?" I asked.

Markowitz shook her head. "No, nothing like that I'm aware of, and I would have been told."

"This isn't for publication," I said, "but how is the collection stored?"

"It isn't," she said. "It's on display so people can see it. It's a big piece of Chicago's history. Something between two and three million books were destroyed in the fire. The donation of 8,000 books from England formed the foundation of the city's free library system. We want people to see what's left and appreciate its significance."

"Are they all still here?" I asked.

"Of the 8,000 donated books, most were meant for frequent public use, as you would expect in a library. Good paper stock, sturdy bindings, and such. Still, after all these years, the bulk of them have fallen apart. There are only about 200 left, the ones that had the least general appeal and therefore got the least wear. We're very protective of all of them, particularly the two donated and signed by Queen Victoria. They are the most valuable in the entire collection."

"Tell me about them," I said.

She described them.

One is an illustrated history of Buckingham Palace. The other is titled, *An Early History of the Prince Consort.* It's the story of the queen's late husband, Prince Albert. Neither book would have made the *New York Times* best-seller list, had the list existed back in the day.

"They are of only historic significance," Markowitz said. She smiled. "Personally, I have no plans to read either of them."

"Understandable," I said. "Do you keep them locked up?"

"No, they're on public display. They rest on special pillows that are inert and non-acidic to keep them as clean and pristine for as long as possible. Those two are only available to researchers and must be read on the special pillows. They cushion the books and keep them from being opened too wide. We don't want the spines broken."

She stood. "Would you like to see the two that Queen Victoria sent?"

"Actually, I would," I said.

I found them remarkably unremarkable except for the plates inside the covers. Printed on them were the words, "Presented to the City of Chicago towards the formation of a free library after the Great Fire, as a mark of English sympathy by . . ." and then in hand-written script, "Her Majesty the Queen Victoria."

"Wow," I said. "These must be worth a fortune."

"They're priceless," Markowitz said, "and therefore impossible to insure. Which is why your interest is of concern to me. To lose these books would be a devastating blow to the soul of our city."

We walked around the ninth floor, Markowitz pointing out the Victorian collection and other items of interest. It was still early in the day but, even so, there were maybe twenty people milling about. No one drew my attention until I saw a man in a baseball cap browsing near the display that included Queen Victoria's books. A quick glance wouldn't have raised my suspicion. But I felt compelled to watch him. His movements, slow and casual, riveted me. Each step he took brought him closer to the treasured tomes until he stood against their display table.

My first impression made the cap a size too large for him, causing it to sit very low on his head, hiding his face. The second was his build, virtually identical to the "plumber" described by Beth Daley, the clerk at Keene's. The third was the way his hand moved slowly under the table where priceless books resided.

Of course all of this ran through my brain faster than I can relate it here. I knew in a millisecond who I was looking at. And, strangely, he looked familiar.

He gave me a quick glance, turned his back, and began to walk away quickly, toward the steps to the lower floors. Then he began running.

"Stop him," I yelled toward the security guard. "Stop him. He has a bomb."

At the mention of a bomb the security guard, who had taken several steps toward the fleeing man, stopped. Apparently he wasn't eager to confront an explosive up close and personal. So I took up the chase, Mary Alice Markowitz right on my heels.

Several library visitors were standing between the suspect and the stairway, which slowed him down enough for me to close the distance between us. I was taller, and my stride was longer. I knew I could overtake him. But what then?

When I saw him take a cell phone from his pocket, I knew I had to be fast.

Trying to dial and run at the same time slowed him down just enough. I caught him at the top of the steps, threw myself into him and punched the phone out of his fist. It skittered across the floor, out of his reach. He lurched and bucked to throw me off, and I kept trying to drag him backward, away from the phone that would trigger disaster.

He was incredibly strong and began dragging me toward the stairway at the same time he fought with me. If he succeeded in shoving me over the edge, I could break bones or be killed in the tumble down the stone steps. It was a long way to the first landing.

I hooked my left arm around the top newel post and hit him as hard as I could in the kidneys, over his heart, and, finally, in the throat. I felt his grip on me loosen marginally, and I took the opening to leverage myself away from the stairwell.

He grabbed me and said something I didn't understand. One word I didn't catch.

We rolled on the floor. I tried to wrap my arms around his chest and hold him still, hoping bystanders would come to my assistance. I called out for help. The security guard responded. But as he leaned over the bomber to drag him away from me, the attacker swung the steel-reinforced toe of his boot into the guard's knee and sent the man sprawling and screeching in agony.

The bomber returned his attention to me. He kicked at me whenever he could get a booted foot free. He hit me whenever he regained control of an arm. In his squirming he managed to roll onto his back, which gave me a chance to bring a knee up hard into his groin. He yelped, but he was able to jerk his right arm out of my grasp. He swung his fist from floor level as hard as he could into the side of my head.

The world went out of focus, and he took advantage of my daze to shed me and get to his feet. He sneered down at me and kicked me in the gut. If he hadn't been slightly off balance, the blow might have ruptured several organs.

Through a red haze I saw him running—limping really, with one hand clutching his crotch—straight for the spot where Markowitz stood over his lost phone. She took a step forward, challenging him to get past her. The guard had regained his feet and stumbled toward the same spot.

"Don't . . ." I muttered toward Markowitz and shook my head. "Get it . . ."

It was cryptic, but the best I could do. And Markowitz understood. She picked up the phone and clutched it tight as she moved away from the arsonist.

At this point the security guard prepared to launch himself at the arsonist, much as I had. But the arsonist, younger and more agile, made it halfway down the steps before the security guard reached the top. I heard the guard radio other security people in the building. He described the fleeing man as best he could and told everyone listening to stop him and be careful in case he was armed. But somehow the guy eluded everyone.

Later his baseball cap and jacket would be found on the seventh floor in a trash bin.

He had ditched his disguise and thus escaped security without being recognized.

I saw Markowitz walking toward where I was still down, cradling the phone as if it were a newborn child. She looked nervous and concerned.

"Don't touch the keypad," I whispered. "Use another phone. Call 9-1-1. Evacuate building. Fast. Bomb."

I put my face down on the cool floor let the world fade.

I woke up to some serious jostling in an ambulance with the siren screaming. An EMT bent over me. I saw her lips move, and I assumed she was asking me questions. But I could barely hear her voice and didn't understand a word she said.

I closed my eyes and went back to sleep.

The next time I woke up it was in a quiet place with a bed, raised at the top. Warm blankets encased me, and I had a bitch of a headache.

I recognized Mark's voice. "Sleeping Beauty awakes."

The lights were low, but I saw Eric Ryland, my editor, standing near the door with Ron Colter.

Mark pushed a call button and a nurse showed up thirty seconds later.

"On a scale of one to ten, ten being a lot, how much pain are you in?" she asked.

I never understood that question and found it hard to give an informed answer. So I took a guess. "Seven. Maybe eight."

"We'll let you have something for it as soon as the doctor sees you," she said.

He arrived a few minutes later and spent as much time looking at my chart as I spent reading a new page on my "Far Side" calendar each morning, maybe fifteen seconds. Apparently the chart wasn't nearly as funny.

He looked up and scowled at me.

"You ever think of letting the cops catch the bad guys?" he asked.

"Every time I find myself in the hospital," I said.

He looked surprised. "Does this happen often?"

Mark interrupted. "Too often."

The doctor opened his mouth, as if he wanted to ask something, then closed it again, raised his eyebrows and shook his head.

He asked, "Do you know what day it is?"

I had to think about it. "Friday?"

"Thursday."

He asked me to track his finger with my eyes. I frowned.

"You okay?"

"That hurt a little."

"Any nausea, dizziness?"

"A little nausea. I get light-headed when I move around in bed."

He nodded, appearing to have expected those answers.

Colter took two steps away from the door, moving deeper into the room.

He said, "Before you give her pain meds, I need to ask her some questions."

Mark got into his face. "You can come back tomorrow or the next day. Right now she needs the meds and rest."

Colter shook his head. "Deuce is the most reliable eyewitness we have to tweak the profile sketch. We need to do it while the memory is still fresh and not clouded by drugs."

"Oh, for God's sake . . ." Mark started before I interrupted.

"It's okay," I said. "He's right. I did get a very good look, and the strange thing is, I'm pretty sure I've seen the man before, but I can't remember where."

The doctor had taken in the debate and set the rules.

"Ten minutes," he said. "Then the nurse throws all of you out."

He turned to me. "Ms. Mora, you have a concussion. We're going to keep you at least overnight and take another look in the morning. For the time being, take it easy. Sleep. Watch TV if you feel like it. Basically stay very quiet."

Given the way I felt, staying quiet wasn't going to be any problem at all.

~

COLTER SUMMONED AARON DEBROSSE, the FBI forensic artist I'd first met at Beth Daley's house. Debrosse had been waiting outside my room and promised to be as quick as possible. He handed me the most current sketch of the arson suspect.

"I think the easiest thing would be for you to tell me what you saw that's different from what Ms. Daley and the other witness recalled," Debrosse said. "Instead of redoing the whole sketch, I can refine it to make it more accurate."

Colter asked a question that was going through my mind at the same time.

"You think you're remembering the sketch when you say you've seen him before?"

"Maybe that's part of it," I replied. "But I don't think so. The vague memory I have of seeing the guy before is quite different in some respects from the sketch."

Debrosse sat down with his iPad Pro and called up the likeness. He looked up at me with expectation.

I said, "Well, for one thing, his face is ruddier, rougher."

"Like old acne scars?" Debrosse suggested.

"No, not pocks. More weathered. He has a scar that cuts through his left eyebrow."

The nurse appeared after ten minutes and tried to end the session. But Debrosse and I were still fine-tuning the new sketch, and I was the one who asked for more time.

"I feel okay," I assured her. "Feeling useful is good medicine."

"Well, make it quick," she said and hurried out.

When the artist and I finished, the new sketch varied considerably from the original.

"That's the man I remember seeing before," I said. "I'm sure of it. But I still can't remember where."

"Damn," Mark said in a low voice. "He looks vaguely familiar to me, too."

Colter almost smiled. "Well, that narrows it down," he said. "We just have to figure out where the two of you have been together when your paths crossed his."

I sighed. "I think my brain is rebelling at any more heavy thinking right now. It feels like wet cement."

Eric spoke up. "Let's find a place in the hospital where we can print that out," he said, nodding at the new sketch. "I'll take a copy back to the office and get it up on the web."

Mark asked Debrosse, "Would you email me a copy of the new sketch?"

Debrosse got Mark's email address, and seconds later I heard Mark's phone chime.

Eric, Colter, and Debrosse started to leave. Colter turned back at the door.

"I'm going to put a cop in the hall," he said. "If you recognized the arsonist, he might know it. He knows where you've run into one another before. He might come after you."

"You really think he'd try to kill me in a hospital?" I asked.

"Yes, actually, I do."

"Okay," I said. "I won't play hero."

Colter turned to Mark. "Are you armed?"

Mark nodded.

"Can you stay until we get somebody over here?"

Mark nodded again.

"You don't have to stay," I told him after Colter left. "After they give me the pain killer I won't be much of a conversationalist."

"I want to stay," he said. "If he comes here while you're asleep, you won't have a chance to defend yourself."

"Don't you have to go to work?"

"Since the library bomb never detonated, there's no need for me to get involved in the investigation right away. I'll get the FBI report later. The first guys on the scene said this one looks like the others probably looked, complete with cell phone detonator."

"You just going to stare out the window while I sleep?"

He showed me the device in his hand, an iPad Mini he used as an e-book reader.

"I have Jack Reacher and Harry Bosch to keep me company," he said, mentioning two of his favorite literary characters created by Lee Child and Michael Connelly.

"I might be asleep a long time."

"I've got Ian Rankin and James Lee Burke in the on-deck circle."

"At least it's not another woman."

"Oh, I've got Patricia Highsmith and Ruth Rendell waiting in the wings."

During the conversation the nurse returned and pressed the pump on my morphine drip. I thought I might have heard Mark's last sentence from the bottom of a deep well.

49

I tried to go back to work after two days at home, but Eric told me if I showed up at the office he'd have me escorted from the building. To be truthful, his threat didn't make me unhappy. Just taking a shower set the world spinning. Headaches and nausea were abating. But I was tired. And I knew I couldn't drive safely.

On the fourth day the post-concussion symptoms relented. I still wasn't certain I should drive, so I called Uber for a ride to the office.

"You were supposed to take a week," Eric complained softly.

"I ran out of things to do," I countered. I remembered a line I loved in a Nelson DeMille novel called *Plum Island*, and I repeated it. "The trouble with doing nothing is not knowing when you're finished."

Eric smiled. "What's wrong with reading? Use that adjustable bed you love so much and inhale a good book. Take a nap. Read another book."

"I ran out of books."

"Buy some new ones. There are plenty out there. Or read your favorites again."

"I'm not going home, Eric. You might as well give it up."

He did, though he didn't like it.

"When, exactly, did I lose control of this ship?" he asked.

Then Ron Colter showed up, and to my dismay, Mason Cross, my nemesis from the National Security Agency followed him through the door. Colter, Cross, and I had dueled during an investigation of a child trafficking ring (and that's all I'm allowed to say about it). Colter and I had come to terms recently. Cross and I never would. I knew Cross had been around because Mark saw him at the K-Town fires. But I hadn't run into him in nine months. There was small likelihood he had come in to welcome me back to work.

If Chicago's arsonists were homegrown and unaffiliated with international terrorist groups, Cross should have backed off and left the investigation to the FBI. His continued presence suggested the jihadist theory hadn't lost its traction.

The two feds stopped only briefly to announce themselves to Eric's secretary, who nodded at them to go into my editor's office. It was only then that I noticed the *Journal*'s lawyer, Jonathan Bruckner, sitting with Eric. I hadn't seen him enter the newsroom. Nobody shook hands. Nobody even offered a hand. Not a good sign.

The vibes became more ominous when Eric sent me a message to join them.

Again, there were no handshakes, though I did see Colter offer a small, quick smile.

"How're you feeling?" Cross asked.

"Strange you should ask," I said. "I was fine until I saw you here."

Eric flashed me a glance that shouted, "Cool it." I ignored him.

"Sit down, Ms. Mora," Cross commanded. "We have a few question to ask you."

"And I'm sure I have no answers for you," I snapped back. "Between the hospital and bed rest at home, I haven't been out in the world much lately."

Cross ignored me and put a copy of the new arsonist sketch in my hand.

"Yeah, I've seen this," I said. "Oh, wait, I'm the one who helped create it."

Again, Cross ignored me. If he was going to continue to be pissy, I wasn't going to waste any more of my best sarcasm on him.

"You know people," the NSA operative said. "You meet a lot of people. You interview a lot of people. You hear tells in their voices, their language. You see them in their bodies. What were your impressions of this guy?"

"He has a wicked right cross when he's lying on his back on a marble floor."

Eric jumped in and ordered me to answer the question.

I thought about the arsonist for a minute, and it made my head ache. But I thought I knew what Cross wanted, and I gave it an honest effort.

"He didn't look like the western stereotype of a native of the Middle East. He didn't look like what we imagine an Arab looks like, however erroneous our images are."

"Italian? Greek?"

"I only have vague impressions of what Italians and Greeks look like, and the impressions aren't homogenous. There's no stereotypic look, at least not that I'm aware of."

"German? Scandinavian?"

"What are you going to do, take me on a world tour? I can't help you. To the extent that I got a good look at a man who was trying to kill me, nothing about him yelled out, 'Canadian,' or 'Finn' or any other nationality."

I paused and felt myself frown. There was something. The man had said something to me while I rolling around on the floor with him that I didn't understand, a word I didn't recognize. I tried to go back to the moment and pull it up.

Colter recognized my effort. "What is it?" he asked.

"He said something to me while he tried to get his hands around my throat."

"What was it?" Cross asked.

I shook my head. "A word. Just one word. He only used it once. I didn't catch it. Or I didn't understand it. It was like 'striped,' or 'stripper,' only it sounded more guttural. If it was a foreign language, maybe German, Russian . . ."

"How did he say it?" Cross asked. "Like a question or an exclamation?"

"Like an epithet."

Cross said, "Now look at the sketch."

I glanced down at the page in my hand.

"Of all the characteristics you see there, what stood out for you the most?"

"The heavy, dark eyebrows and how they sort of grow together over the bridge of his nose. Almost a unibrow, but not that heavy. Also the beard. It looked like maybe two days' growth, but it was dense and heavy, too. The guy was hairy. And, as you already know, the eyes I saw were blue, not brown like Beth Daley described. It's hard to make that mistake. During her encounter or mine, he might have been wearing tinted contacts."

"That," Cross said, "will be hard to use when we don't know which color is natural. But a guttural epithet that sounded like 'stripper,' that gives us a place to start."

"Doing what?"

Cross turned away from me, but Colter answered.

"You wouldn't believe what our computer geniuses can do. Thank you Deuce."

As they made their way out of the office I felt a cold shiver scrabble up my spine.

50

J ust before noon on Monday I got a call from Ron Colter inviting me to pay a visit to the FBI headquarters on Roosevelt Road.

"Is Mason Cross going to be there?"

"Yes."

"Am I going to be held incognito again?" I asked, recalling the last time I occupied a federal building with Colter and Cross.

Instead of answering, Colter hung up. I didn't take that as a good sign.

When I told Eric that I'd been summoned, he asked if I wanted Jonathan Bruckner to come along, assuming he was available.

"I don't think that's necessary," I said. "I'll call if I need backup."

AT FIRST I thought Colter was alone in his office. Then I noticed Cross sitting against the back wall at Colter's conference table. The expression on his face matched his surname. But when didn't it?

Colter indicated I should sit at the table, too. I chose a chair as far from Cross as possible. Colter smiled a little as he sat down. He started speaking without fanfare.

"We believe the word you heard was '*striapach,*'" he said.

The word had a very guttural sound. I had no idea what it meant or what language it belonged to. I rolled it around in my mind and tried to match it to what I had heard the arsonist spit out at me while we were rolling around on the floor. They seemed to pair up.

"Possibly," I said. "What does it mean?"

Cross stepped in. "It's Gaelic, Middle English if you prefer. It means 'whore.'

Now I smiled. "So the man trying to kill me called me a whore. I've been called worse. What made that tidbit of knowledge worth a trip over here? The fact that the man knows some Gaelic is evidence that he's Irish? I think I've been suggesting that for quite a while. His complexion and hair would suggest further than he's black Irish, a descendant of sailors in the Spanish Armada of the 1500s. Most black-Irish people have dark eyes, not blue, but in six centuries there has certainly been enough intermarriage that a blue-eyed black Irishman isn't a far-fetched concept."

Cross asked, "What's to say he isn't dark-eyed? As you suggested, he could have been wearing blue contacts when you saw him and no contacts when Beth Daley had coffee with him."

"He went out of his way to meet Beth Daley," I said. "He intended to give her a vague and possibly inaccurate impression of his appearance, a ploy to lead investigators—you—off the rails. It seems more likely he would disguise his eye color for Beth than at the library, where he never anticipated the need."

Colter agreed. "Even Washington can't ignore your conjecture on his ethnicity any more. The evidence seems overwhelming in support of your theory at this point."

"The caution," Cross said, "would be against dismissing the possibility that we're dealing with a jihadist trained to appear Irish. Or a real Irishman who has self-radicalized and joined ISIS in spirit and action. I still think one of those is the more likely scenario."

I struggled to come to terms with the three possibilities. An ongoing hangover from the concussion still messed with my cognitive thinking.

Colter saw me chewing at the issue. He said, "The problem with dismissing the possibility of jihadists, Deuce, is the lack of a motive for some average Chicago citizen to want to burn and kill on the horrific scale Chicago has experienced."

"It could be something akin to a severe mental or emotional dysfunction," I said. "He could be a former football player suffering from the terrible effects of too many blows to the head. There's plenty of evidence that people afflicted with . . . what is it, CTE? . . . that these men can become unspeakably violent."

"I haven't heard of any CTE victims who learned how to become serial firebombers and attack whole city blocks," Colter said. "They usually go after individuals with handguns or knives or fists."

I felt exasperated. "I'm not saying the guy has CTE. I'm just throwing alternate theories on the table."

"I know," Colter said. "And I'm not objecting. The more possibilities we consider, the higher the chance we'll hit the right one. Which brings us to this. I'll admit I thought you were on a wild-goose chase when you started combing Greenwood Heights. Now I'm not so sure. The apartment building owner who rented to Joe Smith told us utilities were included in the rent, and the guy stole cable TV from a neighbor. That explains why there's no personal info on him in all the usual places. Joe Smith lives entirely off the grid. It's slim and circumstantial evidence, but it is evidence that the arsonist and the handyman could be the same guy. And now we accept that both could be Irish. So we'll keep running with it."

"What's this 'we' thing?" I said. "I've been running with it. I'm still running with it. I haven't seen you leaving shoe leather all over the neighborhood."

"We will now," Cross said. "We're taking over from you."

"The hell you are," I said. "You can't just push me aside."

"Yes," Cross said, "actually we can. We can get a restraining order. If that doesn't work, and we find you in Greenwood Heights, we'll forcibly remove you and even put you under arrest. I don't think either of us wants to go through that again, but we can and will do it if we have to. We have the manpower to complete the canvass quickly. All we need from you is a rundown on places you've been, who you've talked to, and who told you what. We'll take it from there."

"Are you going to release these new theories to the public?"

"No," Colter said. "For the time being we're going to keep it all quiet while we try to grab up Joe Smith."

"And you'll share anything you find out?"

Cross glowered. "No, probably not."

51

"Jonathan says there's nothing we can do," Eric told me when I got back to the office in a fury. I had called Eric from my rental car to tell him the outcome of the meeting. I think he was secretly relieved that I wouldn't be tromping around Greenwood Heights by myself any longer, but he knew better than to say that to me. Instead, he called our lawyer and asked him if the feds had the authority to muscle me aside.

Jonathan said they couldn't bar me from being in the neighborhood. But they probably could get a judge to issue a restraining order to stop me from knocking on doors. It hung on whether they could make a sufficiently compelling case that an amateur sleuth nosing around could complicate the investigation of the biggest criminal case ever to hit Chicago. He seemed confident that a judge would opt for whatever the feds thought they needed to bring the fire bomber to justice.

"You think the suspect doesn't already know I've been there?" I snapped.

"We're pretty sure he does know," Eric replied. "He's already skipped out on one lease, a place he'd lived for several years. The likely reason is that you spooked him."

"And a platoon of FBI agents won't?"

"They would. But if enough of them can act fast enough, they might find him before he can move again."

I slumped in my chair. "That's not fair," I said, thinking I sounded like a petulant child even as the words escaped my mouth.

"Life isn't fair," Eric said.

"That's not the best version of the quote, Eric. Nobody ever uses the best version, which is the full version. 'Life isn't fair, but government must be.' Ann Richards, former governor of Texas. Ann wouldn't have kicked me out of Greenwood Heights."

"She wouldn't have a say," Eric said. "She had no jurisdiction in Chicago. Besides, she's been dead for a dozen years."

I SAT at my desk for a couple of days, glum over the abrupt end of my involvement in the hunt for the arsonist. On the fourth day I felt marginally cheered when I realized the feds apparently weren't making the swift progress they anticipated. I felt guilty about feeling that way. It would have been far better for the city and its populace if Colter, Cross, and crew had found Joe Smith on their first day in the field. Perhaps that failure would teach those guys some humility. They were so cock-sure of themselves that a taste of failure would be a character builder for them.

I knew they had failed. Had they caught up with Joe Smith, or whatever his name was, there would have been a huge presser, a perp walk, all sorts of public back slapping, and deep sighs of relief. Instead, it was deathly quiet.

I didn't want to say, "too quiet," but I could have. It would have been accurate.

THE NEXT TO GO WERE FIVE sightseeing boats parked at the Navy Pier.

The boats, anchored along the north and south sides of the pier, were firebombed in quick succession in the middle of the night by someone described as a lone man who slammed Molotov cocktails into three boats on the south side of the pier then ducked through a garage to the north side and firebombed two more.

Security officers called in the police and CFD, which brought trucks and boats. The police chased the man in what might have looked like in a scene out of the Keystone Kops. They followed him around boats, over boats, into a boat at one point, through the garage, and around more boats. He was dressed all in black and very quick, the officers reported. Nobody got a good look at him. Descriptions were paltry but tended to support the probability that it was the same person responsible for the city's epidemic of arsons.

The boats had been fueled and provisioned during the evening to prepare them for early morning sightseeing trips. As a result, two of them exploded before firefighters could take the blazes down. No one was hurt, but windows were blown out in two restaurants and the Chicago Shakespeare Theater lobby. It was miraculous that no one died.

I happened to be at Mark's condo and got to the Pier with the initial wave of first responders. I got there in time to talk briefly with a woman seriously cut by flying glass. She had witnessed everything and told me about it while EMT's evaluated her and got her ready for transport to the nearest hospital. I didn't hold back anything in describing her injuries. With the next few hours I would come to wish I had showed more discretion—or that one of my editors had.

The Navy Pier opened in 1916, forty-five years after the Great Chicago Fire, and the area where the ships docked lay just outside the Great Fire's footprint. But the boats had been tourist vessels, plying the Chicago River to give passengers awe-inspiring views of that part of the city that had grown up inside the footprint. The loss of the boats would put a prolonged damper on how many people would get a chance to admire the river vista.

Not a direct link to the Great Fire. But it close enough.

Joe Smith was back.

52

"Did you find more butts?" I asked Mark when he came home, dirty and exhausted from his preliminary examination of the cremated remains of the tour boats.

He nodded. "They're almost becoming a cliché," he said. "Maybe he'll stop when he runs out of half-smoked cigarettes."

"Want me to cancel the Diner tonight? You look like you could stand to stretch out on the couch and nibble on some lasagna from Bacchanalia before you doze off."

"I can't eat lying down, not without dribbling food all over my shirt. Otherwise, that sounds like a great idea."

"You could take the shirt off. If you dribble on your bare chest, I'd be happy to get you clean. Very slowly and very thoroughly."

Mark turned his head toward me, his eyes alight with an inner heat.

"I'm suddenly not hungry for food," he said. "But we could pretend, and you could get me clean, anyway."

"Take a quick shower, and I'll get you dry. And, Mark, this works both ways, right?"

"Oh, yeah. In fact we could get to the drying part quicker if you'd shower with me."

And I did.

When Eric called me into his office the next day, the curtness of the order and the expression on his face combined to warn me of incipient trouble.

"You remember that grandmother who complained about you scaring her grandkids?" he asked, without prelude and without inviting me to sit down. "After Christmas, after the firebombing of the sporting goods store on the North Side. She prompted your book-throwing snit, if I recall correctly."

"I haven't thrown a book since. Not even in the privacy of my own home. She wasn't the only one responsible for my anger, just the culmination of a day filled with moronic calls from people without two brain cells to rub together. I entered a twelve-step program. I've apologized to all the books I've thrown and all the walls I hit."

Eric wasn't amused. "She hasn't forgotten you, either. She filed a formal complaint against you with the HR department, cancelled her subscription, and started campaigns on Facebook and Twitter to get everybody else in Chicago to cancel their subscriptions, too."

"After all this time? It's been, what, four months?"

"Grandmothers have long memories and hold unending grudges when it comes to the well-being of their grandchildren."

"What well-being?" I said. I could hear the irritation in my voice. "All I did was write a column on the different ways people respond to terrorism."

Eric's chest heaved in a resigned sigh. "We've taken twenty-eight cancellations just this morning. There's no telling how many more will follow. She can carry on her campaign for as long as she wants. Social media is free."

"Are we in such bad financial shape we can't survive a few dozen cancellations?"

"It's a snowball. You know that, Deuce."

I said nothing while I put together Eric's line of reasoning. As much as I didn't want it to be, I had to acknowledge he was right. If the cancellation campaign caught on, it would make a dent in our circulation, with the potential loss of tens of thousands of dollars in subscription revenue. The lower our subscription numbers the less we could charge for advertising. The combination could add up to losses in the millions. Like most newspapers in the country, we were surviving on razor-thin margins already. Any significant revenue decline could slide the *Journal* right into bankruptcy. Whether we could emerge intact on the other side remained an open and troubling question.

"I haven't seen her posts or tweets," I said, my eyes drifting to the carpet under my feet. "What's she claiming we did that so offended her now?"

"Going back to December, she says you used profanity and hung up on her."

My head snapped up. "That's not true, Eric. Neither of us used profanity, and she hung up on me."

"You're the one with the three-minute egg timer on her desk. How can you be so sure after all this time that you didn't hang up first?"

"How can *she?*"

My egg timer was a little kitchen hourglass I keep on my desk to keep track of how long I will tolerate abusive callers before I thank them for their time and move on. It's also good for timing eggs.

I said, "The egg timer wasn't even in play. I remember who hung up first because I waited to hear her phone slam until I remembered you don't slam smart phones. It made me feel a little foolish."

Eric took off his glasses and pinched the bridge of his nose. I knew it signaled more bad news. The signs were all there.

"This morning's story cinched it," he said. "Couldn't you have showed a little restraint in describing the woman's injuries? One of the TV stations, Fox I think, quoted you and the *Journal* verbatim, and once again, sorry to say, her grandkids heard it. They were so scared they refused to go to school. They're afraid somebody's going to cut their throats. The woman's now convinced you're responsible for all that's wrong with the world."

"Shouldn't Fox bear some of the responsibility for that?"

"Maybe, but you and the paper provided the opportunity."

I dropped into a chair, unbidden. "If I went too far, why didn't the copy desk soften it?" I asked. Then I thought better of trying to shift the blame. "No, don't answer that. I have to admit that I wondered when I wrote the story if I was going too far. But the injuries were ghastly. One big shard of glass lodged in her neck an eyelash from her carotid artery. I asked her permission to describe her injuries."

"What did she say?"

"To write whatever would convey the horrors of what the arsonist is doing."

Eric stared at me for a moment then dropped his eyes. "I'm still going to take you off the story for a while, at least publicly."

"You're suspending me?"

"Not from your job, but from public involvement in the story, yes. I'm also going to write an editorial-page apology to readers for the excesses of your piece today. It's infuriating and embarrassing to have to do that. It wouldn't have happened if you'd used some common sense. I have to call the grandmother back and see if the fact of your suspension—I won't tell her it's limited—and the public apology will assuage her."

I was stunned. "What am I supposed to do while I'm suspended?"

"Stay in touch with your sources. If you learn anything new, write it up and give it to me. I'll decide how to handle it."

"What about my column?"

"We'll run a note saying you're on vacation."

My shoulder muscles bunched. "Nobody's going to believe you let me take off in the middle of the arson investigation. Harry Conklin's going to put two and two together and blast it all over his TV show. He won't let this go, Eric. He's pissed that he couldn't get any traction with his notion that I'm sleeping with Ron Colter. That alone will double his resolve to put the worst possible spin on my so-called vacation."

"What in the world did you do to get on Conklin's bad side?"

"I don't know. I don't really care. I'm not sure anybody has to do anything to get on Conklin's bad side. It probably goes back to the time I wouldn't answer his questions the last time you suspended me, during the Ransom Camp investigation."

"Apparently he holds a grudge longer than this grandmother."

"Don't do this, Eric."

"I have to, Deuce. I need you out of the spotlight and out of the paper for a little while. Maybe that will help calm this thing down." He watched for my reaction. I fought not to give him one. "Look," he said. "It's Thursday. Take the rest of the week off. Come back Monday ready to go back to work. But anonymously for a while."

"How long?"

"Until Grandma cools down."

And that was it.

I gathered my things and went home.

53

T he closer I got to home the more I felt my anger surge. By the time I walked in the back door from the garage my stomach churned with acidic fury.

This woman—I didn't even recall her name, if I ever knew it—had to be nuts. She had a right to be irritated by a newspaper story that rubbed her the wrong way, even if her irritation bordered on irrational. To let it fester for four months, then to allow it to overflow onto an article describing the reality of today's Chicago was bad enough. But to cultivate it to the point of retribution, who has that kind of emotional energy to waste?

I wanted to see what her social media posts said, but without a real name or a user name, I wouldn't be able to find her. I had called the circulation office during the drive home. One clerk said she didn't know what I was talking about. Her supervisor knew but said she couldn't discuss it because of possible future legal action.

The world had gone nuts. A reader attacked my newspaper and me for giving voice to a victim of the city's arsonist, a story that brought home the agony of one survivor. There couldn't be a more accurate version of my job description. And while I sidestepped the matter with Eric, where was the copy desk on this? If the last editors to read the story had problems with its graphic nature, why didn't they bring their concerns to me?

I wondered if I could find the grandmother by searching the internet by subject matter: "*Chicago Journal* subscriptions," perhaps. Or "Deuce Mora profanity." Or "Chicago newspaper boycott."

No, I wouldn't do that. If I somehow managed to find her Facebook posts I'd have to ask Mark to tie me to a tree so I didn't get into a pissing match with the dotty old biddy. Not worth it, I decided. And who was I kidding? If I'd written the story as my head suggested instead of as my heart demanded, none of this would have happened.

I tried to figure out what I should do with myself for a long weekend. Deciding on a new profession was one option, and I didn't reject it out of hand.

Then I perked up. Eric said he wanted me out of the spotlight and out of the paper, but he stipulated specifically that he didn't want me off the investigation. I decided I would take my quasi suspension with grace. I wouldn't argue. I didn't want to give him a chance to change his mind and make it worse.

I pulled my copy of the most recent FBI artist's sketch out of my briefcase and stretched out on the sofa to figure out where I'd seen this man before.

I spent more than an hour staring at the drawing, placing the face in everywhere I could remember being over the winter and into the spring. Our paths probably wouldn't have crossed in my Pilsen neighborhood because the arsonist lived in Mount Greenwood, more than fifteen miles south of me. No one had been able to match up a driver's license or a car registration to the little we knew about him. So there was little chance he owned a car. Chicago had excellent public transportation, but not between Pilsen and Mount Greenwood. The fastest route from the arsonist's home to mine involved walking, a bus ride, two different trains, the red and the orange lines, then more walking. The shortest incarnation of the trip would take at least ninety minutes each way. He could use Uber if he had a credit card, which he didn't, or a cab if he had cash. But for a handyman whose office was on the street, public transportation would be much too time-consuming, and a hired ride too expensive, simply to indulge a desire to hunker behind an oak tree and stake out my house.

Had I seen him at Toast when I was at the restaurant to meet Beth Daley? I didn't recall any lone males at any of the tables. Even if he was there, and I'd missed him, Beth would have noticed. As she walked from the front door to the table where I sat, she eyeballed everything in the restaurant that moved.

Perhaps he had returned to one of his arson scenes at a time I was there. I'd been at the sporting goods store, the South Loop, and K-Town, but I'd been focused on the damage, not the rubberneckers. While he might have seen me, I felt certain I hadn't seen him.

I took a break and made dinner for myself with enough extra to feed Mark if he showed up later.

The weather had turned damp and chilly again, as it often does in Chicago in late April. When I finished eating I turned on the gas fireplace and stretched out on the sofa to continue my trip down memory lane with the FBI artist's sketch. Nothing clicked.

Mark arrived a little before 7:30 and gobbled up my leftovers as I told him about my day. He had the same question I did.

"Why did the grandmother wait four months to lash out?"

I shrugged. "Maybe she didn't know how to use the internet and had to learn."

"It doesn't take four months," Mark said, "to figure out how to tweet or post a message on Facebook. But then again, blaming you for making her grandchildren afraid of Christmas—if that really happened—is proof enough she isn't the brightest ornament on her Christmas tree."

I explained it wasn't the December column alone that set her off. The previous day's story had pushed her over the edge.

"All you did was tell the truth," he said. "That's your job."

He stood and started collecting our plates from the coffee table.

"You were nice enough to cook," he said. "So I'll clean up."

He turned and smiled at me, then did a double take.

"You okay?" he asked.

"I'm fine," I said. But I wasn't. Mark's offhand remark about clearing off the dishes created a shock to my system that left me light-headed. I glanced at the artist's likeness of the arsonist, and my mind transported me to another place. A man lurking in a corner, pressed against the wall. There, and yet not there. Hovering. Listening. Waiting.

I held the drawing toward Mark. "I don't know who he is, but I know where he is."

54

I only half heard Mark as he urged me to tell him what had triggered my eureka moment. I was too preoccupied to answer him. I had to figure out what to do with the memory. I knew nothing for certain beyond the urgency to do something fast.

It wasn't yet 8:30 p.m. The Second City Diner would be open several more hours. I debated briefly whether I could afford to wait until the following evening to check my hunch. I concluded that waiting would be too great a risk. If I had the right man, and if he planned on firebombing the place, it could happen any time, even in the next few minutes. As I considered what to do next, Mark grabbed me by the shoulders.

"Earth to Deuce," he said. "Honey, you're white to the eyes. What's going on?"

I forced myself out of my shock and answered Mark's question.

I said, "He's a member of the kitchen staff at the diner, a busboy, I think. We've got to do something right now. If he's going to firebomb the place, it could be tonight."

Mark released my shoulders and looked at me wide-eyed, but only for a moment.

"I'll handle the CPD and the police," he said. "You call Eric. He needs to be ready."

"As angry as he is with me, he'll really be pissed if I interrupt his evening."

"Oh, come on," Mark said. "This could be the break that closes the investigation."

I didn't respond.

Mark said, "Okay, if you don't want to talk to Eric, call Colter. He'll be able to mobilize a response a lot faster than I can."

"Colter cut me off the last time we talked. He's pissed at me, too. Besides, I can't be a hundred percent positive that Second City is where I saw the guy. The last thing I need to do is send the feds on a wild goose chase."

"Better a wild goose chase than more carnage," Mark said.

He stood and started pacing in front of the fireplace. He shoved his hands in his pockets. He did that a lot when he was thinking.

"So let's go back to the diner and confirm my suspicions."

I saw Mark's shoulders sag. I said, "Look, you don't have to go. I can drop by on the pretext of checking on some reservations."

Mark shook his head. "It's not that I don't want to go. But we need cops and fire backup right behind us. You've got to reach Colter."

We took Mark's truck because he had the lights and siren. In the end I called Eric, but he had left for the day. Next I called Colter on his private cell phone. He wasn't happy to hear from me until I told him the reason for the call. Then he was all action.

I didn't want to play phone tag with Eric, so I called the night city editor. I told him what might be going down, where, and how the reporter and photographer could connect up with the police. Under no circumstance, I warned, were they to approach the restaurant.

THE POLICE, fire, and FBI set up a staging area on a side street just a block from the diner. They would stay out of sight unless and until they were needed. However a SWAT team surrounded the restaurant, trying to blend into the landscaping as much as their body armor and weaponry would allow. Some crouched behind cars. Others shielded themselves inside the fenced trash compound. The plan called for Mark and me to go into the diner, tell maître d' Daniel Weldon what we suspected, and determine whether the suspect was working that night. If he was there, we'd call for the troops, who would come in quickly and quietly and try to take the suspect down without a fight or a fiery tragedy.

I called ahead and told Weldon we were on our way.

"We should have a table available by the time you arrive," he said.

I explained we weren't coming to eat. It was much more important than that.

I told him, "You've got to find a place for us to have a quick and very private conversation. I'll explain when we get there."

He started to press me for details, thought better of it, and said, "I'll be ready."

THE DINER WAS STILL JAMMED when Mark and I entered a little after 9 p.m. A waiter took over the maître d' position, and Weldon led us back to his small office a few feet from the service doors to the kitchen. I forced myself not to look through the porthole windows in case Joe Smith was inside looking out. Instead, I ducked under the windows, and Mark did the same. Weldon walked ahead of us and didn't notice.

When I explained why we were there, he went ashen.

Weldon had the look of a maître d'. I guessed him to be in his mid-forties though his bourgeoning male-pattern baldness could have made him look older than he was. He had a well-tended stubble beard just beginning to show a little gray. His blue eyes sparkled over a straight nose and his smile projected the idea that he was happy to have you in his restaurant. But as he listened to me, he seemed to slouch in his chair behind a cluttered desk. The sparkle melted from his eyes. His abdomen above his belt appeared to go soft and bulge, as if all the blood draining from his face was pooling in his stomach.

He took the artist's rendering from me and studied it, nodding his head.

"He could be one of the busboys," he said. "I've seen this sketch dozens of times on TV and in the newspapers, but it didn't occur to me that he was a lookalike for anyone I know. Now that you tell me he might work here, I see it."

He handed the sketch back to me.

"Yeah. Could be," he repeated. "Joe something. I don't remember his last name. Our cleaning crew employs him, not the restaurant. He stands in a few times a week as a busboy when we need an extra pair of hands. We're always busy, so he works a lot."

"Is he here tonight, Daniel?" I asked.

Weldon nodded and frowned. "What do we do? We've got a full house out there." He got up from his desk. "I must get the chef. He is the owner. He needs to be in on this."

I said. "The head of the FBI's Chicago division and a police superintendent are outside. We need to talk to them. They'll call the shots."

"Not shots, I hope," Weldon said. "Not fire, either." He might have sounded as if he was joking, but he wasn't.

When Weldon returned with the owner/chef, Jaques Bacque, I led them out the back door and around to where Colter waited with the cops in charge.

I introduced the men and told Colter that Weldon believed the suspect was inside the restaurant but wasn't sure exactly where.

The plan called for Weldon and Bacque to return to the restaurant with Colter and pinpoint the arsonist's exact location. Once Colter had eyes on the suspect his team would begin closing in. Meanwhile, Weldon and Bacque would quietly get patrons moving outside and away from the building without saying why. Maybe somebody smelled gas, an excuse that would get people moving without panic. It would have to happen quickly, before Joe Smith noticed anything unusual in the dining room.

It occurred to me the suspect might have rigged the restaurant the same way he rigged Keene's, with firebombs that could be detonated by a cell phone call. I mentioned this to Colter.

"We thought of that," he said. "My men have instructions that if he so much as shows a cell phone in his hand, they take him out. I hope we don't have to kill him, but better him than a lot more innocent people. I got a good look at him working in the kitchen. I'd bet a month's salary we have the right guy."

I hoped that level of certainty would be enough. Killing an innocent busboy would complicate life far beyond my ability to calculate.

BUT BY THE time the SWAT team moved into place, the suspect had disappeared.

"What the hell happened?" Colter asked. "I took my eyes off him for ten seconds."

Nobody had an answer.

SWAT officers searched the building, but the busboy had disappeared.

The police and FBI searched the surrounding neighborhood. Again, nothing.

On the very real chance that he could be hiding a block away getting ready to make a deadly phone call, the evacuation of the restaurant became urgent.

When it began to appear that nothing was going to happen immediately, the bomb squad went in with explosive-sniffing dogs.

But with the bombs wrapped as they were, the dogs couldn't get a scent. Colter called off the search. Everyone looked frustrated.

And infuriated beyond words.

55

T he arsonist had caught a glimpse of the FBI official through the
porthole windows in the swinging kitchen doors and recognized
him immediately from his television appearances and his photos
in the newspapers. Common sense dictated that he was the target of the
agent's search, not a late dinner.

In the three or four minutes it took authorities to realize their suspect
had disappeared and begin a search of the restaurant building, the arsonist
was out the delivery door and running for his life away from the side street
where the rest of the cops were hidden in the dark, awaiting orders to move
in. Under his apron he wore black. He left the apron in the restaurant. No
one saw him leave.

In the six minutes it took for the authorities to begin searching the
neighborhood, the arsonist was five blocks away, running hard south on
May Street, east on Madison and south again on Halsted. He raced toward
the campus of the University of Illinois/Chicago where he could blend in
with the throngs of young people out for fun on a nice night. He didn't
pause until he reached the back of the old Jane Addams Hull-House
Museum. There he paused and bent over, grabbing his knees as he struggled
to catch his breath.

As he started to consider what his next move should be, he realized he had left his backpack in the restaurant. He shrugged it off. Nothing in it would lead authorities to him. The only item he needed nestled snug in his back left pocket, the cell phone that would detonate the bombs hidden in the restaurant's wine cellar. He would take out a lot of cops and federal agents if he blew the place now. But he could think of three reasons to wait for another night. First, he hadn't had time to open the stairwell doors to help the fire spread. Second, the reporter and her boyfriend weren't in the restaurant so far as he knew and would survive its destruction. Third, he had a soft spot for dogs. He didn't want them hurt or killed. They bore no responsibility for their training and their mission.

He would wait for another night, when the reporter and her boyfriend were eating at the diner and felt safe because they didn't see him. The busboy job was finished. He couldn't go back. He wouldn't be able to recover his backpack, an acceptable loss. It would be fun watching the authorities squirm as they tried to explain why they didn't find the bombs during the first search, leaving them to create fiery death and destruction later.

He smiled, remembering a favorite quote from the movie Repo Man.

"It happens sometimes. People just explode. Natural causes."

56

"I cannot leave my kitchen as it is," Jacques Bacque said in frustration and anger. The emotion of the evening seemed to thicken his accent. Though his name sounded French, Bacque was actually from the Basque region of Spain, a territory that produced some of the finest chefs in the world. "My kitchen must be spotless when I leave. I shall tolerate no less."

Colter discussed the situation with the deputy superintendent of the Chicago Police Department and the head of the Bomb Squad. Dogs and a squad of bomb experts using sniffer technology that could detect vapors coming off of explosive materials had searched the building twice, coming up with nothing. The arsonist had probably wrapped his bombs in several layers of impermeable plastic sheathing to prevent the escape of any chemical vapors. Thus Colter and the police decided it was likely, though not certain, that if the arsonist planned to firebomb the Second City Diner he hadn't had time to activate his plan before fleeing.

Colter told Bacque, "I can't guarantee to a hundred percent certainty that it's safe, but if you're willing to take the risk, go ahead. Take as many of your people as you can and get the job done fast. I don't want anybody hanging around in there longer than necessary."

Bacque ordered his *sous chef* to take all the dishwashers and busboys still on site and get started. He would tend to the storage of leftover food himself.

A police cordon circled the restaurant. Several fire trucks and EMT squads waited nearby. They would stay until the building was empty and locked down for the night.

Ninety-five minutes later the crew emerged.

"Wrapped up?" Colter asked Bacque.

"Close enough," the chef replied. "No food left out. Dinnerware clean. Bar tidy. Linen ready for the laundry service. If there's anything more we'll handle it tomorrow."

Daniel Weldon, the maître d', joined us. He said, "We've still got to make good on the meals people didn't get to finish. We'll comp them. That will cost us a tidy sum, but there's no other choice. Can we assure people it's safe to come back?"

"After we do one last sweep tomorrow," the police commander said, "After that you can go in, but if anybody notices anything out of the ordinary, you'll have to evac again and call us immediately. Better safe than dead."

Bacque shook his head. "No, we will close for a week. Our assurances will not overcome the fears of our clientele unless we take this place apart looking for problems. We will start early tomorrow." He turned to Weldon. "Appliance specialists, electricians, plumbers, carpenters, masons—I want them all here first thing in the morning."

As the restaurant crew disbursed, Bacque stayed, apparently reluctant to leave the place that had made him quickly rich and instantaneously famous. I took the opportunity to ask him some sensitive questions.

"Who hired this guy?"

Bacque looked at me sharply. "I believe Daniel explained earlier that the man was employed by the restaurant's cleaning crew. The manager of the cleaning company hired him. When we used him to help bus, we paid additional to the cleaning company for the additional service of one of their people. I know nothing about where he came from."

"Is the head of the cleaning crew still here?" Colter asked.

Bacque looked around and pointed to a man walking away from the restaurant.

"Call him back, please," Colter said.

His name was Menendez. I didn't catch the first name, but Colter and a detective wrote it down. He had a driver's license, a green card, and a Columbian passport. The IDs and the photos all matched up.

"Did you hire the guy named Joe Smith?" Colter asked.

Menendez said, "He is a contract worker, paid for the hours he works. No benefits."

"Social Security?"

"He had a card. I didn't record the number. I don't withhold for contract workers."

Menendez looked at Colter, then at me, then at the police detective. He thought he might be in trouble. The requirement to withhold Social Security was federal law.

"Look," Colter said, "cooperate with us and you can go on your way, do your job, stay out of trouble, and we'll overlook the trouble you're in already."

Menendez nodded, unsure whether he could believe the federal agent.

Colter asked, "What's the guy's name."

Menendez frowned at Colter, then shrugged. "He says his name's Joe Smith. I don't believe him."

"What did his documents say, the license, green card, and passport?"

"Joseph Smith."

"But you don't believe him?"

"Could be forgeries."

"You hired him anyway?"

"Look, since Latins aren't coming into the U.S. so much any more, workers like him are hard to find," Menendez said. "I need a coupla crews workin' different places to stay in business. So I don't ask so many questions any more. He shows up. He does what he's told. He don't steal from the clients. He don't complain. He takes his money and goes home. I don't bother him. He don't bother me. Life goes on."

"You pay him cash?"

"Yeah. Cash only. No records."

I asked, "He speaks English okay?" I knew from Beth Daley that he did. I thought it prudent to get a second opinion.

"Yeah. He speaks good English. Sometimes with an accent a little."

"What sort of accent?" I asked.

"Nothing Latin, like Mexican," Menendez said. "I don't recognize it."

Colter stepped in. "You say you don't believe Joe Smith is his real name. You have any idea what his real name might be?"

"No. Nobody calls him anything but Joe. That's all I know."

That was all any of us knew.

It wasn't nearly enough.

I took a last, long look at the diner. This place I had come to enjoy so much felt sinister in that moment. Nothing bad had happened, but it felt as if tragedy had gone on hold, not been defeated.

It would catch up with us. And it wouldn't take long.

57

Colter called me at 6 a.m. the next day and asked me to meet him for breakfast. He wouldn't say what he had in mind. We met at Toast, the place I'd first interviewed Beth Daley, the only person we knew who actually had a conversation with the arson suspect. It was Friday, and the place was filling up fast. That actually helped us. The din created by a full dining room masked our conversation.

I got there first and grabbed the most isolated of the few available tables.

When Colter arrived, I asked, "What's the haps?"

He did an excellent double-take. "What?"

"What's the haps?" I repeated. "It means what's going on? What's happening? Don't you ever read for fun?"

"No."

"You should, especially James Lee Burke. His two characters, Dave Robicheaux and Clete Purcell, they say that a lot."

"We aren't forming a book club here. I've got no interest in Dave Robicheaux or Clyde what's-his-name."

"Clete, not Clyde. Purcell."

Colter dismissed me with a brief shake of his head.

"I went by the Daley woman's condo on my way here," he said. "It was cleaned out with a 'For Sale' sign on the front gate."

"We knew she wanted to go back home to Missouri," I said. "She had no reason to hang out here. If you catch the suspect, you can always send a photo array to her home town police and ask them to present it."

"When I have witnesses in front of lineups, live or a photo array, I like to watch them," Colter said. "Their reactions to the suspects tell me a lot about how certain they are of their choices."

"Then go down and present the array in person," I said.

He took a swallow of coffee. And then he changed the subject.

"We found the suspect's backpack in the restaurant this morning. I guess he didn't have time to pick it up when he ran."

"Anything in it of any use?"

"Nothing obvious. The lab has it. If we find DNA or prints that don't match Joe Smith, we'll try to run them down and hope they belong to somebody with useful data on file."

I nodded and thought about passing along that tidbit to Eric. As pissed as I felt, I wasn't looking for opportunities to call him.

Colter picked up on my mood, and he knew what caused it.

"What's with your vacation?" he asked.

"The time builds up. I have to use it or lose it."

"I'm calling BS on you, Deuce. You have to use your vacation days or accept pay for them at the end of the year. You don't lose them."

"Really?"

"And I know you too well," he said. "It's not in your DNA to take a day, let alone a whole weekend, in the middle of a big story."

"Maybe I'm just tired."

I didn't want to lie to Colter, but I didn't want to get into a debate over my predicament, either. I tried to let him know I wasn't on a vacation without getting into a discussion about the reasons.

"Why do you care?" I asked him. "Before last night you basically written me out of your will. First you said I was the only reporter you trusted. Then you and Cross turned around and shut me out."

He lowered his eyes. "Sorry," he said. "Heat of a bad moment." When he looked up again, his eyes were deadly serious.

"You're not out of this case," he said. "The *Journal* might have taken you out of the paper but you're still very much a part of the case. There's only one reason the arsonist would come out of his hole to target the Second City Diner. It's the one place he can be certain he'll find you and Mark on the same night every week. You've gotten closer to him than anyone else. He wants you dead."

That dismal thought had crossed my mind, but I dismissed it. It didn't ring true. Maybe because I didn't want it to. Hearing Colter give it voice was scary.

"He's not targeting people," I said. "He's targeting buildings. The toll in the Loop could have been two or three times higher if he'd waited to detonate his bombs until the store opened."

"Nobody at the store posed a threat to him," Colter said. "Beth Daley might'uv, but he engineered that meeting for his own sick reasons. You're a threat. Mark's a threat. That's why I'm certain there are firebombs in the diner. We just didn't find them last night. The place will be closed for the foreseeable future. I gave orders this morning for the bomb squad to take the place apart. Can you imagine what the toll would be if he blew the place at the height of a busy dinner hour on a Friday or Saturday night?"

"But you don't mind if he blows it when it's full of cops?"

"He won't. He'll give up on the plan if you're not in the restaurant. Not to repeat myself, but the diner isn't the target. Cops aren't the targets, either. You are."

"You can't be sure of that."

"Yeah, I pretty much can. I started my career with the FBI as a profiler. I'm quite good at it."

"If you take the diner off the table, so to speak, what will the arsonist do?"

"There aren't many possibilities," Colter said after he finished his coffee. "He could firebomb your house in the middle of the night, but I don't think he'll take that risk."

I asked, "Why not?"

"Because Pilsen is a close-knit neighborhood. Everybody knows everybody else. Everybody keeps a lookout. Lots of cops live there, eat in the Italian restaurants, and drink in the private clubs on Oakley. With the weather getting nice, there are people socializing on the streets at all hours. Too much chance of somebody spotting him and getting suspicious, especially the cops, who've been looking at the artist's sketch for months."

"You think anyone would notice him at three or four in the morning?"

"It would be a risk. Chicago gets up early. The partiers are just going home when the working folks are leaving. They all know each other. Somebody would notice a stranger. Just to drive home the point, we're posting the neighborhood with the artist's sketch. We hope that presents too many chances for him to take."

"He could come from the Blue Island bus stop and through my back alley."

"You've got it well-lighted with motion sensors and bars on the windows."

"So if not my house, what then?"

"The *Journal* building, maybe," Colter said. "But it's three or four times the size of Keene's and has armed guards in the lobby. Nobody can get in without a pass or an escort. I don't think he'd attempt it. You'd be safest if you moved in with Mark for the duration. When you have a date night, go places you've never been before or visit infrequently. Keep the creep from planning ahead."

I said I'd think about it. And I did.

But I couldn't escape the alarming truth that if the arsonist wanted me dead, there were a half dozen ways he could get the job done without firebombing a restaurant during a quiet dinner with Mark.

58

"It might not be such a bad idea for you to get out of town for a while," Mark suggested as we sat in front of my fireplace and waited for the heat to erase the damp chill from the living room. The early May weather in Chicago had warmed, but the rising temperatures often came with rain. A deep chill settled over the city at night as the thermometer dropped. I once went to a Cubs night game in May and couldn't feel my toes by the third inning.

"Not going to happen," I said.

He held out his hands in question. I frowned at him. "For one thing, I'm not leaving until this arsonist is in custody or dead. For another, I don't like taking vacations alone. You and I have plans to spend time in the Rockies this summer. That sounds a lot more appealing than a solo stay in an old cabin in West Texas."

He laughed. "West Texas? Where did that come from?"

I waved him off. "I don't know. It's the first isolated place that came to mind."

Mark moved on. "We've lived together before. We did fine. I've got two spaces in the garage and a king-sized bed. All bases covered. Why not give it a try, at least? It's not a lifetime commitment."

I shrugged. "I guess nobody's going to firebomb your building."

"Not a forty-seven story tower with alarms, full sprinkler system, locked garages, and 24-hour on-site armed security, no."

I took an hour to pack while Mark got the cats and their paraphernalia ready, and the deed was done.

As we drove to Mark's building on the south side of Grant Park in the Museum District, a weird thought occurred to me.

I said, "This is kind of like a shotgun wedding, isn't it?"

In my peripheral vision I saw him throw me a quick, startled glance. He said, "Except there's no shotgun and no wedding."

"And no pregnancy."

He reached over and laid his hand on mine.

"We could change that."

I stared out the window and felt my eyes fill up.

I SPENT most of the night lying in bed with my mind commuting between possible scenarios for the fiery end of my life and the possible explosive end of yet another Chicago landmark. I knew I wasn't going to get any sleep, so I tried to relax and follow my thoughts along whatever treacherous path they carried me.

Dark thoughts and deep fears are always more intense at night when you know you should be asleep but won't get there before dawn. My mind catalogued the many historic buildings in the city that stood within the footprint of the Great Chicago Fire and could be potential targets for the arsonist. They were large places and small. The Grant Park area had to be considered because the park had been built on top of debris from the 1871 fire. The remains of the blaze were dumped into the water along the Lake Michigan shoreline as landfill. The area was then covered over with rock, roads, sidewalks, sod, trees, flowers, memorable pieces of outdoor artwork, and the spectacular Buckingham Fountain. Where South Michigan Avenue had once been land's end along the South Side, there was now a 319-acre green zone buffer between the famed street and the water.

As for me, if the arsonist wanted to kill me he could walk up to me on the street and use a handgun bought on a West Side street corner. He could bump into me and put a chef's knife through my heart. I could avoid some of the dangers if I stayed cooped up in Mark's condo, but I still had to go out for work.

The only good choice was to leave the city, move to some place like the mountains of North Carolina, get a new job, and make a new life. But that would end my relationship with Mark, and I couldn't accept that. The odds of both of us finding new work we wanted to do in North Carolina were small, especially for me. As revenues plunged, newspapers were unloading staff as fast as a sinking ship jettisons cargo. Maybe I could stay in Chicago if I found another profession. But I didn't really want another profession.

I decided to call my brother in the morning and see if he had any ideas. Gary was a prominent lawyer in Denver. He had a lot of contacts. But the thought of asking him for help was anathema to me. I needed to get on with my life by myself.

I just wasn't sure where to start.

THE ARSONIST HAD BEEN awake all night brooding up an anger that reached a boil.

How had things gone so wrong? The owner and the maître-d *at the diner now knew who he was. So did the staff. He couldn't go back to work there. He could set off the bombs any time, from any location, with just a call from the master phone. But it wouldn't make any sense to do that now, when the reporter and her boyfriend weren't inside.*

Morning TV news said the bomb squad and fire department were back to search the building again at dawn. They expected to find something, and the arsonist knew if they were sufficiently determined they would unearth the bombs. They couldn't be spotted with a casual glance, and even the best bomb-sniffing dogs couldn't detect them. But they weren't invisible. A thorough search would find them.

He pushed himself out of the chair in front of the old television set. He had a handyman job at midmorning, and he feared if he didn't show it *would raise questions. Besides, now that he was out of work, he needed to stockpile funds, and this was a job that would pay $2,500, plenty to see him through until he decided what to do next.*

He should think about getting out of town for good. He'd made his mark. He'd left an impact that would last for years, maybe even beyond his lifetime. He wanted desperately to kill the reporter and her boyfriend, but it would be safer to ignore them and just leave. Alaska was appealing, except for the weather. Mexico, maybe, except it was dangerous there.

It was a decision for another day. He knew he couldn't bring himself to leave until he erased the bitch from the face of the earth. If for no other reason, anger and pride wouldn't permit it.

He had to come up with an alternative scenario.

And he did.

59

The next day I was propped up on Mark's sofa with Murphy on the floor beside me, and the cats draped over my legs and cutting off circulation. It was Sunday, and Mark was working, a perfect opportunity for me to start reading Walter Isaacson's biography of Leonardo da Vinci, which I had nicknamed *The Da Vinci Load* because the hardcover, which I had resting on my stomach, weighed nearly 3.5 pounds. My laptop weighed less and didn't have any sharp edges.

When cat pressure started putting my feet to sleep, I shifted enough to convince both Caesar and Claudius to move, one to curl up on the bottom of the sofa, one to stretch out along the back.

My cell phone rang. Caller ID said it was my editor. I had no desire to talk to him. On the other had, I didn't have any choice.

"What is it Eric?" I asked, trying to sound less irate and more disinterested.

"Why didn't you let us know what happened Thursday night?" he demanded with no introduction and no explanation.

"What happened Thursday night?"

"Don't play with me, Deuce."

"I'm not playing, Eric, I'm reading. And I did alert the newsroom

Thursday night. I called you first. The magical, miracle new phone system you have will confirm that if you don't believe me. You were gone for the day. So I talked to the City Desk."

"You remembered where you'd seen the arson suspect before and went to the restaurant with the cavalry to take him down."

"The cavalry was busy, so I took Mark, the FBI, the police department, the fire department, a SWAT team and, oh yeah, the NSA."

"And you didn't think you should call me at home?"

"I was pretty sure you'd find out through your city desk, your photo editor, and your police reporters since the operation was all over the police scanners, and there was a presser after midnight. You couldn't have been too pissed at me. You waited three whole days to call and jump down my throat."

"And then," he continued, "the bomb squad went back to the restaurant over the weekend, tore the place apart, and found six bombs, all ready to detonate on the command of a cell phone ringer."

"You had it well staffed."

"You didn't go."

"Mark went. I read about it in the paper like everybody else."

"Not buying that, Deuce. You trying to tell me Mark didn't fill you in?"

Busted.

"Yeah, he did."

"Why?"

"Why what?"

"Why didn't you go back Saturday? Why didn't you call in after you talked to Mark?"

"Colter held another presser," I reminded him. "He covered everything Mark told me, and, again, the *Journal* had it well staffed."

"You went with authorities Thursday night."

"I knew the owner and the *maître d*. I had access and credibility. I was the one who could most reliably ID the suspect. I didn't want the cops and the feds jumping all over an innocent man, maybe killing him."

"You're incorrigible."

"Thank you."

I SPENT the next hour thinking about the last few days and brooding about my relationship with the *Journal* and with Eric. Over the years it had been a carnival ride with enough ups and downs to keep me vaguely sick to my stomach. When things were good, they were great. When they were bad, it was, well, like now.

I hadn't told Eric about Colter's thoughts on the dangers to Mark and me. I had no reason, really. It was all speculation, and I didn't want to talk about it with anyone except maybe Mark. I felt nervous, no doubt. But I didn't want to broadcast that to the world.

Mark was taking me out to dinner. We would take his personal truck. We planned to leave from the locked building garage, drive directly south to Hyde Park, eat at a place we'd never been, and then come directly home. That should be safe enough.

It was.

But it wouldn't last.

60

I barely had time sit down at my desk and take the lid off a cup of mediocre coffee when my cell phone rang. Caller ID said, "Ron Colter."

With no introduction he asked, "You remember all those people you interviewed while you were canvassing Mount Greenwood looking for the arsonist?"

"I don't know that I remember every one of them," I said. "There were a lot."

"Well, one of the couples you talked to, who had used the guy for some handyman work, saw him working on the roof of a house across the street. The man is a decent amateur photographer. He got out his camera, waited for his opportunity, and took a series of pictures of the guy. Then he called us. We were talking about photo arrays a couple of weeks ago. I'd like to prepare one and swing by and show it to you."

My pulse jumped at the prospect of getting back in the game.

"Sure," I said. "When?"

"I've got a meeting this afternoon that I can't miss. Maybe between 5:30 and 6."

"I'll be at the office, waiting."

∼

IT WAS after six when he arrived.

"Sorry I'm late," Colter said. "I left the meeting early and drove down to Mount Greenwood to make sure the suspect hadn't left. He was on the roof where our informant saw him, and from the look of the job, he'll be there for at least a few more days."

"So what do we do?"

"Let's look at some pictures."

Colter took an envelope from his coat pocket. "I've got an array of six men doing roofing work. I want you to look at them and tell me if anyone looks like the busboy from the diner or the man you wrestled with when he tried to firebomb the library."

We sat at Eric's conference table again. I had made sure Eric knew about the meeting. Colter spread the photos in front of me, two rows of three photos each. Could this really be the beginning of the end of it?

It took me less than thirty seconds.

"Second row, middle," I said.

"Are you sure?"

"Absolutely positive."

"Good girl," he said.

"So now what?"

"While I talked to my office, the guy apparently finished up for the day and left. I didn't see where he went. But he left his tools behind, so he'll be back tomorrow. Overnight we'll put SWAT, under-cover cops, and elements of the FBI and ATF in place and out of sight and put the nearest firehouse on standby. The owners of the house he's reroofing will drive away together in the morning. If the guy's there, they'll tell him they're going to the store and will be back in an hour or so. Nearby neighbors will be evacuated overnight."

"I'd like Deuce to be there in the morning," Eric said.

Colter locked eyes with me for a moment. Then he nodded. "Let's see what the morning brings. If we have dozens of sets of eyeballs on the guy, he won't be a threat to you. I'll see if I can arrange something. Is Mark around?"

"Tomorrow sometime. He had to check a suspicious fire in Naperville. He called earlier and said it was a sloppy job, and he should be done with it tomorrow morning."

"Anything I can do for you before I go?"

"Go with me for a walk outside. I really need to get a little exercise."

"That's too open," Colter said. "I'll take you somewhere for dinner. It's the least I can do. My unit's parked right in front of the building in the circular drive. We can be out of here and into the car in a few seconds."

That sounded good. I accepted.

"Wear a jacket," he said. "It's getting cold outside."

61

I think I remembered from one of my psych courses in college that the fight-or-flight response in human beings is triggered by brain's limbic system, a cluster of parts buried in the cortex and sitting atop the brain stem. Among the triggers are any stimuli that create a threat to survival, real or perceived. When the limbic system kicks in, it floods the body with adrenaline, increases heart rate and breathing, and puts all senses on high alert.

My limbic system was the last thing on my mind as Colter and I crossed the *Journal's* lobby. I saw his car in a no-parking space in the half-circle driveway out front, right where he said he left it.

As we walked to the SUV, I saw a flicker of light to my right. We both saw it, and our heads turned simultaneously in that direction. We saw a man in a dark hoodie standing on the lawn beside the driveway. He had an old flip-top lighter in one hand and a green bottle filled with liquid and a cotton wick in the other. He touched the lighter flame to the wick, and it caught. I heard Colter yell, "Run" as he reached under his suit coat and topcoat for his gun. Trying to reach it proved awkward.

"Deuce, run," he ordered again.

I saw the gun finally in Colter's hand, but I also saw the Molotov cocktail arcing through the air on a trajectory that would land it right between us, splattering both of us with flaming gasoline.

I didn't think about it. I didn't weigh the pros and cons. I just moved.

At six feet tall I had enjoyed rather illustrious sports careers in high school and college: softball, golf, but most of all women's basketball. I could slam dunk and shot-block with the best. I was about to try the most dangerous shot-block of my life.

I heard a gunshot, then another. The bottle was still in the air, the guy in the hoodie staggering but still on his feet. I heard him laughing, and that infuriated me.

I didn't have far to go, but I had to go fast. One long stride. Two. Three. Push off hard. Leap and stretch high.

The bottle was coming down on my left side. I'm a natural right-hander, but I didn't have time to adjust. I caught the bottle with my left hand and hurled it back in the arsonist's direction, all before my feet hit the ground.

It crashed and exploded at the arsonist's feet, and he became a human fireball in a matter of seconds.

Colter and I both ran for him and threw ourselves on his body, succeeding in setting ourselves on fire in the process. We rolled him in the grass. People who saw what happened slipped out of their coats and began beating at the flames, attempting to smother them. Colter and I both choked on the smoke, and I could smell flesh burning.

I heard a loud hissing sound, and the three of us were enveloped in a thick, cool fog. One of the building's security guards had grabbed a fire extinguisher and put the flames down in seconds. I pushed myself to my knees and struggled not to fall over. Colter had rolled off the attacker and moaned softly. I thought he might be semi-conscious. The guy in the hoodie was on his side, lying perfectly still. His position was a ghastly recreation of one of the bodies burned in the warehouse fire in the South Loop so many months before.

I fell into the grass and tried to control my breathing. Ripples of pain spread from my left hand up my arm. I wondered how bad I was hurt.

I didn't want to look.

~

I HEARD a commotion back toward Colter's truck. I turned my head and saw two city cops running toward us, one yelling into his radio. I couldn't hear what he was saying. The other one looked at the three bodies in the grass and knelt by me, probably because I was the only one who appeared to be conscious.

With my right hand I pointed toward Colter.

"Call an 'officer down,'" I said, my voice raspy with smoke. "That man is the FBI's AD for Chicago. And then cuff this guy." I indicated the man in the hoodie. "We're 99 percent sure he's the Chicago arsonist."

The cop glanced at the suspect. He said, "He's hurt pretty bad. Can't risk moving him too much without medics. He's not goin' anywhere right now."

Then he turned his head to me again. "And who are you?"

"Deuce Mora. I'm a columnist . . ."

"For the *Journal*. Yeah." He relayed my information to his partner then turned back to me. "We got buses on the way," he said. "Help is just a few minutes up the road. Can you tell me what happened?"

I tried. It was slow going. When I got to the part about my shot-blocking ability, the officer gaped.

"You did what?" he said.

"I only had two choices," I said, "return air mail to sender or burn alive."

He started to move aside so the doorman could cover me with a blanket he'd found somewhere. I started to tell him to take care of Colter first, then stopped when I saw that Colter was already covered. No one had given the arsonist a blanket, and he probably needed it the most. I pointed that out to the police officer, and he went off to see what he could do to prevent the suspect from going into shock and dying, if he wasn't already dead.

The officer returned to my side. He looked down at me and shook his head.

"Lady," he told me, "you are a piece of work."

I'd heard that before.

It wasn't always a compliment.

62

A s it turned out, my injuries were relatively minor. I had first- and second-degree burns on my left hand, wrist, and forearm, probably from direct, if brief, contact with the hot bottle, its burning wick, and some leaking, flaming gasoline. Somehow the metal clasp on my watchband became superheated and branded its design into the underside of my wrist. I also had burns on my neck. It would have been a lot worse if Colter hadn't told me to put on a jacket before we left the condo. The front of the leather coat burned through, but it protected me long enough to keep the clothes beneath from catching fire and immolating me. My shirt and slacks were scorched beyond repair, but the skin beneath suffered nothing worse than a careless, if painful, sunburn. My hair and eyebrows got singed, too. A haircut would eliminate the burnt ends, and the eyebrows would grow back. All in all, not too horrible.

Ron Colter's injuries were more severe, but not life-threatening. He had second-degree burns on his arms, neck, and chest. He'd be in the hospital a while, and he might require localized skin grafts. With physical therapy he should make a full recovery.

The arsonist, whose identity we still didn't know, took the worst of it: one bullet wound to the arm, another to the gut and second- and third-degree burns over fifty-five percent of his body. Doctors said he could survive unless his injuries became infected or unless the damage to his lungs was so severe it lethally impaired his ability to breathe. They wouldn't cite odds on his life. Inhaling fire is never a good thing, and scorched lungs are an agonizing way to die. For the time being, the suspect was being sustained with a ventilator in a burn unit. He had not regained consciousness.

Somehow, he had avoided serious trauma to his face. The FBI took several good photos of him. They were published in all the city's newspapers and broadcast on television all around the world under the headline, "Who is this man?" To a person those phoning in knew the mystery man as Joe Smith. If he had friends or family, they preferred to remain anonymous and distanced from their notorious relative.

I was lying in a hospital bed with assurances from doctors that I would be released within a day or two, as soon as they packed me full of antibiotics and satisfied themselves that my burns were clean and unpolluted by evil bugs. In the meantime, they hooked me up to a morphine pump in case I needed help with pain.

I used it once, fell into a drugged sleep, and vowed not to use it again unless absolutely necessary. It wasn't. The watchband brand on my wrist formed a focal point for pain but not severe enough to combat with mind-numbing drugs.

Few visitors were allowed to see Ron Colter for several days as a safety precaution. Doctors didn't want anyone carrying an infection into his world. But his wife came to visit me and brought word from Ron that he would be fine, and that my stunt in the *Journal* driveway had been the most incredible "save" he had witnessed in his twenty-six years in law enforcement.

Since the incident involved the Chicago AD of the FBI, a man in a hoodie tossing a Molotov cocktail, and me, it didn't take long for people to figure out the perp was a suspect in the arson investigation.

But still no one called in an ID.

Of course the *Journal* found several witnesses to my leaping catch, one describing it as miraculous as Dwight Clark's iconic grab of a Joe

Montana touchdown pass for the San Francisco 49ers in the back of the Dallas end zone in the final few seconds of the 1981 NFL championship game.

I took a lot of ribbing for that description. I admitted I had seen videos of the catch. I felt compelled to point out to everyone who brought it up that I hadn't even been born when that game was played, and very honestly, folks, as I was jumping up to grab the burning bottle, Dwight Clark never entered my mind.

MY EDITOR, Eric Ryland, was the first visitor to my hospital room after I was transferred from the ER. Mark would be a close second. He was making a mad dash back from Naperville, and the traffic on the Stevenson was brutal, as usual. I had talked to him on the phone twice, assuring him he didn't need lights and sirens to career eastward, that I would be fine. I was reasonably sure he paid no attention to my request.

After Eric assured himself that I was comfortable and not in any danger, he assured me I would be welcomed back at work, but not until my doctors cleared me.

I laughed. "Has it occurred to you that you've now suspended me twice, and each time it resulted in a solution to a major mystery?"

His expression was rueful. "That did cross my mind," he replied. "It makes me wonder if there might be a cause-and-effect aspect to the suspension process. Maybe I should make suspending you part of my journalistic action repertoire. Even when bad things happen that aren't your fault."

"And it occurred to me," I said, "that each time you suspend me I wind up in the hospital. I'd just as soon you didn't try it again."

"I'll keep your sentiments in mind," he said. "Meanwhile, how're you feeling?"

"Not too bad," I said. "I hope to get out of here tomorrow."

"Don't rush it," he ordered. "Meanwhile, in a highly unusual move, the FBI would like you back in the game."

"I thought my Dwight Clark move pretty much accomplished that."

"True. But what they want is to use you to help with calls that come in about the identity of the man in the burn unit."

"Why?" I was genuinely perplexed. "What do they need me for?"

"You know so much about this guy, they figure you're best qualified to make judgments on which calls are credible and which aren't."

"Colter's a profiler. He should do it. I don't have any skills like that. What if I make a bad judgment?"

"Colter's not well enough."

"Then another profiler."

"You won't have to talk to the callers. Another profiler will do that. You'll be listening and evaluating. You'll both work out of this room until you're released, then the FBI will move the operation to your house. Look at it this way. You'll have somebody to talk to while you mend."

The profiler was Emily Ortega, a very serious woman of about forty whose eyes suggested they had seen more of the dark side of life than most people. She was pleasant and businesslike. We talked about how the system would work. We would answer the calls simultaneously. She would do the talking. My job was listening. We would exchange rudimentary hand signals indicating our reactions to what each caller had to say. FBI technicians would attempt to trace each call. If any call paid off, other agents would take over from there.

The first calls that came in mirrored those the FBI had fielded before I got involved. They were from people who identified the man as Joe Smith. Obviously the callers were former clients.

On the morning of the third day I was getting dressed in preparation for my discharge. The feds told me a duplicate phone system had been set up at Mark's condo instead of my house. Mark had insisted I stay with him at least until my wounds healed.

At first the calls had been exciting. Every time one fell flat I fully expected the next one would hit pay dirt. But as each succeeding call proved disappointing, the routine became more and more monotonous. Maybe I could work up enthusiasm again in the brighter environment of the condo, surrounded by our fur babies. Oh, and Mark.

And then we took the call from Keegan Michael Petrauskas.

EMILY PICKED up the phone and, as usual, identified the FBI hotline. She set a trace in motion as I picked up my handset.

"Who's this?" a male voice asked.

Emily identified herself. "Do you have information on the photo?" she asked.

A few seconds passed in silence.

"Oh, shit," the caller said.

"Do you know the man?"

"Yeah. He's my cousin."

"What's his name?"

"Is he the arsonist?"

Ortega and I exchanged glances.

"Do you think he is?" she asked.

"Yeah, I think he might be."

"Who is he?"

"I tole you, he's my cousin. Name's Cameron Conor."

"What's your name?"

"Keegan Michael Petrauskas." He spelled the last name. "Everybody calls me Mike."

I nodded to Emily. The guy sounded like the real deal. She tried to stretch out the conversation to give the trace a chance to succeed. To do that, she had to get chatty.

"Well, two-thirds of your name's Irish," she said. "What's Petrauskas? Greek?"

"Lithuanian. A coupla generations back one branch of the family tree sorta went off the tracks," he explained, mangling a metaphor. "Is Cam the arsonist?"

"Why do you think he is?"

"Look, lady, I really think I should get off the phone."

"No need for that, Mike. We're just talking. Have you seen your cousin recently?"

"Not for over a year. I've been working a construction job in Saudi Arabia. I just came back 'cause my mother recognized Cam's picture in the paper and begged me to come home and take care of this. Nobody else in the family would touch it."

I was now nodding vigorously, certain this was real. I passed Emily a note: "Did Cam ever wear contacts?"

Emily continued. "Your family isn't close?"

He sighed. "Used to be, when I was a kid."

"What happened?"

"Why is that your business?"

"It's not. My family's all chopped up, too. I was just curious what happened to yours."

"Granda Finn happened," he said. "Well, he wasn't my granda. I guess he was my 'grand uncle,' or somethin'. I've never figured out how that relationship shit works."

Another FBI agent opened my door and gave Ortega a thumbs up. They had located the caller. A SWAT team would be moving in momentarily.

"What did Finn do to your family?" she asked, as if she really wanted to know.

"Well," Petrauskas said, "I didn't exactly give you the whole story about my cousin. I didn't give you his last name. He dropped it when he dropped outta school."

I waited.

"The full name of the guy inna pitcher is Cameron Conor O'Leary."

Ortega and I locked wide eyes. Neither of us had seen that coming.

Suddenly the question about the arsonist's contacts made no difference.

∽

PETRAUSKAS DIDN'T RESIST when the SWAT team surrounded him. Ortega had assured Petrauskas he was not under arrest. Yet. But he should go with the agents. He agreed.

Agents took him to the FBI's division offices on Roosevelt Road where the interview continued. He asked for coffee and got a large cup with a fairly decent looking ham sandwich and chips on the side. A peace offering. Nobody bothered to ask me if I was hungry. Or thirsty. At least they allowed me to sit in on the interview after my discharge. The arson suspect's identity hadn't yet been released.

I was shocked when Colter pushed himself through the door in a wheelchair.

"My God," I said. "Should you be out of the hospital? They wouldn't even let us come visit you to avoid infection."

"I'm okay," he said. "I'll explain later."

He introduced himself and complimented Petrauskas for stepping up and being forthright. Then he started drilling down.

"I presume your cousin's last name, O'Leary, puts him in the lineage of the woman who owned the farm where legend says the Chicago Fire began," he said.

"Yeah, we're in that lineage, if that's what you call it," Petrauskas said. "Catherine O'Leary was our grandmother goin' back a lotta generations. I think there's six or eight 'greats' in fronta the grandmother part. But she didn't start the fire. Neither did her damned cow. The fact that people still think she did is what's caused alla this shit."

"How so?" Colter asked.

"Our Granda Finn was a right bastard, he was," Petrauskas said. "Never met a grudge he couldn't hold for life. And he carried a big'un for the legend of Mrs. O'Leary's cow. Said it ruined his life. Every time somebody found out his last name was O'Leary, they jumped him about the fire. Got axed from two jobs over it. Only work he could get was menial labor, and back in those days people'd tell him to his face it was 'cause of the fire. He'd tell 'em time and again the story was a fable, but they either didn't believe him or just wanted to keep persecutin' 'im. The older he got, the more bitter he got. Can't really blame him."

"How did that affect your cousin?" Colter asked.

"Of all the kids in the family, Cam loved Granda Finn the most, and Granda Finn favored him. Granda poured all his bitterness all over the family. Mostly we managed to ignore it. Those who couldn't eventually moved away. That wound up bein' mosta the family. But Cam drank it in, and he believed it, and Granda's bitterness infected him, too."

Petrauskas took a couple of bites of the sandwich, crunched a few chips, washed it down with coffee, then continued.

"Cam's father was always gettin' in bar fights over that fable. Eventually he abandoned his family and left town, and nobody heard from him again. Cam's mum wound up committin' suicide. She left a note sayin' she couldn't stand the family shame any longer. Granda Finn insisted the family had nothin' to be shamed over, that the city should bear the shame. His mum's death pushed Cam over the edge. When Cam started echoin' Granda's ravings, it kinda broke the family up. It wasn't so much that Granda bitched alla time about how he'd been treated. What broke us all up was his constant preaching about revenge. "

"Revenge on who?" I asked.

"The city, like I tole you," Petrauskas said. "He'd say shit like, 'They think we burned the city in the Great Fire, but we didn't. So we got a free lick comin'. We should burn it good the next time.' Cam started watching weird movies about revenge, and he'd quote lines he remembered. They were all about vengeance and blood and death. Really creepy shit. Cam tole me once he could burn the city, that he could learn to make firebombs off the Internet. He asked me if I wanted to help. I blew him off. I didn't take him serious and didn't want to have anything more to do with him. He's one of the reasons I went to the Middle East. Him an' the money."

"You're kidding," Colter said.

Petrauskas raised his eyebrows. "All this seem like a joke to you?"

Colter ignored the rebuke. "And you think Cam took his grandfather's ravings to heart, that more than 100 people are dead and nearly

250 injured because of random acts of revenge against a city where a few people insulted your grandfather?"

"The possibility occurred to me."

"Why didn't you come forward sooner?"

"I already told ya, I was on the other side of the world workin' construction. We only got bits and pieces of the news from here, and I never saw the drawing of the suspect. For all I knew the guy was black or brown or yellow. If I'd come forward earlier, what would I have said? That I think my cousin mighta done this shit, but I don't know where he is, don't know if he's still alive? What good would that've done you?"

"Not us, Mike," I told him. "But it might have saved a few dozen lives. "Think about that for the rest of your life."

63

A nother week passed. My burns had stopped hurting, but the doc kept my hand, wrist, and forearm wrapped and told me to be careful not to bang my arm around and chance breaking the blisters. That would create an open door to infection.

"Does that mean I have to postpone my taekwondo classes?" I asked. "Learning to break boards with my bare hands was my spring project. I was looking forward to it."

He walked out of the room without answering.

Ron Colter was back at work but spent a lot of his day in the wheelchair. His specialists weren't thrilled about so much activity, but they conceded that propelling the chair was strengthening his injured shoulder.

Cameron Conor O'Leary's condition had been upgraded to critical but stable. He was awake but surly and uncommunicative. I actually understood that. If I were handcuffed to a hospital bed, in terrible pain, and being forced to go through debridement, a surgical procedure in which dead and blackened skin is cut away from the burn area, I'd be surly, too. Debridement can be an excruciating process.

While I understood O'Leary's mood, I had no sympathy for him. After the pain he caused so many others, what he now endured was justifiable payback.

～

"How CERTAIN ARE you you've got the right man?" I asked Colter one day when Mark and I were sitting in his office going over the final details of the case.

Colter got out of the wheelchair and walked around a bit.

"Gotta stretch my legs so they don't stiffen up," he explained before returning to my question. "We found his last apartment. His landlord called it in. He hoarded news accounts of his arsons. He had half dozen books about the Great Chicago Fire. He had articles on making firebombs and Molotov cocktails. And—ready for this?—he kept a journal."

"That should about wrap it up," Mark said.

"Did he mention a motive?" I asked.

"Revenge, like the cousin thought," Colter said. "Just what Granda Finn preached. I've heard of kids lashing out after being bullied in school, but O'Leary's in his thirties. You'd think he'd've learned to ignore it. Nobody believes the O'Leary cow fable any more."

"What about a second suspect?"

Colter smiled. "You mean somebody hidden by the grassy knoll? No indication there was anyone else. He had no friends his family knew of, and no indications of anyone else in his apartment. Prints were all his."

I asked, "So, what's likely to happen to him?"

"He could still die," Colter said. "We probably won't get that lucky. He has a court-appointed lawyer, but nobody can question him while he's still in a precarious condition. So we wait. If I had to guess, I'd bet on him being committed eventually and then, if he gets better, he'll probably spend the rest of his life in prison with taxpayers footing the bills."

64

Ron Colter and his wife and Mark and I received special invitations to attend the grand reopening of the Second City Diner. What might have qualified as an occasion worthy of black-tie treatment was not. Chef/Owner Jaques Bacque wanted it to be a normal casual evening for his guests, with the exception of the complimentary bottles of King Brut Champagne Grande Cuvee at each table.

The food was lavish, the service impeccably attentive without being cloying, and the mood upbeat. Diners were grateful one of their favorite eateries had reopened, but the atmosphere reflected the city's relief that one of the most terrorizing periods of its history had been closed.

My arm was out of its protective bandages. There was some scarring, but it would fade. Colter had given up his wheelchair almost two weeks earlier, and only those who knew him well noticed that when he turned his upper body, he still did so gingerly. That, too, would improve with physical therapy.

A few people, including the mayor and city council president, came by to say hello and briefly congratulate all of us on bringing the arson suspect to ground. But for the most part, we were left alone to enjoy the evening.

We avoided discussing the case through dinner. But late in the evening, over coffee and dessert of Bacque's signature Gateau Basque —a tart of pastry cream, brandy, and dark cherries in a buttery crust —we couldn't avoid the arson conversation.

"I have two things I'd like to clear up," I said to Colter. He nodded. "Did you ever figure out where that odd pipe, the medwakh, came from? Since it had that odd residue, it seems like there's a good chance it came from the Middle East."

"We don't know," Colter said. "You can find the pipes and the dokha tobacco in this country. They're not common, but there is a small market for them. And they're not illegal. O'Leary might have gotten his hands on them and used them to steer us toward Islamic jihadists. Unless he decides to tell us, we might never know."

I accepted that and asked, "How do you account for witnesses saying they heard one or two people shout 'Allahu Akbar' as they ran from the fires at Cubs 'n' Stuff and Keene's?"

Colter stirred his coffee. "Either they heard what they expected to hear, or they lied," he said. "If they lied to the FBI, that's a federal crime. And they could be prosecuted. Their statements did mislead us, after all."

Meanwhile, Cameron Conor O'Leary remained in the Cook County trauma and burn unit. His condition remained dicey, an advanced medical term for crappy. He wasn't yet able to try talking, and it didn't matter, really, because he refused to communicate in any way with authorities, including his own court-appointed lawyer.

And still, no one had a definitive answer to the question of who, or what, had set off the Great Chicago Fire or the simultaneous Great Peshtigo Fire in Wisconsin almost 150 years earlier. Despite the arsonist's obsession, the idea that Catherine O'Leary's cow was at fault in Chicago had been relegated to the trash bin of folklore decades earlier. And no one could blame the cow for Wisconsin.

Lily Colter asked, "If the legend of Mrs. O'Leary's cow is a fable, what could the ignition have been?"

I put down my fork with some reluctance. While I had been quarantined in Mark's condo, I had spent hours researching that very question. I'd read all the theories, including vandals, milk thieves, a drunken neighbor, a group of card players who forgot to extinguish the lantern when they left, even spontaneous combustion. None of them worked for me.

"My money is on the wind," I said. "The door to the O'Leary barn faced southwest. The wind was hot and dry and blowing from that direction at gale force. The door could have been left open, or it could have blown open. The wind knocked the lantern off a table or a bench onto the floor. The kerosene spread through the dry straw and wood, the flames rode the current, and that was the beginning of the end."

"But if Mrs. O'Leary was there, milking the cow, couldn't she have put it out, or at least contained it and called for help?"

Mark said, "Nobody knows where she was, or if anybody was in the barn."

Lily Colter was skeptical. "The Chicago area was still largely agrarian in 1871," she said. "People would have known better than to leave a burning lantern unattended."

"You'd think," I agreed.

She said, "I like the meteor theory better."

I grinned. "Well," I said, "it's certainly more interesting. I did learn something during the course of my research. The difference between a meteor, a meteoroid, and a meteorite. A meteor is the flash of light caused by a burning piece of space debris as it passes through Earth's atmosphere. Meteor refers only to the light, not the debris. The space rock is a meteoroid, which can be as tiny as a pebble or as big as a sixth of a mile at its widest point. Most meteoroids burn up completely in the atmosphere. But if part of the debris survives to strike the ground, it becomes a meteorite. If that's what caused the Chicago and Wisconsin fires, it would mean the rock split into at least two pieces during its race through the atmosphere."

Lily nodded. "So why couldn't that have been what happened?"

"It could," Mark said. "But there's no evidence of it. No big rocks were seen headed toward the earth. No meteorites were ever found here or in Wisconsin. Of course searchers might have missed it, or them. Or they might have buried themselves so deep in the ground that there's no observable trace."

"I would think," Colter said, "someone would have heard the explosion of a meteoroid crashing through the O'Leary barn."

I nodded. "Imagine a meteoroid big enough to survive a plunge through the atmosphere, breaking into multiple pieces, shattering the speed of sound, and striking the planet on exactly the same night when the Upper Midwest was coming off one of the driest summers in its history, and the hot winds were blowing at more than sixty miles an hour."

Mark looked at me with a deadpan expression.

"That would be quite a coincidence," he said. "But then, you don't believe in . . ."

"Shut up," I said.

65

Jackson Hole, Wyoming

"This is rated as easy?" I said to Mark.

"Yeah," he replied. "I figured if you liked this hike I might be able to convince you to climb the Grand with me the next time we're here."

I put my hand on his arm and pushed so hard he nearly fell off the boulder we were relaxing on in the center of the most beautiful field of wildflowers I'd ever seen.

It had been more than a month since the Chicago arsonist had been captured. When we flew out of O'Hare headed west, Cameron Conor O'Leary remained in the hospital, handcuffed to his bed. Doctors said he would survive, his burns, the skin grafts would morph into messy scar tissue, and the smoke damage to his lungs would leave him with a permanently raspy voice and susceptible to diseases that likely would end his life early. Whatever time he had left he would spend in a hospital for the criminally insane.

While Chicago slogged through a hot, humid summer, Jackson Hole enjoyed a protracted spring. The saying was that Jackson Hole summers were two days in August.

Right at that moment, I wanted to sit on that rock in the middle of the field of wildflowers for the rest of my life. From my wildflower field guide I was able to identify yellow arrowleaf balsamroot, silvery lupine, red fireweed, scarlet Indian paintbrush, and purple Columbia monkshood among the dozens of varieties that exploded all around us.

I lay back on the solid piece of granite and surveyed the world around me and the sky above. I could see a section of the Teton Mountains called the Cathedral Group, jagged edges of a tectonic plate that pushed straight up from the Jackson Hole valley floor eons before. They didn't appear to have weathered much. The granite edges looked as if they could slice a limb from a careless climber.

The sky could only be described as cobalt blue, so intense it almost hurt my eyes to stare at it. We had hiked nearly 300 feet vertical over several miles and stopped to rest at an elevation more than 7,000 feet above sea level. The atmosphere was thin, the pollution non-existent. Nothing came between me and the sky to muddy up the view.

I asked a child's question. "Why is the sky blue?" It was one of those things I expected Mark to know.

He stretched out beside me. "As I understand it, the sun's light is scattered by the earth's atmosphere, like billions and billions of prisms. Blue is scattered most because it travels in shorter, smaller waves. So when we see the sky, we see overwhelming blue."

I smiled. "And because it would look weird if it was red."

"That, too."

I turned my head and could see String Lake below us. We had started the hike at a trailhead on that milky green lake. It wasn't milky green because of pollution. The color was created by glacier melt that fed into the lake. For some reason the ancient water created the milky green color.

I wanted to ask another "why" question, but even more I just wanted to be quiet.

There wasn't a lot of oxygen at this altitude, and the exertion of the climb had depleted the reserves in our blood. We had been in the area for twelve days, and the feeling of oxygen deprivation subsided as our bodies made more red blood cells to harvest scarce oxygen more efficiently. But full acclimation would take even longer. Exertion here was a humbling experience, even on this trail, that was rated as relatively easy—as opposed to climbing the 13,776-foot tall Grand Teton, from which this park took its name. The top of that mountain was nearly twice as high as our rock in the meadow.

Mark took my hand. "What are you thinking?" he asked.

"About going back to Chicago tomorrow. I don't want to leave here."

"You might feel differently when it starts snowing on Labor Day and sometimes doesn't stop until the Fourth of July."

"But it's gorgeous."

"And thirty below zero."

"Well, there is that."

He propped himself up on an elbow and looked down at me. "If you're ready to leave Chicago, there are lots of places to consider."

"I don't want to leave you."

"You could move to Tierra del Fuego, and I'd follow."

"At the southern tip of South America? You don't think it snows there?"

"Yeah, but in the southern hemisphere it snows from maybe April to October. Here it snows from October to April. We could commute."

I laughed and turned my face to him. "That's a long time to hang in the sky."

"Thank you, John Denver."

"Maybe I just need to find something new to do," I said. "The last couple of years journalism has pretty much roughed up my body and my soul. Newspapers will soon be anachronistic, if they aren't already. I don't want to hang around and watch them die."

"What would you like your next life to be?" Mark asked.

"I don't know. I haven't thought about it. But I have thought about thinking about it."

Now he laughed. "That's a start."

"Yeah," I said. "I guess it is."

ACKNOWLEDGMENTS

The closest I ever got to fighting a fire was shoveling dirt on a campfire. So when it came to setting a city on fire, I needed help in learning what to do and how to do it and, more than that, how to put those fires out. We all owe a great deal to the first responders in our fire departments, who have much more than book learning on this topic.

But for what I know, I'm deeply indebted to the book, "Kirk's Fire Investigation" by John D. DeHaan and David J. Icove. There is nothing you could possibly want to know about fire that isn't in that book.

For learning what happened during those three ghastly days beginning October, 8, 1871, I relied on the book, "The Great Chicago Fire" by David Lowe. It's a fascinating account, complete with interviews with survivors who described their brief stay in hell.

Extreme thanks to Julie Smith and Mittie Staininger of BooksB- Nimble without whose advice, support, and artistic genius this book would exist only in the bottom drawer of my desk.

And, as usual, thanks to my editors, David Ehrman and Win Blevins—great writers of television and books, respectively—for their sharply attuned senses of story. They asked great questions for which I hope I provided adequate answers.

As ever, thanks to the City of Chicago and all of my friends there for their beauty and inspiration and encouragement.

jh

WANT MORE DEUCE FOR FREE?

Sign up at JeanHellerBooks.com to join my mailing list and get *The Storm!*